SYMBOL OF TERR[...]

Chenault looked up [...] you left Earth must ha[...] were its markings?"

A device totally unfamiliar and now almost forgotten. One Dumarest drew with frowning slowness on the paper Chenault pushed toward him.

"This? Are you sure?" Chenault looked up from the paper, rising as Dumarest nodded. "Let me see, now." He moved to a shelf, took down a heavy volume bound in cracked and moldering leather, riffled through the pages to stand, finger on an item. He said, "The clue, Earl. You've given me the final clue. I know where Earth is to be found."

THE TEMPLE OF TRUTH

Dumarest stepped closer to where the statue stood. It was, he judged, about twelve times life-sized, the cupped hands some seven feet across. The ball hanging above the cupped palms was about ten feet across and he studied it, frowning, wondering as to its purpose, the markings blotching the shining, metallic surface. A ball poised before her, one she had just tossed upward or was about to catch. Or was it something more than that? The symbolism had to be important. A ball—or was it representative of something special? A world, perhaps?

A world!
Earth!
It had to be Earth!

Also in Arrow and Legend by E C Tubb

SYMBOL OF TERRA
and
THE TEMPLE OF TRUTH

DUMAREST SAGA 30 & 31

E.C. Tubb

A Legend book
Published by Arrow Books Limited
62-65 Chandos Place, London WC2N 4NW

An imprint of Century Hutchinson Limited

London Melbourne Sydney Auckland
Johannesburg and agencies throughout
the world

SYMBOL OF TERRA first published 1984 by Daw Books, USA
©1984 by E.C. Tubb

THE TEMPLE OF TRUTH first published 1985 by Daw Books, USA
©1985 by E.C. Tubb

First published in one volume 1989 by Legend

Printed and bound in Great Britain by
Anchor Press Limited, Tiptree, Essex

ISBN 0 09 963100 8

SYMBOL OF TERRA

Chapter One

Dumarest saw the movements as he made his way along the valley; small flickers of red which could have been the flirt of a scarlet wing, the nodding of a bloom, the glow of reflected sunlight from a gleaming leaf. Facile explanations and none of them true; a bird would have risen, there was no wind to stir a flower and the sunlight streamed high to leave the valley in shadow.

Halting, he plucked a leaf and chewed it as he studied the terrain. Above and before him, monstrous against the sky, the bulk of a mountain reared in rugged splendor its natural beauty now enhanced by the glowing colors of sunset. At its base time and weather had conspired to form a deep, wedge-shaped declivity, flanked with steep inclines fringed with shrubs and stunted trees; vege-

tation which swept down to soften the bleak out-
lines of dirt and stone and to cover the floor with
flowered sward.

An artifice of man; the ground had been carefully leveled and graded, the plants set with calculated design to form a haven of beauty in which
birds could dwell and exotic flowers fill the air
with their heavy perfume. Faint in the distance
came the tinkle of running water.

Dumarest threw down the pulped leaf, catching
another glimpse of red as he resumed his progress.
Higher this time, but on the same side of the
valley. An enemy or a watchful guardian but one
lacking experience in remaining hidden. Or one
who wanted to be seen so another could remain
invisible.

A possibility but he doubted it. The vegetation
was too still and his sharpened senses would have
warned him of lurking danger. Steadily he moved
on down the valley to where the sides closed in to
meet the rock of the mountain. A great door pierced
it, made of massive timbers now closed and firm.
Windows flanked it, rising high like a multitude of
dark and wary eyes. Above them the sunlight painted
swaths of ruby and gold, orange and amber, pink
and vibrant chrome.

"Hi there!" Dumarest lifted his voice in a shout.
"Is anyone at home?"

His words flattened against the rock to fade and
become lost in the tinkle of water coming from a
stream rilling to one side. A chain hung beside the
portal and he pulled it, hearing the faint tone of a

bell. Repeated as again he hauled on the links. Turning he saw again the flash of red, closer now, lower on the slope.

"Chenault?" Again he shouted. "I've come to see Tama Chenault!"

A clearing stood before the door, set with a bench, and he moved toward it after plucking a fruit from a bush. Steel glimmered as he lifted the knife from his boot, using the edge to remove the rind, laying the blade beside him on the bench.

Eating, apparently relaxed, he listened to the tinkle of water, the soft rustle of leaves, the faint murmur of insects. A bird rose with a whirr of wings behind and to his left. There was a soft, squashy sound as if a boot had trodden a fallen fruit. Silence and then, with sudden abruptness, the unmistakable sound of clicking metal.

Dumarest threw himself to one side, snatching at the knife, hitting the ground as a dull report filled the air. Rising, he turned, blade lifted, leaving his hand in a blur of shimmering light as he spotted his target. As it hit, the woman screamed.

She was tall, slim, her skin the color of sun-kissed grain. The green of her dress hugged a symphony of curves lushed with mature perfection. Her eyes matched the hue of her gown. The color of her hair was one he would never forget.

"Easy." Dumarest was on her before she could move, one hand closing on her wrist. "You aren't hurt."

"I thought . . ." She swallowed. "I felt . . ."

Nothing but the shock of impact as the thrown

9

knife had knocked the weapon she'd used from her hands. That and the fear born of the ruthless savagery of his face. It lingered as he sheathed the knife and picked up the gun. It was crude, a simple affair of twin-barrels with a large bore, the hammer needing to be cocked before it could be fired. An antique, but one as deadly as a laser in the right hands with the right ammunition.

"Yours?"

"No. That is—"

"Chenault's?"

"He—" She broke off. "You're hurting my arm."

Dumarest released her, hefting the gun. "Try to run and I'll use this. Why did you want to kill me?"

"I didn't. The gun fires a harmless dart. It would just have made you sleep for a while." She frowned at his expression. "You don't believe me. Look for youself." She pointed to where a gaudy tuft of feathers stood in the grass beyond the bench. "That's what I shot at you. You can check it."

"There's an easier way." Dumarest lifted the gun and aimed it at her body. Deliberately he thumbed back the hammer. "Two barrels," he said. "Two charges. Let's see if they're both the same."

She watched, wide-eyed as he moved to place her between himself and the bench. A hand lifted to her mouth as he began to close his finger on the trigger but she made no other sign of fear. Not even when he fired.

10

"Well?"

Dumarest looked at the dart standing from the wood of the bench. Perhaps it was as harmless as she'd claimed or perhaps she'd only thought it to be harmless. The latter, he guessed, she hadn't flinched from the decisive test.

He said, "Did Chenault give you the gun?"

"Yes."

"Why? What were you supposed to do with it?"

"Sometimes there are predators. They come into the valley and hunt the creatures here. When they do I take care of them."

"And visitors?" Dumarest shrugged as she made no answer. It was prudent to be cautious on even the most civilized of worlds and, in the Burdinnion, few were that. "Were you born here on Lychen?"

"No."

"Where then? Solis?" A guess and a wrong one as the shake of her head signified. "It's just that you remind me of someone I knew once. She had the same color hair as your own."

A red which burned in his heart like a flame. One which would never die as the memory of Kalin would never die. Kalin whom he had loved. Long gone now, the spirit which had won him dissipated, dead, leaving only the memory of a shape. Of eyes and hair and skin and mouth and . . . and . . .

And, suddenly, she was before him.

*   *   *

11

A bird broke the spell, rising with a thrum of pinions, leaves falling with a rustle—sounds of potential danger which jerked him from a dream. An illusion in which time had encapsulated and a person long gone was again at his side. Standing as she had so often stood before, looking up at his superior height, the long, clean line of her throat before his eyes, the magnet of her body, her chin, her lips, the flaming cascade of her hair. The emerald pools of her laughing eyes.

The hair, of course, it had to be the hair. The red which had betrayed her when she had watched him. That and her shape and her lips and her eyes. The eyes which held more than laughter.

She said, "Are you well?"

"Yes. Why do you ask?"

"You seem disturbed. Would you like to sit?" She gestured toward the bench. "Would you like some fruit? Water? I could fetch it from the stream."

And vanish while getting it but Dumarest felt certain she wouldn't. He watched as she crossed the clearing, noting the movement of her legs, the sway of her hips. A woman, but not the one he had known. Not the one he had imagined standing before him so short a while ago. Yet the impression had been so sharp. An illusion? The effect of the fruit he had eaten? Had the juice held a subtle hallucinogen which distorted reality?

He narrowed his eyes as she returned bearing water in some folded leaves. Against the vegetation she seemed neutral, a figure wearing green, one who could have been anyone—a female, well-made, but without character. An impression heightened by her face as she concentrated on her burden. It was smooth, somehow unformed, a collection of contours and planes. Then, as she noticed his interest, it firmed into what he had seen at first.

"Here." She handed him the folded leaf. "Drink and rest for a while."

Thirst and weariness made it easy to obey. The water was cool, refreshing, and Dumarest swallowed it all. Relaxing he smelt the perfume of the valley, listened to its quiet humming. The susurration of insects and growing things, the rustle of an upper breeze which stirred the vegetation as if to a giant's breath. Peace enfolded him and a calm tranquility.

To the woman he said, "What are you?"

"Who am I? My name is Govinda."

A question he hadn't asked and he wondered at the poetry which had made him liken her to some elemental spirit. One who lived in a tree or a stream, a thing of legend come real, belonging to this place like the stream and the plants, the enigmatic face of the house which was barred like a castle.

"Govinda." The name held music to match her tone. "Just that?"

"Isn't it enough?"

"Of course, but others I've known here on Lychen have several names."

"Nobles. Those aspiring to rank and position. They add names to each other like pearls." Her shrug dismissed the importance of labels. "And you?'' She smiled as he told her. "Earl Dumarest. I shall call you Earl. Were you born here on Lychen?''

"No more than you." He reached out and rested his fingers on her hand. The skin was soft and warm. "Which is your home world, Govinda?"

"I don't know." She met his eyes and answered the question she read there. "I had no real family and must have been passed around. I remember Yakimov. I did most of my growing there. After a while I moved to Kremer, then to Habralova then to other worlds. Finally I came here."

"To stay with Chenault?"

"He looks after me, yes." She withdrew her hand from beneath his fingers. "What do you want with him?"

"To talk."

"Just that?"

"Are you worried I'll hurt him? Is that why you tracked me and tried to knock me out?" Dumarest shook his head and smiled. "You said he looked after you. I think it's the other way around. But why should he need looking after at all?"

She said, "You want to talk. What about?"

"I'll tell him that."

"You can tell me and I'll tell him. Then, if he wants to see you, he will."

"And if he doesn't?" Dumarest let the question hang. "Surely he doesn't live here alone aside from you. There must be others."

"There are."

"In the house?"

14

"You talk too much, Earl, and say too little. Just what do you want with Chenault? To talk, you say, but how can I believe that?" She met his eyes, her own direct. "Why didn't you call ahead to arrange an interview? Why steal into the valley like a thief? How did you get here, anyway? I saw no raft."

"I walked."

"From where?"

Dumarest said, "That I'll tell Chenault when I meet him. And I'm going to stay here until I do. Tell him that and tell him we have mutual friends. Edelman Pryor for one. Tayu Shakira for another." He saw her face alter. "You know Shakira?"

"I—I'm not sure."

"Shakira of the circus of Chen Wei? You know him. Tell Chenault he sent me to him. Tell him now."

"I can't." She looked at the sunlight painting the mountain, the level of mounting darkness beneath it. The warning of approaching night which already filled the valley with dusty shadows. "Not yet but soon. I promise. You'll have to wait." Rising, she added. "If you want to leave do it now. If you see Tama and upset him you'll never leave this valley alive."

He came when the sun gilded the topmost peak of the mountain, turning the ice and snow which crusted it into an effulgent flame. Deceptive warmth. It would soon yield to the star-shot indifference of night. Dumarest heard the sigh as the great doors

15

swung open, and rose from the bench to stand facing it and the figure which came toward him, silhouetted against the light filling the hall.

"Dumarest? Earl Dumarest?"

"Chenault?"

He was tall, broad, thick around the waist. A man old as a tree grows old, as gnarled, as strong. The lines engraved on his face gave him a hard. emotionless appearance, one belied by his sudden smile, teeth flashing white between drawn-back lips. His eyes in their sunken sockets held a bright awareness.

"I'm Chenault. The girl said we had mutual friends."

"That's right."

"Edelman Pryor, for one." Chenault tilted his head a little, the thick mass of gray hair higher than Dumarest's own. "Tell me about him."

"Old, dry, dusty. He deals or dealt in old books, maps, logs, statuettes, legends."

"Statuettes?"

"He gave me one. A small thing he'd had for years. You may have seen it; a woman, grossly emphasized, of a size you could hold in a hand. He said it was the depiction of some ancient goddess. Erce."

"Mother Earth," said Chenault. "Or the Earth Mother. You have it with you?"

"No. Pryor is minding it for me. I didn't want to lose it."

"Neither did he." Chenault nodded, understanding. "You are subtle, Earl, I like that. A gift accepted and returned in a manner devoid of offense. He gave you my name?"

"Yes."

"And Shakira?"

"Yes." Dumarest met the stare of the bright eyes, brighter now with reflected starlight. "Tayu Shakira of the circus of Chen Wei. He said you could help me."

"Tell me about him." Chenault listened as Dumarest obeyed. "Did you know him well?"

"No."

"But if he gave you my name—"

"No one knew him well," interrupted Dumarest. "But if you knew him at all, really knew him, you must know one thing about him. He is—unusual."

"In what way?" Chenault leaned forward, tense. "Tell me!"

Dumarest said, curtly, "He is not like other men. He has hands sprouting from his waist. Extra hands."

"The product of wild genes." Chenault sighed and relaxed. "You know him. Tayu must have trusted you to allow you to live with that knowledge. Later you must tell me about him and also how you managed to make Edelman Pryor feel so indebted to you that he gave you his most prized possession. Govinda was right; you are a most unusual man, Earl Dumarest. I am proud to greet you as my guest."

"It will be an honor to shelter beneath your roof."

"The old courtesies." Chenault smiled his

pleasure. "It is good to hear the traditional words again. But I am remiss as a host. Govinda told me that you claimed to have walked here and must be fatigued. She was also curious as to where you came from. We are somewhat isolated here. The nearest village lies over a hundred miles to the west. The town—"

"I had a raft," said Dumarest, "but I didn't want to be followed. So I dumped it and came here on foot. From the other side of the mountain."

"Where water is scarce and game even scarcer. Well, you are here now, and can have all you need." Chenault gestured toward the open doors. "Shall we go in?"

The hall matched the barbaric splendor of the great doors; a place of vast dimensions, the roof peaked, the floor tessellated in garish diamonds of red and green. Colors repeated on the walls together with others of smoldering vividness set in a profusion of designs which Dumarest found vaguely familiar. As the doors closed behind them the air seemed to vibrate and the designs to blur, to seem to move as perspective changed, to freeze in a series of grotesque parodies.

Faces distorted by the painted masks peculiar to clowns.

A circus!

Dumarest halted as he recognized the vague familiarity for what it was. The floor, the hall, the peaked roof which depicted the summit of a tent, the designs themselves all reflections of a small and bizarre world. Now he could recognize the semblance of cages, the hint of watching beasts, the shape of a ring, the tiered seats, the hanging strands of a trapeze. An illusion created with paint and light and undoubted genius.

"You noticed." Chenault stood facing Dumarest his bright eyes direct. "What do you see?"

"A circus tent, of course. But—"

"Lopakhin created it. He felt the need and I permitted it. Tyner is a genius and, I suppose, I have a weakness for the grandiose. A happy combination and one which allows of such indulgences. Others also find it amusing and, at times, they come to stare and gawk and make their observations. Fools for the most part, but it does no harm to cater to their whims as long as they do not clash with my desires." Casually Chenault added, "Perhaps you have met those I'm talking about. Jaded dilettantes from the great Houses. Those of influence and position with too little to do and too much time in which to do it. At times they visit me and request permission to view my hall. Sometimes I accommodate them."

"You are gracious."

"Sensible. Why arouse antagonism when there is no need?" Chenault turned and moved down the hall. As Dumarest fell into step beside him he said, "I give a little and receive much in return. If they think I am an amusing eccentric then that is to my advantage. Also, from such people, information can be gained."

As to his own presence on Lychen and what had happened since he had landed. Dumarest glanced at his host and wondered just how much the man knew and what he intended. An academic question; if the information he had gathered was true then he had no choice but to stay close to the man until he had gained the coordinates of Earth. The secret Chenault owned—or did he?

Always there was doubt and there had been too many disappointments and yet, this time, Dumarest felt close to success. A conviction based on instinct but which he knew could be contaminated by hope. And if this was another blind lead it would be best to discover the truth without waste of time.

Dumarest said, bluntly, "Shakira gave me your name and that of this world. He said you would help me."

"Of course. And I shall."

"Then it might help if I told you what I'm looking for and—"

"But later." Chenault halted as they reached the end of the hall. "There is a time and place for all things and welcome guests are too rare to be hurried. You are in need of food and rest and other comforts. Later we shall talk." The clap of his hands created echoes which murmured to silence. As they faded, a man appeared, standing, waiting, in the age-old attitude of one who served. "Baglioni," said Chenault. "He will guide you to your room and attend you. Until later, my friend."

A wave and he was gone leaving Dumarest with his guide. Baglioni was small; a man with the body of a child but with the face of an old man. A midget who bowed and gestured for Dumarest to follow as he stepped to a wall. He froze as Dumarest dropped a hand on his shoulder.

"Can you hear?"

"Yes, my lord."

"And speak too, so I see. Are there many like you in this place?" He smiled as the man remained silent. "Would money persuade you to find your tongue? No? I thought not. Your master is fortunate in having so devoted a servant." Without change of tone Dumarest added, "When did you leave the circus?"

"My lord?"

"What were you? Acrobat? Tumbler? Clown?" Pausing, he added, "Or were you in a sideshow with the rest?"

Baglioni was stiff. "I don't understand what you mean, my lord. Now, if you will follow me, I will guide you to your room."

Chapter Two

Bizarre luxury everywhere, the walls painted in striations of complementary colors, the furnishings adorned with grotesque carvings depicting men and beasts and things of the sea and air. The bed was wide, soft, the woven cover resembling an ancient tapestry. The bathroom adjoining was bright with mirrors and gilded metalwork.

Dumarest stripped and stood beneath the shower, washing away the sweat and grime of his journey with blasts of hot and icy water, foaming unguents and cleansing soap. With a sponge he tended to his clothing, removing dirt and stains from the neutral gray plastic. Dried, naked aside from a towel wrapped around his waist, he padded into the bedroom and moved toward the window.

He had seen this window from below, a round

eye which gave a view of the valley, set, he guessed, to one side of the great doors and high in the cliff. The pane was immovable to his touch, locked or sealed to the frame; even if broken it would give only to the sheer face of the cliff. If the door to the room should be locked from the outside it would become a prison despite its luxury.

A fact assessed and dismissed; if Chenault intended him harm the danger lay in the man himself and not the furnishings of his house. Leaning forward Dumarest studied the terrain below. The valley was dark now, filled with gloom alleviated only by the starlight which touched trees and shrubs with a silver glow. A wrongness; the windows should be streaming light unless the glass had been treated to blank it from within. That explained their dark and empty appearance from outside and he wondered how many had watched his progress down the valley.

Turning, he made for the switch and killed the interior illumination. The window, now filled with the silver glow of starlight, painted the chamber with a ghostly luminescence.

One broken by a warm fan of brilliance as the door opened and Govinda stepped into the room.

"Earl?" She had not expected the dimness and drew in her breath as she saw him move. "Oh, there you are."

The door closed behind her and she stepped toward him, her hair black in the pigment-robbing light. Her gown was formal, high at the neck, covering her arms, falling to just above her feet.

23

Around her the air was heavy with the scent of flowers.

"It's beautiful, isn't it?" She gestured toward the window. "It can be darkened if the light bothers you. See?" At her touch the round eye grew dim and finally dark. "You need only turn the control. One way for total darkness the other for as it was." The room grew palely bright again as she demonstrated. "I came to see if there was anything you needed."

"That was kind."

"Tama likes his guests to be comfortable."

"Is it your job to see they are?"

"I don't want you to miss anything. Look!" She pointed at the window. "See?"

Beyond the pane, in the valley, came a sudden dart of brilliance. It was joined by another, more, and within seconds the area was filled with a host of scintillant streaks of burning colors which moved and died as quickly as they had appeared.

"Firebirds," she explained. "They rest and eat and glow as they fly."

Nocturnal creatures and there could be others yielding equal pleasure. Dumarest turned as the woman pressed close beside him, her face and eyes turned toward the view outside. In the pale light her face looked oddly different from what he remembered, even more unformed than it had when she returned with the water. A nondescript combination of basic features, older, betraying lines which should not have been missing. Then, conscious of his examination, she turned to face him and, at once, was younger, more alive.

"Earl." Her hand rose to touch him, long fingers resting on his naked shoulder, falling to move over the pattern of scars on his torso. A gentle touch which lingered, then, reluctantly, fell away. "Dinner will be soon," she said. "You'll find clothing in the cabinet."

"My own will do."

"Not at the table of Tama Chenault. Dinner here is a festive occasion and he has a high regard for what is proper. Please, Earl." Her hand rose to touch him again. "Is it so hard to accommodate an old man?"

The clothing was black edged with gold, the blouse fitting close to match the smooth fit of the pants. Garb to be expected in the great houses where formality was the rule. Dressed, Dumarest looked at himself in the mirror; a tall, wide-shouldered man, the bulk of his torso diminishing to a flat stomach, a narrow waist.

"It fits, Earl, and it suits you." Standing beside him, framed in the mirror, Govinda stared at him with emerald eyes. In the restored lighting of the room her hair burned with a ruby splendor. She too wore black, the skirt banded with gold, her costume complementary to his own. "You look a warrior. A king."

"And you look a queen, my lady."

"Your lady, Earl?" In the mirror her face seemed to blur as if the glass had fogged; then, as he turned to face her, it was firm again. "That would be nice if true. A pleasure but one coupled with pain. How could any woman ever be sure of you?" Her laughter dismissed the question as it eased the moment. The muted throb of a gong echoed through the room. "The first warning, Earl."

"Warning?"

"That dinner will soon be served. There will be two others. On the last the doors will be shut and if you aren't present you'll be denied a meal and thrown from the house." Her tone was light but he guessed she wasn't joking. "Come." She slipped her arm through his. "Let me show you the hall."

A place he had seen but, entering it, he found it altered. The circus depiction had vanished and in its place loomed the brooding magnificence of a cathedral. A vista of soaring columns and arched roofs, groined, carved, set with the smoldering grandeur of stained glass windows. An illusion as had been the circus.

"It changes," said Govinda. "Something to do with various pigments reacting to different forms of light. At one time you see this and at another, something else." She watched the movement of his eyes. "You're impressed?"

Dumarest nodded.

"Tyner will like that. He's proud. If you want to make a friend just tell him how clever he is."

Lopakhin was a squat barrel of a man with a twisted, cynical mouth and hot, restless eyes. He wore vivid hues in a jarring assembly; a garment which could have been taken as a mockery of rigid

26

formality and an affront to his host. One Chenault chose to ignore and Dumarest guessed that the mode of dress was a part of the artist's facade. The mask he wore to cover an inward uncertainty. One augmented by an abrasive and arrogant manner.

"Hail to our visitor!" He rose from his place at the table, goblet in hand, bowing as Govinda led Dumarest into the room. "A brave man who has faced many dangers—and who has yet to face many more."

"Sit down, Tyner." The woman at his side matched him for bulk but her eyes held a patient understanding and her tone was gentle. Her dress was similar to that worn by Govinda, lavender instead of black with silver adornment instead of gold. Differences of no significance when compared to her face which was one mass of intricate tattooing. "Sit," she snapped when the artist hesitated. "You fail to amuse."

"And that, my dear Hilary, is the most heinous crime of all." Lopakhin shrugged and lifted his goblet, drinking, setting it down with a bang as he dropped into his chair. "To be serious. To regard life as something other than a game. Yet, to look at you—"

"Is to see beauty," said Dumarest quickly. "To witness the work of a master of his craft. My lady." He stepped forward and took the woman's hand, lifting it to his lips as his eyes searched her face. "Some are as nature intended," he said. "Many work to gain beauty. A few have it thrust

27

upon them. I know worlds where you would be hailed as the epitome of femininity.''

"So my father often told me." Her voice held the echo of resentment. "I have yet to find one."

"Beretae," said Dumarest. "Sunyasha. On both body-decoration is an art and unadorned flesh is held in small regard. Your presence graces this table." He turned to Lopakhin. "As does yours, my lord. The hall is a work of genius. I tell you it as others must have done. As more undoubtedly will." He reached for a goblet and lifted it. "I salute you!"

"That was well done," said Govinda as Dumarest took his place at her side. "Perhaps too well done."

"No." The man facing her was lean, hard, his skin the color of ebony, his hair a close-knit mass of jetlike wool. "Ian Massak," he said. "I know your name and now I know you've brains as well as guts. A happy combination." To the woman he said, "If you're going to flatter anyone, Govinda, don't use half-measures. Go all the way whether it's to be cruel or kind."

"And he knows how to be kind." The man at Dumarest's side nodded toward the tattooed woman. "Look at Hilary, I haven't seen her so relaxed for weeks."

She was leaning back, smiling, happy as were the others at the table and Dumarest wondered if he'd passed a test of some kind. They had been the last to arrive, a thing Govinda could have managed, and Lopakhin could have acted as he had as part of a charade.

"I'm Toetzer." The man at Dumarest's side smiled a welcome. "Good to have you with us. That's Shior down there, next to him is Vosper, and—" He broke off as a bell chimed. "Later," he said. "Tama is about to give the blessing."

A hush fell as the echoes of the bell faded into a silence that lasted as, at the head of the board, Chenault sat as if carved from stone. A posture adopted by the others as Dumarest noticed with rapid movements of his eyes. One broken as Chenault moved, hands lifting, the left held stiffly upright before him, the palm to his right, the right hand also stiff lowering to rest on the tips of the fingers to form an unmistakable T.

Sonorously he said, "The one became the many and the many shall again become the one. This in the fullness of time."

A rustle around the table as the gesture was repeated and Dumarest was conscious of the scrutiny of a dozen pairs of eyes. A moment in which to make a decision and hope he offended none by following their example. As his hands came to rest Chenault said, "We ask the Mother to grant us strength. To give us aid. To guide our path. To favor us as her children. To her our devotion. Until the end of time."

A whisper like the rustling of leaves as the response echoed over the table. One in which Dumarest joined.

"Until the end of time."

Then, beside him, Govinda dropped her hands as did the others following Chenault's lead. For a moment the solemnity of the moment lasted, then dissolved as doors opened and servants came to lift the covers from steaming dishes, to place new flagons on the table, to bring in a choice of meats and fish and vegetables flavored with a host of herbs and spices, cut and set to form elaborate patterns.

"Here!" Massak leaned forward, his knife extended, a morsel stuck on the point. "To you, my friend."

A ritual Dumarest recognized and which told him something of the man. He leaned toward the proffered morsel, took it between his teeth, used his own knife to spear a fragment and to offer it in turn.

"Peace and brotherhood," he said. "Wars without killing but, if killing there must be, let it be quick and clean."

The talk of mercenaries who had met after peace had removed the reason for their antagonism. The proffered morsel a sign of friendship, the taking of it a sign of trust.

Massak beamed as his teeth closed to scrape on the blade.

"Look after him, Govinda," he boomed. "If you don't then I will."

"But not in the same way, eh?" Lopakhin smirked as he reached for his wine. "But as good as, perhaps? I've heard of you mercenaries and what is it they say? Any port is—"

"Shut up, you fool!" Hilary was sharp. "Some things you don't joke about."

"Was I joking?" Lopakhin shrugged. "Well, let us talk of other things. Of long journeys, perhaps. Of other worlds. Of dreams and hopes and legends. Of children you yearn to go back home to. Home!" He hid his face in his goblet, droplets dewing his lips as he set it down. "Home—another name for hell especially when you're a child. Take Hilary, for example, held down, screaming, while her devoted father drove his needles into her face and body. Turned into a spectacle to titillate the rich and idle. Robbed of her dignity. Forced to sit nude while men goggled and wanted to do more than just look. Why should she ever want to go back home? Why should you?" His eyes met Dumarest's. "Why should anyone?"

"Sometimes they have pleasant memories." Toetzer selected a fruit and peeled it with thin, delicate fingers. "My home world was a kind place with soft winds and purple clouds and, at night, the stars formed patterns like faces with smiling eyes. We grew all we needed and helped each other and had fun at festivals and weddings and even at funerals. A life well-lived is no cause for grief. Why mourn someone who has moved on to better things? Do we begrudge a child a better way of life?"

"Paradise." Massak speared more meat. "But how real was it? Aside from your memories, I mean."

"It was real."

"Then why leave it?"

"Slavers." Toetzer's hands began to tremble.

"They came and they took me. Others too, no doubt, but I can be sure only of myself. They sold me and I was—changed." The tremble had increased, the fruit falling from his fingers to roll on the table as he slammed his hands to the board. "Defiled," he whispered. "Degraded. Demeaned—God, why did it happen?"

Govinda said, "But why didn't you go back? When you had the chance, I mean."

"I couldn't. It wouldn't have been the same. I'd changed and . . . and . . ." Toetzer shook his head. "No. I couldn't go back."

"Of course you couldn't." Lopakhin was emphatic. "Your own good sense wouldn't let you. A man must be a fool to walk with his head turned to look over his shoulder at the past. No one wants to go back to their home world after they've left it. No one!"

He was wrong. Dumarest wanted nothing more.

The meal ended, servants clearing away the dishes, replacing them with others holding comfits, sweetmeats, tasty morsels designed to pique the senses rather than assuage hunger. Tisanes joined the wines, smoking pots containing herbal teas, others redolent of coffee, of chardle, of rich, thick chocolate.

Govinda said, "You can leave if you want, Earl. Or move around. Dance if you choose." Her eyes were inviting as the soft sounds of music stirred the air. "Or just sit and talk. Change places if you like. Would you care to talk to Toyanna?"

"Later, perhaps."

She was a lean and hungry-looking woman with a roach of silver hair and hands resembling claws. She reminded him of a harpy; a creature of carnival who urged clients to chance their luck or test their skills, knowing they had no chance. He wondered what Chenault saw in her and glanced to where he sat. He seemed asleep and had taken little part in the conversation but his eyes were open, bright in the light, slick with a watchful sheen. As Dumarest watched Baglioni came to whisper into his master's ear.

"No!" Chenault shook his head. "I will not be disturbed."

Again the midget spoke, his voice too low to hear.

"Tell them to go. It is not convenient. This is my house and I am its master. No!" His hand lifted to quench Baglioni's fresh appeal. "I don't care who they are. Send them away."

"Visitors." Massak shrugged as the midget scurried from the hall. "They picked a bad time but since when have the rich ever been considerate?" He turned toward Lopakhin, teeth flashing in a smile. "A pity, Tyner. They would have gawped at your hall and complimented you on your artistic merit and even offered you rich commissions to create for them a similar toy. I often wonder why you always refuse them."

"They could not appreciate my art."

"True, but the money is tempting."

"Money isn't everything. As you said, to them

33

such a creation would be nothing more than an amusing toy. I am not interested in entertaining fools." Lopakhin reached for a sweetmeat, bit into it, spat as an unexpected flavor filled his mouth. "Damn the thing! One day I'll have a word with the chef."

"His creations match life," said Massak. "Both are full of surprises. As an artist yourself you should appreciate his skill. For me such things are too subtle. I prefer simpler fare." He swept a space clear before him and set his elbow on the board, forearm lifted, hand spread and empty. To Dumarest he said, "Come, my friend, let us play a familiar game."

Dumarest shook his head.

"No flames," urged Massak. "No bowls of acid. No spikes or naked blades. Just a friendly test of skill and strength. The one who forces the other's hand to the table wins a promise."

"Such as?" Dumarest smiled as the other shrugged. "No. You would win and I'd be in your debt. In any case to gamble for unknown stakes is to wander blindfolded in a mine field. No man wants a friend to do that."

"True " Massak looked at the artist. "How about you, Tyner? No? Vosper?" He called down the table. "Shior?"

Dumarest rose and left the board to wander around the chamber. Alcoves held objects of delicate construction and obvious worth; vases, bowls, statuettes, jeweled flowers, insects fashioned from glinting metal. A polished plaque held the shadowy impression of a face tormented by endless suffering. One which moved as Dumarest leaned toward it. A mirror? A cunning work of art which took a basic reflection and augmented it with previously delineated lines?

"One of Lopakhin's creations." Toyanna stood beside him, the sheen of her silver hair making a brighter spot on the plaque. "He's crude and coarse and drinks too much but there's magic in him. As I think there is in you, Earl. Give me your hand."

"A reading?"

"You mock?" For a moment anger shone in her eyes then, smiling, she shrugged. "I forgot. A man like you needs always to be cautious but I mean you no harm."

"And can do little good." Dumarest was blunt. "The past I know and the future can take care of itself. I've no wish to listen to mumbled warnings of dire events which might or might not happen. Things never specified but only hinted at. Thank you for the offer, my lady, but this isn't carnival and I'm no gull."

"You think you know my trade?"

"I can guess."

"Because I asked for your hand?" She held out her own. "Take it. Does that make you a reader of palms?"

There was strength in the hand despite its thinness, matching the lithe grace of her body, the near-gaunt appearance of her face. Things Dumarest noted as he saw her eyes, watchful, sharp with calculation. A woman, he guessed, who had never been young but always too adult for her years. A trait which rarely yielded happiness.

His fingers touched her flesh, traced lines, paused as he frowned, moved on as, nodding, he released his breath.

"Your past is filled with shadows, my lady. Times of distress and hardship when, too often, you had to suffer the unthinking folly of others. None appreciated your sensitivity and you were hurt by their indifference. You have known rejection, scorn, contempt, anger. Often you have been misunderstood and the love you hold within you cries for recognition."

She said, dryly, "But it will come together with the man of my dreams. There will be recognition of worth and wealth and a long journey. A good try, Earl, but there could have been more detail. No reading should be too fast. You needed to pause, to ask questions in a casual manner, to incorporate the answers in later remarks. Yet, if you were put to it, you would make out."

Smiling, he released her hand. "Is that your professional opinion?"

"Hardly that." She returned his smile. "Hilary is the expert."

"But you've worked carnival?"

"As a healer, yes." She drew in her breath and met his eyes. "Herbs, unguents, lotions, philtres, tablets, pills; all harmless and most useless but the advice was something else. As was the treatment I gave at times. I had the knack for it. I could look at a client and tell if all was well. Sometimes I could be precise as to what was wrong and even take steps to cure it. Certainly I could warn against it. Do you believe that coming events can cast their shadow before them?''

"Fortune telling?"

"A man has a tumor growing in his brain. The signs are there for those with the skill to see. To state that, shortly, he will go mad and die is not to guess at the future but to know it. To be certain of it. The coming event has cast its shadow. You see?"

Dumarest nodded. "Do you still sell pills?"

"Not exactly but I do prescribe them when necessary." Her eyes held the dancing glints of amusement. "We should have been introduced, Earl. I am Pia Toyanna, Doctor of Medicine, Doctor of Psychology, of Radionic Healing and Psionic Manipulation." She added, casually, "I'm also a surgeon."

One who had made Dumarest foolish. He admitted it and she shook her head, smiling.

"No, Earl, you made a wrong conclusion but it wasn't so far out. Now, may I take your hand?" She held it clasped in her own, not looking at him, her eyes half-closed as if she strained to see things beyond the normal range of vision. Then, sighing, she released his hand. "Strong," she said. "In you there is an incredible determination to survive. I guessed as much when I learned you were coming and—"

"You knew I was coming here?"

"Yes." She recoiled a little from the savage

intensity of his stare. "Yes, I did, a day or two ago."

"How?"

"I was told. Tama told me. It was after visitors had come and they had talked and he told me the news. About you coming and the deaths of the Karroum. They were full of it." Her eyes widened a little as she looked into his own. "Did you have anything to do with it, Earl? Is that why you chose to walk from the other side of the mountain?"

"Did Chenault tell you that too?"

"Of course. Me and others—we've been expecting you. But did you have anything to do with the deaths of the Karroum?"

He said, tightly, "Why ask? If you know so much you know the answer to that too. Anyway, what does it matter?"

"It matters." She was bleak. "The rule of the Karroum falls to Mirza Annette. A bitch, Earl. One who believes in revenge."

Chapter Three

In her was steel, granite, the biting chill of winter
ice. Things Vaclav recognized as she was ushered
into his office to stand glowering before his desk.
A tall, broad-shouldered woman in her late middle
age, her graying hair cut short to frame a harsh,
uncompromising face. Her eyes, palely blue, were
sunken beneath thick brows. Her nose was a jut-
ting promontory dominating a thin-lipped mouth.
Her hands, her chin, the column of her throat
belied the femininity of breasts, hips and buttocks.

Without preamble she snapped, "You know who
I am?"

"Of course." Vaclav gestured to a chair and
waited until she had settled herself. "It is an honor
to meet the Lady Mirza Annette Karroum."

"You know why I'm here?"

"To inquire about the unfortunate incident which took place at the Crystal Falls. I assure you that, as Chief Guardian of Lychen, I made the most thorough investigation. Would you care for some refreshment? Tisane? Coffee? Wine?"

"Coffee."

"With brandy?" He reached for the intercom as she shook her head and gave the order. "While we are waiting, my lady, allow me to offer my condolences on the recent loss your House has suffered. The seventh lord was too young to die."

"When is too young?" Impatient anger edged her voice. "Hedren Anao Nossak was a fool. It would have been better for all had he died at birth. As it was he lived long enough to display his weakness, and his death has caused me serious inconvenience. Alone that was nothing but his uncle died with him and I have been forced to take on the leadership of the House of Karroum. As such I have a duty. None may harm a Karroum and escape the penalty."

"I understand, my lady."

"Do you?" Her tone held contempt. "I doubt it. Honor is instilled with the mother's milk, not adopted in later years to be worn as a garment. One too easily set aside for the sake of compromise or expediency. I'm sick of hearing such words. The path of honor is clear-cut, direct, inarguable. A life for a life! A hurt for a hurt! The creed of the Karroum and, by God, while I rule we'll abide by it!"

A fanatic and a dangerous one. Vaclav wondered what she had been doing in her years away from Lychen. Farming somewhere on a hostile world, he guessed, in the Burdinnion such were plentiful. Now, looking at her, sensing the stubborn pride radiating from her, he wished she had stayed away.

"My lady, you must understand that I can only work within the framework of the law."

"I want facts, Vaclav. Not excuses."

"Yes, my lady."

The coffee arrived and she drank it while he gave her what she wanted. He was patient. Old as she might be and intransigent as she undoubtedly was yet she had the power to break him and they both knew it.

She said, as he ended, "So Angado Nossak returned to this world with a man he'd met on his travels. One we know to be Earl Dumarest. He shared Angado's apartment at the falls. Some time later Angado was found dead in the main salon, his uncle Perotto with him, also dead, the room empty but for an injured cyber. And Dumarest?" China clashed as she set down the cup and saucer. "Gone. Running from the scene of the crime in a stolen raft. Is he guilty?"

"Of what, my lady?"

"The murders, what else?"

Vaclav said, "Angado was killed by a dart from the ring-gun his uncle was wearing. The same weapon caused Perotto's death. Cyber Avro was not injured but incapacitated by illness. The only other man in the apartment, a guard knocked out

41

by Dumarest, was not present when the incident took place."

"But Dumarest was. Together with a woman."

"Wynne Tewson. The guard recognized her. Dumarest used her raft."

"To escape." Mirza was curt. "From whom and for why? Innocent men do not run. He must have killed in that room. He certainly killed those in the other raft which followed him."

"An accident. I have depositions. Three eyewitness accounts. The rafts were close and must have collided over the falls. Dumarest managed to reach safety by the use of auxiliary burners. He was fortunate."

"You think so?"

"My lady?" Vaclav sensed he was on dangerous ground. Mildly he said, "He could have followed the others into the falls. His raft could have veered, spun, tilted, anything. He was lucky it didn't."

"Is that why you haven't arrested him? I can't understand why he wasn't held for questioning. It seems to me that you have failed in your duty. To have ignored such an elementary precaution smacks of the most arrant stupidity."

Vaclav looked down at his hands and fought to remain calm. A victory gained at cost—later he would pay for resisting the impulse to tell the bitch what he thought of her and her arrogant manner.

"My lady, you asked for the facts and have been given them. If you find them not to your liking I am not to blame. I am concerned with

42

guilt, not revenge. With proof, not assumptions. As things stand there is no evidence against Dumarest.''

''But—''

''The incident over the falls was an accident, as three witnesses are willing to swear. There is no case to answer. The raft he used could have been stolen, true, but as the owner is dead there can be no complaint. The dart which killed Angado was fired from the ring worn by his uncle, as the evidence makes plain.''

''Evidence can be manufactured.''

''My lady?''

She was brutal in her curtness. ''Use your brains, man. Perotto's body showed extensive bruising. Injuries which could have been caused by savage blows. He could have been beaten helpless, his ring used against Angado and then turned on himself. Can you deny the possibility?''

''No, but where is the motive?''

''Did he need one? Perhaps Dumarest had outstayed his welcome. He could have thought to use blackmail against Angado and Perotto challenged him. He may have tried to steal.'' She made an impatient gesture. ''Do the details matter? Interrogation would have revealed the truth but you failed to hold him. More proof of your inadequacy.''

Vaclav said, stiffly, ''He was in a raft, my lady. It headed into the sky and was gone long before the guardians learned of the situation. I put out a routine trace but nothing was found. It could be anywhere.''

"Find it. Use every man and machine you have. I want it located. The raft and the man who used it. Understand?"

"I'll do my best."

"You'll do more than that—you'll find Dumarest." She drew in her breath then continued, in a milder tone, "As a girl I studied logic. You've supplied the facts as to what was found in that room and I've given an explanation to account for them. One you don't seem to like. Let's look at your idea. Angado killed by a dart from Perotto's ring. A fact beyond dispute. But what then? Suicide?"

"A possibility, my lady."

"Rubbish! If you believe that, you're a bigger fool than I take you for. With Angado dead Perotto had everything to live for." Her voice rose a little, the former mildness forgotten. "He was scum and may have deserved to die but he was of the Karroum and the one who took his life will pay. I swear it!"

The place held the stench she had hated since childhood; an odor of fear, pain, regret, terror. One compounded by the smell of antiseptics, bandages, drips, the sterilizing fluids used to treat the bedding and gowns. Like a prison, a hospital was a world unto itself where values changed and small things took on a tremendous import. As small officials regarded themselves as greater than they were.

"Aside!" The official wilted beneath her glare. "Where can I find Cyber Avro?"

"My lady." He didn't know her but her arrogance betrayed her class. "Please, my lady, if you will be so good as to wait." He gestured with the hand with which he had tried to bar her progress, pointing at a waiting room fitted with hard chairs, dusty walls, faded prints of scenes and men long dead. "I will summon Doctor Kooga."

"You will send him to me," she corrected. "Now direct me to the cyber."

He lay on a bed in a room containing the most expensive equipment the hospital could provide. As the room held the most comfort; things lost on the patient, who rested supine, eyes closed, his head swathed in an elaborate dressing. Beneath the covers his body looked like that of a man in the last stages of deprivation; the stomach concave, the torso a slight mound, the thighs like sticks, the arms resting above the material the same. What she could see of the face reminded her of a skull.

"My lady, I beg you!" Vaclav, beside her, betrayed the conflict which tore at his equanimity. "This is madness! He is of the Cyclan!"

"He was in the room."

"True, but he saw nothing. He was almost comatose when we found him and needed emergency treatment. All this," his gesture embraced the room, the equipment, "is at the order of the Cyclan who have guaranteed to meet every expense. Kooga dropped all other cases to concentrate on this. He is working in close collaboration with Cyclan physicians." He added, as if in justification, "They communicate by radio. If they were present we wouldn't have this problem."

Nor the witness and Mirza drew in her breath as she thought about it. Vaclav had said nothing, her own intelligence had directed her to the hospital, and she could guess why. The Cyclan with its awesome power cast a wide shadow, working its will even when none of its servants were present. If another cyber had been present the room would have been sealed and guarded against any unauthorized entry. Had Avro's aides survived the accident at the falls the same. But they had died, as all Avro's companions had died, to leave him helpless and alone.

"They will be here soon," said Vaclav as if reading her thoughts. "A special ship is carrying Cyclan physicians to Lychen. They will take over. But, my lady, Avro must be alive when they do."

A threat implied with a hint. One backed by the reputation of the organization which spanned the known galaxy. Obey or pay for disobedience. Pay in the subtle destruction of the economy, the ruin of established Houses, the blasting of ambition and hope. If Avro died too soon Lychen would be ruined.

But Avro could tell her what she needed to know.

"He saw," she said. "He was there. He had to be. He knows how Angado died and who killed Perotto."

"He was helpless. Unaware."

"When you discovered him, yes, but earlier?" Mirza shook her head. "I doubt it. And why was he present at all? Or the woman? No. There are

46

too many questions left unanswered. He will answer them.''

Vaclav caught her arm as she stepped toward the bed. He was sweating, fear overriding the inherent danger of the act. To her the contact of his hand was an insult, an offense against her pride.

"My lady! For God's sake! A touch could kill him!"

The truth and she recognized it and she halted to look down at the skull-like features. A fool, she thought dispassionately. A man who had become a living, thinking machine. One who regarded food as fuel for his body and fat as unwanted surplus. An attitude which robbed him of needed reserves so that in times of strain he drew on basic needs and when, as now, he needed the energy to aid healing, it was not available.

Yet a clever man despite the stupidity. One who could take a handful of facts and extrapolate from them to formulate the logical outcome of any sequence of events. The power of the Cyclan; to guide those who hired their services and to assure success. To become so indispensable that they and not those who used them became the real rulers of worlds, the real dictators of policy. The power behind the throne, unrecognized, unassailable, undefeatable—in time they would own everything.

But not yet and never her.

"Please, my lady!"

Vaclav's hand fell from her arm as again she stepped toward the bed, but she made no effort to touch the patient, looking, instead, at the roll of record paper spilling from a monitoring machine at his side. She frowned in puzzlement at the patterns, checking the machine before again studying the paper.

A push-button was set in an oblong of plastic close to Avro's limp hand. She thrust her thumb against it, held it down until a nurse came running into the room.

"What—" The girl stared, eyes wide with shock. "You! What are you doing here? This room—"

"I ordered Kooga to meet me here." Mirza cut short the protest. "Where is he?"

"Doctor Kooga is off-duty. Resting. He—"

"Get him up and get him here. Fast!" The snap in her voice made the nurse jump. "Move, damn you! Get him!"

"But you shouldn't be here. It isn't allowed. The regulations—" Flustered, the girl turned toward the door, relaxed as she saw the man filling the opening. "This is Doctor Kooga."

He was tall, slim, a face masked by the need to maintain detachment, one too used to the sight of pain. A man younger than Vaclav, who was a decade younger than herself. His voice, while calm, held the tone of one accustomed to obedience.

"Why are you here, nurse?"

"The bell summoned me, sir. When I arrived these people were present."

"Thank you. You may go." He waited until her footsteps had faded down the passage. "Now I

48

suggest we have less shouting and less giving of orders. In themselves neither is capable of achievement." He looked at Vaclav. "I think I know you—Chief Guardian, correct?" He continued at Vaclav's nod. "We've been having a little trouble lately over unauthorized parking. Too many have grown into the habit of leaving their vehicles too close to the hospital. It causes congestion and noise we can do without. See to it."

Vaclav closed his lips against the bile rising from his stomach.

"And you, madam?"

"I am the Lady Mirza Annette Karroum. I have an interest in your patient. But first let me ask you about the patterns you are getting on your encephalograph. They are most unusual and—"

"A matter for medical confidence." Kooga was bland as he interrupted. "The patient is in good hands and is as comfortable as can be expected in the circumstances. Now that your curiosity has been satisfied you may leave. The Chief will escort you from the premises."

She said, "Chief Vaclav will leave us. You will remain." To Vaclav she said, "I'll see you later."

Dismissal which he accepted but in the passage he paused, looking at a reflective surface, not proud of what he saw. A man too old, too established in set ways; he had somehow lost his original zest. Not as tall as he would have liked, not as slim, and far less handsome. Not as clever as the doctor who held the literal power of life and death in his hands. He could only hold and question and send for trial or release. Suffer the burning of stomach acids eating into ulcers when he was forced to swallow his pride. Know tormented nights when, for expediency, he acted more like a servant than a free man. Feel self-revulsion when he was spoken to like a dog and treated like an object of contempt.

Maybe he should have let the bitch kill the cyber and so make an end.

In the room Kooga waited as before for the sound of departing footsteps to fade then he said, firmly, "Let us get one thing straight, madam. Here I am the master. I give the orders. I am the one to be obeyed."

"You are bold," she said. "But stupid. I rule the Karroum—does that mean nothing to you?"

"It means you're rich but—"

"I own this hospital. I own the research facilities attached to it. I probably own your house and the schools your children attend. You have children?"

"Two boys and a girl. What has that to do with it?"

"Children and a wife and, maybe, dependent relatives all enjoying the good things of life. All coming from you, Doctor, and, through you, from me. What promises have the Cyclan made?" She pursed her lips as he made no answer. "Wealth? Position? A place in one of their hospitals?"

"They will appreciate all I do for Cyber Avro."

"So it seems you have a choice. You can rely on their promises or risk the certainty of my anger. On the one hand you stand to gain—what? On the other you will lose your position here. You will lose your house. Your children will be denied their schools. No one claiming affinity with the Karroum will employ you. You will be ostracized. You, your wife, your children, your relatives—need I say more?''

He said, flatly, "You can't. You wouldn't."

"You challenge my power?" Her face became ugly. "I could break you as you could break that nurse who came in here. This is your world, Kooga, but it is only a part of mine. Who is going to fight for you? Who will dare to defy me? Within a year you'll be ruined, your children begging in the streets. And never think I'd hesitate at doing it. The honor of the Karroum is at stake. Make your choice, Doctor."

The promise of friendship from a vast power against the angry spite of a fanatical old woman. If he refused her would the Cyclan restore what she would take? And what if, despite his care, Avro should die before they arrived?

He said, "The pattern from the encephalograph is dictated by an unusual growth in the cyber's cortex. A mass of what seems to be alien tissue which has become incorporated with the basic structure."

"Alien? A cancer?"

"I'm not too sure. The Cyclan has ordered no samples to be taken or investigations made. Those advising me seemed to be aware of the condition and ordered me to take steps to relieve the pressure. This I did by extensive trepanning. The exposed areas of the brain are now covered with plastic domes containing a sterile vapor.''

The brain almost naked, pulsing beneath transparent bowls, the whole covered with dressing to hold them in place and hide them from view. And she had been tempted to slap the lax and empty face!

"Can he be revived enough to talk?" She altered the question. "Does he have periods of loquacity?"

"At times he rambles but seems to be unaware of what is near. Almost it is as if he is vocalizing dreams.''

"Such as?"

"Birds. Flying. Falling." Kooga shrugged. "Just ramblings.''

"Does he answer direct questions?" Again she altered the question. "Can you arrange for him to do so?"

"He is resting in a delicate metabolic balance and to stimulate his consciousness could have unfortunate results. His constitution is poor and I am attempting to bolster it. He is too weak for slow time to be effective—he would die of starvation before any cure could be effected. The alternative, cryogenic treatment, I am reserving for any later emergency.''

Frozen, drugged, held in suspended animation with all life-processes slowed. Had Kooga already used it Avro would be beyond her reach. Thoughtfully Mirza looked at him, at the push-button by his limp hand.

"Why the bell if you don't expect him to revive?"

"An elementary precaution. Aside from the growth in his skull he isn't really ill. His distress is caused by side effects of the pressure and, if it could be removed, he might regain full use of his faculties. In such cases remissions are common. Momentary flashes of awareness or periods which could last some time."

"In which he would be lucid?"

"Of course. There is no viral or bacteriological infection. No broken bones. No organic degeneration to flood the system with toxic wastes. His sense of awareness is distorted by the growth which has disorganized his normal cerebral function."

Like a tumor causing headache, madness and final death. Pain through inpact with the appropriate center, apathy, loss of muscular control. And yet Kooga claimed he wasn't really ill. Not in the strict medical sense, maybe, but certainly in the engineering. Yet, if he had remissions, he could still be of help.

She told Kooga how and he frowned.

"It will be difficult."

"Tell me how? All we need is a bone-conductor speaker and a larynx-mike. I'll make a tape for continuous play. If it breaks into his awareness he'll know what I want. If he has a remission he'll be able to whisper the answer." She added, sensing his waning reluctance, "Do it and you'll have my favor. Anything you get from the Cyclan will be a bonus."

"I won't risk his life."

"All I want is to use his ability. His special skill. The answer to a single question." She drew in her breath. "Where the hell to find Dumarest."

Chapter Four

He slept late, waking to find the window filled with glowing light, uneasy at his tardiness. As he stirred a pounding came from the door, sound which must have woken him, and Dumarest reared on the bed, calling out as his feet touched the floor.

"What is it?"

"Please, sir, a message from my master. He will receive you at zenith."

Baglioni's voice and Dumarest frowned. "When? At noon?"

"At zenith, sir. Food is waiting your pleasure downstairs."

Dumarest stood upright and felt a momentary nausea. The product of too great an effort maintained too long or the lingering traces of an insidious drug. It could easily have been administered in the food or wine served at the dinner but if so for what purpose? He glanced at the door to his room, firmly held by a chair rammed beneath the knob, if he had been drugged to sleep deeply then no one had been able to get to him. Unless the intent had been merely to keep him out of the way.

Standing beneath the shower he recalled the final events of the previous night. Toyanna, Shior whom he had met later, a man built like a whip, slim, graceful, one who could have been a high-wire artist. Vosper who had played with a deck of cards and betrayed a gambler's skill. Others, faces and voices, among them Govinda's, and then the midget guiding him to his room.

To the bed in which he had slept like a log.

Ice-cold water lashed his body to drive away the last of his somnolence. The clothing he had worn at dinner lay where he had thrown it. He ignored it, donning his own, checking the edge of his knife before thrusting it into his boot. Downstairs a servant led him to a small chamber furnished with a table and chairs.

Lopakhin sat in one if them, eating, grease shining on his lips. He waved a fork in greeting.

"Earl! Good to see I'm not the only laggard. Help yourself." The fork pointed as he spoke, halting at the dishes on the table, many of them steaming. "Broiled fish in that one. Eggs in that. Spiced meat over there. Fruit, bread, porridge—God know's who eats it, and this holds something like jam. In the other pots is coffee or tisane. Two kinds, mint and something else." He busied himself with his food. "Don't stand on ceremony, just dig in."

Dumarest chose a portion of fruit, some of the porridge, a piece of bread accompanied by a cup of mint tisane.

Sitting he said, "Is every night like last night?"

"No. That was a special occasion."

"To greet me?" Dumarest added, "I was expected, but how did anyone know I was coming?"

"A call, maybe." Lopakhin wiped his mouth and put down his fork. "Someone you asked direction from could have warned Chenault you were coming." He saw the shake of Dumarest's head. "No?"

"I'd heard of Chenault but didn't know just how to find him. It took time to find out."

"And you didn't want to ask direct. Why? Because you didn't want anyone to know your destination. And you walked the last, what? Hundred miles?" Lopakhin pursed his lips in a soundless whistle. "I see what you're getting at."

"Things like that worry me," said Dumarest. "I'd like to know how it was done."

Lopakhin looked at his plate as if trying to read an answer in the smeared mess of his food. Then, with an abrupt gesture, he pushed it aside.

"You've met Hilary. We fight and argue at times but we're close. Two of a kind but on her it shows more than it does on me. Can you imagine what it must have been like for her? A child, tormented, made different from any other she knew, set up as a spectacle to be laughed at, goggled at, used, abused. Most in that position would have become little better than animals. Some would have gone mad. A few could have found escape in some other way. Closing in on themselves and finding something inside of them they didn't know they had. A trait. A talent. Something given as compensation, maybe."

"Like your artistry?"

"I didn't say that."

"I know. You were talking about Hilary." Dumarest pushed aside his barely touched food. "So she's a sensitive. Able to tell if strangers are approaching. Is that it?"

"Something like that."

"Is that why Chenault keeps her?" Dumarest rose as Lopakhin made no answer. "Never mind. It isn't important. But thank you for telling me."

"If you're one of us you should know. If not then it doesn't—" The artist broke off. "I'd rather you didn't mention who told you."

About the sensitive or the near-spoken threat? Dumarest thought about them both as he headed toward the great doors. They were locked but a postern yielded beneath his hand and he stepped into the clearing before the house. It was deserted, silent but for the musical tinkle of water, and he stepped across it to where the side of the valley reared high before him. A glance at the towering mountain still hiding the sun and he began to climb. Halfway up he halted to sit and look at the Valley of Light.

It was well named: at sunset it would be filled with golden hues, at night the burning darts of firebirds and the flare of other nocturnal creatures together with the sheen of plants releasing stored energy in pale effulgence. At dawn would be the ghosts of dying brilliance, the fading gleam of vanishing stars but now, with the sun sending streamers of brilliance to halo the mountain, it held a muted softness. A lambent glow in which details were blurred and perspective distorted.

A small world which Chenault had made his own. A house which was more like a castle. Guests and servants who acted as retainers. If they didn't accept him as one of their number would he be killed?

Lopakhin had hinted as much and it was a real warning. Had he been drugged to keep him somnolent while his fate had been decided? Did Chenault summon him as a friend or as an executioner?

"Earl!" He heard the voice and rose as Govinda called again. "Earl! Where are you!"

"Here!" He waved as he saw the scarlet flash of her hair. "I'm up here!"

"It's getting late." The pale blur of her face stared at him, framed by the mass of her hair, a face which, suddenly, became achingly familiar. "Earl?"

He stumbled as he ran toward her, his boot hitting a root, causing him to fall, to roll down the slope and come to rest hard against the gnarled bole of a stunted tree. One which showered him with droplets and eye-stinging pollen from the profusion of pendant tails adorning the branches. Rising, rubbing at his eyes, he saw her running toward him but now she looked as she had before.

"We must hurry." She looked at the sun now burning at the peak of the mountain. "It's zenith and Chenault will be waiting."

He sat in a room flanked with shelves bearing old books, moldering files, logs, reports, journals, ancient manifests, recordings dusty and faded with time. An assembly interspersed with brighter, newer items; globes, star charts, almanacs, computer read-outs all set in neat array. The room was windowless, light coming from glow-plates set in the roof, a soft illumination which dispelled all shadows.

"My hobby." Chenault's gesture embraced the room. "Or my obsession, some would say. It rather depends on your point of view. Tell me, Earl, what do you know of legends?"

"I know that others claim that in every legend lies a grain of truth."

"Others? What of yourself?"

"I wouldn't know." He saw Chenault smile and added, bluntly, "You know why I'm here and what I'm looking for but what I hope to find is no myth. Earth exists. I know it. I was born on that world. To me it is no legend."

"But to others it is nothing else."

Dumarest shrugged. "A point of view. Some would say you are mad for wasting your time with old papers and idle dreams. Because they say it does it make it true? A man I trusted told me you could and would help me. That is why I'm here. If he was wrong tell me and I'll leave.''

"He wasn't wrong."

"Shakira," mused Dumarest. "The circus of Chen Wei. He owned it but he hadn't founded it. That was done long ago. By your father? Your grandfather?''

Chenault said, "How did you know?"

"Your name. The appearance of your hall. Those you keep around you. Once the circus gets into your blood you can't get rid of it. Chen Wei— Chenault, the coincidence is too strong. Do you ever regret letting it go?''

"At times, yes. Then it is like a pain. But I had no choice and Tayu's need was greater than my own. We reached agreement and I retired to follow my own pursuits. The money from the sale allowed me to do that, to help others and . . . and . . . well, all that is history. But, yes, I did know you were coming and what you hoped to gain.'' Chenault smiled, relaxing. "You're a hard man, Earl. I knew it the moment I saw you. A hard and determined man. Only a fool would take you for one. Now, let us talk about legends.''

A subject which had become his life and he glowed as he spoke of mythical worlds, of strange regions reputedly discovered and later forgotten, of mystical plants and beasts, of isolated areas on lost and forgotten planets. Tales Dumarest had heard before but he sat patiently, listening, waiting, knowing the other must take his time.

"Eden, Paradise, Heaven, Avalon—all legendary worlds, Earl. All with one thing in common; places of ease and beauty where pain is unknown and no one ever falls sick or grows old or dies. Hope-worlds, Pearse calls them. Planets built of imaginative longing. Born in conditions of despair and hardship; tales whispered to children to console them for their bleak and hopeless lives. Live, be good, and when you die those worlds will be waiting. With time the essential qualification became forgotten and now men actually believe such worlds exist and are waiting to be rediscovered together with others, El Dorado, Jackpot, Bonanza —a dozen others including Earth.''

"Which is no legend.''

"Pearse says otherwise. Have you read him? And the study by Mikhailovik on the subject? The work of Dazym Negaso?'' Chenault rose and moved to a shelf to return with a thick volume. "The third edition,'' he said, "Completely revised. Listen.'' He turned pages then, in a flat voice, read, "Earth, the name of a mythical planet held in veneration by the Original People, a backward sect found on various planets scattered throughout the galaxy. The sect is a secret one and neither seeks nor welcomes converts, fresh adherents being obtained from natural increase. The main tenet of their belief is that Mankind originated on a single world, the mythical planet Earth, and after cleansing by tribulation, Mankind will return to the supposed world of origin.'' Chenault closed the book. "Well?''

"There is more," said Dumarest. "He talks of the Original People and their esoteric rites. He also mentions the inconsistency of a variety of human types developing on one world beneath one sun."

"The main argument of those eager to discount the theory," said Chenault. "But all using it overlook the obvious. We have varied types of human now, yes, those with black skins and with brown, with yellow and white together with a range of hair colors and consistencies; curled, lank, oval, round, kinked—and even divergencies in physical shape; long-armed, broad-shouldered, round-headed and peaked. But all can interbreed. All belong to the same species. To any ethnologist the answer is obvious." Chenault set down the book and leaned forward over the table at which he sat. "One race, Earl. One type—the changes took place after leaving the Mother Planet. After!"

Born of wild radiations found in space and on worlds close to violent suns. Genes altered to form new patterns. Mutations many of which must have died as unviable but some had survived to pass on their altered characteristics. Dumarest had seen them; catlike men, wolflike, women who had the markings of serpents, haired like goats, some with skin thickened in places into scales. And Chenault must have seen more; things of nightmare, creatures distorted beyond easy recognition, shaped in mockeries of birds, beasts, spiders, fish.

Freaks to stock sideshows.

"It fits, Earl," he said. "If Mankind originated

on one world they couldn't be as they are now. The changes must have come after they had left. Perhaps they had to leave because of the changes." He paused. Then, in a voice which held the roll of drums, he intoned, "From terror they fled to find new places on which to expiate their sins. Only when cleansed will the race of Man be again united."

The creed of the Original People—was Chenault one of them? But if he was why had he revealed himself? Or was he throwing out bait to win support and, maybe, more information?

Dumarest said, "You are confusing legends. As I understand it Earth is supposed to be a world loaded with riches. Rivers of medicinal wine, trees heavy with fruit, hills studded with gems. Find it and you find the wealth of the galaxy."

"The things left behind," said Chenault. "The goods which had to be left, the installations, the buildings, the facilities, the treasure of knowledge, Earl. Of knowledge. Can you imagine what secrets they must have known? No, there is no conflict. Not when you study it with an open mind. Not when you delve a little beneath the surface. Did you know that Earth has another name?"

Dumarest nodded. "Terra."

"Exactly. Now it begins to make sense." Again Chenault intoned the creed. "From terror they fled . . . Not 'terror,' Earl, but Terra. Terra! They ran from Earth!"

*   *   *

It made sense but words, like figures, could be made to supply a variety of truths. Chenault had chosen his some time ago; despite the timbre of his voice, the deduction wasn't new, and Dumarest remembered the ritual of the blessing, the symbolic gesture and the words intoned, the response.

He said, "Tayu, Tama, Toetzer, Toyanna, Tyner—how many of you have names beginning with T?"

"Why?"

"It's a mistake unless you want to advertise yourselves. Coincidence can be stretched too far. And if you're using it as a means of identification there are better ways."

"Such as this?" Chenault made the gesture he had made at the table, hands forming a T. "How many would know what it means? Would you? But if I did this?" He drew a T on the table with a finger dipped in ink. At the upper junction he added a circle then, deliberately, quartered it with a cross.

"The symbol of Earth," said Dumarest. "Of Terra. But I'm not interested in legends. All I want is to get back home."

"We share the same ambition."

"You act like a secret society. Why? There is no need."

"No?" Chenault leaned across the table. "I don't agree. Think about it, Earl. How long have you searched for the coordinates of Earth? How often have you been frustrated? If the planet

65

exists, and you know that it does, why can't it be found?"

A question Dumarest had pondered too often and still the answers remained the same. It wasn't listed in the almanac and, as all planets were listed, it couldn't exist. The logical answer which refused to recognize its absence of logic. Another, equally vapid: Earth was a legend and who could believe a legendary world was real? And how could an actual world have such a stupid name? Earth was dirt, soil, the stuff you grew crops in. Worlds had proper names or they weren't worlds at all.

Words to deny the obvious, but men believed in them and not his living, breathing assertion of the truth. To state it was to invite mockery, contempt, arrant disbelief. A weaker man would have been made the butt of cruel jests, one less controlled would have wasted strength in angry combat.

"A lost world," mused Chenault. "Your world, I mean. You left it, wandered on the ship which carried you and, when you tried to return home you found no one believed it to be real. Well, stranger things have happened. I remember one time when—" He broke off, one hand lifting to his chest.

"Something wrong?"

"No. Give me a moment." Chenault lowered his head as if to hide his face and eyes. Time during which Dumarest sat listening, his face impassive, his eyes half-closed. "Forgive me."

66

Chenault straightened in his chair. "The penalty of age."

"You want me to get something? Water? Wine? Some brandy?"

"No."

"A doctor?"

"No. I'll be—" Again the hand lifted as Chenault almost slumped to the table. Dumarest rose, touched his shoulder, the exposed column of the throat. "No!" Chenault twisted. "Leave me. Get—" His voice faded. "Tell her I need her. Hurry!"

"Who?"

"Pia. Pia. Tell her."

Dumarest left the room, almost running, reaching the dining room, a chamber holding musical instruments, another set with gaming tables. Vosper sat dealing himself a hand.

"Chenault's ill. He wants the woman, Toyanna. Where can I find her?"

"The laboratory or in her room on the first floor but—" He shrugged as Dumarest moved away, concentrating on his cards.

Pia Toyanna was halfway down the stairs when Dumarest found her. She wore a simple gown, green edged with black, belted snug to her slender waist. She carried no satchel and her hands were empty. She listened to Dumarest with an air of impatience.

"Yes. Yes, I understand." She nodded dismissal. "Just leave this to me."

"Do you need help?" Chenault was a big man. "If he needs to be moved you could have trouble."

67

"I can manage." She faced him, eyes and voice determined. "You've done all you can do. Now please leave things to me."

Dumarest watched her go, following her as she headed to where he had left Chenault, frowning when she moved on to a door lower down the passage. As he made to follow a figure stepped before him. Baglioni, small but determined, lifted his left hand. The dart gun in the other glimmered with reflected light.

"This area is restricted, sir. Please do not force me to use this against you." The dart gun lifted in his hand.

Dumarest said, "Do you think it would stop me?"

"I'm certain of it." The midget remained calm. "It fires a spray with a cover four feet in diameter at a distance of as many yards. I shall fire as soon as you lessen that distance. One dart must surely hit your face and one will be enough to knock you out. To cost you an eye, perhaps, if you should be unlucky. Personally I wouldn't care to gamble on the odds."

Too high against him but not for Dumarest. He knew he could close the distance between them and reach the man before he could fire. But to do it would reveal his speed and make an enemy and all to no purpose. Chenault had the right to act as he chose within his own house.

Casually Dumarest said, "I wouldn't either. Will Tama be all right?"

"He will receive the best of attention, sir. That I assure you. You need have no concern. Now, if you would care to return to the dining room, refreshments have been served."

Cakes and sandwiches and drinks of various types together with a collection of condiments.

Vosper, selecting a cake, sprinkled it with an aromatic red powder and tasted it with the tip of his tongue.

"Too sweet." He added more powder. "You shouldn't have been in such a hurry, Earl. I could have saved you that run-in with Baglioni. And Toyanna knew she was needed."

"Why didn't she go directly to Chenault?"

"Didn't she?" Vosper shrugged. "Maybe she went to get her medical kit. She couldn't have done much for Tama without one." He tasted the cake again, nodded his satisfaction, and began to eat. "Care for a game? Anything you like as long as it's for real money. I lose interest when playing for fun. Your choice; Starsmash, Spectrum, High, Low, man-in-between. You name it."

"Poker?"

"Sure." Vosper beamed. "My favorite." Finishing his cake he glanced toward the gaming room. "Want to eat or shall we get at it?"

"You sound like a shark," said Dumarest. "Are you?"

"No."

"A telepath? How did you know about my run-in with the midget?"

"A shrewd guess. When Tama's in trouble Baglioni comes running to protect him. It happens every time." Vosper laughed. "A telepath. I wish to hell I was. I'm just an engineer."

Chapter Five

Like a mouse the nurse moved down the corridor
and into the room where Avro lay like a corpse on
the bed. A routine visit; monitors did a good job
and normally were trusted but this was a special
patient and Doctor Kooga had made it plain that
any failure would bring harsh penalties.

Quietly she stepped to the side of the bed, looking at the flaccid, skull-like face, one seeming
more dead than alive, yet the monitors registered
the beating of the heart, the passage of oxygenated
blood through the brain. Only one thing seemed
out of place: a tiny, flickering lamp on the panel of
the encephalograph, the signal of high current
demand. Nothing to worry about, activity of the
recording pens always registered above a certain
level, but this was unusual in terms of duration.

The cyber's mental faculties were working at high pressure and she wondered why. He should be comatose, drifting in a mindless lethargy, thoughts at a low ebb. Instead his mind seemed to be acting like a dynamo.

Leaning over the inert form she gently touched his face. A gesture without the intention of a caress; part of her duties was to administer drops in each eye. A thing done with practiced skill and she wiped the surplus from the waxen cheeks, trying not to think of the orbs she had seen, the spark which seemed to glow in their depths. The reflection of light, she guessed, it had to be that. The cyber was drugged, asleep, resting like the dead man he would soon be unless things took a turn for the better.

Even so she tiptoed quietly from the room when she left.

Avro didn't register her going. He floated in a void shot through with swaths of warmly glowing colors illuminating shapes of unusual proportions. Vistas which rolled endlessly through the chambers of his mind. Stored impressions, memories, speculations, all now released to flood his questing awareness, but confined to the limits of his brain.

A foretaste of what would be when his cortex had been removed from his body and sealed in a vat to become a part of the tremendous complex which was Central Intelligence. There he would become one with the gestalt which directed the Cyclan, using cybers and agents to spread the dominance of the organization until, in the end, it would rule the entire galaxy.

A concept which yielded mental pleasure and he swam in a sea of ceaseless attainment during which problems were solved, new worlds based on unusual chemical combinations created, new frames of reference established to bring into being new and exciting universes.

A time of euphoria which faded as the colors dulled and the vast shapes diminished to form a rocky plain on which stood a solitary figure. One clad in the scarlet robe he knew so well, the breast glimmering with the Seal of the Cyclan.

Marle? Had the Cyber Prime come to visit him in his vision? A companion? Someone he had previously known? Avro strained his eyes but could make out no detail; the drawn cowl masked the figure's face.

"Master?"

His words died without acknowledgment but he was not surprised. The vision matched others he had experienced before; illusions born of his distorted mind. The Homochon elements grafted within his brain were now growing like a cancer running wild. Normally, when activated, they established rapport with Central Intelligence, placing him in direct mental communication with the great complex. An organic communication which was almost instantaneous. But, illusion though it seemed, this too could be the product of rapport.

He said, "Who are you? Am I to be interrogated?"

Sound which did not exist beyond his enclosed

world, just as the movement he made as he stepped toward the figure had no reality but in his mind.

"You failed," said the cowled figure. "You failed."

Not once but twice and Avro felt the shame of inadequacy even as he admitted the truth.

"I admit it," he said. "I failed. But it was not wholly my fault. The affliction I now suffer struck me down. I had Dumarest in my hand, safe, captured, but I collapsed at the wrong moment. Even so he should have been held. The arrangements had been made. Those with me should have taken him." In memory he was again the sight over the falls; the rafts almost touching, the flames, the bodies falling and Dumarest rising like a bird into the sky. "Luck," he said. "I knew of his luck but thought I'd taken every precaution. I made a mistake, one, but it was enough. Who could have known I would be stricken down when I was?"

"You had the data. You knew of your condition."

"Yes."

"You should have predicted the logical outcome."

"I did. But there was time."

"Time is a variable."

"A trait accounted for. The probability of my staying active and successfully completing the capture was 98.5 percent. Almost certainty."

But it nor any other prediction could ever be that. Always there remained the unknown factor which, as had happened, could negate the highest

74

probability. A factor which seemed to act to Dumarest's advantage with consistent regularity.

"Even so you failed. A proof of your inefficiency. Can you deny that you merit the penalty of failure?"

Avro felt the cold chill of what was to come. A cyber did not fail. If he did not succeed then he ceased to be a cyber. The reward for which he had dedicated his life was denied him. Instead he was given total extinction.

And the colors would be gone, the shapes, the endless drifting in a void thronged with mental attainment. There would be no created worlds, no new universes, no communion with others of his kind. No near-immortality in which to plan domination and guide the Cyclan to the fulfillment of the master plan.

"No," he said. "I have not failed. Not yet."

"Then where is Dumarest? The secret of the affinity twin which he holds still eludes us. We must recover the sequence in which the fifteen biomolecular units must be assembled."

Avro said, "To repeat the obvious demonstrates a lack of efficiency. I am aware of the need to obtain the secret."

One which would give the Cyclan total domination over all others. By its use one intelligence could take over the body of another. Become that other, using the host as it willed, defying all barriers of time and space. Each cyber could control a ruler and the brains making up Central Intelligence could experience bodily life again and rid the

75

Cyclan of the fear that they hovered on the brink of insanity.

"He must be found," said the figure. "Where is he? What happened in the main salon of the apartment by the falls. What happened?"

"Dumarest killed and escaped," said Avro. "Killed the man who had killed." He couldn't think of names but the incident was clear.

"Where is Dumarest?"

"Gone." Rising into the featureless sky on a trail of flame. "Gone."

"Where is Dumarest?"

A problem to be answered; find the man and find the secret and, at the same time, prove his efficiency, his right to his reward. Avro examined the evidence, the smattering of facts he had gleaned as to what Dumarest had done since his arrival on Lychen. The people he had met and the interests he had shown. Data which he incorporated into a web of other facts, isolating, evaluating, arriving at a logical conclusion.

"Where is Dumarest?"

A question answered then ignored despite repeated demands as he concentrated on the figure standing on the rocky plain before him. A simulacrum created by Central Intelligence? A novel means of rapport? Something special to himself or was the whole thing a fantasy?

"Who are you?" he demanded. "Show me your face."

He watched as a hand rose to throw back the cowl. He felt no surprise; logic had told him who and what the figure must be and he stood, in the world of his mind, looking at the accuser who was himself.

Vosper said, "Open for five. Jem?"

Toetzer took his time, pursing his lips as he studied his cards, the middle finger of his left hand flicking the pasteboards. A habit Dumarest had noticed since the man had joined the game hours ago. As he had noticed others from those who had joined the school.

"Call and raise ten."

Toetzer wasn't bluffing. He played with mathematical skill; paying strict attention to the odds, assessing the worth of each hand, the potential of each draw. Massak was different, using guile to mask his real intent.

"I'll just lift that another five."

A killer waiting to strike. To use the power of his money to crush the opposition as he would use the strength of his body to destroy an enemy. Shior matched him but in a more subtle fashion. A rapier as compared to a club smiling as he, too, lifted the raise by an equal amount. A ploy to test the opposition, buying the right to act in his own manner, one akin to Massak's but not so blatantly obvious. A man who would appear to be a reckless fool—and who would take those who thought so for all they had when the time was ripe.

"Earl?" Vosper looked to where he sat. "You in?"

Dumarest shook his head, following the instinct

which told him to fold his hand. Lopakhin joined him, grunting when Vosper met the raise and doubled it.

"Here it comes. The hammer. The trouble with Ron is he's greedy."

But too engrossed in his own hand to pay due attention to the others. Dumarest sat back in his chair, looking, listening. The players had gathered as Vosper had said they might and, as was the habit of men playing cards, they talked. Small talk, banter, jests, idle remarks but, from such talk information could be gained. Dumarest had made the most of the opportunity.

Vosper was an engineer, Toetzer a mathematician, Massak a mercenary, Shior a fighter, Lopakhin, aside from an artist, was also a communications expert. Grain garnered from chaff and Dumarest added it to other facts. Toyanna a skilled doctor, Hilary a sensitive, Govinda?

He felt the touch on his shoulder as Massak, laughing, scooped up his winnings. The woman stood beside him, hair a scarlet aureole, her face smooth, her eyes luminous.

Vosper glanced at her and shook his head. Toetzer, cards in hand, paused as he was about to deal.

"No offense, Earl, but if Govinda stays then I'm quitting the game."

"You think she's helping me to cheat?"

"No, nothing like that, it's just that—" Toetzer broke off, then appealed to the others. "How can I explain? Can any of you tell him?"

"She reminds him of his mother," said Vosper. "The one who—"

"Not my mother!" Toetzer was harsh. "The bitch who bought me. Who defiled me. Who— The hell with it. She stays I go." He slammed down the cards. "What's it to be?"

"I'll go," said Govinda. Stooping, she whispered in Dumarest's ear. "I just wanted to be close to you. To ask if I'll see you again later. We could go for a walk or something."

"Yes," he said. "Later."

"Not now?"

He glanced at the cards, the players, the money on the table. As yet he still had to win. "Later," he said again. "I promise."

Massak shook his head as she left the room. "A beautiful woman," he said. "What do you see in her, Earl?" He hurried on as Dumarest frowned. "I mean what does she look like to you?"

"What you said—a beautiful woman."

"Yet she reminds Toetzer of everything he hates. To Vosper?" Massak looked toward him. "What do you see in her, Ron?"

"I had a sister once. She looks the same."

"Someone you loved and would never hurt, right?" Massak turned to Lopakhin. "And you? What do you see with your artist's eye?"

"Beauty." Lopakhin was curt. To Dumarest he said, "They're having a game with you. Toetzer doesn't like her, that's true, or he says he doesn't like her, which isn't the same thing. Personally I think he fell in love with the woman who bought

79

him and taught him how to live. Certainly he can't forget her. If she stood naked and defenseless before him all he'd do would be to try and kill her with kisses."

Toetzer said, "That's a lie!"

"When you look at Govinda you see her. Right?"

"Yes, but—"

"That proves it." Lopakhin shrugged and again looked at Dumarest. "She's a mentamorph," he explained. "It's a survival trait, I guess. She appears to those who might possibly threaten her as something they would never hurt. With Vosper it's his sister. With me it's a model I knew once and for whom I'd have walked over burning coals. Who Massak likes is anyone's guess but Shior had to stop him once when he tried to get his hands on the woman. And you, Earl? What does she look like to you?"

A woman, soft, appealing, one haunted by a hidden yearning.

One who, twice now, had wrung the strings of his heart.

The first he mentioned, the second he did not. Shior nodded, understanding, his voice serious as he said, "You've hit it, my friend. Govinda is more than what she seems. Inside of her she carries a deep hurt. Of all the gifts that anyone could offer her, motherhood is the one she would take."

"She's barren," said Vosper. "Sterile. God knows how much she spent and how hard she's tried but—" He shrugged. "The thing she wants most is the thing she can't have."

"Adoption?"

"The easy answer, Earl, and the most obvious solution, but it's not for her. She needs to have an affinity with the child. She isn't an ordinary woman and can't accept an ordinary baby. Toyanna could tell you why; it has something to do with the rejection syndrome, a mental repulsion due to her attribute." Vosper shook his head and sighed. "A pity. I hate to see anyone living in hell especially someone like Govinda. She's a nice person."

"Maybe too nice." Massak frowned at Toetzer. "Are you making love to those cards or stacking the deck? Come on, let's play."

Vaclav came out of the dusk like a nocturnal bird of prey, scowling, infuriated at the brusqueness of the command which had brought him to Kooga's office. To the doctor when they were together he snapped, "You summoned and I've responded. But if you have any more complaints as to unauthorized parking I shall not be amused."

"Sit." Kooga waved to a chair. Like the office it was of good quality and excellent taste. "Let us understand each other. As Chief Guardian of Lychen you have a duty to—"

"Protect the persons, property and privileges of the ruling Houses," interrupted Vaclav. "Basically that is the sum total of my responsibility. To take care of the Insham, the Vattari, the Cerney, the Karroum. Especially the Karroum."

"You don't like them?"

"They own most of the planet. They crack the

81

biggest whip. When they say 'jump' we ordinary people ask 'how high?' I think you know that, Doctor.''

"And if I do?"

"You have the answer to your question." Vaclav added, impatiently, "There are things needing my attention. Why did you send for me?"

"A problem." Kooga opened a drawer and produced a recording. He laid it before him on the desk. "After our last meeting Mirza Karroum had me do something for her. She was convinced the cyber could help her locate Dumarest. At her insistence I connected a microphone to an electrode connected to the cyber's cranium so as to feed in the output of a tape. I also connected another from his larynx to a recorder. It was her hope that, by verbal stimulus, he would gain remission and be able to respond.''

Vaclav said, "Would it work?"

"Theoretically, yes."

"Did it?"

For answer Kooga touched the recording with the tip of a finger and said, "We are dealing with the Cyclan. On Lychen the Karroum are powerful but we both know that if the Cyclan wished they would be ruined and destroyed. Also, and this you can understand, I do not take kindly to threats.''

Vaclav studied the doctor's face, seeing beneath the surface to the injured pride, the resentment which he knew so well. Familiar emotions which he had seen and used often before, but Kooga was not the subject for interrogation even if a charge could be made. Even so he could be led.

"So you made a decision," said Vaclav. "What?"

"This is in the strictest confidence, Chief."

"Of course."

"I had to make a decision and arranged a compromise. I made sure that the skull-connection was inoperative. The connecting wire wasn't quite making contact."

"So you got nothing." Vaclav mimicked a report. "Too bad, my lady, I did my best but the cyber failed to respond." He shrugged. "Where's the problem?"

"A nurse went into his room to make a routine check. During it she noticed unusual activity of the encephalograph. She also made physical contact with the patient. This was within the scope of her duties but—" Kooga paused then finished with a rush. "She must have moved the wire or touched the skull-connector and made it operable. She probably thought it a part of the monitoring device and did a routine check. This is the result." Again he touched the recording. "The final part contains the cyber's prediction of where Dumarest is to be found."

"Where?"

"Chenault's. The Valley of Light."

"Are you sure?"

"No. How can I be? The prediction comes from the cyber, not myself, but how often are they wrong?" Kooga frowned. "You seem troubled."

Vaclav said, "At Mirza Karroum's insistence I

ordered a wide-scan, high-fly survey. Costly, but what the Karroum want they get. Something which could have been the raft Dumarest used was spotted to the east of the mountain where Chenault has his home. But it was over a hundred miles distant. Why would he have wanted to walk so far?''

"To hide.''

"From us?''

"From the Cyclan. Listen.''

The voice from the recorder was weak, thin, drifting from fast to slow as if time, for the speaker, held a dimension different and more variable than for others. Words which blurred, changed, struck with sudden, crystalline clarity.

"It ends there,'' said Kooga. "The part where he mentions Chenault. That's the part Mirza took notice of.''

"She heard it?''

"I couldn't stop her. I thought the recording would be blank so there was no need to antagonize her. Later, after I'd played it again, I sent for you.''

"Why?''

"I told you the encephalograph showed unusual activity,'' said Kooga. "The wild variations from the normal seemed to be aligned to these spoken words. That was to be expected but there were other, wilder variations, all unfamiliar, but it's my guess there's a connecting link. The stimulus must have jarred his awareness and concentrated it on a special area. Now listen again. Really listen.''

Again the words, the thread of varying sound,

but this time Vaclav concentrated harder, using his skill and training to filter noise from the relevant data, to fill in the missing pieces.

As the recording ended Kooga said, "He was explaining what happened in the room. How Dumarest killed a man who had killed. That must have been Perotto. Then comes the interesting part; the reason the Cyclan are so interested in Dumarest. It seems he holds a secret they want. A pity it isn't made clear but there is no doubt as to his importance to them." Pausing he added, meaningfully, "His importance and his value."

"Alive."

"What?"

"Dead he would be valueless," explained Vaclav. "Mirza was right; he didn't kill Perotto in self-defense. If they fought it was because Perotto wanted to save his life. We know that he failed. Which makes Dumarest guilty of murder."

"A technicality." Kooga dismissed it with a gesture. "Avro was the only witness and he would never put the man he came to find in danger. Soon the representatives of the Cyclan will arrive on Lychen. If we can hand Dumarest over to them, alive and well, we can ask our own price. Do I make myself clear, Chief?

"You want me to find him, hold him, keep him from harm while you negotiate with the Cyclan."

"Yes." Kooga nodded, satisfied. "I assume you have no objections to making a fortune? To being rich and freed of your present restraints?"

"None."

"Then we are partners?"

Vaclav said, dryly, "In what? If Mirza Karroum knows where Dumarest is she's on her way to kill him by now."

Chapter Six

She came with the night, the stars, her rafts making dark, moving splotches against the nacreous glow of the sky. Riding high and proud as they arrowed toward the Valley of Light.

"Three of them." Massak lowered his binoculars. "She'll drop one to each side to provide crossfire and come in with the other." He sucked thoughtfully at his lower lip. "If we take her out the others will open up in revenge. If we hit them she'll blast the house. Clever. The lady must have had experience."

"That's good," said Shior from where he stood at the mercenary's side. "At least she'll know when she's been beaten."

"If she's beaten." Massak used his binoculars

again. "There's always doubt in these matters. Right, Earl?"

Dumarest made no comment, standing, watching the sky. The rafts were closer now, making no attempt to adopt evasive action, probably unaware they had been spotted. A reasonable assumption; Hilary's talents were unknown outside the house. Her warning had come in good time now that she, and others, were safely lodged in the cellars far below the surface.

Dumarest said, "How many and how are they armed?"

"Four in each of the side-rafts together with a driver. Five in all. Ten when put together. They seem to have machine rifles."

"Lights?"

"That too."

Men to spread along the facing crests, lights to illuminate the clearing, weapons to cover it with a murderous crossfire. Dumarest said, "We need to get behind them so as to attack from the rear. They'll be facing inward against the glow. Easy targets, but we'll have to be in position before they land."

"Good thinking, Earl." Massak smiled, teeth white against the ebon of his skin. "This isn't the first time you've seen action."

"No."

"I thought not. You have a way of sizing up the situation. How about the other raft? Any ideas?"

"Once the flankers are knocked out they'll be in the center of fire. We can hit them from both sides." Dumarest added, pointedly, "If we get into position in time."

"Us, Earl. Shior and me. This one you stay out of. Chenault's order." Massak glanced at the other man. "Let's go!"

As they vanished into the shadows Lopakhin called from the open postern.

"Earl! Here, man! Get inside—fast!"

Good advice and Dumarest followed it; if firing should start he would be a clear target. As the heavy door thudded shut behind him the artist gestured to a screen beside it.

"It's hooked to a scanner higher up," he explained. "A good view and a safe one. You never know what these crazy bastards will do next. Look at her!" He gestured at the screen, the raft it depicted, the woman standing within it. "What the hell does she imagine she is?"

A warrior-queen riding to war as others of her House had done in ages past. Snatching the power left by slain men to lead their forces to victory and establish the Karroum as the thing it was today. A Family secure in its pride, jealous of its honor.

As the raft lowered, her amplified voice echoed from the sides of the valley.

"Chenault! This is Mirza Annette Karroum! I demand audience!"

Silence then, as the raft landed, her voice again.

"Chenault! I come to parley. Unless you appear I'll blow open your house!"

A threat backed with the potential of action. As lights blazed from the flanking rafts to illuminate

89

the clearing Dumarest could see the snouted weapon in the woman's vehicle. A heavy-duty laser or a missile-launcher. The latter, he guessed, a laser would have been less efficient given the vehicle and its load.

"Chenault, damn you! I'll wait no longer!"

"Wait!" His voice boomed from a speaker. "Give me time. Is this a way to come calling? What ails you that you make such threats? Has the Karroum gone mad?"

"This is a matter of honor. I shall not be denied."

"Honor? What is this talk of honor? How have I offended you? Why come with arms to my house? What do you want of me?"

"Open your doors. Come out and face me."

"Yes. Yes, but give me a moment. All can be settled with a little patience. Mirza Annette Karroum, you say?"

Talk to gain time as Dumarest knew and, on the crests, men would already have died if Massak and Shior knew their jobs. Gasping out their lives to the thrust of a blade or rearing, necks broken by the twist of a thong. Silent death dealt to the unsuspecting. A natural attribute of war.

Watching, Dumarest saw the woman look at her driver, speak to him, turn frowning to stare at the crests on either side. A loss of communication or some noise lacking explanation: something which troubled her.

He said, "If Chenault means to show he'd better do it fast. She's suspicious."

"He'll make it."

90

"Open the postern. Pretend he has. Hurry!"

He appeared as Lopakhin swung wide the panel, standing in the opening, gesturing as if to someone beyond. Mimicry made truth as Chenault stepped toward him. Past him. Through the door and out into the clearing to stand, tall and grim in the artificial glow.

A man who scant hours ago had collapsed now apparently in the best of health. His voice matched his stance, harsh, arrogant.

"This is my home. You intrude. Go before I feel insulted."

"Feel as you please. I stay until honor has been satisfied. Where is Dumarest?"

"Who?"

"Dumarest. Earl Dumarest. He is here and I want him. I want him dead. The honor of the Karroum demands it." She leaned forward over the snouted weapon in the raft, her face made ugly by light and shadow, flesh and blood turned into a chiaroscuro of ice and iron forming the lineaments of a bestial mask. "Him or you, Chenault. Make your choice. Your life, your home, all you possess— or you give me Dumarest. And you give him to me now!"

There was power in her and determination and an iron will which would brook no interference, no opposition. She would gain her way or do as she had threatened and, even as Chenault made no move, Dumarest knew that time was running out.

"Earl!" Lopakhin tried to catch his arm as

Dumarest reached for the door. 'Don't, man. Don't! Let Chenault handle it!''

A man who stood as if turned to stone, his head uptilted a little, his arms held from his body, shoulders stooped and strangely at variance with the massive torso.

As Dumarest came level with him Chenault turned and said, tightly, ''Go back. Don't interfere. Just leave things to me.''

''I can't.''

''Why not?''

Because if the man was killed the hope of finding Earth would go with him. The knowledge stored in his brain, the facts he must have garnered, the coordinates Dumarest felt he must have. And if he defied the woman he would die. The weapon mounted on the raft would fire and spread a hail of destruction. Shrapnel and flame which would turn the clearing and all it contained into smoldering ash.

The woman would do it. Even if she died giving the order yet she would still give it.

Dumarest walked toward her to halt in the pool of illumination thrown by the light on her raft.

He said, ''You want me. Why?''

''You are Dumarest?''

''Yes.''

''I came to kill you. I want you to know that.''

''I know it.'' He met her eyes. ''Now tell me why.''

''Why I want you dead?'' She stepped from the

raft and came close to him, her eyes raking his face, his body. "You killed one of the Karroum. That is answer enough."

"For you, obviously. But not for me. I assume you are talking of Perotto. I killed him, yes. If I hadn't he would have killed me. As he had already killed Angado. Or didn't you know that? Angado was of the Karroum, too. In fact he was the titular head of the House. Would you have hunted down Perotto if he were still alive? Or does the honor of the Karroum stop when it comes to dealing with murdering filth bearing the same name?"

"You go too far!" She fought for breath, trying to master her rage, mouth open as she filled her lungs. "Perotto was—"

"A killer. One without the guts to face his victim face to face. An assassin in the dark. One who paid others to do his dirty work." Dumarest fired the words like bullets. "Scum, as you'd admit if you weren't so blind in your prejudice. I killed him to save my life."

"No!" She was vehement in her denial. "He would never have killed you!"

The truth, but how did she know it? Only at the last when, knowing he would die, had Perotto tried to eliminate his destroyer. Working for the Cyclan he knew the value they placed on their quarry. Knew too how ruthless would be his punishment if he had failed to obey their orders. Avro? Had the cyber managed to survive? Had he told the woman what had happened?

93

A possibility and Dumarest considered it. One which could lead to an even greater danger than the one he was in. Armed, with Chenault as a hostage, who could stop the woman from taking him prisoner?

"My lady, let us understand each other." He faced her, smiling, at his ease. A man talking to an equal on a subject they could both appreciate. "I killed Perotto and I admit it. But it was a matter of honor as I'm sure you will agree. In fact I had no choice." He made a small gesture with his hands. "As you feel that you have no choice. Honor is a hard master to those who follow its dictates."

She said, tightly, "Explain."

"Perotto killed Angado. He was my friend. In fact I owed him my life. What else could I have done?"

The question was like a slap in the face and she stood, considering it, sensing that, somehow, she was being manipulated. A feeling which stiffened her earlier resolve.

"Nothing, perhaps, but for each action there is a penalty. Your honor has been satisfied. That of the Karroum has not. As you had to kill so must you be killed. Mharl!" A figure loomed behind her, a weapon lifted in its arms. "Aim and—"

"No!" The voice echoed from the crest as Massak shouted. "Fire and you're dead!" The bark of a rifle tore the air, slugs ripping into the

94

ground, whining from buried stone. "Lower that gun. Lower it, I say!"

"My lady?"

"Obey." She didn't turn to look at the man. To Chenault she said, "What does this accomplish? Tonight you win—tomorrow your house will lie in rubble. How can you hope to oppose me?"

"I must try."

That answer gained nothing; trying he would fail and, failing, all would be lost. Dumarest glanced at him, then back to the woman, remembering how she had appeared on the screen, standing upright in the raft, face and body belonging to another age. As her code of honor belonged to a time long past. One of chivalrous concepts which had probably never existed but which still lingered to exert their charm.

He said, "There is a way, my lady . . . to settle this dispute with honor. To end it here and now and for all time. The old way." He saw by her eyes she understood. "The way of those who tread the narrow path. One against the other and let right prevail."

Trial by combat—he'd had no other choice.

Mharl was her champion, tall, younger than Dumarest by a decade, strong from a lifetime of arduous labor. Stripped, his torso was ribbed and roped with muscle, his biceps huge, the pectorals betraying his bull-like strength. A machine of flesh and brawn equipped with a shrewd and agile mind.

95

He stood poised, like a dancer, his eyes darting flickers beneath his brows.

In turn Dumarest studied the opposition.

Like Mharl he was stripped down to pants and boots; garments which gave mutual protection and offensive capability. A kick, correctly placed, could kill as effectively as a club or gun or knife. Weapons banned because of the advantage they could give to one or the other. In matters of honor Mirza liked to be precise. But her champion was trained, accustomed to wrestling, kicking, fighting with his hands. This Dumarest sensed from the way he stood, moved, shifted to present himself, the hands crossed before his loins, his weight always resting on one foot so as to free the other to kick.

"Ready?" Mirza Karroum looked from one to the other. "You know the rules: the first to yield admits defeat." An arrangement not as fair as it seemed; if Dumarest yielded he would admit his dishonor and merit summary execution. A fact she chose to ignore. "Begin!"

Dumarest moved, circling to put his back against the light, facing Mharl with the watching windows of the house before him. A small advantage, but lost as the man moved in turn, then, before he could settle, Dumarest dived in, throwing himself down to pivot on one hand, his boot lashing out to slam against Mharl's left knee.

That blow should have crippled but did no more than bruise; Mharl jumping back as it landed. A move preparatory to his own attack and he came in before Dumarest could regain his feet, kicking out, the toe of his boot like a club as it slammed against the hip. As Dumarest grabbed at it Mharl closed in, the hammer of his fists beating at Dumarest's face and torso, leaving ugly welts on the body, the taste of blood in the mouth.

The tattoo ended as Dumarest backed away, stooped, appearing more badly hurt than he was.

"Soon, my lady!" Mharl, excited, called the promise. "Soon honor will be satisfied."

The talk gained Dumarest time. He came in, watchful, noting the position of the hands, the feet, the tilt of the head. Ready when Mharl struck to dodge the blow, to strike in turn, to parry a driving fist, to strike at the corded throat, the edge of his stiffened hand lashing at the windpipe.

Speed offset by the other's massive build, his trained reactions.

Skill gained in the gymnasiums, added to by harsh experience, but Dumarest had lived longer, harder, had learned more. Stooping, he grabbed dirt, flung it into the other's eyes, followed it with a low attack, fist driving into the junction of the thighs. As Mharl screamed he struck again, higher, lifting a boot to rasp its edge down the man's shin. Stabbing at the eyes with his hand formed into a blunted spear, using the other to again attack the throat as Mharl threw back his head to defend his sight.

And felt the universe explode as hands crashed against the sides of his head.

Blows which would have killed had they been delivered with a little more force, a little more direction. Twin hammers driving at his ears in near-synchronization as Mharl, desperate, gambled on a quick victory. One he lost as Dumarest backed, blood streaming from his nose to dapple his chin, his naked torso.

"Mharl!" Mirza Karroum snapped her instructions. "Be wary. Wear him down. Don't let him get too close."

Good advice but Dumarest didn't let him follow it. Again he closed in, kicking, slashing, parrying the driving punches of the other man. Using his arms as if they had been swords, his hands as if they had been knives. Calling on the hard-won experience which had saved him so often before.

A blur and flesh yielded to his attack, blood marring the other's mouth and torso to match his own. Another and Dumarest grunted as a fist ground into his stomach, his own hand reaching out, stabbing, the tips of his fingers hitting the throat and driving deep. A blow followed by another in the same place then, as Mharl doubled, retching for breath, Dumarest was on him from behind, one arm rising to lock beneath the chin, the other completing the vise which held the head hard against his shoulder.

"Yield!" Dumarest jerked at his arm. "Yield, you fool, before I break your neck!"

He sensed rather than felt the lifted foot, the savage, backward kick which would have shattered bone had it landed. As Mharl staggered, his balance lost, Dumarest freed his right hand, lifted it, slammed it down hard on the other's temple.

As it locked back into place he said, "Why die when there's no need? Yield and let's have done with it."

"No! I—"

The words died as Dumarest crushed his left forearm against the windpipe. Against him Mharl squirmed, blood smearing, making a sticky film. As, again, he tried to kick, Dumarest sprang upward and wrapped his legs around the other's waist.

"Your last chance, Mharl. Yield or die."

It was no empty threat. Dumarest felt strength drain from him as he fought to retain his hold. Mharl was too dangerous to be given a chance, too determined to be underestimated. Too strong to be resisted if he should break free.

"Don't be a fool, man! Lift up your hands. Yield!"

A long moment then, as the hands fought to grip him, Dumarest began to close the vise formed by his arms. One powered by the muscles of his back and shoulders, the biceps, the corded sinews of his arms.

Mharl sagged, hands lifting to tear at the constriction, twisting, dropping to his knees as the pressure increased. He was dying, ears filled with the roar of his own blood, vision darkening, his chest a flame from need of air. Yet he would never yield: if nothing else he had pride.

A fact Dumarest guessed and, as Mharl fell toward the dirt he released his hold, lifted a hand, struck once and stood up with the unconscious man at his feet.

"My lady? Do you accept defeat?"

"He did not yield! He—"

"Is beaten." Chenault spoke from where he had stood, watching. "Would you prefer him dead? Dumarest was kind but if he made a mistake it can be rectified. Earl, if her honor demands it, finish the job. Kill him."

He said nothing, watching her face, the play of emotions it portrayed. In the old days things had been more simple; a champion won or he died and those for whom he fought did not have to make life or death decisions. Or so, at least, the stories she had heard as a child had convinced her. As they had instilled the concept of honor which had led to Mharl lying on the dirt at her feet.

Dumarest said, "He did his best for you. He fought well and tried to kill me. Despite that I'm willing to spare him. Are you?"

For a moment she hesitated, then, with an abrupt gesture, extended her hands before her, palms uppermost.

"Honor is satisfied. Right has prevailed. The dispute between us is ended. I offer you my friendship."

He accepted by placing his hands on her own. Beneath his fingers her skin was dry, rougher than he would have expected, warm with a febrile heat.

100

A woman tricked by her femininity, responding to his maleness, the euphoria of witnessed combat. Catching his fingers, holding them as, on the ground at their feet, Mharl groaned and twisted in his waking pain.

Chapter Seven

Lifting his goblet Massak said, "A thing neatly done, Earl. If ever you are in need of employment I know a dozen who would give you rank and a command. I salute you!"

He drank and Lopakhin followed his example. "Fast," he said as he lowered his glass. "The way you moved in, dodged, reacted—like lightning. Mharl didn't stand a chance."

A lie as he must have known; no fight could ever be a certainty and Mirza's champion had been dangerous with speed and skills of his own. Dumarest turned from the group around the table set in the great hall. Vosper's doing or Baglioni's, though neither was to be seen. An oddity; the midget was never far from his master yet now there was no sign of him. As there had been none during the fight when, surely, a bodyguard would have felt his charge needed protection.

A fact Dumarest noted as he moved to stare through the open doors. Mirza had gone, taking her rafts with her, her guns, her dead and hurt. Now the valley lay in shrouded darkness, the glow of starlight broken by the brilliant streaks from the firebirds, the fan of brilliance spilling from the open portal, diminishing as the panels closed to seal the house as it was before.

"Earl?" Govinda was beside him. "Earl?"

She looked lovelier than ever, the mane of her hair a cascade of flame, the lines of her body delineated by the close-fitting gown she wore. One which left her shoulders bare, her arms, revealing the long, silken curve of her thigh at every other step.

"I was worried, Earl," she said. "When Mharl hit you I felt my heart move as if it would burst. Then, when you didn't go down, I knew you would be victorious."

Had she been watching? Dumarest frowned, trying to remember, but Mharl had demanded all his attention and she could have stayed in the shadows.

"Tama was worried too," she said. "I sensed it. As I sensed how that old bitch felt toward you after you'd won. At that moment she would willingly have made you her equal had that been your ambition. It made me jealous." Govinda rested her hand on his arm. "Would you have gone with her had she asked?"

"No."

"Refused the chance to share the power of the Karroum? Do you mean that?"

He said, bluntly, "I'm not in the habit of lying."

"But—"

"It would be power short-lived. No Family would tolerate the introduction of a stranger on such terms. There are too many with too much to lose." A threat settled by the use of an assassin, a subtle poison slipped into food or drink, a convenient accident—there were too many ways of dealing with the unwanted. "Where is Toyanna?"

"What?" The question startled her. "Why, with Tama, I suppose."

"No." He looked to where Chenault stood at one end of the table, leaning against it, using the board to steady his balance. "No, she isn't there."

"Why do you want her?"

"To talk." He smiled at the expression in her eyes. "To share a drink with her. To enjoy her company."

For a moment her face seemed to blur, to become hateful, ugly, then it smoothed and she smiled as she looked up at him, the gleam of her eyes emerald in the shadow of her brows.

"You're teasing me, Earl. Trying to make me jealous. You're not really interested in Toyanna. No more than you are in Hilary. Not as a woman, that is. Not as someone you need to hold close."

"Need?"

"Need." Her voice lowered as she repeated the word. "There is an ache inside of you which has

104

lasted too long. A yearning for something you once had and hope to have again. Can you deny it?" Then, as he remained silent, she laughed and moved away. "Perhaps you will find it, Earl. Stranger things have happened."

She moved on, passing the group at the table, the servants attending them, becoming a blur as she blended in with the decor of the hall. The circus adornment he had seen before; the bars and cages and visage of clowns. The smoldering colors, the bizarre and fanciful decorations. Symbolism he could appreciate and a message which was plain; he had been accepted by the others of the entourage of Chenault. Tama Chenault who had once owned a circus—and the circus took care of its own.

"A happy ending." Chenault nodded a greeting as Dumarest joined him at the table. "A difficult situation neatly solved. For that you have my gratitude; I have no wish to be enemies with the Karroum."

"Gratitude." Dumarest helped himself to wine. "Is that all?"

"I don't understand."

"Words are only vibrations of the air. The cheapest form of repayment there is. From you, Chenault, I want more."

"Such as?"

"You know the answer to that. The reason I came to see you. When are you going to give me what you promised?"

"Soon." Chenault lifted his goblet, wine rilling to stain his chin. "It will be soon."

"Tomorrow?"

"I think so. Yes. Tomorrow."

"I'll anticipate the meeting." Dumarest took the goblet from Chenault's hand, refilled it, handed it back. "A toast, my friend. To life!"

"To life!"

Again wine stained Chenault's chin, the goblet shattering as he lowered his hand. Dumarest reached for a cloth but Toetzer was before him, a napkin busy as it soaked up the wine. If the hand had been cut there was no trace but the red wine could have masked any blood.

"You must pardon me." Chenault swayed a little as he straightened. "Stress and fatigue together with my recent indisposition—I'm sure you understand. A momentary weakness but I think it best to retire. Jem, please attend me." He turned as he neared the side of the hall, Toetzer at his side. "Goodnight all." He waved his hand at the assembly. "I bid you all good night."

As he left the hall Massak turned to Dumarest, smiling. "Well, Earl, what now?"

They gambled, one against the other, elbows to the table, biceps straining as each tried to force the other's hand to the board. Mercenary's fun with a candle glowing to give added incentive to win. A game Dumarest had played often enough with glowing coals instead of candles and, at times, the bared steel of a naked point. A hard game for hard men and he guessed why Massak insisted on playing it.

"You're hard, Earl." Massak rubbed the back of his hand. "Hard and fast and as tricky as they come. The kind of man good to have at your back when the trouble starts. Once more for luck? Double or quits?"

"Try it with someone else."

"I can beat them all. Even Shior." A man hurt with a dislocated shoulder; the last of his targets had been alerted and had fought back. Now Shior rested in drugged slumber and Massak was impatient to regain his eminence. "Once more, Earl. I insist."

And, losing, would be sullen. Dumarest knew the type too well and, even if he beat the man, would gain nothing from his victory. Yet to yield was not enough; like the mistress of the Karroum, the mercenary had his own concept of honor.

"The last time, then." Dumarest took his place at the table. "Double or quits."

"As you say." Teeth flashed white as Massak grinned. "The candles, Tyner." He waited as flames rose from the wicks Lopakhin kindled. "Now!"

A surge and he had thrown all his strength into the combat. Dumarest felt his arm begin to yield and fought back, not to win but to give the illusion of a hard-won battle. A moment of strain and, slowly, Massak's hand was forced back, to stand almost upright, to bend slowly toward the other side. Sweat shone on his face as, baring his teeth, he resisted the pressure, forcing Dumarest's arm back, back, bending it until the back of his hand hung over the leaping flame of the candle.

Lifting as Dumarest fought back.

Falling again to hover as hair singed and the flame licked flesh. A guttering flare which died as Massak forced the hand to quench the wick.

"I won!" His roar of triumph filled the hall. "By God, I won!"

"Try him with knives!" Toetzer, returned, yelled the challenge. "Face him with naked steel and I'll give you odds of twenty to one."

"No!" Dumarest was curt.

"Why not?" Elated by his victory Massak was eager for combat. "First blood, Earl. Just a touch to decide who is the better man."

A single cut which would lead to others and to final maiming or gory death. A combat without reason, profit or cause. Dumarest recognized this but knew he could never get Massak to accept. The mercenary was too much a barbarian for such logic and, his blood heated, wanted nothing but to fight.

"Wait!" Dumarest looked at the ring which had formed, the avid faces. "You want a battle, right? Then we'll give it to you. Here!" Steel flashed as he drew his knife and sent it to quiver, point in the board, halfway down the table. "You at the far end, Ian. Jem, give us full goblets." Dumarest lifted his own, Massak doing likewise. "We drink and go for the blade. Who'll give the word?"

"I will!" Toetzer shouted down the others. "You ready? Go!"

Dumarest sipped his wine, threw the goblet and its contents at Massak, was down the table and gripping the freed knife before the mercenary guessed what was happening. His roar of anger echoed from the roof.

"You cheated! By God, you cheated!"

"Did I say we were to drink it all?" Dumarest sheathed the knife, smiling, one hand falling on Massak's shoulder in apparent friendship. "If you can't win fair, my friend, then you have to win foul." In a lower tone he added, "Stop this before one of us winds up dead."

And Massak had no doubt as to who that would be. The shower of wine had sobered him, that and the sight of the naked blade, the face of the man who had held it pointed at his throat. Death had been close then and he knew it. Knew too that Dumarest, by cheating, had given him an out.

One he took as, laughing, he clapped his own hand on Dumarest's shoulder and called for wine to celebrate a draw.

"To the finest companion any fighter could hope to find. One hard, fast, cunning—and who can take a joke." He lifted his goblet. "To Dumarest!"

That toast was followed by others and it was late when Dumarest finally made his way to his room. His head ached a little though he was far from drunk, having pretended to drink far more than he had actually swallowed. Under the cold sting of the shower he thought of Massak and how he had left him; swaying, bawling mercenary songs and reliving old campaigns. A man who could have been an enemy but who now swore he was a friend. As Mirza Karroum had done. As Chenault had promised to keep his word.

The spray ceased and Dumarest stepped from the shower to dry himself and, killing the lights, lay naked on the bed. Starglow from the window filled the room with silver, making a screen of the ceiling on which he projected mental images. Chenault standing in the clearing, tall, silent, almost as if graven from stone. Chenault in the hall leaning against the table as if for support. The same man who had rilled wine over his chin. Who had smashed a goblet in his hand.

His face had been the same as it had in the study before his attack. His body, even his stance, but had there been a subtle wrongness? A man affected by drugs would have acted as he had done, a little unsteady on his feet, a shade unaware. Had Toyanna doped him so as to make a necessary appearance when Mirz had arrived with her demands? And, if she had, would he be fit enough to tell what he knew about Earth?

A worry accompanied by another: if Avro was still alive then his personal danger was very real. He could have guided the woman to him—but no, the last thing he would want was for her to take her revenge. Instead he would use other methods and Dumarest never made the mistake of underestimating the power of the Cyclan.

He dozed, starting awake to a faint rattle from the door, the sound as of someone trying to get into the room. Rising, he jerked away the chair

110

holding it fast and opened the panel. In the passage outside Govinda shrank from the glittering menace of his knife.

"Earl! I—"

"Come inside." The door closed behind her, the chair again rammed into place. "What do you want?"

A stupid question; the answer was in her eyes, her face. In the heat of her body felt as she stepped close to him. In the message of her arms as they lifted to close around his neck.

In the burning demand of the kiss she imprinted on his lips.

"I love you," she whispered. "Earl, my darling, I love you."

He said nothing, the knife hanging at his side, his free hand rising to caress her hair.

"Since the moment I saw you I knew we belonged together. I can sense such things. As I sense the void in your heart. The space you ache to fill." The pressure of her body was a warm and succulent invitation. "A space I can fill, my darling. My dearest darling. My love!"

A woman enraptured, enamored, hopelessly in love—or one pretending to be.

"Hold me, Earl! Take me in your arms, my darling. Kiss me! Kiss me!"

Words to excite the senses, and gestures to match but all were the province of every actress and even the most inexperienced harlot knew how to emulate passion. Again he caressed her hair, running his hand over the contours of her body, finding

111

nothing but heated flesh beneath the gossamer thinness of her robe. Yet weapons could be hidden in unsuspected places; drugs placed beneath the nails could bring quick unconsciousness once their points had pricked the skin and an ampoule, crushed between the teeth, could vent numbing vapors when impelled by a kiss.

Yet she had kissed and touched him and he was unharmed.

"Earl, what is wrong?" She stepped back from him, eyes wide, luminous in the starlight. Dark pools of shining brilliance as her hair was dark in the starglow. As were her lips and nails and darting tongue. As the thin fabric of her robe which showed betraying glints as she moved. As the dark areolas of her nipples surmounting the breasts which shifted with wanton, unfettered abandon. "Earl?"

The magic was too strong. The web spun by perfume and starglow and warm, feminine flesh. Of soft lips and yielding contours and the ache in his heart which she seemed to know too well and which never ceased to hurt. The pain of what had been and would never be again. Could never be again until the end of time.

"Earl?"

"No!" He moved, reaching for the light, his head turned from her, eyes blinking, narrowing at the sudden, warmly yellow glare. "Don't say anything. Just leave me. Just—" He turned, falling silent as, around him, his universe collapsed.

"Earl!" Kalin stepped toward him, arms lifted, mouth curved as he had seen it curve so often,

112

eyes filled by the light he had never thought to see again. "Earl, my darling. My very own wonderful darling!"

An illusion. Govinda using her talent and making herself appear to him as the thing he most wanted to see. The woman he most ached to possess. The one he missed most of all—and now had found again.

Had found again!

The joy of it blazed through him as he folded her in his arms. The touch of her lips, her hands, her body banishing all thought of illusion from his mind. She was what he wanted her to be and, becoming it, made him see her in that guise. See her and love her as he had never stopped loving her.

"My darling! My love!" She cried out in the bittersweet pain of his caress. "My love!"

Later, when again starglow filled the room, Dumarest turned to where she lay beside him, seeing the cascade of her hair spread on the pillow not black as it seemed but flaming red as he remembered. As red as the flame which she had set to burning within his heart.

In the dimness the lights were like the eyes of watching insects; red, yellow, blue, green, flashing and changing even as Kooga watched. The telltales on the instruments he had added; extra monitors which even now recorded every variation of the electromagnetic fields of the cyber's brain. Among them Avro lay like a corpse, mummified, immobile. The oxygen which kept him alive now pumped directly into his bloodstream by the mechanism which had bypassed both heart and lungs.

A man, dying as all men must die, but the manner of his passing was something novel to Kooga's experience. The vitality was incredible as if, like an animal, the cyber clung to existence against all odds. And, as he sank even deeper toward final extinction, the cerebral activity increased against all logic. The patterns recorded by the pens of the encephalograph were of a complexity Kooga had never seen before: presenting a puzzle he itched to solve.

"Doctor?"

The nurse had arrived to make her routine check and stood, deferential, waiting for him to clear the area. A good worker, obedient, deft with her hands. Too deft for her to have done what he had told Vaclav she had done; such a nurse would never have disturbed any connection. But the lie had been a facile explanation of what he would rather the Chief did not know.

"Doctor? Shall I attend the patient?"

"A moment." Kooga forced himself to soften his normal, brusque manner. "Have you noticed any change in his condition?"

"None that has not been recorded, Doctor."

"No blame is intended," he said quickly. "I was thinking more of some intuitive feeling you may have had which did not register on the monitors. An impression," he urged. "A personal assessment which you may have felt. Such things

114

happen." Too often for the peace of mind of those dealing with the bricks and mortar of ordinary medicine; sensations which defied analysis, guesses, hunches, odd certainties which led to unexpected results. He added, appealingly, "You know this is a special case and any help you can give will be appreciated."

"I'd like to help, Doctor, it is my duty but—" She paused, frowning. "I don't think I can be of assistance."

"Let me be the judge of that."

"It's just that when I was attending him before the bypass was introduced I had the oddest impression that he was shouting at someone. It was as if—"

"A moment, nurse. Was that after Mirza Karroum paid her visit?"

"Yes, just after you had attached the recorder to the patient's larynx." Her eyes met his, wide, innocent. "I noticed it, of course, while making the routine check. The higg-load light was showing on the encephalograph and, as I touched him, I seemed to hear a voice. Well, not hear it exactly, but—"

"Sense it?"

"Yes." She smiled her thanks at his help. "Almost as if a finger had touched my brain. But not quite that either. It was just a feeling. I can't explain it and, naturally, didn't report it. I'd almost forgotten it until you asked."

A burst of cerebral activity which could have been triggered by her proximity and, because of the subtle affinity with the sick gained during her years of service, she had sensed it with a talent barely suspected. Kooga studied her as she stood beside the bed. An ordinary, honest, hard-working woman with an ingrained deference to those in authority. Questioned by the Cyclan physicians she would repeat what she had said and their questions as to the recorder he would do without. To discharge her would be simple yet that, in itself, could give rise to questions. Good nurses were simply not thrown aside without cause.

He said, "As I remember it, nurse, you are due for a vacation. Certainly you merit a reward for your dedicated service. A month, I think, would not be too long. Starting immediately."

"Doctor?"

He saw her puzzlement and guessed its cause; he was not noted for generosity or undue concern with the welfare of those beneath him. Deliberately he grew brusque.

"Aren't you due for vacation? I must be mistaken. However I am making other arrangements for this patient and you will no longer be needed. I was thinking of the Bilton Resort—you could fill in as emergency medical staff. I owe the resident practitioner a favor and you could help to repay it." To explain too much would be a mistake; one he avoided by an abrupt termination of the subject. "I will make all arrangements. Be ready to leave by morning."

Alone he looked at the figure lying supine on the bed. Closing his eyes he tried to capture the feeling the nurse had mentioned but he lacked her affinity and gained nothing from the experiment. Opening his eyes, he studied the interplay of the telltales, the winking gleams which held a subtle mockery.

The visible signs of cerebral activity of a man with a brain grown too big for his skull. One more dead than alive yet who, if the nurse was correct, was screaming for help.

To whom?

Chapter Eight

Chenault said, "I owe you an apology, Earl. We should have met earlier."

"Two days ago." Dumarest was blunt. "I had your promise."

"I was not allowed to keep it." Chenault lifted his shoulders in a shrug. "At times Toyanna can be a veritable bully and she has the means to enforce her will. However, as I hear it, you have been pleasantly occupied."

With the realization of a dream but Dumarest made no comment, looking instead at the study in which they sat. It was as it had been before; filled with the musty smells of old paper, leather, ancient oils. The repository of things long dead and things he hoped were still alive. On the table before him a decanter of ruby wine threw a warm patch of luminescence on the polished wood.

"Legends," mused Chenault. "Stories from ancient times each holding a grain of truth. Dazym Negaso claims that a legend is, in reality, a means of passing a message from one generation to another. In order to be effective that message has to be simple and repetitious as well as holding its own attraction. So we talk of Eden, a place of ease and plenty. A place in which none knows pain. One in which all needs are satisfied. Things all find enticing. Bonanza is much the same; a world with seas of rare elixirs, mountains of precious metals, plains studded with gems. El Dorado much the same. Jackpot, Lucky Strike, a host of others." Pausing he added, softly, "And, of course, we have Earth."

"Which is no legend."

"As we agreed. The Original Home of Mankind from which they fled because of some devastating catastrophe." Chenault lifted his hands to make a T. "From Terra they fled—"

"Yes," said Dumarest. "We've been through that."

Chenault ignored the interruption, finishing the quotation, then, lifting his hands still in the position he had placed them, added, "The one became the many and the many shall again become the one. This in the fullness of time."

A ritual and Dumarest repeated it.

"You are wise." Chenault lowered his hands. "If we are to learn then we must learn to read what the ancients have left us. One race, leaving Earth and becoming the multitude of diverse types we now have. In time they will conjoin to become one again. This, I think, is clear. What is not is what they left behind. A planet devastated, destroyed, deserted—yet you are the living evidence that some remained. How did they survive? How far have they shifted from the original norm? What have they become?''

Dumarest said, bitterly, ''Savages.''

''You are sure? Remember, you can only speak from your own experience.''

''That and others. I was a boy when I left Earth. Stowing away on a ship and deserving to be evicted into space. The captain was kind, he spared me. He also kept a journal.'' Dumarest reached into a pocket and produced a folded sheet of paper. ''Shakira had a sensitive, Melome, who had the ability to throw a person mentally backward through time. She managed to get me back in the ship, in the captain's cabin, looking at his open book. I read what he had written. This is it.''

Chenault took the paper, opened it, read aloud, '' 'The cargo we loaded on Ascanio was spoiled and had to be unloaded at a total loss. A bad trip with no prospect of improvement so I took a chance and risked a journey to the proscribed planet. A waste of time—the place is a nightmare. God help the poor devils who lived here. Those remaining are degenerate scum little more than savage animals. Found a stowaway after we'd left, a boy who looks human. He claims to be twelve but looks younger and could be dangerous. Decided to take a chance and kept him but if he shows any sign of trouble I'll have to—' " Chenault looked at Dumarest. "It ends there."

"I know."

"Were you the boy he mentions?"

"Yes."

"Dangerous," murmured Chenault. "He was right in that but he should have added lucky as well. Not many stowaways are treated so gently. But this is no proof the planet he landed on was Earth."

"I am the proof of that." Dumarest looked at his clenched hand, lifting it to slam hard on the table. "Damn it, man! I know where I was born!"

Silence followed the fading drum-echo of the beaten table, broken by a soft click and, turning, Dumarest saw Baglioni standing before an open panel, one hand buried in a pocket.

"It's all right," said Chenault. "It's quite all right." He smiled at Dumarest as the midget retreated behind the closed door. "I appreciate your impatience, Earl, but we must be objective. The evidence, alone, does not support your contention. Yet, obviously, you must have left the planet of your birth. A ship must have carried you. As you rode with it you must remember its name." He paused, waiting. "Do you?"

"It had more than one name," said Dumarest. A fact he hadn't understood at the time. "When I joined the ship it was the *Cucoco*."

"And the captain?"

"Petrovna. Zuba Petrovna."

"You see, we make progress." Chenault gestured to the wine. "Help yourself and relax. A tense mind and body do nothing to help solve any problem. One we can now look at from another angle. During your search you must have found clues. They are?"

The spectrum of the sun which was Earth's primary; the Fraunhofer Lines forming a unique and identifiable pattern. The circle of the constellations forming designs when seen from Earth. A moon resembling a pocked skull when seen in the full. A direction. A region in which the planet must be; one toward the edge of the spiral arm where stars were few and the nights lacking the splendor of Lychen.

Items over which Chenault mused as if he were a jeweler studying gems.

"The spectrum will tell us where we are when we find it but to isolate one from so many stars is a formidable task. One you have tried, perhaps?"

"Yes," said Dumarest. "The cost was prohibitive."

"Understandable and the effort would be wasted if the computer consulted lacked the essential data. As it is missing from the almanacs such a probability is high. The constellations?" A shrug dismissed their immediate value. "Like the spectrum they will only tell us where we are when we get there. The direction; the seventh decant, well, that covers a vast area. As does the bleak night-time sky. The moon is of little more help as many worlds have oddly fashioned satellites. You have more, perhaps?"

"Names," said Dumarest. "Sirius 8.7. Procyon 11.4. Altair 16.5. Epsilon Indi 11.3. Alpha Centauri 4.3." He added, "The numbers are the distances of the stars from Earth's sun."

"Signposts in the sky." Chenault nodded as he considered them. "Valuable data, Earl. A relationship could be established and the central point found. A simple matter of mathematical determination. Surely you must have checked the data?"

Dumarest said, bleakly, "I tried. The stars are not listed."

"Or their names have been changed. Even so, the correlation remains. The seventh decant, you say?" Again Chenault brooded over the data, leaning back in his chair, his eyes like glass as they gleamed with reflected light. "One other thing; the ship on which you left Earth."

"The *Cucoco*?"

"It must have had more than a name. What were its markings?"

A device totally unfamiliar and now almost forgotten. One Dumarest drew with frowning slowness on the paper Chenault pushed toward him.

"This? Are you sure?" Chenault looked up from the paper, rising as Dumarest nodded. "Let me see, now." He moved to a shelf, took down a heavy volume bound in cracked and moldering leather, riffled through the pages to stand, finger on an item. He said, "The clue, Earl. You've given me the final clue. I know where Earth is to be found."

It was something he had dreamed of a thousand times; the occasion when, in answer to his question, he would receive not blank stares or mocking laughter but the affirmative which would signal the end of his quest. The person who knew where his home was to be found. Now, incredibly, he had found him.

Yet he had to be sure. "You mean that?"

"Yes, Earl. I mean it."

Dumarest said, slowly, "I want the truth, Chenault. No guesses, wild assumptions or vague promises. If you know the coordinates set them down on that paper and I'll be in your debt. But if you're toying with me—" He broke off, looking at his hands resting on the table, the fists they made, the knuckles white beneath the skin. "I'm in no mood for games. Not now or ever on that subject. If you don't mean what you say admit it now."

"Or you will kill me?" Chenault read the answer in the face turned toward him, the hard stare of the eyes. "A fair warning, Earl, but unnecessary. I know where Earth is to be found."

"The coordinates—"

"Have yet to be determined." Chenault lifted a hand to still any protest. "It is merely a matter of time. The puzzle is now complete. I promise you I know the answer. I swear it."

His voice carried the truth and Dumarest relaxed. Wine gushed from the decanter as he tipped it over a glass, the ruby fluid like water in his mouth, warming as he refilled the glass, both drinks joining in his stomach to wash away the residue of tension. A time of celebration, the drinks a libation to ancient gods who, at last, had been kind.

"You gave me the final clue." Chenault resumed his chair, the heavy volume to one side on the polished board. "The device was the sigil of the House of Macheng. They operated in the seventh decant, running a fleet of small trading vessels. The *Cucoco* must have been one of them." Pausing, one hand touching the book, he said with an abrupt change of subject, "Did Shakira ever tell you what his specialty was?"

"He had the ability to recognize talent when he saw it. Even when it had still to be developed."

"And mine is the ability to solve puzzles." Chenault stroked the book with a gesture like a caress. "Anagrams, acrostics, crosswords, riddles— all, to me, are difficulties which do not exist. Elaborate incantations containing hidden meanings, jumbled formulae, the mazes in which men try to hide true meaning all yield to my skill. Can you wonder why I turned to harder problems? Using my skill to unravel the truth hidden in legends? Most are just fanciful stories dreamed up by desperate people to provide a modicum of comfort in harsh and bitter times. The promise of pleasure to come in some distant time. Tales taken and embroidered with added glitter to become worlds of vast and incredible riches. Many such worlds are basically the same—Bonanza, Jackpot, Lucky Strike—all sharing the same promise of vast fortunes. Others offer different rewards; ease, health, youth, tranquility but, again, too many bear the same similarities. Eden, Avalon, Elysium, Heaven, Paradise—you understand the point I am making?"

"Legends and the growth of legends," said Dumarest. "One kernel of fact becoming two, four, a dozen. But Earth is no legend."

"Neither is Ryzam."

Dumarest reached for the decanter and poured, looking at Chenault, setting aside the wine as the other shook his head.

"Ryzam," said Chenault. "I'll wager you've never heard of it but you must know what it offers. Youth, restored vigor, health, the crippled made whole again, the maimed and the dying given new life. A magic place with a dozen names—give me one."

"Argentis."

"Argentis," murmured Chenault. "And Farnese, Djem, Delyon, Mytha, Elagon; the names are legion. But all stem from one and Ryzam is the source. Ryzam, the origin of a score of wonderworlds, and yet it isn't a world at all. Just a place on a planet which legend has enhanced beyond all recognition. I must go there."

Dumarest sipped at his wine and said, "We were talking of Earth."

"And now we are talking of Ryzam. A fascinating place, Earl, one steeped in legend and fanciful tales but all stemming from undeniable truth. I stumbled on the essential data while pursuing my studies in kindred legends and soon decided that, somehow, various threads had become tangled to present a false whole. Unraveling them took years, isolating pertinent information occupied decades. Then a trader sold me an old log and in it I found the essential clue. As important to the solution as the one you gave me appertaining to Earth. Ryzam,'' Chenault looked at the decanter, the pool of ruby shadow at its foot. "A place as important to me as Earth is to you. As I said, I must go there."

Dumarest said, "Do you know where it is?"

"Yes."

"Then you'll have no trouble finding it. As I'll have no trouble finding Earth once I have the coordinates." Dumarest paused then added, "The ones you will give me."

"Give?" Chenault turned to meet Dumarest's eyes, his own direct. "Why should I give them to you?"

"In return for the information I gave you. The clue you said was all-important."

"And what of my years of study? The expense of rare and ancient books? Logs? Charts? A host of kindred data? And my skill—is that of no value? Come, my friend, be reasonable. Surely you don't expect charity?"

The goblet Dumarest was holding quivered a little; the movement betrayed by the shimmer of the wine it held. Carefully he set it down, withdrawing his hand, feeling the polished surface of the table beneath his fingers. Wood which fretted beneath his nails.

"I want those coordinates, Chenault."

"And you shall have them. I swear it. But not as a gift but as a reward justly earned." Chenault made a gesture, smiling, but the iron of his voice matched the cold hardness of his eyes. "Earth, Ryzam, the two sides of a coin. You need to find one and I must go to the other. Help me and I will help you—it is as simple as that."

On the bed Govinda stirred, mumbling, uneasy in her sleep. Standing before the window Dumarest glanced at her then looked again through the pane. In the shadows fire burned as the nocturnal life of the valley followed its normal path. Streaks of color he noted but ignored as again he tasted the bile of angry defeat. To be so close, to have been led to believe so much—then to have the prize he valued so much snatched from his hand to be held at a tantalizing distance.

If the prize existed at all.

A thought which drove him from the window toward the door, halting as Govinda stirred again, mumbling, rearing up to cry his name.

"Earl! Hold me—Earl!"

The fragments of nightmare which he soothed away with gentle hands, feeling the warmth of her body close to him, the silken mane of her hair soft against his cheek. Only when, at last, she was sleeping quietly did he move, easing free the door, opening it, closing it behind him as he moved down the passage. The stairs were deserted, the great hall, the corridors beyond. The study door was firm and he leaned against it before lifting the knife from his boot and driving the steel to disengage the catch. Inside it was black with a smothering darkness, one destroyed as he found the switch and illuminated the room with an even glow.

It was as he had left it, the wine still on the table, the goblets, one clean the other still holding what he had left. The chairs and, close to where Chenault had been sitting, the massive tome he had consulted. Dumarest opened it, finding the paper on which he had drawn the marking adorning the hull of the *Cucoco*. One repeated on a page followed by scant information.

House of Macheng. Traders. Main field of operations 7th Dec. XVB34TYCS23R.

The truth as Chenault had relayed it—the following figures and numbers were probably some condensed coding which told him nothing. Yet, to Chenault, they could hold the secret he had hunted for so long. In which case there would have to be an appendix.

Dumarest lifted the pages, began to riffle them, then halted as, frowning, he looked at the symbols. Many were alike and he studied the one he had inscribed. Loops, bars, slanted lines and yet . . . and yet. . . .

Then, suddenly, he was a child again, crouched shivering behind a dune, staring at the strange vessel lying before him. The open, unguarded port, the daubed symbol plain against the scarred hull.

Not the one he had shown Chenault but one almost like it. One with two extra bars and one less loop. One which he saw lower down on the same page.

Ukmerge Combine. Traders. 7th and 8th Dec. Fringe. BAS92UGSA73C

The same decant—but why had Chenault made such a play on the importance of the clue? One Dumarest now knew to be false. If the code-figures were the heart of the matter then they couldn't have yielded the correct data. Which meant that Chenault had lied as to his knowledge or had known the answer all the time.

Closing the book Dunarest looked around at the tomes, the charts, the latest introductions. Any researcher needed a system to enable him, if no one else, to file and retrieve his discovered information. The computer? A musty folder? One of the ranked books? If the entire program had been reduced to the essential coordinates it could be anywhere.

Dumarest moved to the computer and tapped keys. The screen lit, flared with the negation symbol, went blank again. What he had expected: lacking the operating code the machine refused to obey his command. A folder marked with a crossed circle held nothing but sheaves of closely typed figures. Another contained computer read-outs useless without the cypher-code. A book yielded nothing and was tossed aside. Others followed it. As he reached for a mnemonic cube Dumarest heard the sound of movement and spun, hand falling to knife, staring at Chenault standing at the end of the table.

"Wine, Earl?" He moved the decanter again, the glass rasping over the wood. "I offer it freely— you have no need to steal."

"I'm no thief!"

"No?" Chenault shrugged. "Then why break in here? What did you hope to find?"

"You know damn well what I wanted." Dumarest took a step toward the other man, another, a third. "I warned you not to play games with me. Not to lie."

"I haven't. I—"

"You're using the oldest con trick ever known: sell someone a promise then make them sweat blood for fear of losing what they never had. You tried it on me. Dangled the carrot then demanded the price. All right, I'll pay it. Give me the coordinates and I'm with you every step of the way." His voice deepened to a snarl, matching the savage mask of his face. "Deliver, Chenault. Play it straight. I warned you what would happen if you didn't."

Dumarest moved, jerking to one side as the decanter Chenault held hurtled toward him to splinter against the far wall with a crash of glass. As he lunged for the door the man caught him, gripping with fingers which reached bone, jerking him backwards with savage force. Dumarest twisted, snatched out his knife, drove the blade directly at the massive torso. It struck, grated, slipped from the chest

131

to slash at the arm. The injury had no effect and Dumarest felt hands close around his windpipe.

"Fool!" Chenault tightened his grip. "You fool!"

Dumarest arched his back, drove up his knee, missed the groin and slammed the pommel of his knife hard on the other's forehead. A blow followed by another a little to one side, more as the hands eased their grip and he tore free.

"No!" Chenault backed, hands lifted to protect his face. "No! Please I—" He broke off, slumping, one arm lifting in appeal. "Help. I need—please!"

He caught at the table as Dumarest reached the door, falling to the floor as he dived into the passage. Turning to follow the path Toyanna had taken, halting as, again, Baglioni appeared before him, dart-gun in hand.

"That's enough!" The midget lifted the weapon. "You know you can't beat this so—"

He didn't see the knife Dumarest threw, didn't feel it until it slammed against his weapon and knocked it from his hand. Didn't see him move until, suddenly, he was suspended in the air, his face inches from Dumarest's own.

"Where is he?" Dumarest snarled his impatience and shook the diminutive figure. "Where the hell is he?"

"Who? What—" Baglioni squealed as Dumarest dug fingers into his neck. "Don't!"

"Then take me to him." Dumarest slammed the man to his feet. "Take me to Chenault!"

Chapter Nine

He lay like a mummy in a crystal tomb; a pale shred of humanity festooned with wires and the pipes of a life-support system. His face was drawn, corpse-like, the mask of an ancient time. One shadowed by an elaborate construction of pads and lenses, microphones and receptors. Looking at him Dumarest was reminded of an insect caught and cocooned by a predatory spider. One who came to stand before him, tall, somber in her black.

"You guessed," said Pia Toyanna. "How?"

"He seemed too young for the age he had to be." Dumarest looked at the figure in the transparent cabinet. "And the first time I sat with him in his study I felt there was something wrong. I couldn't hear his heartbeat or sound of breathing. Other things." Small things added to the one big thing his basic nature had recognized; the absence of a living organism. Sitting with Chenault had been like sitting with a machine. "How long?"

"Since shortly after he sold the circus. His health had been bad for a long time and, suddenly, it grew worse. Myositis, myotonia, myasthenia gravis—his muscular system just fell apart. Toward the end he couldn't even lift a finger."

And so the surrogate. The machine shaped like a man which reacted to the amplified impulses caught by the receptors covering Chenault's body. Lying in his box he would see what the machine saw, hear what it heard and, in return, it would move as he wanted to move, say what he wanted to say.

"Vosper built it," she said. "He's an engineering genius and Lopakhin helped. Basically it's just a sophisticated version of a remotely operated mining robot; one using radio to transmit the impulses instead of wires. A machine—but to Tama it is more than life itself."

"And to Baglioni?" Dumarest glanced at the midget where he stood before the door, silent, rigid in his anger. "He used it too, didn't he? When Chenault was too weak to operate it. The time Mirza came, for example, and the master of the house had to show himself."

"How did you know?"

"He was unsteady, unsure of himself and his control was bad. The glass he smashed by too great an application of pressure. The wine he attempted to pour into his mouth and sent to dribble

134

over his chin. Other things. But it was a good try.''

"But Baglioni? It could have been anyone."

"You? Hilary? Vosper at times? The rest were accounted for. And only Baglioni was so fiercely protective of Chenault. A return for Tama giving him the opportunity to feel a fully grown man." Dumarest looked at him, then at her. The midget's loyalty was accounted for but what held her to Chenault? The others?

She said, when he asked, "Tama is a good man. We owe him much."

For her the opportunity to stretch her skills to the ultimate, fighting death and decay with everything she had or could get. For Vosper the chance to prove himself a genius and the same for Lopakhin. For Hilary a refuge. For Toetzer the same. For Govinda?

A woman crippled with her need to become a mother. Toyanna shook her head when, bluntly, he asked the question.

"No, Earl, you can't father her child. No man living can do that. She is barren, sterile beyond all hope of ever bearing life. Transplants are rejected. I've put a half-dozen foeti within her womb and all have failed to survive. And yet still she hopes." Her face softened as she looked at him. "Take my warning, Earl, don't fall too deeply in love with her. Remember, she isn't what she seems."

Not to him or to any man but if the illusion was strong enough did the harsh reality matter? What if her hair lacked Kalin's true flame? Her body was not quite identical? Her mind not the savage flame of true affinity he had once known but a shadow of that overwhelming joy? It was there. It existed and against it the ghost of what had been had no chance. This was a woman he could hold in his arms, feel her, possess her, respond to her own passionate demands. And, on the foundation of wanting, grew the substance of fact.

He loved Govinda.

Govinda . . . Kalin . . . Kalinda.

Now, for him, the two were the same.

Baglioni said, "What are you going to do?"

"Do?" Dumarest saw the anxious inquiry in the midget's eyes. "Nothing."

"I don't understand. If it means so little to you then why force your way into here?"

"I wanted the truth," said Dumarest. "And I grew tired of being taken for a fool. I came here to learn something and I think you all know what it is. Chenault swore he could give it to me. He can still give it to me. Once I have it I'll leave."

"With Govinda?" Toyanna fired the question then shook her head as Dumarest nodded. "She won't go with you."

"I'd prefer her to tell me that."

"She'll tell it—her life is tied in with the rest of us. And we are bound to Tama."

"Bound? Held?" Dumarest echoed his impatience. "That mummery at the table? The secret society? The cult? There is nothing mystical about Earth. It is a planet. A world circling a sun. It knows heat and cold and bleakness but there are no ancient sages there, no magicians, no gods. No answers either," he added, "no matter what you may choose to believe. No superior race from which all others sprung. I know. I was born there."

"And so must be a part of that race if ever it existed." Toyanna pressed her point. "Be a child of those who were left. Carrying in your body their genes, their attributes—tell me, Earl, do you regard yourself as normal?"

He said nothing, staring at her, waiting.

"Your speed," she said. "I saw you fight and, at times, you seemed a blur. Such reflexes are rare. And the way you knew Chenault's surrogate was not really a human being—how many ordinary people would have sensed the difference? With Govinda you—but never mind that, enough to say that you have a certain charm which appeals to the basic in a woman. I've felt it, Hilary, even Mirza despite her age. A defensive mechanism, perhaps, certainly a survival trait. For your genes if not for yourself. And there is more. Why are you so enamored with returning to Earth? What attraction can that world have for you? Or is the need to return based on something deeper? A drive dictated by a compulsion beyond your comprehension?"

Questions for which he had no answers but only another question.

"Are you saying that I'm not human?"

"No, not that. If anything you could be more than human. An improvement, taking humanity as we know it, a better breed of person." Toyanna made a gesture of resignation. "As a doctor I've

137

seen too many divergencies from the norm. Any norm we care to establish so that now the word itself has ceased to hold meaning. A man is an animal who can breed with others of his kind. No matter what shape he has, what color, what size—as long as he can breed, he belongs to the same species. Even mutants as long as they remain sexually viable must be termed human no matter how they appear. Even freaks.''

The disfigured and distorted and deranged. Those who drooled and lived in dreams and sloughed their skin as if they had been reptiles. Giants and midgets and women who had found another world within themselves. Artists and fighters and the woman he loved who was not what she seemed and could have no offspring.

Dumarest narrowed his eyes at the thought, wondering if Toyanna had deliberately planted it and why. Was Govinda a mutant who had progressed one step too far? Something which, despite her shape, could no longer be called human?

He said, ''We've talked enough and I've waited too long. Wake Chenault and ask him what I want to know.''

''He's worn out. The effort of your fight weakened him.''

''A few words,'' said Dumarest. ''A few numbers; the coordinates of Earth. Something he can give and lose nothing in the giving. He swore he could help me.''

''He can.''

"Then wake him." Dumarest stepped toward her as she made no move. "Do it!"

"And if I don't?" She added, quickly, "Don't answer that, I can guess. But why?"

"I warned him but he still tried to trick me."

"A fault, but—" She broke off, gesturing at the cabinet. "An old man, weak, dying, afraid, doing the best he could. Wanting to survive and knowing only one way to do it. Needing you as we all need you, Earl. Your speed, strength, courage, determination. Your luck." She met his eyes, his frown. "Yes, Earl, your luck. If we are to succeed we need all we can get."

"For what? Ryzam?" Dumarest thinned his lips with impatient anger. "You want me to join you chasing a fable, is that it? All right. I agree. Give me the coordinates of Earth and I'm with you all the way. That's what I told Chenault. The offer I made. He refused to accept it."

"He could have cheated you. Given you false data."

"He could have tried."

"But you would have made him verify the figures as far as possible. You wouldn't have trusted him. Yet you can't seem to understand why he couldn't trust you. You could have taken the figures and left."

Dumarest said, flatly, "I gave my word."

"One he should have taken, perhaps, but, in his place, would you?" She paused then said, before he could answer, "I promise you this; after we've

139

been to Ryzam he will give you what you want to know. All you want will be yours."

Or Chenault would be dead and the knowledge he held lost with him. A gamble Dumarest was reluctant to take and yet there seemed to be no choice.

He said, bitterly, "The old and weak have a strength of their own. All right, tell Chenault he's won. I'll have to trust him—but if he cheats me not even Ryzam will save him."

On the side of the valley something flashed, died, flashed again. Gleams Dumarest noted, assessing time and direction before running toward the slope, bent low, blending into the vegetation his boots soundless on the loam. Halting to wait, to move again, to make a sudden dart and to lift Govinda high in his arms.

She squirmed, writhing, resisting his grip with spring-steel reaction, relaxing as she recognized him, slumping to lean against him, masking him with her hair, the mounds of her breasts warm against his cheeks.

"Darling!" She brushed back her hair as he set her down. "I didn't see you. What were you doing—spying on me?"

"I saw a flash and was curious."

"About this?" She lifted a pair of secateurs from the basket which had fallen to one side. Fronds covered the bottom. "I was collecting herbs. Hilary is going to make a potion for me. Something special. Once you taste it, my darling, you will never leave me.''

''You don't need a potion for that.''

''No?'' Her eyes held his, bright yet vacant of humor, glinting with reflected light as they moved to search his face. ''Do you mean that? Would you settle down here with me, grow old with me, spend the rest of your life in this one place so as to be at my side? Would you do that for me, Earl? Would you?''

Massak rescued him from the necessity of an answer. He called up, his voice flat, dampened by the contour of the terrain.

''Earl! Come down here. We need a referee.''

He was stripped to the waist, his torso a mass of ugly scars, livid patches of paler hue which patterned his skin in abstract designs. Shior faced him, also naked to the waist, his hairless chest unmarked.

''A challenge,'' explained the mercenary. ''I say Shior isn't fit yet and he claims he is. If he can beat me I'll agree. If he can't then he goes back to his bed.''

Dumarest said, ''Fit for what?''

''To live. To fight. To survive.'' Massak shrugged. ''Does a man need an excuse for combat?''

''Not an excuse, a reason.'' Dumarest looked at the other man, smaller, slighter built, but equally as dangerous as the mercenary. One now completely healed. ''Run to the end of the valley,'' he suggested. ''The first to return will be the winner.''

"Run?" Massak snorted his disgust. "What kind of combat is that? A warrior does not run."

"Sometimes it pays. Too often a stupidly brave man ends up a dead one."

"True." Shior nodded his agreement. "But some never learn. My thick-headed friend, for one. Even though his scars are a constant reminder. Fire," he explained. "Flame throwers on Appanowitz. I heard the warning and ran but he had to be stubborn. Gambled that he could cut them all down with a laser before they got him. Had there been one less he would have won the bet."

"As it was, Shior had to finish the job and, for me, the war was over." Massak scowled at the memory. "Fire," he muttered. "Those who use it should be roasted over a slow flame. Head-down over a camp fire as we did to the swine who tried to feed us poisoned wine. That was on Amara and it took him a long time to die."

"You fight old wars too often," said Shior. "Come, let's run. The exercise will do you good."

They vanished into the vegetation, Govinda watching them go, shaking her head as the rustling died.

"Men! Always they talk of death and battle and conflict. Why, when there are so many other things to talk about? Small, helpless, loving things to cherish and nurse and watch as they grow to full stature?" Without altering her tone she said, "Have you ever given a woman a child, Earl?"

Dumarest remembered what Toyanna had told

him. "I can't give you what you want, Govinda. No man can."

"Is it so much to ask?" Her eyes, her face, mirrored her pain. "Why when I need it so much? Why must I be denied? Why? Why, Earl? Why?"

The question asked by all born to suffer. By all railing against their fate. Why? Why me? Why?

As always there was no comforting answer.

"You're wrong." She stepped back, shaking her head, chin lifted in sudden defiance. "There is a man who can give me what I need. Tama can. He promised. He swore that everything would be all right. Once we get to Ryzam—" As suddenly as it had come the brave defiance left her and she was weak again, sobbing, broken by the weight of too much yearning, too hopeless a dream. "Earl! Hold me! Tell me it will be all right!"

He obeyed, caressing her hair, holding her close as he murmured words of reassurance. Only when she had calmed did he rise, stooping to pick up her basket, the herbs it contained.

"We'll give them to Hilary," he said. "For that special potion."

"Do I need it?" Her eyes met his and she smiled at what she saw. "Never mind the herbs, Earl. Take me for a walk. To the edge of the valley."

Where the vegetation was thick and the ground soft and the air sweet with the scent of flowers. Where her hair spread in a scarlet mantle on the sward as she lay in the age-old attitude of demanding surrender. Where, afterwards, Dumarest turned to lie supine to stare at the burning vault of the sky through a screen of leaves. Seeing the sun and the tiny mote of the raft which hovered high above the valley like a watching bird of prey.

Vaclav was annoyed and showed it, making no attempt to mask his face as he glared at the image on the screen.

"I'm limited," he said. "I told you that. There's nothing more I can do."

Kooga, equally annoyed, maintained his professional calm. "We had an agreement, Chief. I can't understand why Dumarest isn't in your custody."

"I explained all that. Mirza Karroum has made her peace with him and has withdrawn all accusations. More; she seems to have become his friend. I can't defy the Karroum."

"And Chenault?"

"Alone means little but he also has friends. I can't break into his house to arrest his guest, especially as I've no reason. I've a raft watching the area. If he leaves I'll know it and maybe something can be done."

Justice outraged, his own concept of law turned into a mockery and his office used for personal gain. Things which made a sour taste in his mouth and the fading image on the screen didn't help. Kooga had his own world; one in which he was almost supreme, and the habit of demanding obedience was one which had become a part of his nature. A trait Vaclav found more than irritating and he sat back, glowering at the communicator, his desk, the far wall of his office.

A box in which he had spent too many years of his life.

Kooga had hinted of a means of escape; money to gain independence and freedom from the need of pandering to those who ruled Lychen. The big Families with their whims, their degenerate off-spring, their cruelties and unthinking demands. Once he had accepted it and had been glad of the security the Guardians offered. An organization in which he had risen to become its Chief but Luccia had died and their child with her and the driving need to provide for them had ended with their funeral.

A bad time which work had helped to push to the back of his mind, but always their memories lingered, his wife with her youth and beauty and wonderful understanding and the child they had both wanted so much and which had cost so dear.

A drawer opened to reveal their faces; hers still beautiful but traced with lines of strain, the boy's empty, vacuous, a smiling mask which conveyed no humor. A fault in the cerebrum which normal medicine had been unable to cure. A genetic weakness, perhaps. One stemming from the mother but he hadn't been sure and had never wanted to risk repeating the tragedy.

So no wife, no child, just endless work which filled the hours, his only consolation that he was making sure the job was well done.

Now Kooga with his hints and promises and the

growing pressure of his impatience. A man needing a cat's-paw and covering the need with lying
talk of partnership.

Yet, if he was right, one thing at least was true.
Dumarest could provide the escape he yearned to
obtain. The way out if he could stomach the price.

Kooga had no such problems. Dumarest was an
item which Vaclav should have collected by now—
Mirza's change of mind had left the field wide
open. The Chief had the men, the means, the
authority to arrest on his own volition. Why did he
delay? Was he hoping to deal with the Cyclan
direct?

A thought which accompanied him as he left his
office and made his way to the room where Avro
was lying. It was as before; dimmed, the monitors
flashing as they maintained and recorded their
surveillance. On the print-outs the complex pattern
of lines held their own fascination.

Kooga studied them as he had studied the earlier
ones, adding minutes to the hours in which he had
struggled to grasp their meaning. The normal
encephalographic patterns could be ignored; to him
they were as familiar as the fingers of his hand.
But they only formed a background to the pattern
obtained from the cyber. The added lines, their
waverings, their codelike repetitions presented a
mystery he felt on the edge of solving.

Communication?

He felt it had to be that. Comparison with the
words gained by the recorder, matched to the wavering lines, showed a certain correlation. Elemen-

tary cypher-breaking techniques had shown certain positive extensions and a more sophisticated investigation must extend the range of that knowledge. In time, with enough data, he would be able to solve the mystery.

And with it the secret of the power of the Cyclan.

The print-out trembled in Kooga's hands and he let it fall as he indulged in the pursuit of a dream. Power and authority all guaranteed by the Cyclan in return for his silence. A vast medical complex in which his words would be law—and no arrogant bitch like Mirza Karroum would ever again make him feel like dirt.

He looked at the unrolling paper with its mesh of lines. Dumarest was money but this was power and, soon, it would be his.

"Doctor?" He turned, startled, meeting the eyes of the new nurse. "A message, sir. From the Cyclan." She glanced at the silent figure on the bed. "Cyber Zuber will arrive at dawn."

Chapter Ten

Zuber was of his kind; cold, calculating, a stranger to emotion. A living machine who was a physician who had never learned to be a man. The robe he wore was in direct contrast; a warmly glowing scarlet, bearing on its breast the gleaming Seal of the Cyclan. Framed in the thrown-back cowl his head bore the likeness of a skull, hairless, the cheeks sunken, only the deep-set eyes revealing the keen mind within. His hands, his limbs and body, were the parts of a functional machine. Flesh and blood now directed to a single purpose; to serve the organization of which he was a servant.

To Kooga he said, "You have done well, Doctor. At least Cyber Avro is still alive."

"Thanks to your instructions."

"They may have helped but more was needed.

You provided it. Did many help you?'' Zuber paused, ''There must have been others, surely? Nurses? Assistants? You can be open with me.''

Interrogation concealed by courtesy and a continuation of the questioning which had commenced the moment the cyber had entered the hospital with his aides. Men who had vanished on mysterious errands, returning to whisper their reports, moving on about their business. Taking over the patient; Kooga had been refused entry when he had gone to Avro's room. His protest had been met with a facile explanation and he had known better than to argue. Now, and until he was ready, he must act the part of the innocent.

''Was there any unusual occurrence? Anything which could be termed a crisis? Or, if not that, any unusual activity? I mean, of course, in regard to the patient's condition.''

''Nothing which has not been reported.'' Kooga had answered the question before. One differently phrased but identical in meaning. ''You have my records and they are complete. Every detail of medication, surgery, dressings, after-care, all are there. A most interesting case but I must confess to feeling relief now that you have taken over. The responsibility was not one I would care to repeat.''

''You did your best,'' said Zuber. ''No one could have done more.''

And his best had been good enough. Kooga was not deluded by the cyber's compliment or the smooth, even monotone in which it was delivered. One designed to avoid all irritant factors. Had he failed the tone would have been the same even while ordering his death.

Yet he hadn't failed and Zuber seemed satisfied and would soon be gone taking Avro with him. Then he could return to his study of the print-outs, copies of which now lay safely hidden. Work which had occupied him all through the night leaving traces of fatigue stamped on cheeks and eyes.

Details which Zuber had noted and dismissed; men in Kooga's profession were always the victims of weariness.

He said, "There is, however, one small point which I would be gratified if you would explain. According to my information the nurse who tended Cyber Avro has left the hospital by your order. She is now in a distant region. The explanation?"

A shock but Kooga had rehearsed the explanation.

"She was tired. She had worked hard and long and I wanted to avoid the possibility of risk. Nurses get accustomed to routine and tend to lose their fine edge by repetition. They take minor things for granted. Usually such carelessness is unimportant but, in this case—well, I dared not take the chance of an avoidable complication."

"Such as?"

"A change in temperature signaling a potential source of infection. A shift in the position of the patient's body. A stain on a dressing. The malfunction of a monitor." Kooga shrugged. "You know how it is."

Not from personal experience; those who served the Cyclan did not fail, but Zuber could assess the probability. Those subjected to the poison of emotion could never wholly be trusted. Not even Kooga, loyal as he seemed, could be above suspicion. Why had the nurse been sent so far? Why hadn't it been included in the report—his aides had discovered the move while making a thorough check. What had Kooga to hide?

Nothing, perhaps, and yet Zuber knew that the smallest scrap of data could have unsuspected importance. That to ignore it would be to betray a lack of efficiency.

He said, "Regarding the monitors—it seems you went to extreme lengths in order to obtain the most detailed information. Especially as revealed by the encephalograph."

"I assumed you would want me to obtain such data." Fear made Kooga curt. "If you wish it can be destroyed."

"It is complete?"

"Of course."

"Yet the same system of monitoring was not used throughout. A more sophisticated machine was introduced just after the nurse was removed."

"It may have been." Irritation edged the doctor's tone. Questions as to his conduct, even from the cyber, were unwelcome. "I worked on your behalf and you have said you are satisfied. Now, it seems, you question my professional integrity. I did what I did because I judged it should be done. The result justifies my decision."

"Of course. Did you find the print-outs interesting? Unusual in any way?"

"No." Kooga added, "I didn't study them. The data was for you alone."

A lie and Zuber knew it; no physician would have failed to check for possible deterioration in the cerebrum and no one of Kooga's experience would have failed to note the unusual pattern. Anger and fear had betrayed him and had marked the need to terminate his existence.

"I understand." Zuber nodded as if satisfied. "Just one other thing while we are on the subject and then you will be left in peace. To enjoy your reward," he added. "One you have richly deserved."

"Thank you. The point?"

"There was a slight commotion; a woman insisted on entering Cyber Avro's room. The receptionist recorded the incident. She was not alone."

"No."

"The details?"

A matter he had overlooked and Kooga cursed his forgetfulness. The receptionist had been too efficient—or had the power of the Cyclan cast its shadow before it? How many eyes had been watching him? Checking everything he had done?

"The woman was Mirza Annette Karroum," he said. "The man was Vaclav, Chief of the Guardians. They, that is she, wanted to question Cyber Avro. Naturally I didn't allow it."

"Question?"

"Yes, I don't know the details. I ordered them from the room immediately."

"One of the Karroum?"

"Yes, I—" Kooga hesitated. The cyber would

know of the power held by the Karroum and the other big Families. On worlds such as Lychen such were not ordered as if they were inferiors. "She was stubborn," he admitted. "I had to explain how useless it was to talk to the patient, to get any response. Once she understood that she left."

"Thank you." Zuber rose, extending his hand, the broad ring on his finger gleaming in the light. "I think that will be all."

The administrator was a woman, no longer young, her hair long, graying, dressed in a bun which accentuated the sharpness of her features. A face now marked with the stamp of anxiety.

"I don't understand it," she said. "Doctor Kooga seemed perfectly well when I last saw him. A little tired, perhaps, but that's all. Then, an hour later when I had to go to his room to ask his decision on a matter, he was dead. Naturally I sent for you immediately."

"Why?" Vaclav met her eyes. "Did you suspect a crime?"

The answer lay in the room where Kooga lay sprawled on the floor, one hand extended to where the carpet had been drawn back. Vaclav knelt beside him, sniffing at the pale lips, lifting the lids to examine the glazed eyes. No scent of familiar poisons or traces of familiar drugs but that meant nothing. The room itself told him more: the furnishings were ripped, paintings thrown down from

153

their hangings, the entire place looked as if it had been searched.

By whom?

Vaclav looked at Kooga's extended hand. It lay clenched and, as he forced open the fingers, he found a scrap of paper clutched in them. A fragment from a larger piece which bore the tracery of lines. The paper itself was from a photocopying machine.

The administrator waited outside. To her Vaclav said, "Whom did the doctor see this morning? Cyber Zuber? Anyone else, I mean after his interview with Zuber? No? I see. What time did you see him? The exact time, please. Good. And it was an hour later you called on him?"

"About that, yes."

"And found him like this? Has he been touched? No? Good. That will be all."

"But—" She looked past Vaclav at the body sprawled on the floor."

"Leave him for now." Vaclav stepped back into the room. "I'll let you know when he can be removed."

A man dead, trying to reach for something, but why? The room gave the answer, one Vaclav sensed with his years of experience and, standing, looking around, he read the message it conveyed. Kooga, tired, seeking his bed, entering the room and finding it bearing the marks of an obvious search. If he had hidden anything in it he would have gone immediately to it—and those who had set the trap would have what they wanted.

Vaclav stepped again toward the body. Kooga had died but he bore no sign of an obvious wound. Poison was the logical instrument but how had it been administered? As Vaclav looked at the drawn-back carpet, the reaching hand, he saw the minute spot of reddish brown on the pad of the palm. Something which could have been dirt or a fragment of dried blood.

Straightening he looked at the room. A recorder lay where it had been thrown, tapes scattered around it. He examined them, remembering the one Kooga had played, the gained response of Avro with its whispered directions on where Dumarest could be found. Had he told the cyber of Dumarest? Was the tape still here?

He searched them, reading titles, halting as he found one with a single word. Ardestum—an obvious anagram. He played it, listening again to the whispering voice, then rewound it to hit the erase. If Zuber had killed Kooga to get his hidden papers he wouldn't get this. A small revenge but better than none—the power of the Cyclan would give the cyber immunity of punishment for his crime.

Outside, Vaclav threw the tape into a bin with items waiting for incineration. An assistant collected it as he reached the end of the passage, making his way to Kooga's office. As he entered Zuber turned toward him from where he stood at the desk.

"Chief Vaclav. It is good to meet you. I assume you are here to investigate Doctor Kooga's demise. A regrettable loss. You knew him well?"

155

"No."

"But you had met him. With the Lady Mirza Annette Karroum. You were together in Cyber Avro's room. May I ask why?"

Vaclav said, curtly, "She was unhappy with my report on the death of the previous head of her House. She wanted confirmation from Kooga as to the cause."

"And chose the room of a sick man to conduct her investigation?"

"It happened that way. Naturally Kooga wasn't pleased."

"But he answered her?"

"He satisfied her, yes. Now, if you will excuse me, I've work to get on with."

"Of course," Zuber's hand appeared from the wide sleeve of his robe, the ring glowing on his finger. "I must not delay you. I have little time to spare either. We must be leaving soon."

On the ship in which they had arrived, taking Avro with them, his inert body wrapped in a cryogenic sac and frozen against the ravages of time. To be transshipped and sent to Cyclan Headquarters there to be wakened, tested, probed so as to gain every scrap of information from his body and mind. The direct order of Marle, Cyber Prime, who, like all of his kind, abhorred waste.

"I wish you a safe journey."

"Thank you, Chief." The ring glinted as Zuber moved his hand to touch Vaclav's own. "And I wish you success."

The desk was void of anything of value, the

office the same and, back in his own, Vaclav sat brooding on what he had learned. Kooga dead, murdered for something he had possessed. Papers taken from where they had been hidden; copies of something the Cyclan wanted to remain a secret. The one Dumarest held? No, the tape hadn't been taken and so, obviously, Kooga hadn't mentioned it. And the questions Zuber had asked—why had he been so interested in who had been in Avro's room?

A pattern had to be present and Vaclav strove to find it, scowling as the communicator hummed, reaching out to hit the button, his hand freezing as he saw the tiny fleck on his skin.

Something which could have been dirt or a fragment of dried blood.

A match to the one he'd found on Kooga—and Kooga was dead. The communicator hummed again but he ignored it, thinking, remembering. Zuber and his ring and the way he had reached out to touch hands in a farewell gesture. One alien to his breed; cybers did not entertain emotional ceremony. An act, then, to get within range and Vaclav was no stranger to rings which were not as they seemed. A touch of anaesthetic to numb the pain of the dart which penetrated the skin to instill its poison and the thing was done. A man dead but not knowing it, walking, talking, smiling even as the delayed action drug did its work.

How much time did he have?

Kooga had died within an hour after the administrator had seen him but he could have fallen minutes after reaching his room. How long before that had he met Zuber? A computation which carried a bleak answer—time was short and getting shorter.

Vaclav reached for the communicator, killing the incoming call, his hand pausing as it rested on the keys. Perhaps the Cyclan could save him, neutralizing the poison, and the bribe of Dumarest could persuade them to do it. But he had destroyed the tape and had no proof. They would need to check and that would take time he didn't have. But if he could talk fast enough and be persuasive enough—.

A desperate hope and a futile one. Vaclav recognized it as he withdrew his hand from the communicator. No matter what was promised his life was still forfeit. Knowing of Dumarest and his value to the Cyclan they would assume he knew the secret he held. And he had been in the room with the others. Avro's room with the mysterious knowledge it held which must never be revealed. The reason for Kooga's death and his own. Two out of three with only Mirza left.

Soon the bitch too would be dead!

A moment of gratification then it vanished in a deeper anger. She was what she was but the cybers were something else. Killers without emotion, manipulators, devoid of mercy or tolerance or sensitivity. Using death as a convenient instrument. Red swine who had taken his life. To cheat them was now his only revenge.

The communicator beckoned but he rose; who knew what tendrils might lie in his department? It was better to play it safe and he left the office, the building, moving quickly down the street to a public phone. Punching the number, snarling at the delay, curt in his demand when, finally, the screen came to life.

"Get me Mirza Karroum!"

"But—"

"Get her, damn you! Chief Vaclav here! Move!" A pause, a time of nothingness, then her face appeared, hard, cold, impatient. "Listen!" He spoke before she could protest. "Kooga's dead and I'm dying. You could be next." He told her why. "They know nothing about Dumarest but they want him. He could be an ally. In any case you need to watch yourself. Agents could be left to take care of you."

A girl brushed past him as he left the booth, young, well-made, with wanton, inviting eyes. A sight he ignored, looking instead at the street, the houses, the traffic, the bowl of the sky which covered all. Things more precious now than ever before and he drank them as if to store memories against another time.

How long?

The curse of knowledge which all men had but most managed to forget. The fact of inevitable death but, for him, it was close. Reaching for him at this very moment, touching him, causing a shiver to run up his spine. Had Kooga sensed what was happening? Known, too late, that he was dying? Would there be time for him to reach the grave where his love lay buried?

159

He began to walk, faster, faster, breaking into a run. To halt as the light seemed to flicker. To fall as it died.

In their way the Cyclan had been kind. There was no pain, no terror, just a soft darkness on which two faces were portrayed in a golden light. Luccia's and next to her the boy. Smiling as she was smiling, as he had always smiled but, now, there was no emptiness in his eyes.

The valley looked different than it had before but then it had been night and now it was bright with the glory of a dying day. Beauty Mirza Karroum did not appreciate and she sent the raft down to land with a jar which shook her teeth. At the door Chenault was waiting, hand lifted in greeting, a salutation she ignored, brushing past him into the hall.

"You made good time," he said, following her. "I didn't really expect you until tomorrow."

"Where's Dumarest?"

"With some of the others in—"

"Send him out here to me." She glared her impatience. "Now. We must talk in private."

"He's busy."

"And I've no time to waste. What I have to tell him is important. He won't thank you for delaying our meeting. Now move, man! Move!"

She prowled the hall, trying to gain comfort from what she saw; rocks and boulders and writhing streaks of mineral color all forming the illusion of an entrancing grotto. But it didn't appeal and she turned as Dumarest came toward her, hands lifting as if to embrace him, lowering as she realized the incongruity of the gesture.

She said, bluntly, "You're in danger. The Cyclan has men on Lychen."

He said nothing but she saw the slight tensing of his body; the reactive response of nerve and muscle as if he had readied himself for a fight. Things another would have missed but she noted them as she sensed the subtle change in his attitude. Before the news he had been a man tall, calm, smiling a greeting. Now he was an animal, sharply aware, questing with mind and sinew the danger he recognized.

"They came for Avro," she explained. "He told me where to find you."

"How?" He nodded as she explained. "And?"

"Kooga's dead. Vaclav too. Cardiac failure so they said but I don't believe them. Both were murdered. Vaclav knew he was going to die and warned me to be careful. He thought I was to be the next victim. He suggested that you could be an ally."

He said, "Do they know I'm here?"

"No. Not unless Avro's told them and I can't think he did. He was in a coma and will be in a cryogenic sac by now. Vaclav destroyed the evidence. They don't know you're here, Earl." Pausing, she added, "Not yet."

Two words which told him the situation and he looked at her, seeing the hard face, the eyes to match, the rigid line of chin and jaw. A woman almost twice his age and one determined to survive.

"Betraying me to the Cyclan won't help you," he said. "You'd still follow the others and for the same reason. As a precaution against your talking to others about something you may have learned about the Cyclan."

"But there's nothing! I swear it!" She fought to remain calm. "But I can never prove that and they'll never take my word. Earl! What can I do?"

"Run."

"What?"

"Leave Lychen. Travel to other worlds and keep moving. Get lost if you can. Trust no one and say nothing. Make no commitments, no friends, have no ambitions. Learn to be always alone." His voice was bitter from personal experience. "In time they might accept the fact that you know nothing and call off the chase. If you stay here you're dead. Tomorrow, next week, the month after—the Cyclan never gives up."

"But if you were with me? Guarding me?" She saw his expression and shook her head as she recognized the impossibility of gaining total protection. "No. It wouldn't work. You're right, Earl, I'll have to run—but you come with me."

"I can't."

"I don't want to betray you but—"

"I can't," he said again. "I'm going with Chenault. An expedition. There's no point in arguing. I'm going."

"I'll come with you." She had spoken on impulse but it made sense. "Where's Chenault?"

He sat alone in a room bright with flowers, papers scattered on the table before him, a pile of books to one side. Old books which filled the air with the scent of dust and dulled the sweetness of the blooms.

He frowned as he heard Mirza's demand.

"No."

"Why not? I can help. How did you intend to travel?"

"I've a ship."

"Where? What? Your own working as a trader or one you intend to charter? Whatever it is I've a better one waiting on the field at this moment. The *Kasse*. I can have it ready to leave by midnight."

"I won't be ready by then."

"Get ready. What do you need? Supplies? Goods? Weapons? Give me a list and I'll have them loaded from the Karroum warehouse. Damn it, man, why do you hesitate? I've the ship, the supplies, the crew—"

"No crew," said Chenault. "I'll use my own."

"Why? Who do you have?" She glanced at Dumarest then back at Chenault. "What's the mystery?"

Dumarest waited then, as the silence lengthened, he said, "Tell her."

"No. She—no!"

"We're hunting a legend," said Dumarest. "Chasing a ghost. One we may never find but the search itself will be rewarding enough." He saw by her expression she had grasped his meaning. "And the sooner we go the better. Time is against us. It could be fatal to wait too long." Another message but this time with meaning to Chenault also. "I think it would be stupid not to take advantage of what has been offered. Others may think so too. If they do the search is over before it begins."

Mirza said, "And you, Earl?"

"If you go then I go with you." One way to escape the trap Lychen had become and, while they were together, he was safe from her betrayal. "Tomorrow, you said?"

"No!" Chenault slammed his fist on the table. "You can't! We have an agreement!"

"One based on mutual help. The two sides of a coin, remember? I help you and you help me—but what help are you stuck in a chair? How long am I supposed to wait?"

"If you leave me you'll lose—"

"Nothing." Dumarest was harsh. "I lose nothing —you can't lose what you've never had. It's your decision, Chenault. Make up your mind."

He leaned forward across the table with a face the other remembered. One he had seen before when steel had flashed at his torso to cut the artificial flesh of his arm. The face of a killer attacking a machine but one just as willing to attack the man behind it. One too dangerous to be frustrated for long.

"All right." Chenault voiced his surrender. "She can come with us."

"Good. I'll order the *Kasse* to be readied for

flight.'' Mirza glanced at Dumarest. "Give me a list of what we'll need. And we'll use my crew—I don't trust amateurs in the Burdinnion. Where are we heading?"

"Ryzam. It's a place on a world somewhere. Chenault knows where it is."

"So do I. It's Skedaka on the far edge of the Burdinnion." She looked from one to the other. "Are you serious? Is that the ghost you're hunting? The legend of Ryzam?"

Dumarest said, bitterly, "The place of eternal youth. Of endless health and vitality and all the rest of it. Now you say it's a matter of common knowledge."

"Not common, but it's known. By spacers and traders and those who live on Skedaka. A lot of people have tried to find it." She paused, looking at them both. "A lot of people," she repeated. "But none who reached it has ever returned."

Chapter Eleven

Captain Lauter was a broad, thick-set man, old, experienced, loyal to the Karroum, more than loyal to Mirza Annette. From the depths of his big pilot's chair he lifted a hand to point at the screen before him.

"There," he said. "Skedaka."

A world which was a child of death; seared, torn, gouged, warped by the tremendous cataclysm which had created the Burdinnion. Standing beside the chair Dumarest studied the image set against the background of stars. One which seemed disfigured, diseased, blotched and mottled with drab colors.

"Where's the Ryzam?"

"There." Again Lauter pointed. "That patch to the north."

166

The image swelled as he increased the magnification, growing to almost fill the screen, the patch looking like a crusted scab on leprous flesh. One composed of soaring spires, jagged, edged with sawlike serrations as if rock had been rendered molten then flung upwards to solidify in flight to form a pattern resembling the gigantic bristles of a monstrous brush.

"You can't land on it," said Lauter. "No clear space for one thing and the forces which stream from it for another. Get to within a certain height and the generators fail. Some ships tried it. None came back."

"None?"

Lauter said, dryly, "It happens about five miles up. When the ships hit the ground—" He clapped his hands together, the sound sharp in the control room. "We'll have to find a spot well clear of the area."

A good spot and a safe one; Lauter had a high regard for his vessel. Dumarest watched as the image shifted, shrank to normal size, looking forlorn and alone in the bright immensity of the cosmos.

"You've been here before, Captain?"

"Yes."

"Then you've heard of the legend. Do you believe in it?"

"No."

"Why not?"

"Because I'm not a fool." Lauter was blunt. "Ryzam is unusual, that I'll admit, but so are a thousand other places on as many worlds. Most of them have legends, tales, stories invented in taverns and spread by the credulous. Usually it's because the natives want to encourage tourists and the money they bring. Expeditions, even. Skedaka is no different. People live there, poor devils trying to scratch a living from dirt that's mostly ash. Sometimes they find gems and rare metals and there's a kind of herb which grows wild. Maybe the legend grew from that—the stuff can give energy and tighten the skin so as to reduce wrinkles. Instant youth. It doesn't last though no one down there will admit that. They have a vested interest in maintaining the legend. In the town they'll sell you everything you need to explore Ryzam. Maps, guns, everything. Sell," he repeated. "They never hire."

"Because no one ever comes back?"

"That's right."

"Do you know why?"

For answer Lauter magnified the image again, this time larger than before, the scab shown in greater detail, accentuating its bleak harshness.

"A maze," said the captain. "Go into it and it's certain you'll get lost. No food. No water. There could be predators and God alone knows what else. The only thing you can be sure of is that there's nothing to find. I guess, when the searchers realize that, they've passed the point of no return."

A facile answer; one to be expected from a man who had spent his life in the ordered confines of a ship, the predictable regions of space. Yet Chenault with his dream was just as bad; his obsession blinding him to what could be an obvious explanation.

He sat in the salon of the vessel together with Mirza and the others; Toetzer, Lopakhin, Massak, Shior. Hilary was with Govinda, and Toyanna, together with Baglioni, was in the cabin holding the casket. Working at the major task of keeping Chenault alive while, in the salon, he planned the next steps of the operation.

"We shall land to the north," he said. "Opposite to the town. The section we want is marked by a cluster of spires resembling a pair of lifted hands. We must pass between them to a space shaped like a star."

Massak said, "And then?"

"Once we have reached it I'll give further instructions as to direction."

"No." Dumarest stepped into the room and up to the table at which the others sat. "That isn't good enough. So far we've followed you blind but no longer. I want to know why you think you can succeed when so many others have failed."

"Because I have information they lacked." Chenault rested his hand on the papers before him. "Ryzam is a mystery, a trap for the unwary, as events have proved. But one man found the solution to the problem and set it down in his journal. I have the relevant passages from it here. Lydo Agutter was an educated and knowledgeable man. I say 'was' but the chances are that he is still alive.

169

He discovered the truth and set the details down in his book. I have them here.''

Shior said, ''The secret of eternal life?''

''Yes.''

''If he found it why didn't he sell it?'' Mirza snapped the question. ''Such a secret would have made him rich enough to buy a world.''

''Money.'' Toetzer echoed his disgust. ''There are more things in the universe than the lust for wealth. If Agutter were intelligent he would know that.''

Dumarest said, ''How old is the information?''

''Two centuries at least.'' Chenault lifted a hand to silence any protest. ''Time is meaningless when compared to immortality.''

''True, but in a couple of hundred years things can change.'' Massak voiced the obvious. ''Even if he did find the way how can we be certain it's still open?''

''We can't,'' admitted Chenault. ''But knowing it exists gives us the vital clue as to the necessary direction. We follow his instructions, circumnavigate any obstacles, regain the given route as soon as possible. With the talents among us it should be simple.''

Talents? Dumarest glanced around the table. Shior and Massak to provide protection with their fighting skills. Vosper, now asleep, and Lopakhin to maintain the surrogate. Toetzer? A sensitive of some kind as was Hilary to warn of danger or discern the correct direction. Toyanna to keep Chenault alive. Baglioni to act as personal bodyguard. Govinda a magnet he couldn't resist. Mirza a passenger and himself?

"You will be in charge, Earl." Chenault adjusted his papers. "When we land you will take over the expedition."

The cabin was small, dark, full of ghostly whispers; the transmitted sounds of activity vibrated through the stanchions, decks and hull. Noise no living ship in space was ever without and one which served as a background to his thoughts. Dumarest turned on the narrow bunk, turned again, feeling metal against his temple, the ghost-sound growing louder, fading as he moved away.

Rising he snapped on the lights and stood breathing deeply before stepping into the mist-shower. The thin spray cooled his flesh and, dressed, he left the cabin and walked down the passage outside. Doors flanked it; cabins holding sleeping figures, one more important than the rest. Dumarest tested it, found it locked, tapped and waited.

"Earl?" Pia Toyanna looked at him through the open door. "Is something wrong?"

"Maybe. Can we talk?" He saw the movement of her eyes and stared beyond her to where Chenault rested in his casket. "Inside? Can he hear us?"

"He's asleep." She stepped back, closing the door as he stepped into the cabin, locking it behind him. "What is it?"

Dumarest looked around before answering. The cabin was much larger than his own, one adapted for its special occupant, a clutter of medical appara-

171

tus lying close to the casket itself. A cot near it showed the recent imprint of a body, Toyanna's he guessed, and the puffiness of her eyes told of her fatigue and recently broken sleep.

"I'm sorry if I woke you but—"

"That doesn't matter." She was impatient. "Get to the point."

"Can Tama stand the journey?"

"What?"

"The expedition. He intends to accompany us. Personally, I mean, not just his surrogate." Dumarest glanced to where the machine rested in a chair, slumped a little, looking like a corpse. "Is he strong enough to survive?"

"Yes, if—" She broke off, confused, then said, with a rush, "He isn't as old as he looks. The muscular dystrophy has weakened him but his vital signs are strong and, aside from fatigue, he is in no worse condition than when we left Lychen."

Dumarest said, bluntly, "Don't misunderstand me. I don't give a damn whether he lives or dies but he has something he promised to give me. I want to be sure he has it."

"He has."

"Tell me how you are so sure."

"You gave him the names of stars and their distances from Earth. The names have changed but their relationship remains the same. A box enclosing Earth's primary. It is a simple matter of association to find that box and, when you do, the coordinates of Earth are revealed. And there are other clues which lead to the inescapable—"

"He knows," said Dumarest. "He knows how to find Earth. He knew it long before we met." He read the admission in her eyes. "Why, wanting to reach Earth as he does, didn't he go there?"

"Like this?" She glanced at the casket, the figure it contained. "Look at him. He can't stand. He can't walk. He needs help even to talk. He can barely open his eyes. Yes, he knows where Earth is to be found, but the discovery came too late. Can you appreciate the irony of it?" Her voice grew brittle with emotion. "At times the Gods are more than cruel. They give but demand too high a price. For him it was the culmination of a lifetime of searching—a dream he could never enjoy."

Not unless the secret of Ryzam could be found and he could be made young again and strong and able to walk with pride on the Mother World he considered Earth to be.

Dumarest slowed as he neared his cabin, hearing movement from within, slamming open the door to stare at the woman on his bunk.

"I've been waiting." Govinda threw back the scarlet mane of her hair. Framed by the tresses, her face held an aching familiarity. "I want to talk to you, Earl. Why am I to be left behind with the ship while that old bitch is going with you?"

"A matter of policy." Dumarest crossed the cabin to sit beside her, taking her hands in his own. "We can't always do everything together. Sometimes we have to part as we did that time on Chron. You remember—" He saw the puzzlement in her eyes and changed the subject. The way she

173

appeared to him was familiar as if time itself had folded back on itself, but the memories they shared were limited to recent events. "Mirza insisted," he explained. "She may be old but she's tough and can handle herself."

"She wants to be with you."

"I'm glad of it." He softened the admission with a smile. "While she's with me I'll have no fear of the ship leaving us stranded. And, if you're with the ship, I'll have no fear of losing you, my darling." His hand reached out to touch her hair, her cheek, the smooth line of her throat. "Don't you know how much I care for you?"

"Show me!"

A demand he couldn't refuse and for a time the cabin became a palace filled with wondrous delights and the murmurs of their passion added strength to the ghost-sounds roving the vessel.

"Earl!" Her hand was the warm caress of a kitten. "I love you, my darling. Always remember that I love you."

"For ever and ever?"

"Until the end of time. Earl, my darling, I swear it! I've never felt this way before. I can't imagine life without you. Please be careful."

"I will."

"Ryzam!" She shuddered in his arms. "A deathtrap. Everyone says so. Even if you find what you're looking for you'll never come back. I'll be alone again. Alone. Earl, how can I bear to be without you? How can I live?"

Fears he soothed with soft words and gentle

caresses until, exhausted, she fell asleep in his arms. A warm, soft and yielding bundle of feminine loveliness. A woman who was all he could ever hope to find. One reborn, resurrected, more precious to him than anything in the universe aside from the one thing which dominated his life.

Ryzam could provide it.

Once Chenault had solved its secret and had gained what he was after Dumarest would finally learn where Earth was to be found.

The *Kasse* landed at dawn as near to Ryzam as Lauter could manage, and an hour before noon the expedition was on its way.

From his position in the lead raft Dumarest looked back at the others strung out in line to the rear. One, the third, was bulked with Chenault's casket, the surrogate itself, Toyanna and Baglioni who, armed and grotesque in his armor, looked like a malevolent gnome from some tale of an ancient time.

Behind them, at the rear, Hilary rode with Shior and Vosper together with supplies of food, water and other essentials for survival. Toetzer and Massak held second place. Mirza and Lopakhin completed the complement of the lead vehicle.

All wore mercenary combat armor complete with air tanks and radio communication. All were armed.

"It's like an army." Mirza turned to look back at the line. "I've seen pictures like this in old books. Men wearing metal casings and going out

175

to fight. They looked like machines and I guess we look the same.''

"Killing machines," said Lopakhin. He leaned forward to gain a better view of what lay before them. "And there's another." He gestured at the forest of bleak and serrated spires now clear in the russet light of a sullen sun. "There it is, Earl. A graveyard if ever I saw one. Let's hope to God we don't add to its reputation."

"Men don't die without reason." Dumarest adjusted the controls and sent the raft higher, watching to see if those following did likewise. "And we can't be sure that no one has ever come back. Maybe they did and decided not to talk about it. Or, if they did, their stories never got around."

"Or they found the secret and wanted to keep it for themselves." Mirza turned to face forward, her machine rifle falling to clash on the side of the raft as the sling slipped from her shoulder. "Damn! Sorry, Earl!"

"Is it cocked?"

"No. I'm not that stupid. I told you I knew how to handle these things."

The truth and he hoped the others had been as honest. Shior and Massak placed among them would provide a steadying influence and yield fast action if it was needed. Chenault was another matter. His casket was fitted with antigrav units for easy handling but nothing could lessen its bulk. If an attack came the other rafts would provide covering fire.

Details settled on long before the *Kasse* had landed and put into operation with the minimum of delay. Ryzam was too harsh, too foreboding to be contemplated for long without imaginary fears rising to augment any real dangers. And those, if they existed, were still unknown.

"An army," mused Lopakhin. "You'd think a force like this could go in and search and find whatever is to be found. Given enough men and firepower who could stop it? That's what makes nonsense of most legends. If the lure is strong enough the truth will be found. Even curiosity will do it. Any problem which—" He broke off pointing. "Earl! Quick! There!"

"What did you see?"

"Movement. Something—" Lopakhin shook his head. "It's gone now."

Dumarest searched the area and saw nothing. An illusion, perhaps, one born of the light and shadow and an active imagination. Even so he tripped the radio switch within his helmet.

"Movement reported directly ahead," he said. "Can anyone verify?" His listened to the chorus of negatives. "All right. It was probably a trick of the light. We'll lift another hundred yards."

The height would betray them to a greater number of watchers if any existed but gave a sense of comfort to those unaccustomed to the dangers of the unknown. As the sun passed its zenith they neared a configuration of spires which held the vague likeness of a pair of uplifted hands.

"There!" Chenault was triumphant. "The hands Agutter mentioned. Beyond will lie the star."

The beginning of the journey discovered in the

old journal and Dumarest hoped it would be as uneventful as the trip so far.

Mirza voiced his suspicions. "It's too easy," she said. "Just fly in and land and then keep moving. I don't like it."

Dumarest made no comment, eyes narrowed as he stared ahead. Ryzam was beneath them now, the area ringing the edge and, he guessed, relatively harmless. But to plunge on would be to invite destruction.

"All rafts halt," he said into the radio. "Massak, Shior, bracket Chenault between you. I'm going ahead to see what's waiting. Keep alert." To the others in the raft with him he said, "Keep watch to either side. If anything comes at us shoot."

He sent the vehicle rising, aware of the turbulence which must exist close to the sun-warmed spires, the danger of being swept against their serrated edges. As it moved forward he searched the crevasses, most shrouded in shadows cast by the spires, haunts of mystery and menace. On, the configuration of hands passing to one side. Farther, the star-shaped clearing a splotch of relative brightness; then, as it drew level, he felt the raft lurch beneath his hands.

"Earl!"

He heard Mirza's cry, ignoring it as he fought to maintain height, the raft wheeling as it fell, tilting, Lopakhin shouting his fear as he was thrown against and over the edge. A clutching hand saved him, fingers which caught in the straps restraining the supplies and he hauled himself back into the body of the vehicle as it juddered, veering to drop as Dumarest sent it back the way it had come. A fall which threatened to send them hard against the spires to be impaled by the jagged peaks then, abruptly, the vehicle was alive again and heading up and out from the heart of Ryzam.

"God!" Lopakhin was sweating within his helmet. "I looked at death just then. What the hell happened?"

"No power. Something cut the engine." Dumarest cautiously tested the controls. "It's all right now."

"A fault?" Mirza thinned her lips. "These rafts were supposed to have been checked."

"They were." Dumarest glanced at the handlike spires as they fell to the rear. "Captain Lauter told me of a force which comes from Ryzam. Something which cuts out ship generators. It must affect rafts the same way."

"So we can't just fly in." Lopakhin grunted. "It's obvious when you think about it. If rafts worked Ryzam would be mapped and charted by now. So what now, Earl? Do we walk?"

"Not all the way." Dumarest spoke into the radio telling the others what had happened. "Come in to meet me, Shior. We'll unload, move back out and transship the supplies. Chenault comes in last."

"What about the rafts?"

"They stay outside. All but one. Let's get moving!"

The uplifted spires rose to enfold them with a symbolic embrace, one too like a grasping prison to be comfortable. The star-shaped clearing was smooth, the seven pointed rays set equally at the circumference of the central space. There they landed to stack the supplies. By mid-afternoon it was done, only Chenault waiting for transshipment.

"I'll get him." Dumarest climbed into the sole remaining raft. "Take over, Ian. Set guards and keep everyone on combat alert."

Massak saluted. "You expect trouble? Here?"

"Everywhere. Keep the women among the bales and have men watch from every angle." Dumarest glanced at the surrounding spires, their bases wreathed in thickening shadows. "Stay put. No exploring. We shouldn't be long."

A wind had risen by the time he reached Chenault, small dunes piling against the sides of the grounded rafts. Chenault himself, impatient, looked at the lowering sun.

"We're wasting time," he complained. "This shift could have been completed in one move."

"We can afford wasted time," said Dumarest. "We can't afford mistakes." He glanced at Toyanna and jerked his head. She followed him to one side out of earshot of the others. "Tell me something," he said. "Can Tama operate his surrogate by a cable?"

"Yes. Why?"

"It could be necessary. One other thing, the midget stays behind."

"I can see why," she admitted. "But he won't like it."

Baglioni was furious. "No. I refuse. You can't make me."

"You stay." Dumarest was firm, then softening his tone, explained. "I'm leaving two rafts here, one under the hands and the other in the clearing. There'll be a gun in each. We may have to come out in a hurry and we'll need all the help we can get. The raft, the guns, someone to come to the rescue. That's you, Baglioni. You're the best suited." He allowed of no argument. "Pia, follow me in your raft to the hands and pick me up. I'll ride with you to the clearing."

Where the camp had been set and death was waiting.

Chapter Twelve

It came as the dying sun gilded the tips of the spires and Chenault was busy probing the star rays for signs Agutter may have left behind. A search as yet barren and which would have created disappointment in an ordinary man but which only caused him to move faster as he touched and scanned the walls. Toetzer had joined him, Shior following as if by accident. It was Hilary who screamed the warning.

"Look out! Danger! Be careful!"

Then, the harshly strident blasting of a gun.

Shior had been fast, reacting by instinct, firing at something he hadn't recognized. A broad, disc-like creature edged with scrabbling legs which dropped from the side of a spire to land and rear with snapping mandibles. A thing six feet across, two thick, armoured like a crab, the carapace the dull hue of the spire on which it had lurked.

One followed by others, a flood as it died beneath a storm of shattering lead.

"Helmets! Close helmets!" Dumarest snapped the order into the radio as he snatched up a gun. Vapors could be emitted by the things, acid sprays, numbing gases—in Ryzam no possibility could be ignored. "Massak! Guard the women! The rest of you—move!"

They advanced behind a hail of bullets which smashed through armor, spilling greenish ichor, pulpy flesh, oddly shaped organs. A curtain of protection from which Chenault stumbled, Toetzer following, Shior standing to cover their retreat. An act which cost him his life.

Dumarest saw the movement as, again, Hilary screamed a warning. Things seeming to peel from the spires, falling to land, scrabbling, rearing, darting forward with startling speed. Swamping the lone figure, muffling the blast of his gun, absorbing the missiles Dumarest poured into them.

"Hui!" Massak roared his anger. "Those damned things! They've got him!"

Tearing through his armor with mandibles like shears. Ripping at the soft flesh exposed beneath the protection. Feeding on his body and blood.

"Back!" Dumarest caught the mercenary and threw him toward the bales. "Hold your position. All of you! Back! Back, I say! Back!"

He fired again, a long burst which emptied the clip, sending more broken and shattered disc-things to join the others twitching on the ground. Reloading he looked at the spires, seeing them flake into new creatures which glided down to join the feast. Tearing into their injured fellows with savage ferocity. Cannibalism common among all such predators living in a hostile environment.

"We must press on." Chenault lifted a hand, pointing. "I thought I saw Agutter's sign down there."

"We can't." Dumarest fired again, a short burst which sent broken things twitching to one side. "There must be millions of them. They coat the spires. Waiting dormant until aroused." He fired again adding, grimly, "They're waking now."

There were too many to kill and he knew it. Already they must fill the crevasses behind them, blocking off the path to the hands, the edge of Ryzam. The raft couldn't carry them all and it would take too long to return with the others. The only hope of survival was to keep the creatures away from them. To hide their scent and presence.

"Cease fire! Freeze! Seal your suits!" Dumarest snarled as Vosper continued to fire. "Obey, damn you! Obey or I'll gun you down!"

Movement had attracted their notice and the scent of water vapor expelled from lungs and sweat had brought the things in for the kill. Shior's death had provided irresistible bait. Sealed the suits would prevent the smell of water escaping and, while motionless, the small party could ape the rocks, the lifeless surround.

"Lice." Toetzer echoed his disgust. "Like a

swarm of lice. Vermin lusting to feed. Fruit of evil and degeneracy and the instrument of vengeance against those—"

"Shut up, Jem!" Hilary was sharp. "This is no time for you to start preaching."

Massak, more practical, said, "What now, Earl?"

Dumarest studied the situation. The creatures had fed, those replete now clinging to the rock, blending into it, their carapaces, he guessed, absorbing the weak energy from the sun. Others, still questing for food and water, had slowed and would soon again become dormant. The sun, lowering, would be giving less energy and, with darkness, the things would probably enter some kind of brief hibernation.

But the night could bring other perils less easily seen and combatted.

"Tama, move slowly and check on that sign you saw." The surrogate, a machine and not a man, needed no armor or suit, yielding no attractive scent. Only its movement could bring unwelcome attention. "Don't go too far and freeze if anything shows an interest. The rest of you rip open the bales. Load up with food and water. Set extra containers to one side. Toyanna, pick those you want to carry the casket." Dumarest waited, then, into the radio, said, "Tama?"

"There's an opening. A wide crack, narrow at the top, fretted at the bottom. Debris is lying around. I think some of your bullets must have shattered a wall of some kind." Chenault added, "Agutter's sign is to one side and above it."

185

The path they needed to take if the old instructions were valid.

Dumarest said, "All of you get ready to move. Head for that opening. You stay with me, Toetzer. Massak, you cover the rear. Ready? Move!"

He stood, waiting, Toetzer at his side, a pile of cans of water at their feet. Before them gaped the mouth of a ray leading from the clearing, one of the seven points forming the star. It lay opposite the one with the opening. As the column crossed the clearing and the creatures began to stir Dumarest picked up one of the cans.

"Now, Jem. Do as I do. Throw them as far as you can."

The container left his hands, thrown with all the power of back and shoulder muscles, hitting to bounce and slide deeper into the opening. Another, a third, Toetzer's falling short. He gave a strangled cry and, without warning, ran after it, snatching it from the rock, unsealing it before hurling it from him in a rain of glittering droplets.

"Feed, you spawn of hell! Drink the blood of man and give him the fruit of his earned torment! Drink, you vileness and filth of degeneracy!"

"Come back, you fool! Back!"

Dumarest snatched up his gun, its blast cutting short the sound of the thin, insane babble coming from the speakers. Bullets ripped into the other containers and smashed racing creatures into twitching pulp. As Toetzer came stumbling toward him Dumarest backed, following the others.

"Here, Earl!" Massak was beside him, gun blasting flame. "He'll never make it."

A judgment based on experience. Toetzer was too far, moving too slowly, falling as they watched to be covered with a mass of ravenous creatures. His screams echoed from the speakers, dying as the two men fired and continued to fire until the creatures and the man were dead, unfeeling flesh.

Firing again as they backed into the opening to bring rock showering down from the roof. A barrier Dumarest sealed with a final burst then, satisfied, turned to look at a cavern of nightmare.

There was a glow in it, a pale luminescence stemming from things which hung like elongated fruit from points high on the walls and roof. Others glowed lower down, some of different shapes from the others, some, as he watched, appearing to twitch.

"Bunch up," he ordered. "Keep a sharp watch— you women watch the roof."

He studied the floor as they moved forward to where the cavern narrowed to a gaping tunnel. It was littered with debris, scraps and fragments of darkish brown material, the sheen of broken metal, shreds of what could have been plastic. The residue of earlier inhabitants or those who had followed Agutter's path. As he neared one of the glowing bundles it moved, bobbing on its stem, jerking as if it contained something alive and struggling to escape.

As Massak lifted his gun Dumarest said, sharply, "No. Don't fire."

"It could be dangerous."

"It is, but not yet. We were lucky. My guess is that whatever is inside those sacs sealed the wall. Maybe in order to breed. Later we'd have been their food."

To be taken, cocooned, planted with eggs which would hatch to devour the helpless, paralyzed prey. Now, replete, the creatures were ready to break free, open the wall and stream like a tide after new prey. A cycle, repeated endlessly, life living on life. The normal way of nature but in Ryzam so concentrated as to defy understanding.

The tunnel held more of the sacs, their number diminishing, to be replaced with masses of softly glowing fungi in a variety of convoluted shapes. A fairyland of deceptive beauty through which Chenault led the way, brushing strands from his lenses, stirring dust with his shoes.

"It's hot!" Mirza voiced what they all felt. "God! I'm roasting!"

The heat increased as they progressed, wending their way along and down a winding slope, breaking out into a vaulted cavern to pause beside a cairn bearing an eroded can.

"Agutter's!" Chenault snatched at it, lifted the paper it contained. Reading he said, "To those who have followed me so far—congratulations! The path now lies to the left. At the next cairn it will be safe to rest."

As he turned to follow the directions Dumarest said, "Hilary? Is it safe?"

"I can't be sure." Her voice echoed her indecision. "I sense something but I'm not sure what. Toetzer could have told you—he had an ability to sense inimical forces. I—I wish he was here."

But the man was dead, paying for his insanity, his skills now lost to the expedition. As the party moved on Massak stepped beside Dumarest, resting his gloved hand on his helmet, the fingers tapping in a signal he recognized.

"What is it?" Dumarest put the question after he had switched off his microphone and had touched helmets to form a conductive link. "Something worrying you?"

"A lot of things, that cairn for one. Why should Agutter have left a message? If he was going in how would he know where it was safe to rest? If he was coming out how the hell did he get through those creatures?"

Questions Dumarest had already considered. "Things could have been different then. Anyway, what choice do we have?"

"None, I guess." The mercenary grunted his acceptance of the situation. "But, if it comes to it, we stand together, right?"

"We all stand together."

"Sure, unless—well, you know what I mean." Massak swore as sweat stung his eyes. "This damned heat! It isn't natural. If it gets worse we'll have to take off the suits."

That would mean walking comparatively naked

in a realm of unknown dangers advertising their presence with every step.

"We'll wait," said Dumarest. "We can stand a lot more of this."

Vosper couldn't.

He walked at the front of Chenault's casket, guiding it together with Lopakhin at the rear, stumbling at times, his breathing harsh within his helmet, loud over the speakers. Watching the roof, the walls, checking their rear, Dumarest didn't see him lift his hands to raise the visor and expose his face to the air of the cavern. Only his voice, breathing his relief, told of his action.

"By God, that's better! I was burning in there, the air searing my lungs, but this is sweet. Try it. All of you, try it. Hilary. Mirza. How about you, Tyner? Keep this up and you'll run to melted lard."

"Better that than what you're risking."

"An artist voicing his fear." Vosper was mocking. "Admitting he's a coward. Open your helmet, man. Taste what fresh air is like. It'll open your mind. You'll be able to create a masterpiece when we get back. A vision of unsurpassed beauty to stun the eyes of men. And women, too, naturally." He broke off to giggle. "It's like wine. The air, I mean. I've never felt so good."

Totanna said, warningly, "Earl, he sounds as if he's been drugged."

"From the air?"

"What could be carried in it. Those fungi could

190

shed spores and many types produce hallucinogens. I think you should make him reseal his suit.''

"You could try it.'' Vosper laughed as if delighted at the prospect of amusement. "But you'd have to kill me to do it. Want to try, Earl? You, Massak? Maybe the two of you could manage it. Maybe we'd all die in the attempt. Stupid, isn't it? Here we are, looking for eternal life, and we're talking about killing each other. No need for that. Just leave me alone. I'll be all right.''

A possibility, already his voice was gaining its normal sobriety and the impact of what could be in the air might have passed. Certainly it was too late to prevent any damage and, if the air was harmless, it was well to know.

"Earl?'' Toyanna again. "What shall we do?''

"Leave him.''

"But—''

"Just leave him.''

The rest moved on into the depths of the cavern, to where tunnels gaped, to the one on the left which led to a long gallery crusted with distorted figures of stone glowing with the pale sheen of organic decay. To a place where the floor was gouged as if by mighty claws and walking was difficult.

They camped when they could go no farther, sleeping in sacs inflated and washed clean by tanked air. Stripping to lie close as Dumarest and Massak shared the watches sitting alone in the brooding stillness of a world beneath a world.

* * *

There had been no cairn. Chenault looked at the hand Dumarest extended toward him, then, slowly, produced the paper he'd found in the eroded can.

Reading it Dumarest said, "I can go no farther. May God help all poor fools who search for an empty dream. If any find this be warned and think of Samu Lowski." Folding the sheet he handed it back. "You lied."

"Can you blame me? How far would any of you have gone after reading this?"

"As far as we've come now. Too far, perhaps." Dumarest looked at the sacs, those within. Awake now, eating from cans, drinking, easing their bodies. "You could have picked a stronger team."

"I took what I could get." Chenault dismissed the subject. "We're here now and must make the best of it. The source can't be too far—Ryzam isn't that large. If it lies at the center a few more days should do it. Less if we have no trouble."

And, after they found it, they would have to get out.

A problem Dumarest ignored; worrying about future difficulties made them no less.

He said, "How are you? Physically, I mean."

"I can manage."

"That isn't what I asked. You should conserve your strength. What are the coordinates of Earth?"

"They're—" Chenault broke off his near-automatic response. "No. Not yet. I'll give then to you when we find what we're looking for."

They pressed on, suffering from weariness of previous effort, the debilitating effect of heat and the dehydration it caused. The helmets were open now; Vosper's continued good health having proved the safety of the air, but still the enervating heat remained. Lopakhin provided the explanation.

"It must be due to hysteresis. Look." He waved his gun violently in the air and held it out for Dumarest to touch. The metal was uncomfortably warm. "We must be cutting through lines of force of some kind. That generates the heat."

"At our speed?"

"I know, Earl. It's unusual. Normally it needs a high velocity but, apparently, not in Ryzam." The artist shrugged. "All I can suggest is that we remove the suits."

A suggestion followed, the weight and bulk tucked in a niche to be retrieved on their return. A pragmatic arrangement: if they could survive the journey in they should be able to survive it out. Massak marked the spot with a daub of paint sprayed from a can, lifted it, smiling, sent more to mark the wall higher up.

"I've used it all along," he explained. "I've been in caverns before and once fought an engagement in an underground installation. I got lost then and if it hadn't been for someone with more brains I'd have died. He used wire to mark the path but paint is just as good."

An elementary precaution and Dumarest had taken it but his markings had been more subtle. If any of the group panicked and wanted to run he didn't intend to provide them with an easy path to follow. Now, more than ever, safety lay in numbers.

The column had lengthened a little, stretching as difference in strides accumulated to create gaps and openings. Dumarest called a halt, bunching them close, moving forward to check what lay ahead. The vast gallery they had been following changed to a vaulted cavern with low-sweeping roofs, curved walls, a floor which undulated like a rolling ocean. It levelled as it ran beneath a convex roof cracked, pitted and scarred with crater-like blotches. The air held an acrid, acid smell which caught at his nostrils. The glow from the rock was dimmer than that they had passed.

"Wait!" Hilary caught his arm as he returned. She stood with her head tilted a little as if she heard things silent to others. "Up ahead," she whispered. "I sense it." Her voice rose, the scream chopped off by Dumarest's hand.

"Danger?" He spoke softly into her ear. "Like that you sensed before in the clearing?" He felt her nod. "From above?"

"I can't be sure." She gasped as he uncovered her mouth. "It's just that I know something's going to happen. Something bad."

Lying in wait somewhere in the area ahead. When it struck, Vosper died.

It happened quickly; a blur which ended at his throat to become a thing of nightmare, scaled, spined, the shears of mandibles tearing at his throat. A spider-like thing two feet across swinging on a thread from a crater in the roof. More followed it, bodies which jerked to the impact of bullets to hang broken, spinning like grotesque ornaments on the end of glistening threads.

"Run!" Dumarest barked the order as he fired. "Get clear of this roof! Massak! Mutual cover!"

He ran to the wall behind him, dropped, crouching, gun lifted to blast in rapid but aimed fire at the menace from above. The mercenary followed, both men firing to protect the other, the rest around the casket. A trained maneuver free of the danger of panic-firing and the wildly aimed bullets which could deal unintentional death.

Bodies fell between them to lie twitching on the ground, mandibles tearing at oozing flesh, the creatures feeding as they died.

Hilary screamed, screamed again, the sound ended by the blast of a gun. Mirza shouted curses as she cleared the air above the casket. Running, firing, Dumarest and the mercenary joined the others as they reached the far side of the area. Pulp and ooze marred the transparent surface of the casket. Blood at the throat of the tattooed woman. It jetted through Toyanna's fingers as, looking at Dumarest, she shook her head.

"Hilary!" Lopakhin dropped to his knees beside her, blood on his cheek, more streaming from a lacerated scalp. "Please, for God's sake—"

"Tyner." Her hand rose to touch his cheek. "You're hurt, my dearest. I'm sorry. I didn't want to leave you. But I'm so tired. So very . . ."

Her voice faded, dying as she died and for a moment there was silence. Then the artist rose, gun in his hands, tears streaming down his cheeks as he emptied the magazine at the craters blotching the roof, the lurking horrors they contained.

Chapter Thirteen

Dumarest turned, gun lifting, lowering as he recognized the woman coming toward him. He sat with his back against solid rock, beneath a roof barely eight feet from the ground. A branch cavern and a safe place for the camp.

"Mind if I join you, Earl?" Mirza Karroum sat as he gestured to the spot at his side. "I couldn't sleep," she explained. "Too many thoughts, I guess."

Accompanied by too many worries. It had been three days since Hilary had died and she looked what she was; an old, tired, disheartened woman. She needed the consolation he could give.

He said, "You should ask Pia to give you something."

"To make me sleep? No. Would you?"

"I'm working."

"You're always working." She looked at him as he sat limned against the glowing rock. A man naked but for shorts and boots; the protective mesh of his own clothing had forced him to discard it because of generated heat. "On guard. Keeping watch. Pushing us all and keeping us a unit. Chenault couldn't have found a better man."

"He needs to rest."

"He's dying." She was blunt. "Pia tries to hide it but I know the truth. He's drawing too deeply on his reserves. Maybe he won't make it. Maybe none of us will."

"We knew that from the beginning."

"True, but still we came. The lure of a dream." She stretched out her hands, turning them to show the brown blotches on the skin. Her left wrist bore a scarlet tattoo. "The brand of the Karroum." She had noticed his interest. "It's applied as soon as possible after birth. To avoid any substitution. Angado had one—you must have seen it."

"His wrist was scarred."

"Then he must have had it removed. He never did like his heritage." With a gesture she dismissed the subject. "Why did you join this expedition, Earl?"

"Chenault has something I want. Why did you?"

"I told you—the lure of a dream." Again she extended her hands. "Look at them, Earl. Old like me. Ugly as I am ugly. As I've always been ugly. They used to laugh at me when I was young, not to my face for I was of the Karroum, but behind

198

my back. Somehow it seemed more cruel that way. Then, when I grew older, I could see pity in their eyes. Pity!''

She turned her head and Dumarest waited, saying nothing. When she faced him again she had regained her composure.

''I looked too much like a man so I acted the man and became harder than one, more feared, more hated. But I was born a woman, Earl, and I want to be one. A young and beautiful woman. One whom some man would love.'' For a moment she looked at her hands, strong, square, the fingers blunt, spatulate. ''I'd follow Chenault to hell if he could promise me that.''

''You have.''

''Yes.'' She leaned back, pleased with his answer, glad that he hadn't tried to lie to her, to soften the truth she knew too well. ''And so far I've been lucky. Hilary wasn't. Neither were Vosper, Shior—''

Dumarest said, sharply, ''Don't count the dead.''

''Why not? Superstition?''

''Just don't count them. They are gone. The living remain.''

''To be cherished, cared for, guarded, loved.'' She was bitter. ''I've heard that before, somewhere. From a mercenary. A man blinded by a laser—for a while he was my lover.'' She paused as if expecting comment then, when none came, she said, ''That was a lie, Earl. If it was true what would you think?''

''That you were kind.''

"To give a cripple the use of my body?"

"To have given a man in need the pleasure of being wanted."

"And that is important?" She answered her own question. "What could be more important? To be wanted, needed, loved. Did you guess that Hilary and Lopakhin were lovers? That he felt so deeply about her. Tell me, Earl, if it had been Govinda who had died would you have shot the spiders or Chenault?"

"He didn't say it would be easy."

"No, he didn't, but if we find what we're looking for and get back alive will you bring her down here to gain what she most needs? Do you love her enough for that?"

"You doubt I love her?"

"Govinda? No. That is obvious to all with eyes. But is your love big enough to include a child of her body? Could you share her with a baby?"

Dumarest met her eyes then, smiling, said, "There's an old recipe on how to cook a meat pie. It begins—"

"First catch your animal. I know. I'm sorry, Earl, at times I ask too many questions." Her hand reached out to rest on his own. "But I warn you, if I get what I'm after, your lady could have a fight on her hands."

"You flatter me."

"Is the truth ever that?" For a moment her hand lingered with unmistakable warmth then, as if annoyed at having betrayed herself, she lifted it to gesture at the cavern around them. "The Karroum

200

own mines. I inspected them once and learned something of geology. I've been studying these fissures and galleries and, to me, they seem wrong. Almost artificial as if formed by some unnatural process.''

"As if something had weakened the crust of this world to release the magma,'' said Dumarest. ''To let it fume upward in a fountain of bubbles and froth.''

"Which cooled too quickly. You've noticed that? The surface formation is unique in my experience and is geologically impossible. No natural eruption or weathering could ever produce such a configuration.''

"And the glow?''

"Natural minerals within the rock which fluoresce to the impact of radiation.'' She added, ''It could be the same force which produces the hysteresis. Lopakhin told me about it. He also noticed that the glow isn't steady; it fades then brightens again. The deeper into the caverns we go the more pronounced the change becomes.''

"Which means we're getting closer to the source of energy.'' Dumarest had observed the change. "One which pulses but I've not been able to establish its rhythm. There could be peaks and valleys. Times when this entire region could be almost dark and others when it might be filled with destructive energy.''

"A mystery,'' she said. ''One to add to the rest. Why no attacks since Hilary died? We could have passed through the habitable environment of Ryzam but, somehow, I doubt it. My skin crawls too much and too often. As if something is watching me. Waiting for me to get closer. You've hunted?''

Dumarest nodded.

''Then you know what I mean. A predator has its territory and it waits until its prey is within reach. When it is it strikes.'' Her hand slapped against her thigh with a flat, meaty sound. ''We've had it too easy since Hilary went and it worries me.''

''You'd rather be fighting for your life?''

''We do that every second of every day in one way or another. No. I want to see my enemy. The thing which gave Ryzam its reputation. We could turn round and go back and, with luck, make it to the rafts and on to the ship. If we've met all the dangers we could return with men and flame-throwers. Armored domes, machines, drills to blast an opening from the surface. It would take money, yes, but if the reward is high enough the money could be found. So what lies ahead, Earl? What is it that, once found, can never be left?

In the lead Chenault lifted his arm. ''There,'' he said. ''There . . . there . . . there. . . .''

The words slowed, slurred as the surrogate took a step, the manlike figure staggering, remaining upright to lean against the wall. Touching it Dumarest found the synthetic skin warmer than it should be. At his side Lopakhin swore as he eased open a panel to release a puff of acrid vapor.

''Heat! I told him not to move this thing too fast! Now he's burned out a junction!''

"Can you fix it?"

"I can try but Vosper was the engineer." Lopakhin looked around. They were in a rounded gallery ending in a triple junction of narrower passages. Chenault had pointed to the one on the right. "I'll need room so had better get down to it here. Space could be limited farther on. The light's good, too."

Blazing patches which shone with scintillant brightness to dispel all shadows. At the casket Toyanna was busy checking dials and registers, straightening to look at Dumarest with a worried frown.

"It's all right," he said reassuringly. "Just a shorted connection. It won't take long to repair." He glanced at the casket, the corpselike figure it contained. "How's Tama?"

"Alive—just." She echoed her fear. "But there's something else. The power's going. If the antigrav units fail we'll be stuck unless we can carry the entire weight."

"We can't."

"But—"

"There are five of us not counting the surrogate. One man must stay on board." Which left four to handle the burden, two of them women. Dumarest said, "You'll have to lighten it. Dump all emergency supplies and equipment. You'd better start doing it now. The radio-units can go first; when we move off we'll use a cable to link up the surrogate."

"Tama won't like that. He wants to maintain full mobility in order to guide us."

"He can do that verbally. In any case the surrogate can be put to better use. Get busy now. Stand guard, Mirza. Watch the rear. I'm going ahead to see what's in front of us."

Massak had preceded him. As Dumarest passed into the narrower passage he saw the mercenary standing lower down. He too had stripped to shorts and boots, the scars on his body making a livid tapestry against the rich darkness of his skin.

"Listen!" He held up a hand as Dumarest halted at his side. "Hear it?"

"No."

"Try again. Hard." Massak grunted as Dumarest shook his head. "It's gone now anyway."

"What was it?"

"A sound, high, thin, something like that made by a generator. But it had something extra to it. Something like—" Massak shook his head. "I can't describe it. Maybe it was just imagination." He looked at the passage with its rounded roof and concave floor. "This place can give you all sorts of ideas. Look at it—it's just like a burrow."

One which could have been made by a gigantic worm slithering through plastic magma or grinding its way through rock with adamantine teeth. Fancies enhanced by the silence, the smooth walls, the mounting tension as the party moved along what could easily become a trap.

"If anything comes at us, anything really big, that is, we wouldn't stand a chance." Massak gestured with his gun. "No niches," he explained. "No cracks to duck into. No side passages. We

204

could be caught front and back and turned into pulp.''

"If anything came," agreed Dumarest. "If we couldn't stop it."

"You don't think there's any danger?"

"Not from things as large as you're talking about."

"Maybe not," admitted the mercenary. "Things that big would have to eat and there's damn all around here that I can see. But that brings up another matter—where are all those who came this way before?"

"If any did."

"They must have done if they were following the lure of what's supposed to lie ahead. I've been trying to figure out these caverns and galleries and they seem to me to all be leading to a common point. Maybe Chenault's found a shortcut but, even so, others must have used it. So where are their bodies? Discarded equipment? Supplies? Clothing? We've left enough behind us and others must have done the same."

One, at least, had done more.

Dumarest saw it as they emerged into a vaulted chamber set with patches of brilliance, the mouth of a tunnel gaping opposite the one they had left. Close beside it, set upright against the wall, rested the unmistakable tracery of a skeleton.

"Bones!" Massak stared at the place, gun lifting with automatic reflex in his hand. "Someone died there."

"A woman." Toyanna stepped back after making her examination. "Look at the shape of the pelvis, the set of the thighs. The skull, too, bears feminine characteristics. And yet there's a strangeness about it. As if it wasn't wholly human."

Dumarest said, "Can you tell the age?"

"Of the woman? About middle-age, I'd say."

"No. How long it's been here."

"Impossible." Toyanna's shrug was expressive. "What we're looking at seems to be an imprint of the skeletal structure rather than the bones themselves. Something like a negative print—see how white they are against the dark background?"

Lopakhin said, "I've done work like this. You take an object, a leaf, flower, animal, insect— anything will do. You place it on a prepared and sensitized surface then expose it to a blast of high-intensity radiation. The result is an image of the object but one containing more detail than can normally be seen. A kind of aura." His hand lifted to rest on the stone. "See? This faint blurring following the bones. And here. And here." His fingers moved to halt over the pelvic area. "Could she have been pregnant?"

Toyanna shrugged. "It's possible, I suppose. Why do you ask?"

"This." Lapakhin moved his finger. "See? This part. And this. There's a different kind of shading." His hand dropped to his side as he moved away. "But what killed her?"

Dumarest stirred, waking instantly, one hand reaching for the knife in his boot. Kneeling beside him Massak shook his head.

"No need for that, Earl. Listen."

The air was filled with a thin, high singing sound that wavered, carrying overtones of bells.

"Is this what you heard before?"

"Yes, but it's louder now. Closer." In the dimness the mercenary's face was tense. "Much closer—and it's coming nearer."

Wailing and singing from the air, the stone, the gaping mouth of the tunnel beside which the tracery of the skeleton kept warning guard.

One almost invisible now; the gleaming patches had dulled to somber glows, the chamber gaining a new menace with the loss of illumination. A good place to stay, he'd decided. One in which to check their gear and rest. To sleep as he had slept while Massak had stood watch. As the others were still sleeping.

"Earl?" The wailing, undulating sound had touched the mercenary on the raw. "What the hell is it?"

A question echoed by Mirza Karroum as she woke, eyes bleared, rubbing strength into her sagging cheeks.

"I don't know." Dumarest touched Lopakhin on the shoulder, found Toyanna already alert. "Spread out. Make no sound and don't move. Whatever it is we don't want to attract its attention."

Good advice but not easy to follow. Not when the sound grew louder; shrilling, tinkling, sweet with the music of bells, strong with the whine of generators. Resting his fingers against the casket, Dumarest felt the transparency quiver beneath his touch. Beneath the somnolent figure it contained, a warning lamp began to flash in pulses of red.

"Give me room!" Toyanna had spotted the signal. A panel lifted as Dumarest moved to one side, her fingers deft as she manipulated keys. "His heart," she explained. "If it gets any worse I'll have to introduce a bypass."

"I thought you dumped all nonessential equipment."

"This is essential." She sighed her relief as the red lamp ceased its flashing. "His heart is a muscle too, remember, and as weak as the rest of him. I had to provide for an emergency."

One drowned in the present problem. The singing, chiming, wailing sound which now filled the chamber with demanding noise.

"Look!" Lopakhin pointed. "The skeleton!" The tracery was glowing as if each bone had been delineated in fire. "The light!"

It filled the mouth of the tunnel, eye-bright, scintillating, glowing as if it was made of ice and diamond and cold, cold flame. A writhing something which flowed from the opening to hang in a shimmering mist of glowing radiance. One which shifted, changed, adopted new and enticing configurations. A thing of beauty, bright, clean, wonderful. One which sang.

Sound which dominated the ear as the glowing mist dominated the eye. As the subtle pulsing of it dominated the mind with its hypnotic spell.

"Don't look at it!" Dumarest forced himself to turn away, lifting a hand to cover Massak's eyes.

One the mercenary jerked away as he turned, snarling. "Don't look," snapped Dumarest. "Don't let it get to you."

"It's harmless. Just a cloud of brilliance. It shows me things."

"It's sucking your mind."

"No. That's stupid. It—"

"Damn you! Do as I say!" Dumarest lifted his hand, the fingers clenched, a fist which he poised to strike, then dropped as Lopakhin rose to his feet. "Tyner! Sit down! No, man! No!"

"Hilary!" The artist stepped toward the glowing radiance, hands extended, his face illuminated by something more than reflected light. "Hilary! My darling! You came back to me!"

"No!" Dumarest tried to rise and was thrown back against the wall by a sweep of the mercenary's arm. "Let me—"

"Stay put. There's nothing you can do. It's too late."

Lopakhin had closed the distance between himself and the shimmering cloud. He walked up to it, into it, froze as it closed around him.

"God!" Massak lifted his gun. "It's eating him!"

"Don't shoot!" Dumarest slammed down the weapon. "It's too late."

"I can give him an easy out."

"He doesn't need it. Look at his face."

It was calm, peaceful, the artist smiling a little as if he saw something which pleasured him. Smiling as his clothing dissolved into the mist, as his skin followed, the fat, the muscle and sinew, the bones and internal organs. Smiling still with bared teeth as his skull sat on the livid horror which had once been his body.

Then that too had vanished and there was only the mist which sang and pulsed and glided away down the facing tunnel to send murmurs and whispers of itself back in diminishing cadences.

"God!" Massak shook his head. "What the hell is it? A leech? A parasite of some kind? Why didn't it it take us all?"

"It had fed." Dumarest looked at the tunnel down which it had gone. "Lopakhin ran to it, remember. It didn't have to search."

But it would find them in its restless drifting, scenting them with alien organs, responding to the heat of their bodies, the electromagnetic activity of their brains. Or perhaps simply their bulk and composition, one different from rock. As were the things they had discarded. The debris which must have been left by others. All gone, cleared away, converted to basic energy to keep the thing alive.

"So we found it," said Mirza. "Or it found us. The thing I felt must be waiting. The guardian," she explained looking at them. "There's one in every legend. The monster which guards the treasure—but where the hell is it?"

"We'll find it," said Dumarest.

"When?"

"Soon." He looked at the casket, the flash of warning lights. It would have to be soon. "In a few hours, maybe."

Massak saw it first.

Chapter Fourteen

It was a bowl set in a cavern and centered by a column of lambent blue. Impressions fined as Dumarest studied it; the bowl was filled with a thinner mist the same color as the column, which was twenty feet high and half as large in diameter.

"It's like a fountain," said Massak. He stood in the opening from which he had discovered the column. "A fountain of mist, water, smoke—what the hell is it?"

Radiation made visible; energies trapped in a revealing medium which showed their writhing complexity as the beam of a flashlight was made to look solid in a dusty atmosphere. Forces which twisted, weaved, following a pattern impossible to grasp. Forming a substance which hovered between that of solid and gas. One alien in its fabrication.

It rested in a cavern shaped like the interior of an egg, the rock bearing a polished sheen. Stone shaped and worn by unknown years of attrition from the force it contained. The glow from it was caught, reflected, emphasized, enhanced by the near-mirror finish. The bowl formed a shallow pool, the edge resting ten feet from where they stood.

"We've found it!" The gun trembled in Massak's hands. "The thing Chenault dreamed of finding. The secret of Ryzam. Look at it, Earl! The source of renewed youth. Of health. Of life itself. You can feel it. Feel it!"

Dumarest inhaled, feeling the tingle coming from the column, hearing the soft susurration which could have been the rustle of breaking atoms. Material created, changed, recreated to form a continuous cycle of pulsing energy.

One which held the same hypnotic fascination as the shining predator.

"Wait!" Dumarest caught the mercenary's arm as he stepped toward the pool. "Let's check it out."

"What's there to check? We've found it."

"As others must have done. Where are they?" Dumarest looked around the chamber; it held two other openings, each, like the one they stood in, fashioned like a soaring arch. "We can walk around the pool and see what's behind those openings. You take the left and I'll go right."

He strode forward before Massak could argue, seeing him hesitate, then, shrugging, following his example. The opening gave on a passage with a peaked roof, the walls smooth and glowing with patches of brilliance. A twin to the one which had led them to the chamber. As he stepped back into it Dumarest saw Massak's arm waving in a signal.

"What is it?"

"Look." The mercenary pointed. "Another skeleton."

One traced in the smooth rock as had been the other, the only difference being in size. The first had been that of a mature woman. This was of a child.

"Barely three feet tall," said Massak. "How old would that make it, Earl? Ten? Twelve?" His tone hardened. "Who the hell would bring a child down here?"

"Maybe it was a midget."

"Like Baglioni?" Massak shook his head. "No, it was a child. Dying, maybe. Brought here to be cured. Then that shining thing caught it—and turned it into lines on a wall. One of those who never came back." He looked at the gun in his hands. "If I see it again I'm going to shoot. Don't try to stop me."

It would be like trying to kill the air but Dumarest didn't argue. "Let's get back to the others." He added, "Don't tell them about this."

The casket lay fifty yards from the opening at the junction of galleries, too narrow to permit of easy passage. Mirza sat with her back against a wall. Her skin was gray and she breathed through her open mouth. Toyanna was almost as exhausted and sat, crouched against the casket, her fingers busy on the keyboard. The red gleams of warning lights illuminated her face and hair with touches of false comfort.

"The power's gone," she said as Dumarest halted at her side. "The antigrav units are dead."

"It doesn't matter. We haven't far to go."

"You've found it?" Relief washed some of the fatigue from her face, her eyes. "Tama! You heard? We've found it!"

The surrogate at the end of its cable stirred, lifting its head, its hands. Self-powered it fed energy back through the wires to the pads transmitting Chenault's muscular impulses.

"How far?"

"Too far to carry the casket. We'll have to take you out."

"No!"

"And there's something else." Dumarest faced the surrogate as it rose to its feet. "You know what it is. Give me the coordinates."

"No. Not yet. Not until . . . until . . ." Chenault broke off, the surrogate jerking. "Must be sure that . . . that . . ."

Toyanna said, sharply. "We have no time to waste. Tama is dying."

And would die if left in the casket. A coffin which would hold more than the withered corpse of an old man. Dumarest looked at the surrogate, at the casket, at the machine again.

He said, harshly, "Listen to me, Chenault. I get the coordinates or I'll leave you to rot. I swear it."

"You can't!" Toyanna looked at his face and knew she was wrong. "Please, Earl, you mustn't!"

"It's his choice."

"Tell him!" Mirza had risen to her feet and now stumbled toward the surrogate. "Tell him, you fool! Tell him!"

"No."

"Then to hell with you." Dumarest turned. "Come on, Mirza, let me show you what we've found."

"What about Tama?"

"Forget him."

Dumarest heard the rustle of clothing, the scrape of feet, the touch of air compressed beneath a moving object. Warnings which triggered his instinctive reaction and he ducked, lunging to one side, dodging the swing of the metal hand which smashed into Mirza's face.

Sending her down to lie sprawled on the floor, blood streaming from her nose, her mouth, the empty socket of an eye.

Toyanna screamed, a shrill sound followed by Massak's roar of anger.

"You bastard! Earl! Watch him! He's gone crazy!"

He jumped to one side as the surrogate lunged toward him, gun lifting, finger poised on the trigger as he sought a clear field of fire. One blocked by the casket, the woman, Dumarest himself as he dodged, weaving, ducking to avoid the murderous swings of the surrogate's fist.

"Chenault! Cut it out! Chenault!"

A man driven insane by his own stubbornness now finding an anodyne in action. To attack and destroy the man who had defied him. The obstacle in his way. A rage in which logic had no part.

And the surrogate was strong.

The proof lay on the floor and Dumarest had already experienced the strength of the artificial limbs. Then Chenault had intended no harm but now he meant to kill.

"Earl! Down!" Massak bared his teeth in a snarl of impatience. "Down!"

Fire blasted from the muzzle of his gun and a hail of bullets slammed into the massive torso of the surrogate. A natural error and one he corrected, swinging the gun to aim at the casket, lifting the barrel to rip apart the man it contained.

"No!" Toyanna threw herself forward. "No!"

A cry of protest drowned by the roar of the gun, the slamming impact of the bullets which churned her body to a broken, oozing ruin. A mistake; she had moved as the mercenary had closed his finger. As he went to fire again the surrogate was on him. Fist lifted, swinging down in a vicious arc.

One terminating at Massak's skull, breaking it open like a hammered nut, driving into the soft mass of the brain, causing it to spatter in a rain of red and gray particles.

Before the hand could be freed Dumarest was on the tall, grim figure.

To fight normally was to commit suicide and he took opportunity to leap on the machine's back, wrapping his legs around the thick waist, one hand reaching to probe at the eyes while the other lifted his knife and drove the point hard at the junction of neck and shoulder.

A gamble which failed; the blade slipping from buried metal to cut a gash in the artificial flesh. As an arm rose to grasp his neck Dumarest struck again, this time sending the point into an eye, feeling the plastic covering yield, the lens beneath shattering under the blow.

Half-blinded Chenault sent the extension of his body into a spinning whirl which threw Dumarest from his position to slam hard against the cabinet. That followed by a fist scraped against his head, tearing his scalp and filling his mouth with the taste of blood. A blow followed by another which he dodged, running toward the opening leading to the column of light, stumbling as his foot slipped on Toyanna's blood.

As he recovered his balance Chenault was on him, fists pounding, swinging like sledges to smash his ribs and lacerate his lungs with their broken ends. To fill his throat with blood and his eyes with blazing, darting flashes.

Dazed, Dumarest hit the edge of the opening, moved through it and, doubled, spitting blood, lurched toward the glowing light.

Chenault followed, the connecting cable unreeling from its spool with a thin humming sound. One which stopped as the surrogate came to the end of its lead, its momentum tearing the connection from its body.

It crashed to the ground, jerking, twitching as if the metal and plastic held a life of its own. Charged relays mimicking direct, human action. Responding to the power that was flooding into it from the column so that it looked like a helpless cripple striving to gain a safe refuge.

When, finally, it stilled Dumarest moved slowly back to where the casket rested. He felt weak, giddy and every move filled his chest with the pain of tearing knives. He was dying, drowning in his own blood, every breath accentuating the internal damage.

As he passed Mirza she groaned, lifting up a hand, her voice fogged with pain.

"Earl! Earl, help me!"

A plea he ignored, dropping to his knees beside the cabinet, fingers searching for the catch he had seen Toyanna use. A panel lifted to reveal a selection of drugs; measured doses in sting-ampoules. He selected two and drove the needles into his throat. The pain-killer acted almost instantly and he hoped the hormone-based cellular sealing compound was as effective. Emergency treatment but it enabled him to see clearly, to think free of pain, to select more drugs and to cross to where Mirza nursed her pain and fear.

"Here." He sent the sting deep into the artery of her throat. "That'll take care of the pain."

"I'm half blind. My eye—"

"Is ruined." He injected another dose of drugs

around the empty socket. "He knocked out the ball, pulped your nose and must have broken your cheek. The temple too, I think." He probed gently with his fingers. "Yes, I was right. Still hurt?"

"No, it's just numb." She sat upright and leaned against his supporting arm. "The others?"

"Dead."

"Chenault?"

"Hanging on." Dumarest glanced at the casket with its warning lights. "I misjudged him. I thought he'd yield when I threatened to leave him. Instead he went crazy."

"He was obsessed. He should have trusted you but—" She broke off, listening. "Earl?"

He had heard it too, a thin, high singing sound, accompanied by the ghost of bells. A sound they had heard before.

"It's coming back!" Mirza strained against his arm and climbed to her feet. "Earl! That shining thing! It's coming back!"

It came with the beauty of a drifting cloud, of light and brightness and of sad, sweet songs. Seeming to pause as it entered the space where the casket rested then to glow even brighter as it moved slowly forward. Watching it Dumarest felt his muscles grow tense even as his eyes drank in the alien beauty. It would be good just to sit and watch and let himself be absorbed by the glittering shape. To rest and cease from struggle and surrender to the inevitable. Death was a termination for him as for all things and where was the point in struggling when the final passing could be so enjoyable? To die. To sleep. To let himself be enfolded in the majestic pattern of nature. To become a part of the shining thing as the food he ate became a part of his own body and mind.

Then the shape he held against him slipped a little and he stared at a dead, tormented face.

Toyanna, her body smashed to pulp, blood marring her clothing, her face, her hair. A doctor who had tried to protect her patient and who had died in the attempt. Had she loved Chenault? If so she could still save him and others with him.

Dumarest rose, the body of the woman held upright in his arms, her head lolling against his chest. A weight he carried from behind the casket to where the shining thing waited as if aware that nothing living could resist its glowing beauty. To hold it out before him, to press it against the gleaming radiance, to feel it held as if by a multitude of tiny, invisible hands, then to release his hold and step back and sag against the wall where Mirza waited tense with expectant dread.

"God!" She closed her eye as if to shut out what she had seen. The feeding which stripped a victim layer by layer. One she had seen when Lopakhin had died and had now seen again. "Earl, will it come back?"

He listened to the dying cadences of its passage. As before, when it had fed, it had moved on. Satisfied with a willing victim, perhaps, following some age-old pattern established on some alien world. Speculations he set aside as, rising, he dragged the woman to her feet.

"I need your help. We've got to get Chenault out of the casket."

Touching her face, she said, bitterly, "Let the bastard rot!"

"Do as I say!" He was sharp; lifting the dead woman had filled his chest with the pain of new injuries. "I can't carry him, you'll have to do that. Hurry, now!"

He coughed and spat a stream of blood, feeling his lungs fill with more of his life's fluid as he tore open the casket. Mirza reached within, lifted the frail shape, brushed away the wired pads.

"You're a fool, Earl. If what you found can help you get to it. Forget Chenault. He deserves to die. In fact I think he's already dead. Leave him."

"I can't." Not while there remained the chance that the information he held could be gained. No matter how slender that chance might be. "Hand me those drugs."

They helped but not enough and Dumarest staggered as he led the way to the opening giving onto the column of light. It blazed brighter than he remembered, the soft susurration like voices calling from across vast distances, the tingle stronger now as if it were some form of atomic gas.

Mirza said, "That? Are we supposed to walk into that?"

"Have we any choice?" Again Dumarest vented a carmine stream. Fighting for breath he said, "It's a chance but what can we lose? We'd never

221

get out in the condition we're in. Move, now. Carry Chenault into the column. I can't help."

"But you'll be able to manage?"

"Yes."

"To hell with Chenault. I'll drop him. Lean on me, Earl. We'll go in together."

"Just do as I say." *And hurry, woman! Hurry before the old man is dead and it's too late!* "Please, Mirza. Do it for me. Please!"

For a moment she stared at him and then she was gone, leaving him with the memory of her ruined face, the body of the old man held like a baby in her arms. Dumarest saw her step into the pool and walk without hesitation directly toward the central column. The mist-water-smoke-like blueness rose to her knees and, after she had reached halfway, he followed her as he had promised.

Slowly for he was heading into the unknown and every instinct warned him against it. The column could consume everything within it to atomic ash. Like the shining thing it could exist only to feed and yet it still was the only chance they had. One they couldn't afford to ignore.

Dumarest stepped into the pool.

Something like a tingling perfume rose around him and he inhaled, doubling to cough his pain as agony tore into his lungs. Sacrificing Toyanna's dead body had negated the healing medication and now even the pain killers had lost their power. He coughed again, staggering as the column spun in his sudden giddiness. One which dominated his actions, causing him to sag, to fall, to immerse himself in the pool as Mirza and her burden reached the column and vanished inside.

Too weak to move, Dumarest drifted like a dead fish in the lambent mist.

One which held magic.

The world was what a world should be with hard, clear seasons, a moon and stars a man could recognize and use to guide his way. A place where, at times, it was gentle and at others harsh. One where it was necessary to work and that was good, for to be idle was to grow weak. A planet which donated a heritage of pride.

"Earl!" The woman was tall with hair the color of flame, pendulous breasts above a belly swollen with child. She smiled and waved as he looked at her. "Take care of your son, Earl. I've enough to do teaching our daughter to cook."

A girl with a winsome face and hair the color of her mother's as the boy matched his father. The first-born who stood straight and strong and looked older than his years.

"I want to learn how to throw a knife," he said. "I have one, see? Mother doesn't want me to learn but I think I should. Please teach me."

"Why doesn't your mother want you to learn?"

"She thinks it will get me into trouble."

"Or out of it." Dumarest lifted the blade from his boot. "A knife is a tool, son, and only as dangerous as the man who uses it. With it you can cut, slice, chop, stab and throw. Like this." His hand moved, a blur as the knife was a blur, one which halted against the bole of a tree the sharp point buried deep.

"Like this?" The small hand rose, the knife it held spinning to fall far to one side of the tree. The eyes masked his disappointment. "I failed."

"You have yet to learn," corrected Dumarest. "Now, son, hold it like this." He placed the recovered blade firm on the palm and adjusted the fingers. "Hold it firm and make it a part of your arm. Now look at what you want to hit. *Look* at it. Forget the knife. Just concentrate on the target then, as if you're throwing out your hand, you throw the knife." He watched as, again, the blade fell to one side. "It takes practice."

"Lots of practice?"

"As much as it takes."

Dumarest smiled as he watched his son recover the blade, throw it, pick it up again with a dogged determination to succeed. It was good to have had the boy and extend himself into new generations and so ensure the continuation of his genes. Good to have a woman he loved and who loved him. Good for her to have children and to know that his love for her was big enough to encompass them all. Good to be home where Chenault—

Chenault?

Chapter Fifteen

Dumarest opened his eyes and frowned at the rock in front of him. Stone illuminated with a bright blue radiance on which he lay half-out of the mistlike pool. As if even in his sleep he had struggled to gain familiar ground and he climbed higher to draw his legs free of the pool and to lie, eyes narrowed against the brightness of the column.

One he had failed to reach but he felt no regret as he felt no pain. His only sadness was induced by the fading memory of a dream but the joy it had contained was something which still could be. Govinda was waiting with her warm, soft body and her wondrous scarlet hair. Kalin's hair but Govinda's talent could absorb the ghost of what had been and make it real again. And, soon now, he would be taking her home.

If Chenault was still alive.

A thought which sent him to his feet to stand as he examined his body. The pain had gone, the grate of broken, tearing bones. Beneath his fingers the ribs were whole again and strong. The breath he drew into his lungs brought exhilaration not agony. He felt no thirst, no hunger, no fatigue. The magic of the lambent pool had made him well.

Proof of the legend of Ryzam—if not renewed youth at least he had restored health. And the others?

The column was enigmatic, pulsing a little, flaring into a new brightness even as he watched. Flaring to fade a little as it followed the pattern of its nature. A pulse which must have been repeated many times as he lay drifting and dreaming in the pool. He had awakened naturally—if the others were still alive they would probably do the same.

Waiting, he did what had to be done.

The surrogate lay where it had fallen, a ghastly travesty of a man, too heavy for him to lift. Dumarest passed it, slowed as he neared the place where the casket had been left, slipped into it as he spotted no danger. The air stank of blood, Massak's corpse lying like a broken, headless doll in a dull brown puddle. Dumarest ignored it, uncoupling the cable from its junction, returning with it to the surrogate, looping it around the massive torso and then, sweating, dragged it to where Chenault had rested.

The casket yielded treasure; rods of heavy metal

226

and power packs now exhausted but still composed of compact atoms. Other things which he set aside then moved the surrogate to rest on the spread-out components. On it he placed the body of the dead mercenary.

At the opening, his hands filled with a wire-lashed bundle, he looked at what he had done. A funeral pyre lacking fuel but the composition was the same and, if the mercenary was watching, he would approve.

As a thin, high, familiar sound began to fill the air Dumarest hurried down to the chamber of light. The hollow egg, he was certain, would provide sanctuary from the shining thing. An assumption proved correct as the bell-chimes came no nearer, fading, to be lost in the soft susurration from the column.

One which, together with the varying intensity, cast a hypnotic spell almost impossible to resist.

Dumarest sat, his back against the wall, nails driven hard into his palms. To wait was never easy and now it was harder than at any other time he had known. Was Chenault alive? Would he emerge unscathed from the column? How long would it be?

Questions coupled to others and Dumarest retraced their path through the caverns a dozen times, mentally reviewing each turn and junction, each mark he had left, every danger they had faced.

Of them all the shining thing was the worst.

He rose finally, impatient to know the result of his calculated guess, moving softly back to where he had fashioned the mercenary's pyre. It had been without fuel—but now it glowed with fire.

With writhing movement and shimmering coruscations. With a covering of radiant beauty as the shining thing engulfed it, seeming more solid now, more inert. Condensing on itself, the writhings slowing even as Dumarest watched, the aura deepening, solidifying as if mist were turning to water and water to ice. A subtle change accompanied by a diminution in the bell-like singing. Down the bulk of the thing, in a line no thicker than a hair, a shadow slowly began to form.

One which widened as he watched. Growing darker as Dumarest turned and ran back to the chamber and the glowing column of light.

"Chenault!" His voice echoed from the curving walls. "Chenault! Mirza! Chenault!"

A flicker and the column was as before.

"Chenault! Can you hear me? Come out, damn you! Come out!" Dumarest stepped into the pool and headed toward the column. "It's time, man! Hurry! Hurry, I say!"

The column flickered again as, within it, something moved. A patch of darkness bearing the silhouette of a man. One who stepped from the column to stare at Dumarest with wide, clear eyes.

A stranger.

One tall, strong, dark-haired. A man of about twenty-five years with smooth skin and a generous mouth.

Looking at Dumarest he said, "Who are you?"

"Dumarest. Earl Dumarest. Chenault?"

228

"Yes." The man smiled, pleased at being known. "That's right. I'm Tama Chenault and my father owns the circus of Chen Wei. Where are we? What is this place?"

"The coordinates." Dumarest held out his hand as if to receive the precious figures. "Give me the coordinates."

"What coordinates? I don't know what you're talking about."

"The coordinates of Earth." Dumarest stared at the blank, uncomprehending face. "You swore you had them. You promised to give them to me. Damn you, Chenault! Keep your word or—"

"What word?" Chenault recoiled from what he saw in Dumarest's eyes, the knife lifted to hang poised before him. "I swear I don't know what you're talking about. I've never seen you before and I've never heard of Earth. But I've something else—see?"

He turned to reach within the column, turning again as he straightened to display the bundle in his arms. One which kicked and gurgled and stared with bright, shining eyes.

A naked baby girl—the red blotch of a tattoo bright on one wrist.

Captain Lauter reached for the decanter, poured, handed a glass to Dumarest before lifting his own.

"A wonderful achievement, Earl. I drink to it. The journey must have been incredible."

Dumarest looked at the glass; one mirrored to reflect the salon in bizarre configurations. His own face was that of a stranger; warped, distorted, the thin lines of newly dressed wounds lying like lace on the taut flesh.

"Without the casket we could make faster time."

"But the perils?"

"I laid a trap for the shining thing; one of a huge amount of heavy metal together with Massak's body. As it absorbed the man it began to absorb the rest. I gambled on it being a reactive creature and the extra food triggered off its reproductive cycle. It became dormant as it condensed prior to splitting."

"Like an amoeba." Lauter nodded, understanding. "Which means there are more than one now. But the rest? The spiders?"

"We ran through the place where Hilary and Vosper died. I had taken rods from the casket and they made good weapons. Chenault managed to protect the baby."

While he had beaten off the swinging, gnashing, spined and feral insects. Looking at the lacerations on cheeks and neck the captain wondered how he had managed to save his eyes. The wounds on face and torso would heal but, inside, something would continue to bear the scars.

"And the rest?"

"We had suits—more than we needed. They yielded spare oxygen and other things. I rigged up a flame-thrower of sorts and used fire and smoke to get us to the surface."

Where luck had been with them. It had been dark and the flat creatures hugging the spires somnolent from lack of sunlight. Even so something had caught up with them as they reached the raft and, in the mirrored surface of the glass Dumarest saw, in memory, the bulk of it, the sting, the tearing, pincer-like jaws. A predator of the night which had died beneath the hammering impact of bullets from the gun he had left.

Then to where Baglioni waited and back to the ship and help and sanity. To the drugs which had eased the pain of injected venom. To dressings and sleep and now to satisfy Lauter's curiosity.

"How's the baby?"

"Govinda's taking care of her." Lauter refilled their glasses. "It's Mirza, right enough, the tattoo leaves no doubt. But how? How?"

"The legend," said Dumarest. "Youth restored—well, she got what she wanted."

"And so did Chenault. But she didn't want it in that way. She just wanted to be young and beautiful and get what she'd always wanted and never seemed to find. I guess you know what that was."

Dumarest nodded, thinking of the conversation they'd had in the caverns, the way she had touched his hand. A gesture which had betrayed her as had so many other small things when the facade she had built for protection cracked to reveal the true person it had shielded.

"She'll find it," he said. "She'll grow and, this time, she may know better than to believe that to be pretty is to be beautiful. That comes from within. And love can recognize it. It is the person

231

which is important not the shell. Once she learns that, her life will be happy.''

As Chenault's would be; Lauter would look after their interests. And Mirza was free of the Cyclan—they would never look for their prey in the form of a baby.

Lauter said, thoughtfully, ''What is it, Earl? ''That thing in the caverns. What the hell is it?''

''A machine.''

''What?''

''I think it has to be a machine. Mirza said the area was unnatural and I agree with her. No natural force could have created it. Something must have come from outside, a ship of some kind, out of control and crashing with tremendous velocity. The impact broke the crust and its own internal forces molded the magma into the shapes we see. A long time ago, now, of course. A millennium at least. Maybe more.''

An accident which had ruined a world. One which must have seared the surface with flame and molten stone, turning metals into vapors, destroying all intelligent life. Only the insects would have had a chance to survive and their mutated descendants dominated Ryzam.

''The drive must have remained functional if only in part.'' Dumarest picked up his glass and drank and in the surface saw the lambent beauty of the glowing column. ''The drive,'' he said. ''It has to be that. One working on a different principle from our own. The Erhaft field cocoons us against the restrictions imposed by the speed of light but the alien mechanism works in the distortion of time."

"A guess, Earl?"

"We can do nothing but guess but the evidence supports it. Look at Mirza and Chenault. Both entered the column old and both came out young."

"An intensification of the process which healed you."

"No. I stayed in the pool. In fact I must have crawled almost out of it fairly soon. The energies loose in the mist reshaped me. Maybe they were designed to do exactly that; to isolate the DNA blueprint and to shape the body back into what that blueprint said it should be. Another guess but it's good enough. The column was something else."

"Time reversal." Lauter frowned, nodding. "The tattoo on Mirza's wrist was recent; the flesh was still puffed. That makes her almost newborn. If Chenault hadn't picked her up—"

"She would have reverted to a blob of sperm. A zygote."

"Then nothing." Again the captain nodded. "No wonder those who found it never came back."

The column saw to that, luring them into its embrace, stripping away the unwanted years as it moved them back in time. Restoring the youth they craved—but as their bodies shed years of age so their brains shed the accumulated knowledge of those years.

"Chenault didn't recognize me," said Dumarest. "He didn't know me because, to him, we'd never met. I had to explain to him where we were and

233

what we were doing. Luckily he was a quick learner."

Lauter said, looking at his glass, "Are you going back, Earl? Govinda—"

"No. It would be of no use. The pool doesn't cure and it can't help her. It can only restore you to what your blueprint tells it you should be. It can't take Baglioni and make him a normal-sized man. And the column can only make you young."

"Only? Men would give a fortune for that alone."

"Would they? Would you? Think about it. To be a boy again as you were before. A young man with it all to do again. The growing, the learning, the pain and frustration. The fear and hate and—" Dumarest broke off; not all had had a childhood like his. In a quieter tone he said, "It's a form of death, Captain. You retain nothing of what you know now. Nothing!"

"So much for legend." Lauter drank and reached for the decanter. "Join me, Earl, I insist." He waited until Dumarest set down his empty glass, then, pouring, said, "The treasure of Ryzam and it's something no one in their right mind would ever want to use. The pool, maybe, but any good hospital could do as much. And there's the danger— what was the shining thing?"

"Another guess," said Dumarest. "But I think it was a parasite of some kind. Vermin which managed to escape the destruction. Or it may even have been a cleaning device." He looked at his wine, red as the blood which had been shed in the pursuit of the unknown. Was Massak laughing at

234

the joke? Vosper? The artist who had contained so much genius? The others? But they were dead and only the living held promise. "To the living," he said, and drank.

A toast in which Lauter joined. "So we face the future, Earl. Mirza and Chenault I can take care of but what about you?" He added, without waiting for an answer, "Mirza told me a little on the journey here. I'm not fond of the Cyclan and I'd like to help. I can take you to where you'd like to go. There are some nice worlds close to the Burdinnion; good climates, cheap land, plenty of space and no one asks too many questions. You could pick one. There's money; Mirza signed a note before she left the ship. Your reward for having helped her and I guess there's no doubt you've earned it." Lauter drained his glass and rose from the table. "Think about it," he urged. "Let me know what you decide."

Alone Dumarest drank his wine, then, refilled, lifted the glass and stared at the mirror surface. It seemed to hold more than the reflection of the salon and his own face. The dream was there and the disappointment. Chenault had reverted back to before he became interested in Earth and had learned the coordinates only when he was too weak to utilize them. Now the knowledge he'd held was lost as if it had never been.

Dumarest drank, the wine stinging with a bitter-sweetness, sliding like water down his throat to rest in his stomach.

A search of Chenault's study might reveal clues; but on Lychen the Cyclan would be waiting and would capture him within hours. A gamble with the odds set too high and the possible reward too vague. Another world then? A new place with new faces where, perhaps, he could find new clues? The search to continue until, like Chenault, he became too old to profit by anything he might find?

Had the dream been just a wishful longing instead of the certainty he had felt could materialize?

Need it be?

Govinda was real and here and she loved him as he loved her. Worlds, as Lauter had said, were plentiful and Mirza's gift would make life easy. There would be no children of her body but, given time, something could be arranged. A surrogate mother; his sperm and what could be salvaged from her genes. Not what she yearned for, nothing could ever be that, but as good as he could provide. And, if there were no children, no daughter who carried her mother's scarlet hair, no boy who wanted to model himself on his father, at least there would be peace.

Peace and love and an end to the obsession which had dominated his life. The search which had cost him so much and had yielded so little.

Earth!

In the mirrored glass he saw it, distorted as he was distorted, twisted, ravaged, suddenly hateful. An image which shattered beneath the closing pressure of his hand to leave the ruby of wine and scratches which yielded the carmine of blood.

A sacrifice to seal a bargain. One conducted by himself for himself with himself as the victim. Blood and wine and shattered crystal to seal his new resolve.

Outside the air was warm, perfumed from small tufts of flowers growing thickly around the ship. In the distance the spires of Ryzam loomed with somber menace, a picture in sharp contrast to that at the other side of the ship where the ground sloped to a stretch of sward soft beneath the foot and gentle to the eye.

"Earl!" Baglioni came running from the ship, his short legs pumping. "I wanted to talk to you," he said as he halted before Dumarest. "I had no chance before. You were all beat up and—" His hand made a vague gesture.

"I wanted to thank you for saving my life."

Dumarest said, dryly, "It's the other way around. If you hadn't waited we'd never have made it."

"And if I'd gone with Tama I'd be dead by now. Like the rest. A pity about Pia, I liked her."

"I know."

"And Lopakhin. Tyner was a genius."

"And Vosper was a good engineer." Dumarest, impatient to find Govinda, sensed the man was keeping him for some reason of his own. "But they're all dead now. Memories. Like Chenault."

"He's still alive."

"Not the man you knew." Dumarest hesitated, the midget and Chenault had been close. "Did he

237

give you anything before we left? A paper? An envelope?"

"No."

"Are you sure?"

"He didn't leave the coordinates with me, Earl, if that's what you're asking. Maybe Lauter?"

Dumarest shook his head. Nothing had been left by Chenault with the captain. Nor with Baglioni—a hope that died like the rest and he wondered why he had asked the question. The search was over. He had made up his mind. Now and for always his future lay with the woman he had lost and found again.

"Govinda!" He waved as he saw her coming over the sward, Chenault following her, the baby in his arms. "Here! Govinda! Over here!"

The sun was in his eyes and she looked blurred as she came toward him, the glow subduing her hair a little, making subtle alterations to her shape. She seemed less mature than he remembered.

"Govinda!" He held out his hands to grasp her own, his fingers remaining empty as she ignored the gesture. "You remember that question you asked me once? Back in the valley? The one about would I ever leave you? Now I know the answer. I'll never leave you. We'll be together for always. Govinda?"

She wasn't looking at him, turning to face Chenault and the baby, her face no longer resembling the woman he had loved.

"Be careful, Tama! Don't hurt her!"

"Please!" Dumarest reached out to catch her

238

arm. ''We must talk. About the future. Our future. We'll find a nice place on a good world and . . . and . . .''

She wasn't listening. She hadn't listened to a word. For her he had ceased to exist and now she had eyes only for Chenault and the baby in his arms. One she reached for to hold to her breast, crooning, her face radiant with an expression Dumarest had never seen her wear before.

''I'm sorry.'' Baglioni said softly at his side. ''I wanted to tell you. It happened almost from the first—when you were being treated. She's found what she has always wanted.''

A baby she could call her own. The oddity spawned by the power of Ryzam and which her mind could accept. The baby and the man who had shared its experience and so, to her, had become its father. The man who would now share her life.

Dumarest turned and walked back to the ship and the endless stars, the search which he would follow, for now there was nothing else.

Beyond the ship, traced against the sky, the spires of Ryzam signposted the graveyard of dreams.

THE TEMPLE OF TRUTH

DEDICATION

To Glennis McCourt

Chapter 1

Karlene shivered. Thirty dozen perlats had been slaughtered to provide her furs yet still she felt the cold. An illusion—born of snow and ice and the pale azure of an empty sky. The visual effects overrode the electronic warmth cossetting her body and she lifted her hands to draw the soft hood closer about her face.

"Cold?" Hagen had noticed the gesture. "Are you cold?"

"No."

"Then—"

"Nothing." An answer too curt and she expanded it as she swept a hand at the vista before them: a landscape of white traced with azure and flecked with motes of nacreous sheen. Out there perspective was distorted so that the mound she looked at could have been a hundred yards distant or a thousand, the dune a thousand or ten.

"There's no warmth," she complained. "No shelter. It's all so bleak. So inhospitable."

He said, "Erkalt is a frigid world, but it has its uses."

"Such as?"

"Low-temperature laboratories. Some mines. Some—" He broke off, knowing she knew the details. "As a site for the games," he said. "As a frame for your beauty. An ice queen should rule over a world of ice."

Empty flattery but she restrained her annoyance. Instead she walked to the edge of a shallow ravine, one barely visible against the featureless expanse. It was empty; a gash cut deep into the snow, pale shadows clustered in its depths. No trace of life yet; looking at it, she felt the familiar touch in her mind.

"Something?" Hagen was beside her, his eyes searching her face. "You catch the scent?" His tone sharpened as she nodded. "When? Soon? Late?"

"Late." The touch had been too gentle: "Sometime ahead but too weak to tell when."

Time and cause—variables beyond her control. Duration weakened impact so that a dire event in the distant future would register as a small incident almost due. An irritation, but one he had no choice but to accept. Now he slipped an arm around her shoulders and led her from the treacherous lip of the ravine.

"Probably a perlat slaughtered for its hide or some other small animal ending its life." He kept his tone light, casual. "Victim of some predator, no doubt. Don't worry about it."

Good advice; to brood on death and fear was to invite madness. Yet, at times, it was hard to ignore the shadows which stretched back through time. In that ravine a creature would die and would know terror before it expired.

"We'll try over to the east," said Hagen. His tone, still light, masked his impatience. "Once we find the right place we can set up the scanners."

"If we find it," she said. "And if it's the right one."

"It will be—you'll see to that."

His assurance held the trace of threat, but she said nothing as he led the way to where the raft stood on the frozen snow. The driver, muffled in cheap furs, touched a control as they climbed aboard, and a transparent canopy rose to enclose the body of the vehicle and protect them from the wind. It droned as they rose, a bitter, keening sound, and she shivered again as the raft moved away from the lowering sun.

"Still cold?" Hagen was concerned. "Perhaps you are ill. I think you should see a doctor when we get back to town."

"No!" Her refusal was sharp. "There's nothing wrong with me. It's just this damned planet."

The snow and ice and shriek of the wind. A sound as if a lost soul was crying its grief as it quested empty spaces. Beneath the raft the ground was a blur of whiteness; a board on which, soon, a bloody game would be played. What did a quarry feel? Fear, that was certain, a rush of terror prior to a savage end, but what else? Hope, perhaps? The belief in the miracle which alone could bring

245

safety? Regret that greed and love of life had led to a frigid hell?

The heaters had taken the chill from the air within the canopy and she loosened the hood, throwing it back from her head and face to release a cascade of hair. It fell in a cloud of shimmering whiteness over the pearly luster of her furs; hair as white as the snow below, as white as the blanched pallor of her skin.

An albino; beneath the silver-tinted contact lenses she wore, her eyes held the pinkness of diffused blood.

"You're beautiful!" Hagen was sincere in his appreciation, eyes studying the aristocratic delicacy of her face; the high cheekbones, the hollow cheeks, the thin flare of nostrils, the curve of lips, the rounded perfection of the chin. Beneath the furs her body was lithe with a rounded slimness. "An ice queen, as I said."

A mutant and hating it despite the wealth it had brought her. Hating the talent she possessed which set her apart, now again making itself manifest within the secret convolutions of her mind.

"Karlene?" Hagen had seen the sudden, betraying tension. "Something?"

"I think so."

"Strong? Close?" He ceased his questioning as she raised a hand. Waited until it lowered. "No?"

"A scent, but it was weak. Where are we?"

Too far to the east and distant from the city. The raft turned as he snapped orders at the driver, slowing as it circled over the too-flat terrain. Hopeless territory for the games as the fool should have known. The vehicle straightened, humps rising in the distance, to become mounded dunes slashed with crevasses torn by the winds, gouged with pits fashioned by storms.

"Anything?" Hagen glanced at the sun as she shook her head. Soon would come the night, the winds, the impossibility of further search. To the driver he said, "Drop lower and head for the north. Cut speed."

"But—"

"Do it!"

Too low and too slow over such broken terrain could lead to disaster; sudden winds, rising from uneven ground, could catch the raft and bring it to destruction. Fears the man kept to himself as he handled the controls.

Waiting, watching, Hagen forced himself to be patient. There was nothing more he could do and his tension could affect the woman's sensitivity. Now Karlene was in command. Until she scented the node, they must turn and drift and turn again in an ever-widening circle. He had chosen the ground, the decision based on skill and experience, but only she could determine the node.

"You've found it?" He had spotted her tension. "The scent?"

She nodded, one hand to her throat, eyes wide at the touch of horror.

"Close?"

"Close." She inhaled, fighting to be calm. "Close and strong. God, how stong!"

The node. The spot where the game would end. Hagen sighed his relief. Now he could relax. The rest was just a matter of routine.

*   *   *

Leaning back in his chair, Dumarest looked away from his hungry guest. Brad Arken was more like a ferret than a man; thin, sharp-faced, with eyes which quested in continual movement. His clothing was shabby, his skin betraying chronic malnutrition. To feed him was a kindness, but Dumarest was not being charitable.

"Earl?"

"Help yourself. Eat all you want."

The bread, the vegetables, the bowl of succulent stew. He had barely touched them but he had guessed the other's hunger. Could guess, too, at his desperation; the reason he had selected him from those hiring their labor, the reason he had invited him to dine.

Now, as Arken ate, Dumarest looked around. The restaurant was contained within the hotel in which he had a room. Warm light bathed the area enhancing the comfort of soft carpets and heated air. To one side a facsimile fire burned against a wall, the bed of artificial logs glowing red, gold, amber and orange in a framework of black iron.

A glow which merged with the yellow illumination from the lanterns and threw touches of color on the flesh and finery of the others seated at their tables. A crowd, mostly young, all apparently wealthy. They were in an exuberant mood.

"Voyeurs," said Arken. "Here to enjoy the games. Watching in comfort while others do the work. At least they'll keep warm."

His plate was empty, the bowl also. The vegetables were barely touched but the bread had vanished and Dumarest guessed it now reposed beneath the other's blouse. He lifted a hand as Arken wiped his mouth on a napkin. To the waitress who answered his signal he said, "Wine. A flagon of house red."

It arrived with glasses adorned with delicate patterns engraved in the crystal. Dumarest poured, Arken almost snatching up his glass, downing half its contents at a gulp, then, almost defiantly, swallowing the rest.

As he reached for the flagon Dumarest clamped his fingers on the neck.

"Later. First we talk. I'm looking for a man. Maybe you can help me find him. He's old, scarred down one cheek, gray hair and, maybe, a beard." Scant details but all he had. "Celto Loffredo. Once he was a dealer in antiquities."

Arken said, "Erkalt's a big world but sparsely inhabited. The city here, a few installations at the poles. They are staffed by technicians employed by the companies who own them and they're choosy about who they take. An old man, even if indentured, wouldn't be worth his keep. Which brings us back to the city. I guess you've checked the usual sources? Hotels and such?" As Dumarest nodded he continued, "So he isn't living easy and a man without money has little choice. If he's alive he must be on the brink."

"As you are?"

Arken said nothing but the answer was in his eyes and, as he reached again for the wine, Dumarest released his grip on the flagon.

As the man filled his glass Dumarest said,

249

"This is free but it's all you're going to get. Locate the man I want and it's worth a hundred."

"That isn't enough."

"All I want is a time and place."

"I'll have to check the warrens." Arken was insistent. "Spread the word and ask around. On Erkalt no one does anything free. I'll need cash for expenses, bribes, sweeteners. How badly do you want to find him?" Dumarest didn't answer, and Arken drank and shrugged before drinking again. "All right, so it's your business, but we'd find him quicker if I could put others to work. And it would help if I'd more to go on."

The man was right, but Dumarest had no more to give. A name, a vocation, the hint that the man could have information he wanted. Details gained on another world and a hope followed because he had nothing else.

"How much will you need?"

"For expenses?" Arken didn't hesitate. "A hundred, at least. More if you want to hurry things along. I'll need to hire men to go looking and there are a lot of places Celto could be. But a hundred should do it."

He refilled his glass, looking at Dumarest, hoping he had struck the right note, named the right price. Too little and he would have undervalued himself and lessened the chance of profit. Too high and he could have lost an opportunity. It depended on his host but Arken thought he recognized the type. A man who lived soft and could afford to be generous; the food and wine was proof of that. He dressed plain but that was not uncommon; many tourists tried to seem what they were not. The grey tunic, pants and boots looked new and the knife carried in the right boot could be for effect.

"Well?" The wine had bolstered his courage and Arken pressed his advantage. A man alone, looking for another on a strange world, would need local help. And, if he was in a hurry, he wouldn't want to waste time. "Is it a deal?"

A parasite eager to suck blood—Dumarest recognized the type. Had recognized it from the first and had set the stage to achieve the result he wanted. Arken's greed, channeled and contained, would make him a useful tool.

"Here. A hundred for expenses." Coins rattled on the table beneath his hand then, as Arken reached for them, steel whispered from leather as Dumarest lifted the knife from his boot. In the illumination the blade gleamed with the hue of burnished gold but the needle point resting against Arken's throat held the burning chill of ice. "Rob me and you'll regret it. I want you to believe that."

"I—" Arken swallowed, cringing from the knife, the threat clear in the eyes of the man who faced him. No tourist this, despite his soft living and casual hospitality. No easy gull to be robbed while fed empty lies. "Man! For God's sake! There's no need for this!"

For a moment longer the steel held his eyes, then it vanished as quickly as it had appeared. Arken touched the place where it had rested, stared at the fleck of blood marring his hand. A minor wound, barely noticeable, but the blade could have as easily opened his throat. Wine spilled as Arken tilted the flagon, a small pool of ruby resting on the polished wood of the table. One which looked too much like blood.

He said, unsteadily, "Why do that? We had a deal. You can trust me."

"I'm glad to hear it."

"I'll find him," promised Arken. "If Celto Loffredo is alive I'll find him."

"Tell him nothing when you do. Just bring me word."

Arken nodded, gulping at the wine in his glass, looking at the soft comfort of the room. Those present had seen nothing of what had taken place; Dumarest had masked the incident with arm and body. He remembered the speed, the sting of the point, the naked ferocity he had seen in the eyes and face of his host. There had been no pretence. It had been no empty threat.

"A hundred?"

"Five," said Dumarest. "Less a hundred for each day I'm kept waiting. Keep me waiting too long and I'll want to know why." He touched a finger in the pool of wine and drew a ruby streak over the table. "If you want to quit leave now."

Arken resisted the temptation. His head tilted as Dumarest rose to his feet, yellow light casting a sheen on the smoothness of his clothing. Somber garb but as functional as the man himself.

A hard man who followed a hard road—Arken's hand shook as he reached for more wine.

The restaurant had two doors: one which led through a vestibule to the outside, the other leading into the hotel, the bar, the small casino the place contained. Dumarest heard the click of balls, the chant of a croupier as he fed a spinning wheel.

"Pick your combination. Red, black or one of each. Three chances of winning at every spin of the wheel. Place your bets, now. Place your bets!"

An adaption of an ancient game but one with a false attraction. Winners gained two to one which made the house margin unacceptably high to any knowledgeable gambler. Even so the table was crowded, a matron, her raddled face thick with paint, squealing her pleasure as both balls settled in the red.

"I've won! Jac! I've won!"

Her escort, young, slim, neat in expensive clothing, dutifully smiled his pleasure at her success. Dumarest watched as he helped pile the winnings into a rounded head, two chips vanishing as, deftly, he palmed them from sight. A bonus to add to his fee for the company he provided, the kisses he would give, the caresses she would demand.

"Earl!" The voice was high, clear, rising above the sound of the tables. "Earl Dumarest! Here!"

She was tall, slender, hair neatly cut in a severe style which framed the sharp piquancy of her face. Her smile widened as Dumarest moved toward her. He smiled back; Claire Hashein had once been close.

"Earl, it's good to see you again." Her hand, strong, long-fingered, rested on his arm. "What brings you to Erkalt?"

"What brings you?"

"Business." Her shrug was expressive. "Some

253

fool of a manufacturer thinks the local furs are unique and insisted that I make a personal selection of the best. Nonsense, of course, any competent furrier could do the job as well as I can, but why should I argue when all expenses are being paid? Anyway, it suits my purpose. You?"

"It suits my purpose also."

"Naturally."

Her hand fell from his arm and she stared up at him, head thrown back a little to expose the long, clean lines of her throat. Now, no longer smiling, she looked older than she had. A skilled and clever woman who wore exuberance like a mask. Then, abruptly, she was smiling again.

"I'm really pleased to meet you, Earl. You came on the *Canedo*?"

The last ship to have landed. "Yes."

"I've been here days. We traveled on the *Gual*. A ghastly journey. The talk was all of the games. I was bored to tears but Carl loved it. He's a natural-born hunter. We met on Servais while I was completing an assignment. Creating a wedding gown for the daughter of the local magnate," she explained. "I guess her recommendation got me my present commission."

She was talking too fast and explaining too much and Dumarest wondered at her confusion. They had met on a journey and parted on landing and the odds were against their ever meeting again. Yet here she was and she was not alone.

"Carl!" She turned as a man thrust his way toward them. As he joined them she said, "Carl Indart—meet Earl Dumarest."

He was tall and broad with close-cropped rus-

set hair, a thin mouth and a pugnacious jaw. His
eyes beneath heavy brows were a vivid blue. His
ears were small, set close to his skull. He was,
Dumarest guessed, younger than the woman and
himself. When he smiled he revealed neat, white
teeth.

"Earl!" His hands rose, lifting to show empty
palms. His grip was warm, friendly, as they closed
on Dumarest's own. "Where has Claire been hiding you?"

She said, "Earl is one of the most interesting
men I've ever met. You could learn from him,
Carl."

"I don't doubt it." The rake of his eyes was the
searching glance of a hunter; checking, assessing,
evaluating. "I guess you're here for the games.
There should be good sport. Are you booked yet?"
His eyebrows lifted as Dumarest shook his head.
"No? A pity. I've a spot in tomorrow's event. Cost
me plenty to get another to yield his place but I
figure it's worth it. Maybe I could find another
place if you're interested."

"No thanks."

"Don't you like to hunt?"

"It's a chance, Earl," said the woman before
Dumarest could answer. "The two of you would
make a good team. You'd sweep the board and
gain the trophy. It could yield a nice profit."

"We'd break even, at least," urged Carl. "Buying
a place won't be cheap and there'd be the hire of
gear if you haven't brought your own. But we
could make extra on the bets." To Claire he said,
"I like the idea. It would add spice to the game.
Try and talk Earl into it."

255

"Why don't you?"

"Bresaw's waiting. He's got the runs from the previous dozen games and thinks there could be a pattern. See you!"

He left with a lift of a hand, brash, arrogant, intent on his own concerns. Dumarest glanced at the woman at his side, saw the shadow on her face, one which vanished as she smiled.

"A boy," she said. "Carl's nothing but a boy at heart. All he can think of now are the games."

"And you?"

"Work. Furs, pelts, hides. Dealers who will try to cheat. Liars who will claim a match where none exists. Well, that's for tomorrow. Now let's have a drink."

The bar was quiet compared to the casino and Dumarest led the way to a secluded table. A waitress came to take his order, returning with tall goblets filled with lavender wine laced with a drifting mist of silver bubbles. Claire snorted as they stung her nose, sipped, laughed her pleasure as her mouth and throat filled with a familiar pungency.

"Earl! You remembered!"

Lavender, lime, some osteth and a touch of chard. The constituents of a drink they had shared in the snug confines of a cabin during a journey which, for her, had ended too soon.

She said, "This is nice but you shouldn't wake old memories. It isn't kind. You know how sentimental I am. Earl—"

"Tell me about Carl."

"What?" She blinked at the abrupt question. "Why talk of him?"

"Why not?" He smiled, masking his interest. "Maybe I'm jealous. How well do you know him?"

"Well enough. He's a hunter. He had some skins for sale and we met, as I told you. I sensed something within him. The strength I'd known in you. It set him apart from the others. God—if you only knew how weak most men are!" She reached for the goblet and drank, almost emptying the container. As she set it down she said, softly, "But Carl isn't you, Earl. He hasn't taken your place. No one could ever do that."

Was she a woman in love—or one acting the part? Dumarest signaled, the waitress bringing fresh goblets filled with the same lavender wine. As she left he smiled at the woman beside him.

"You flatter me."

"I tell the truth. Are you annoyed?"

"Of course not."

"I'm glad." Claire moved closer to him, the long line of her thigh pressing against his own, the touch of her fingers a subtle caress. "You'll never know how much I missed you, darling. Work helped to fill the time and—"

"Carl?"

"To hell with him!" Her voice was harsh, betraying her irritation at the change of subject. "Why talk about him? He doesn't own me."

Dumarest doubted if the man would agree with her. He had radiated a proprietary air and his searching look had been more than a casual examination. Carl Indart, he guessed, could be other than what he seemed. Certainly he was a dangerous man.

Chapter 2

They ran him down at the edge of the foothills close to Ekar's pass and Thorn gloated over his monitors.

"Hell—just look at those peaks! The guy's lost control of his sphincters." His laughter was ugly. "Sure glad that I'm not downwind."

He was a squat, greasily fat man, with mean eyes and a snubbed nose. The twig clamped between his teeth exuded a purple ooze which stained gums and teeth. His furs were worn, stained in places, but he knew his job. Even as Hagen watched, he adjusted the balance on the input; accentuating the terror, the panic and fear. An unnecessary refinement—the quarry faced his end, and those watching would know it. But such attention to detail had made Thorn a top man in his trade.

"Boost visual." Hagen narrowed his eyes as the

screen took on sharper tones. The scanner was floating high and wide but the fisheye lens relayed enough data for the monitor to compensate. "Adjust color."

The scene altered as Thorn obeyed; a subtle shifting of hues which diminished the overriding white and gave greater prominence to the quarry. Crouched between a pair of ice-encrusted rocks, he looked like a ragged doll. One with ripped clothing, dirtied, bruised, broken. Blood showed bright on buttocks and legs. More rested like a badge on his right shoulder.

"That's it." Thorn was matter-of-fact. "They'll get him anytime now. The run's over."

The run but not the end. That would come almost a mile away in the small crevasse Karlene had pinpointed. Already the scanners were in position for wide-angle and close-ups. Others would follow the progress of the hunters. Even now more and more who followed the games would be switching to his channel and paying for the enjoyment of his broadcast. Later there would be tapes, stills, sound recordings of the final moments.

"Move!" Hagen snapped into his radio as the quarry rose unsteadily to his feet. "Close in and seal—you know where."

He had a good team and he relaxed as winking lights on the monitor showed they had swung into action. In twenty or so minutes the quarry would have reached the spot Karlene had noted. The hunters would be close behind. Thirty minutes from now it would all be over.

He had misjudged by five.

"It was crazy!" It was hours later after night

259

had fallen before he'd had time to join the woman. Now, glasses of sparkling wine in his hands, he relived the moment. "He was dead, down and finished—I'd have offered a hundred-to-one on it. Yet, somehow, he managed to make a final stand." He handed her a glass. "A toast, my dear. To another success!"

"You call it that?"

"What else?" He sensed her mood and became serious. "You aren't responsible for the games, my dear. You merely determine where they will end. There's no cause for guilt in that."

Nor in the furs her talent had brought her. The soft living, the luxury, the comfort she enjoyed. No guilt either in success—Hagen had fought hard to gain what he had. To demean his achievement was to be unfair.

"You're right." She tried to shake off her mood—always she was pensive after a game. "Tell me what happened."

"It was unexpected," he said. "That's what made it so unusual. You know how these things normally end—the hunters close in and it's over. But this time they had to work. The quarry dug himself in and—" He broke off, shaking his head. "Never mind. It's over now. It's all on tape if you're interested."

"Later, perhaps."

Which meant never and he knew it. The thing which others bought and played and gloated over gave her no pleasure. Too often she had felt the touch of death and fear. What for others was a titillation was for her a torment.

He said, abruptly, "Karlene, we've done well

and could do better. I've had offers from the Chi-Hsung Combine. A monopoly on the Vendura Challenge with overlap on the Malik Rites. A three-year contract with bonuses and copyright guarantees. It means less work and more money."

"For me?"

"Of course."

"And you?"

She turned to face the window as he shrugged. Outside the night pressed close despite the triple glazing. Darkness illuminated by starlight which, reflected from the snow, threw a pale, nacreous shine over the landscape. A quiet, peaceful scene, but it wouldn't last. Soon would come the winds filling the air with swirling particles of ice and tearing at the frozen snow. Temperatures would fall even lower than what they were. Predators, now buried deep, would be stimulated by the cold to hunt for prey.

"Karlene?" Hagen was beside her, his face reflected next to her own in the pane. "More wine?"

She had barely touched what she had and she shook her head.

"Then—"

"You drink," she urged. "You have cause to celebrate."

She watched as he turned, noting the movement of his head, the profile of his face as he refilled his glass. A hard face but one which could be gentle. A hard man who could have been her father but who inwardly yearned to become something closer. A partner who wanted to become her lover. Why did she resist him?

"Are you taking the offer?"

"That of the Combine?" He shrugged. "It's a possibility, but there are others. If—"

"Don't let me influence you," she said quickly. "You must do what you want."

"I know what I want." He looked at his glass as if coming to a decision then drank and set it down and came toward her, his face growing large in the window. "Karlene, I have money and I can work. There is no need for you to follow the games here or anywhere else."

"Please!"

"Let me finish." He was stubborn. "You must know how I feel about you. I'm not asking you to love me. I'm just asking you to be with me. Here or on any world you choose. If—" He broke off, looking at her face reflected in the window. "Karlene!"

He turned, catching her as she swayed, recognizing the tension, the strain distorting the lines of her face.

"The scent? But—"

"Here," she gasped. "Close."

"Here? In the hotel?"

She nodded, swallowing, one hand rising to mask the quiver of her lips. Death had warned of its coming and, as always, she wondered if that death were to be her own.

Arken said, "I'm sorry. I've done my best but as yet it hasn't been good enough. The man you want is hard to find."

He stood muffled in a stained and patched thermal cloak, the hood drawn tight, breath forming a white cloud before his face. Dumarest, similarly attired, stood at his side, both men hugging the shelter of an alcove.

He said, "You've spread the word?"

"All over." Arken was bitter. "They take the cash and make the promise and that's as far as it goes. I've run down a dozen leads and all have turned out to be a waste of time. Information I paid for and those giving it swore they had seen Celto Loffredo alive and knew just where he'd be. Liars. Damned liars the lot of them."

Men living on the brink, desperate to survive, willing to say anything for the sake of a night's shelter. Setting immediate food and warmth against the prospect of future punishment. Dumarest understood them as he understood Arken: a man reluctant to admit his failure but more afraid to be thought a cheat.

"I've scanned the streets," he said. "Checked the warrens and now it's down to this." His hand lifted and pointed down the street. "Fodor and Braque. Braque's down the street; two zelgars the night. Fodor charges three. Food included. I'll take Braque."

"No," said Dumarest. "I'll take it. Down the street, you say?"

"To the end then turn left. A green lantern." Arken stamped his feet and glanced at the sky. The stars were dimmed by scudding mist. "Better hurry. The wind's rising."

The wind droned louder as Dumarest made his way down the street, pulling at his cloak, stinging his face with particles of ice. The starlight faded as the air thickened, died to leave a solid darkness broken only by the pale nimbus of high-set lanterns. Light which died in turn as the street filled with a blinding welter of snow.

Dumarest had headed to his left and stood with his hand pressed against the wall. A guide which he followed as he fought the wind. The wall ended and he followed it around the corner tripping as his boot hit something soft. Kneeling, he examined it, finding a body which moved, hearing a thin voice pleading above the wind.

"Help me! For God's sake help me!"

A man, thin, frail, clutched at Dumarest as he helped him to his feet. The wind eased a little and he saw a shapeless bundle of rags, a face half-covered by a cloth, eyebrows crusted with ice.

"Braque?"

"There!" The man lifted an arm. "Don't leave me!"

He clung like a burr as Dumarest moved toward the opening he'd indicated, set beneath a pale, green glow. The light flickered as he approached, vanished as the wind resumed its onslaught. Snow blasted around them as Dumarest forced a passage through heavy curtains. Beyond hung others, a door, a table behind which sat a broad, stocky man.

"Cash." His hand hit the table, palm upward. "Give or go." He grunted as Dumarest fed the hand with coins. "Right. You're in. You?"

The man Dumarest had rescued was old, a ruff of beard showing beneath the protective cloth covering his face. He beat his hands together, shivering, then fumbled at his clothing.

"Where—" His hands moved frantically. "I had

it! I swear I had it! I must have lost it when I fell. Or—" He looked at Dumarest, looked away as their eyes met, thinking better of making an accusation. Instead he tried to plead. "You know me, Sag. I'll pay."

"That's right," agreed the doorkeeper. "And you'll do it now." He frowned at the coin the old man gave him. "Where's the other one?"

"I haven't got it. I'm short, Sag. But I won't eat anything. Just let me stay the night." His voice rose as the man shook his head. "I'll die out there! The wind's blowing hard. For God's sake— you'd kill me for a lousy zeglar?"

For less—Dumarest read the man's intention as he rose from his stool. His hand moved, the coin he held fell, ringing as it hit the floor at the old man's feet. A five zelgar piece.

He said, "Is that what you were looking for?"

"What? I—" Necessity made the old man sharp. "That's it! I knew I had it! Thanks, mister!" He scooped up the coin and slammed it on the table. "Here, Sag, give me my change."

Dumarest looked at the doorkeeper as the old man passed into the shelter.

"Sag? Is that your name?"

"Sagoo Moyna. Why?"

"I'm working for a man who wants to find someone. Celto Loffredo." Dumarest gave what description he had. "If you know where he could be found it could be worth money."

"So I've been told."

"Would he come here?"

"He might. We get all kinds. If he does I'll let

you know. Staying?" He grunted at Dumarest's nod. "Better hurry if you want supper."

It was the swill Dumarest had expected. The shelter, as he'd known it would be, was a box with a low ceiling, poorly illuminated, the air fetid. From the huddled mass of humanity on the floor rose a susurration of groans, snores, ragged breathing, mutters, sighs.

A bad place but outside it would be worse. There the only hope of survival was to find others, make a crude shelter and spend the night huddled together for mutual warmth. A gamble few could win.

Dumarest picked his way through the somnolent bodies and found himself a space. He settled down, fumbling, lifting the knife from his boot and lying with it in his right hand; both hand and blade masked by his cloak. The floor was hard, the smells stronger in the lower air, but the place was warm from the heat of massed bodies and he had known worse.

He relaxed, ignoring the taste of the swill he'd eaten to maintain his pretense, ignoring, too, the odors and susurration around him. Things easy to forget after a time of relative comfort. Beside him a man groaned, turned, one arm moving, the hand falling within inches of Dumarest's face. A gnarled hand, the nails cracked, grimed, the knuckles raw and swollen. A finger was missing, another black from frostbite. As he watched, lice crawled among the thick hairs of the back and wrist.

From somewhere to one side a man screamed.

It was a short, sharp, sound muffled and followed by a blow. Another cursed. Anger at broken rest and a dream which had turned into a nightmare. Dumarest moved a little, closing his eyes, the cloak wrapped tight around his body.

Resting he thought of Claire Hashein.

She had been demanding in her passion; memories and wine inducing a feral desire. His room had become the cabin in which once they had traveled. His bed the stage on which she had enacted a familiar scene. A woman protesting her love, making plans, extracting promises. Demanding more than he was willing to give and offering more than she was able. A game in which he had participated, remembering how wine affected her, how she had talked in her sleep.

Yet, when she had sunken into satiated slumber she had said nothing of value.

Dumarest saw her face as he slipped into a doze. Pleasant features which could be the mask of danger. Had their meeting been truly coincidental? Was she being used without her knowledge?

And what of Carl Indart?

A hard man, ruthless, one with the sadistic streak forming the nature of most who hunted for sport. One who had attached himself to the woman for reasons Dumarest could guess. If the man was hunting him what better way to get close?

He stirred, the prickle of danger warning him as it had so often before. The woman, the hunter, Celto Loffredo whom he had come to find. That man could hold the answer to the question which dominated his life, but had apparently vanished from the face of creation.

Dumarest sighed, sinking deeper into his doze, a montage of faces flickering like the glows of a stroboscope as sleep engulfed him. Men he had known, women he had loved and lost, those who had hated him, those he had been forced to kill.

Fragments of childhood and a life in which the shelter he now occupied would have been the epitome of luxury.

Images which shattered as he woke to the sting of a knife at his throat.

The smells had grown thicker, the mumble of sound new a susurration like the wash of restless waves on a distant shore. The illumination was too weak to throw strong shadows but Dumarest had chosen to rest beneath a light, and on the sleeping body beside him something threw a patch of darkness.

A man, kneeling at his back, stooped, the knife in his hand resting on the hood of the cloak. A slender blade which had thrust through the material to touch the flesh just below the ear. A thief's trick; should he wake and pose a threat the knife would drive home bringing silence and death at the same moment.

"Hurry!" The voice was a whisper. "Get on with it!"

An accomplice; one who would search while the other stood guard. Dumarest lay still as the cloak was moved away from the lower part of his body. Fingers probed at his legs, his boots, the

lower edge of his tunic. Places were money could
be hidden. He sighed as they reached a pocket.

"Jud?"

"Keep looking."

The man with the knife was a thief not a
murderer, reluctant to strike without need. Dumarest built on that advantage. As the fingers
delved into a pocket, he grunted, twisted a little,
hunched his shoulder, shifting his arm beneath
the cloak. Movements which trapped the searching fingers and caused the man to lift the knife
from its place. It returned at once to rest lower,
the point hard against the collar of Dumarest's
tunic.

It thrust as he reared upright, the blade slicing
through the plastic to slip harmlessly from the
metal mesh buried beneath. Before the man could
strike again Dumarest had moved his own knife,
the steel shimmering as it swept up and back in
a vicious slash, dulling as the edge bit deep.

"God!"

The accomplice cringed as blood fountained from
a severed throat, a ruby flood which fell like
rain, dying as Dumarest turned, knife stabbing,
the point reaching the heart. Blood dripped from
the steel as it swung toward the other man.
Dumarest recognized the man just as the blade
took his life.

"Scum." Sagoo Moyna looked down at the man
Dumarest had rescued from the storm. "He sold
you out. That's the thanks you get for saving his
life."

"The other one?"

"Jud Amnytor. I've had trouble with him before. Most don't complain when they've been robbed. Too scared to, I guess. Well, to hell with them." His foot spurned the dead. "How do you want to handle this?"

"Quietly."

"That's what I figured. I should report it to the guards but they must be busy and who wants to buy trouble? What's it worth for you to stay out of it?" He blinked at Dumarest's answer. "That all?"

"Report it and the guards will ask questions. One might be how Amnytor managed to operate so long. Another might be why no one's complained. They might think you and he were working together." Dumarest met the other's eyes. "I might even begin to think you set me up."

"No!" Sagoo glanced at the dead. "It wasn't like that."

"Then we have a deal?" Dumarest added, as he looked at his cloak now thick with drying blood, "Call it the price of a change."

It was dawn when he left the shelter, the wind-swept streets empty, bleak. Mounds of frozen snow had piled in corners and hung thick from the eaves. Brilliant white which hid the dirt and stains of poverty, the bodies, the debris of the day. Like a cleansing tide the wind swept clean the place men had made their own.

As he neared his hotel he heard a man call and slowed to a halt as Arken ran to join him.

"I'm glad you're early." Arken gasped, beating his hands as he fought for breath. "This damned cold tears at the lungs. I tried to wait for you in the hotel but they wouldn't let me in."

"News?"

He gave it in a small cafe sitting at a table over a mug of steaming tisane. A place catering to those who had finished their term of duty or were about to start work.

"I didn't find the man you want but I met someone who sold me something he owned. A book. I paid fifty for it."

The price Dumarest had paid to dispose of two bodies but, if it was what he hoped, the book was worth a hundred times as much. He took it from Arken's hand. A small, stained volume the covers a dull, mottled green. The pages were brown with age, thick with faded writing. Beneath the cover, printed on an attached insert, he saw the lines and curves of a neat calligraphy.

"Celto Loffredo," said Arken. "That's a bookplate. He put it in to prove the book was his."

Or someone had done it to make that exact point. Arken? It was possible, his time had run out and it was his last hope of earning a reward. Or it could be genuine. Coincidences happened and it would be wrong to be over-suspicious.

Dumarest said, "Is this all? Was there anything else? Clothing," he explained. "Jewelry; rings, bracelets, medallions." Personal items on which figures could have been stamped. Garments which could hold secrets within their seams. "No?"

"Clothing doesn't hang around. It's used, worn, ripped up to make patches. As for the rest—" Arken shrugged and sipped his tisane. "Anything that can buy food or shelter gets sold."

As books got burned but this one had survived. Luck, perhaps. It happened.

Dumarest fingered the volume, wanting to open it, read and examine it, but this was the wrong place and the wrong time. Fatigue would dull the sharpness of his mind and he could miss essential information; a scrap of data which could lead to the answer. He needed to rest, to get rid of the stench of the shelter, the sweat of recent action. The cloak he wore was slimed with dirt and he remembered the lice he had seen.

Arken said, "I'll keep looking if you want. There could be other things, papers, maps, old stuff like the book." He lingered on the word. "Was I right to buy it?"

"Yes."

"Should I buy more if I find them?"

"Not until I've seen what it is. Fifty, you said?"

An inflated price; Arken would be a fool not to have made a profit. His eyes widened as Dumarest thrust coins across the table.

"A hundred! But—"

"This closes our deal. If you find anything new let me know. Here." He dumped the cloak on the table. "A bonus."

"Thanks. It'll pay for some steam. Why don't you join me?"

"No need. I've got my own."

The bath and shower in his room which he yearned to use. The hotel admitted him without hesitation and he climbed the stairs too impatient to wait for the elevator. The corridor was empty aside from a woman busy with a broom who smiled then returned to her duties as he headed for his room. The door swung open to reveal the compartment with its window, furnishings, carpeted floor. The bathroom lay to one side and Dumarest headed toward it, jerking to a halt as he saw the bed.

The bed and the woman sprawled across it. Claire Hashein, naked, lying on her back, arms lifted, legs asprawl, a glint of metal in one hand.

Behind him the cleaner screamed as she saw the blood.

A ruby tide stained the sheets and painted the torso with carmine smears from the gash which marred the throat.

Chapter 3

Prisons held a universal sameness but the one on Erkalt was better than others Dumarest had known. His cell was a box containing a bunk, toilet facilities and nothing else. One wall was made of bars, But there was warmth and light and he was alone. They had taken his clothes and possessions, giving him a pajama-like garb of soft yellow fabric, but had allowed him to retain the book. A selfish act of charity; prisoners who were engrossed did not scream, yell their innocence, shout abuse. Noises Dumarest ignored as, lying on the bunk, he studied what Arken had found.

The book looked old, but age could be simulated. Acids could have browned the pages and faded the ink. Mechanical friction could have fretted the covers. Dyes could have added the stains. Celto Loffredo had dealt in antiquities and he would have wanted to maintain a supply of saleable items. If not found they could have been made.

Would it have been worth his while?

Collectors were willing to pay high for items they wanted and desire of possession would blind them to the possibility of forgery. Even on Erkalt such collectors could be found. Would a man, cold, hungry, living on the brink, have hung on to something of worth?

Or had the book meant more to its owner than the comfort its sale could have provided?

The pages made small whisperings as Dumarest turned them, frowning as he tried to decipher the crabbed, faded script. A journal, he guessed. A diary relating the important events of a man's life. A trader; many pages bore figures which could have been a record of profits and losses.

On one page, soiled by a stain which could have been caused by water or wine, he read barely discernible words.

> "... loaded three bales of ossum ... will try and get ... passage on the *Gillaus* to ... Blackheart ill and I sat with him. Fever, I think; he rambled on about.... Crazy but some of it made an odd kind of sense. Will try.... If true then...."

The light was too poor, the writing too faded for Dumarest to make out more. He turned the pages, tried to read another, his eyes moving over a column of figures, the last heavily underlined. As he frowned at it the bars rattled, the door sliding open beneath the hand of a guard.

"A visitor," he said. "Your advocate."

Shanti Vellani was small, neat, his face sharp, his eyes like those of a bird. Clear, brown, always on the move. He remained silent until the guard had locked him within the cell and had moved away.

"You're looking well, Earl. I'm pleased to see it. There's no sense in anyone beating their head against a wall."

"You've news?"

"Of course, but first a small matter of business." Vellani took a slip of paper from an inside pocket. "Your account to date. It includes expenses. If you'd like to authorize payment?"

Dumarest took it and studied the amount. It was high but the best did not come cheap and he needed the best. He rolled the ball of his thumb over the sensitized portion.

Handing it back he said, dryly, "I take it the news is bad."

"It could be better." Vellani tucked the slip into his pocket then sat down beside Dumarest on the bunk. "I'll be frank with you. On the basis of available evidence you haven't a chance. The prosecution has a watertight case."

"I didn't kill her."

"So you say." Vellani lifted a hand as if to still any protest. "But look at it from the other side. You and the victim were lovers. She was close to another, Carl Indart, and you could have wanted her to break with him. She refused, you lost your temper, there was a brief struggle and—" His shrug was expressive.

"That's assumption, not proof."

"The cleaner saw you enter the room."

"Which is proof that I wasn't in it. Hell, I wasn't even in the hotel that night. I told you that."

"Your alibi." Vellani pursed his lips. "As regards the hotel you could have left it anytime after killing the woman. All the porter can swear to is that you demanded entry shortly after dawn."

"So?"

"Claire Hashein was killed approximately three hours before sunrise. You could have sneaked out just before dawn and returned to establish your innocence. I merely relate the possibility."

"I've a witness."

"Brad Arken. All he can swear to is that he met you close to the hotel that morning."

"We met the previous night."

"And parted." Vellani shook his head. "It would have been easy for you to have returned to the hotel after leaving him. The public rooms were still open and, in the crowd, you wouldn't have been noticed. Then to your room, the rendezvous with the victim, the argument, the act, the attempt to establish your absence. It's speculation, true, and I could argue it out of court, but there's more. The report made by the examining investigator, for example. The victim was lying supine on the bed. She was naked. Her hands and arms were upraised. Bruises were found on her cheeks as if she'd been slapped. The fingers of the right

277

hand clutched a key which fitted the lock of your room."

"I didn't give it to her."

"Can you suggest how she got it?"

"Borrowed a spare from the desk. Had a copy made—your guess is as good as mine." Dumarest added, bitterly, "Does it matter? The key didn't kill her."

But it may have led to her death. Dumarest imagined the scene, Claire, in love, wanting to surprise him. Entering his room, stripping, bathing, lying on the bed waiting for him to join her. Not knowing he was absent from the hotel. Falling asleep, perhaps, to wake and meet her death.

Who would have wanted to kill her?

Why?

Vellani said, "The collar of your tunic was scarred as if by a metal instrument. It could have been the key."

"It could have been many things. Assumption isn't evidence."

"Medical testimony is. The bed was soaked with blood. It must have sprayed from the severed arteries of her throat and traces were found on the carpet and far walls. The medical conclusion is that such a violent and sudden release of blood would have given the murderer no chance to have escaped contact." Pausing, the advocate added, "Tests revealed flecks of blood on your clothing. They are of the same group as the victim's. More blood was found on your knife and, it too, belongs to the same group. As far as the prosecution is concerned that's all they need."

Motive, means and opportunity—and the damning evidence of the blood. A coincidence; the blood spraying from the thief he had killed had been of the same group as Claire's.

Dumarest said, "If the murderer was stained he'd have to have washed off the blood. Were traces found in the bathroom?"

"Yes. Smears around the edge of the shower drainpipe." Vellani added, "It doesn't help. You—he—could have washed down but missed the traces later found."

"My alibi?"

"It doesn't stand up. Sagoo Moyna denies he's ever seen you."

"He's lying!" Dumarest looked down at his hand where it rested on his knee. It was doubled into a fist. Deliberately he forced himself to relax. As the hand opened he said, "Others must have seen me. There was a man serving the food, and plenty used the shelter that night. They couldn't all have been asleep."

"They weren't."

"Then—"

"Listen to me, Earl, and follow what I say." Vellani edged a little closer, his voice lowering as if he were afraid of being overheard. "I'm not a fool. Scum like Sagoo Moyna will lie for the sake of it but he had a reason. I sent men to find out what it was. You killed that night. I'm not arguing how or why but it happened. Two men dead and Sagoo was paid by you to dispose of them. Do you honestly believe he's going to stand up in court and admit to that?"

"As long as he admits I was there."

"It's too late for that. The prosecution will want

to know why he's changed his story. They'll probe, use devices to check his veracity. Use them on you, too, once they are introduced. The truth will come out—but will it do you any good?"

He had killed an armed thief who had tried to rob him. Self-defense and so justified on the majority of worlds. Even on Erkalt where to kill was to commit the most heinous of crimes. But the other one? The old man?

Dumarest had struck out in unthinking reflex, killing before he had seen the face, recognized a deadly threat. To have delayed could have cost him his life—an assumption he was not permitted to make.

"You're in a bind," said Vellani. "If I get you off one hook you'll be stuck on another and the end will be the same. Twenty years' slave-bondage—need I tell you what that means?"

Locked in a collar which could tear at his nerves or blow off his head at the whim of the controller. One which would detonate if he tried to break it free. A life of helpless obedience.

"You'd be sold to a low-temperature laboratory," said the advocate. "If you manage to serve your time you'll be the first. The record is five years." Pausing Vellani added, "I've spoken to the prosecutor. He's willing to give you an out."

"Such as?"

"You can volunteer for quarry."

The games had started as fun, developed into a sport and were now a bloody slaughter. An attraction which brought tourists flocking to Erkalt during the season. Their money stimulated the economy and fed the parasites that fattened on the ritual; people like Meister and Travante who supplied gear for the hunters; Yegorovich and Mickhailovich who dealt in miniatures, souvenirs, mementoes of the ritual; Pincho and Barrass and Valence with their tapes and stills and tips as to where the quarry could be found.

Entrepreneurs like Hagen.

Murderers like herself.

Karlene moved through the crowd like a silver ghost, tall, impassive, acknowledging greeting with a twitch of her lips, a gesture of a hand. Always it was like this before a hunt; the crowd gathered to discuss the prospects, assess chances, probable routes, odds, the time the quarry would be able to remain free, the moment when he would be run down and his blood sent to stain the snow.

But, more than the rest, they had come to see the man himself.

"Hard." She heard the comment as she passed a man talking to a companion. "I know the type. A killer, too, from what I hear. He'll make a run for it. It'll be good sport. You in for a place?"

"Who isn't?"

The initial raffle. A score would win and be charged extra for the privilege of taking part. Half their fees would be placed within the trophy; the prize for the hunter who won. Given to the quarry together with his freedom should he be lucky enough to make it. Some had gone free—a few spread over the years; enough to maintain the conviction that the quarry had a chance, though that was almost eradicated now by her talent.

"Karlene!"

Hagen waved to her from where he stood with a bunch of others. Hunters from their clothing and interest. She waved back, expecting him to join her, but he was too engrossed in conversation. Business, she guessed, he rarely wasted a moment in his determination to be the best. Alone she moved on to where a wide pane of clear glass almost filled one wall.

Behind it was the quarry.

She had seen them before, Hagen insisting, thinking it helped to refine her talent. Men who stood and looked defiantly at those who had come to gape. Others who paced like restless beasts; nerves too tense to rest. Some had huddled in corners defeated before they had even begun.

Dumarest sat, apparently asleep.

The chair was large, ornate, bolted to the floor so as to face the window. Its arms and high back were covered with scarlet fabric, emphasizing the plain neutrality of his garb. A book, closed, lay on his lap, held by the weight of one hand. His head was supported by the high back of the chair, his face like a mask carved from stone.

Hard, the man had said, and she could see why. The face, the shape of the body, the hand on the book—all gave the impression of strength. Then she realized that he wasn't asleep at all but merely resting. A man conserving his energy, waiting, wrapping himself in a web of isolation. A disappointment to those who had come to stare.

"A killer!" The woman at her side hissed to her

companion, voice low as if afraid the quarry would hear. "He was charged with murder—I had it from a friend in the prosecutor's office. A woman. His mistress. He cut her throat."

"There was doubt."

"But—"

"The evidence was against him, true, but still there was doubt." The man was emphatic. "That's why he was given the chance to volunteer for quarry."

"He could escape!"

"I doubt it. A score of the best will be after him. Nitscke, Sparkissian, Ivanova—Indart has offered ten thousand for a place should he lose out on the draw. You're looking at a dead man, my dear. He hasn't a chance."

That prophecy she would help make come true.

Karlene stepped closer to the glass, curious as to the book, the reason why he should have chosen to read. A religious work of some kind, she guessed, one filled with messages of comfort. As her hand touched the pane Dumarest opened his eyes. Looking at her, he smiled.

"Karlene?" It was Hagen finally coming to join her. "Are you ready?"

She ignored him, looking at Dumarest. He was no longer smiling but the expression had been unmistakable. Almost as if he had recognized an old friend and had smiled a greeting and then, too late, had recognized his error. But his eyes remained fastened on her and, as he straightened in the chair, the book fell from his lap. Small, old, mottled—if it had a title she couldn't see it.

To Hagen she said, "The woman who was killed—describe her."

"What?" He blinked at the question then obeyed. "Why?"

"Nothing." Their appearances were totally dissimilar so he could not have imagined he was seeing a ghost. Someone else, perhaps? "Tell me how she died."

She frowned as she listened, looking at Dumarest, understanding why there should have been doubt. A brutal act of savage, uncontrollable rage—but the man who was supposed to have done it simply wasn't the type. No one governed by such emotions could have sat calmly reading while death was so close.

Did he realize there was no escape?

That the chance was a gamble? An adventurer certainly; one who had long learned to rely on no one but himself. A man who now had no choice but to play the murderous game others had devised.

"Karlene?" Hagen was growing impatient. "We're behind time, my dear and—" He broke off as a man thrust his way toward them. A hunter and one with a question. "Not now!" Hagen cut him short at the first word.

"But—"

"Later." To Karlene he snapped, "We've a lot to do and not much time to do it in. The raft's waiting. Let's go."

A summons she reluctantly obeyed, lingering, hoping Dumarest would smile again, wishing she were the person for whom he smiled.

* * *

Small things were important if he hoped to survive. With Loffredo's book safely tucked in a pocket of his tunic Dumarest concentrated on the meal before him. It was a good one: meat, wine, rich bread, nourishing pastes. He ate well, his guard nodding approval.

"Good. You've got sense. A quarry needs all the energy he can get. I know. I've been out there."

"As quarry?"

"A hunter. A real one. I was after pelts and they don't come easy. Finally I went too far and stayed too long. When I got back they took off most of a leg." The guard slammed his hand against the prosthesis he wore. "The cold," he explained. "Frostbite and gangrene. It finished me as a hunter and I was lucky to be taken on as a guard."

Dumarest said, "Tell me about the others. Quarries, I mean."

"Fools, most of them. They picked at their food as if it would poison them. Some spent half the night praying when they should have been getting their rest. A waste—if they hoped for a miracle they didn't get it. Some used their heads and a few even managed to make it. Not many and not recently, but it can be done."

"How?"

"Luck. Skill. Hell, if I knew for certain I'd volunteer myself." The guard looked at the table, the remains of the meal. The wine was untouched. "Finished?"

"I've had all I want." Dumarest gestured at the wine. "It's yours if you can use it."

"Well—"

"Go ahead. Drink to my success." He waited until the guard had obliged. "Can you tell me anything about what's out there?"

His public ordeal was over. Now, at midnight, he had been fed and a cell waited to hold him while he slept. The guard would stay in the room in which he had eaten. One man to keep watch, but there would be others close by. Even if he broke free there was nowhere to go.

Relaxing, Dumarest listened as the man explained what he had to face. Snow, ice, winds which changed the terrain and made maps useless aside from permanent landmarks. Gullies which formed twisting mazes; blind alleys, open spaces devoid of cover. And the cold—always the cold.

"You'll want to rest," warned the guard. "Don't. If you do you'll find it hard to get going again. You'll slip into a doze and when the hunters find you you'll be dead. Keep moving and stay alert." He finished the wine, burped, looked at the empty glass. "I hope you make it."

"So do I."

"You'll get an hour's start before the hunters are loosed and anything goes. Killing is allowed. All you've got to do is to reach home before they catch you."

Home: one of two points, each spelling safety. Get to one and the rewards would be his.

"Money and freedom," said the guard. "And more." His wink was expressive. "You could be in for a nice surprise."

The choice of women eager to try a new experience. Those who would have added their names to the rest. Money too in return for his attentions. Harpies common to the arena, stimulated by the sight of blood and combat—the spectacle of pain and death.

Dumarest said, dryly, "You have to pluck the fruit before you can eat it."

"True, but it's nice to know it's there."

"I'm more interested in you having worked as a hunter." Dumarest was casual. "I've done some hunting myself but never in the conditions you've got here. I guess it's hard to make a living."

"You can say that again." The guard slapped at his artificial leg. "Too damned hard at times. But it can be done. Sometimes you can get a few really good pelts and cash in."

"If you know how," agreed Dumarest. "But how do you learn? Were you taught or did you do it the hard way?"

These questions supplied details and led to others in turn. It wasn't hard to guide the conversation. The guard was eager to talk, pleased at the chance to display his knowledge and gratified at Dumarest's unfeigned interest. It was two hours later when, yawning, he suggested that it was time to sleep.

Locked in his cell, lying supine on the bunk, Dumarest stared up at the ceiling. Reflected light from the other room cast a pearly shimmer on the unbroken surface. A screen on which to cast mental images and he reviewed what he had learned from the guard; the shape of native predators, their habits, their ferocity. An hour after dawn he would be thrown among them.

The shimmer blurred a little as he began to drift into sleep, the mental images fading, merging to blend into a new pattern. One of a face and a cascade of silver hair, skin with a pallor emulating snow. A woman who had reminded him of another now long gone in space and time.

Had she bet on his success?

Would she be watching as the hunters came after him to take his life?

Chapter 4

It promised to be a good day. Later there might be a little wind but now everything was clear, cold, crisp and hard. From her seat in the raft Karlene could see the empty spaces below, the small huddle of men around the hut at the starting point. This time it was close to Elman's Sink, an expanse of rough, undulating terrain. In it a quarry could founder and lose his lead.

"I wish they'd hurry." A woman beside her was petulant in her complaint. "The hour must be up by now."

"Another five minutes." Her companion, a middle-aged man, glanced at his watch. "Look! One of them is impatient!"

A man had broken from the huddle to stride over the snow. A marshal ran after him, signaled for him to return. After some delay the man obeyed.

"Indart," said the woman. "I bet that was Indart. He has a special interest. Well, it shows the marshal's are fair."

And she would think the games were fair. Many would agree with her. A man, running, given a start. Others following, picking up his trail, chasing him as he headed for safety. All would be protected against the cold. All equally armed.

But the quarry would have no electronic heat warming his body, no food, no stimulants, no drugs. He would be wearing eye-catching brown and be plunging into the unknown. One against twenty—how could he hope to survive?

Karlene closed her eyes, seeing again the man in the chair, his opened eyes, his sudden smile. Something had touched her then as it never had before. The feeling had ridden with her in the raft as she had hunted for scent.

Which had made her do what she had done.

"Now!"

The shout jerked open her eyes as, below, the hunters streamed after their quarry. A score of running figures, some too eager, others, more experienced, holding back in this, the initial stage. They scattered as she watched; human dogs searching for the trail, questing over the frozen snow.

"That's it." The woman next to Karlene sighed her disappointment. "I'd hoped to see the quarry. Sometimes you can but this one's out of sight. Why can't they let us follow the games from the air?"

A matter of policy; rafts would follow the quarry

and the hunters would follow the rafts to make an easy kill. It was better to ban the rafts and force those interested to pay for the use of broadcast-action. Even so the skies wouldn't be clear. Scanners would be riding high and they would be thick at certain areas.

Karlene could do nothing about that and she forced herself to relax as the raft headed back toward the city. She had done all she could—the rest was up to the quarry.

Dumarest was in hiding.

He crouched in deep snow; a small cave gouged from the side of a mound, sheltered him from viewers above. He wore rough clothing topped with thermal garments which enfolded his body, legs, feet and head in a thick, quilted material. Gloves protected his hands. He had not been allowed to retain his knife but had been given a spear; a five-foot shaft of wood tipped with a foot of edged and pointed steel.

A weapon which could be used as a probe, a balance, a staff, it emulated the natural weapons of a beast of prey. With it he could kill if faced by a hunter.

It lay beside him as he crouched in the snow, the blade showing him the position of the sun. It was rising in the east; the shrunken ball of a white dwarf star, radiating light but little heat. In three hours it would be at zenith; in eight, night would close over the land. A freezing, bitter darkness which would last for six hours. If a quarry failed to reach a point of safety before then he was reckoned to be dead.

Dumarest moved a little, feeling the numbing

291

bite of the cold. He had rested too long, but to run without a plan of action was to invite certain death. To run east or west? A "home" lay in each direction. If he ran east the rising sun would dazzle the eyes of his pursuers but not for long enough. To run west would be to reveal his dun-colored clothing against the snow. He looked at it, knowing what he had to do. The risk he had to take.

Waiting, he looked at the blade of his spear.

Albrecht was enjoying himself. His first visit to Erkalt and he was thrilling to the game. Luck had drawn him a hunter's place and he tingled to the crispness of the air, the physical exertion which sent blood rushing through heart and brain. He had hunted before and knew how a quarry would act. He would run and keep on running, heading directly for safety, driven by panic and fear as were all hunted things. Bursting his lungs to gain speed and distance then, when exhausted, to sink in a quivering heap to wait final dispatch. Beast or man it was all the same—his real opponents were his fellow hunters.

He looked at them where they had scattered. Algat far to his right with three others with him; they would probably have agreed to work as a team and to share the trophy. To his left Lochner, tall, determined, raced ahead as if speed alone would give him victory. Others. Indart among them, trailing a little as if satisfied to let others do the work of eliminating false trails and deceptive starts. Cunning, men waiting to isolate the true line of flight, conserving their energy for a time of greater need.

A crevasse opened before him and he jumped it, holding his spear high. Another, too wide to jump, into which he descended, following traces which could have been made by running feet. Following it he dropped below the surface and out of sight of any watchers. A white, fur-clad figure almost invisible against the snow.

One which threw a shadow on polished steel.

Dumarest watched as it grew, turning the blade so as to avoid betraying reflections, tensing as the sound of footsteps came close. A soft padding which made it hard to determine true distance. Hard to decide whether or not the man was alone.

A gamble; one man he could take, two he could handle, more and he would be the target of killing spears. A risk he had to take.

Dumarest rose as the footsteps neared the hide. Snow showered from his head and shoulders as he straightened, lunging forward, the butt end of the spear slamming at the head of the figure before him. A blow softened by the thick fur of the hood and Albrecht staggered back, his own spear lifting in defense—but was knocked aside as Dumarest struck again, the blunt end of the shaft driving beneath the hood and impacting the temple.

As the hunter fell, Dumarest looked around, spear at the ready, eyes narrowed as he searched the crevasse, the snow and ice to either side.

Nothing, but speed was essential. He pulled at the fallen man's garments, tearing free the furs and the wide belt holding fat pouches. Stripping off his own thermal garments he donned the furs. The belt followed and he paused, listening, eyes again searching the area. Only then did he dress the unconscious man in his discarded clothing.

Karlene said, firmly, "It was an act of mercy. "He could have left Albrecht to die."

"He did." Hagen was burning with excitement. "Why can't you see that?"

"He could have killed the man."

"Speared him, yes," admitted Hagen. "But that would have soiled the furs with blood. Instead he chose to stun—have you ever seen a man move so fast? I barely saw the blow and the hunter couldn't have stood a chance. Dumarest wanted his furs and supplies and, by God, he got them."

And had left the hunter dressed in a quarry's garb. Only luck had saved him—the hunter running in for the kill had recognized him almost too late. The thrust of his spear, barely diverted, had caught him in the shoulder instead of the chest.

"A decoy," said Hagen. "The attack served a double purpose; while hunting the decoy they allowed him time to escape." He frowned at his maps, his monitors. "Which?" he murmured. "East or West? Are you sure about the node?"

"You know what I told you."

But not all she knew—suspicion, lying dormant, had suddenly flowered after she had seen Dumarest in his prison. Small things: men too eager to talk, hunters intent on private conversation, expressions she recognized from those more keen on winning bets than following a sport.

Inside information—had Hagen found a way to add to his income? Bets as to the result, the time and place? Tips to the hunters as to where the quarry would meet his end?

Suspicions which had caused her to be reticent. She said, "What happens now?"

"Nothing. The game goes on."

"With Dumarest dressed the way he is?"

"There's nothing against it in the rules." Hagen was patient. "Now the hunters know what's happened they can guard against it. Work in groups," he explained. "Stay close together and ready. All Dumarest has gained is a little time."

The time factor diminished as he lunged through snow and over ice. The furs helped, but he had been unable to take the electronically heated undergarment Albrecht had worn and the cold was an almost tangible enemy. It numbed feet and hands, clawed at his face, sucked at his energy. Stumbling, he fell, rolled down a slope, rose to his feet to stagger on. Behind him the betraying traces he had left showed like gashes on the smooth landscape.

As every footstep he took showed the path of his progress.

Only the wind could cover his trail and, with the wind, would come the blizzards, the freezing chill of incipient night.

And the hunters were close.

"There!" Indart pointed with his spear at the straggling line of footsteps. "Some of you follow. I'll cut ahead to wait before Easthome." He snarled at an objection. "To hell with the trophy—I want the man!"

He lunged ahead before any could argue, four at his heels, following a man they could trust. Others, less influenced, moved on their own paths, some toward the other point of safety, the rest following the trail. If they could move no faster than Dumarest they would never catch him but it was easier to follow a path than to make one. Given time they would spot the hurrying figure. None had any doubt as to what would happen when they did.

Dumarest shared their conviction.

He had halted to examine the contents of the pouches, eating the food he found there, taking some of the stimulants they contained. The place he was heading for was marked by a beacon but first he had to get close enough to spot it. The sun was now well past zenith and the snow crackled beneath his feet. Clouds now flecked the sky and he studied them as he checked time and distance. Already the hunt had lasted longer than usual; he had deliberately taken a winding route.

Now he turned and moved in a direct line along the path of a gulley, rising to slip into a crater-like pit, rising again to lope along a ridge.

His movement was spotted and he heard the yell behind him as he raced on, exertion making him dangerously warm. Sweat would soak his clothing, would freeze, would cover him with a film of ice. Yet to delay would be to take too big a gamble.

Above him, floating high, drifted the eyes of watching scanners.

He ignored them, watching the sky, the gathering cloud. The sun grew darker, shadows thick over the azure-tinted snow. Dark patches into which his own shadow merged and blurred and, suddenly, disappeared.

"Gone!" Hagen shook his head. "Thorn? Any sign?"

"None."

"What is it?" Karlene had insisted on joining Hagen at the monitors. "What's happened?"

"Dumarest's vanished. At least we can't spot him. Damn!" The hunters were close, coming in for the kill, but without a quarry they would look stupid. As would his broadcast. "Thorn? Get in close. Use infra-red. We've got to locate him."

"No!" Karlene shouted her objection. "That isn't our job. Do it and I'll report you!" .

"Damn you, woman, I'll—" He saw her face, read her determination. Swallowing his anger he said, mildly, "We need it for the broadcast. It'll make no difference to the game but it makes a hell of a difference to the entertainment value of what we put out. Surely you can see that?"

"Do it and this is the last time we work together. I mean that!"

A threat he recognized. Turning to the monitors he said, "All right, Thorn. Leave it for now. Concentrate on the node."

Dumarest had gone to ground, burrowing into the snow, kicking it after him so as to block the entrance to the passage he was now making. Inching forward with twisting wriggles of his body, compacting the snow around him as if he

297

had been a worm. Moving silently, invisibly as the guard had told him hunters on Erkalt had to do to reach a nest of perlats. The cold was a burning shroud around his body, the air limited so that his lungs panted for oxygen, the exertion sapping his reserves, but he kept on, the spear dragging behind him.

Halting he moved it forward, thrust it ahead, used it as a probe. It touched something hard and he moved to one side. A boulder, a long-buried mass of rock or a somnolent predator—all things he wanted to avoid. Instinct guided his direction; a wavering half-circle which should take him back far from where he had dived into the snow. Behind it and the hunters who even now could be probing at it with their spears.

He saw them as he cautiously thrust his head through the snow. A tight cluster with others standing closer to him, all looking at the place where he had entered the mound.

"Anything?" One called out to those busy with their spears. "Did you get the swine?"

"Don't kill him if you find him," said another. "Let's make him pay for what he did to Albrecht."

"Indart wants him."

"Too bad. He should be here." A figure thrust his spear into the snow. One humped and monstrous in his furs. Wind caught and lifted the crest of his hood. "Come on the rest of you. Let's dig him out."

The wind gusted as Dumarest eased himself from the mound. Rising he blended with the background, white, furred, indistinguishable from the others. Thrusting with his spear, trampling the snow, he masked the signs of his egress.

"Gone!" The big hunter snarled his anger. "He's gone!"

"How?" Another straightened and looked around. "If he's not here then where is he?"

A question answered as soon as someone thought to count heads. Dumarest moved forward, stabbing at the snow, probing to find the mass he had avoided. Rock or stone would be of no help but the luck which seemed to have deserted him could have returned.

"Here!" He called out, voice muffled, one arm waving. "There's something down here!"

He moved aside as others came to probe with their spears. One grunted as his tip found something more solid than frozen snow. Grunted again as he thrust harder, the grunt turning into a shout as, beneath him, the snow erupted in a burst of savage fury.

A beast half as large again as a man. One with thick, matted fur covering inches of fat. The limbs were clawed, the jaw filled with savage teeth, the short tail tipped with spines. A predator woken from somnolence by the prick of spears. Enraged and seeking blood.

A hunter screamed as closing jaws shattered the bone of his leg. Screamed again as the tail dashed the brains from his splintered skull. Another, foolishly courageous, tried to fight. A paw knocked the spear from his hand, returned to tear the hood from his head, the flesh from his face. Blinded, shrieking, he died as a blow snapped his spine.

The rest began to run, two falling beneath the predator, another stumbling to sprawl on the ground as Dumarest thrust the shaft of his spear between his legs. Bait for the beast should it come after him; one opponent the less to worry about if it did not.

The wind rose a little as he raced on, stinging particles filling the air, blinding, confusing his sense of direction. In the distance he could hear shouts as a hunter tried to gather the rest to form a mutual protection. He moved away from the sound, halted, waited until the wind fell and the air grew clearer. The sun was low now and he moved on, away from it, relaxing as, far ahead, he saw a winking glow.

The light of the beacon which spelled safety.

Men rose from the snow as he neared the hut on which the beacon was mounted.

He slowed as he saw them; hunters lying in wait, now closing in for the kill. Three of them and there could be more. His back prickled to the warning of danger and he guessed others were behind him.

Blood spilled by the awakened predator had stained his furs and Dumarest staggered, limping, a man wounded and in pain. He halted as the others came close, one hand lifting to gesture at his rear.

"A beast," he gasped. "It came out of the snow. Killed the quarry and got two others. We scattered. I was hurt but—"

"Your name?"

"Ellman." Dumarest muffled the sound but knew better than to hesitate. "Brek Ellman."

A gamble—one he lost.

"Liar!" The hunter lifted his spear. "He sold his place to me!"

Dumarest dropped, the thrown spear lancing above his head, turning, rising to meet a furred shape rushing at him from his rear. Wood made a harsh, cracking noise as he parried the other's thrust, his own blade darting forward to penetrate the open hood, the flesh beneath. As the man fell, screaming and clutching at his face, Dumarest snatched up the fallen spear, hurled it at another hunter, followed it with a savage lunge. One which penetrated fur, hit metal, the point glancing upward. Dumarest continued the motion, coming close, feeling the cold burn of steel as a blade gashed his side.

As the man tried to strike again Dumarest ripped the hood from his face, jerked free his spear, sent the blade deep into the throat.

As carmine gushed to fill the air with a ruby rain he turned to face the rest.

Three of them, two closer than they were before. One had thrown his spear and now, weaponless, backed away. He would try to rearm himself but, for the moment, could be ignored. The others meant to kill.

Dumarest acted while they were still cautiously advancing. The wound in his side was leaking blood and the cold was a mortal enemy. To wait too long was to waste his strength and he had none to spare. He stooped, snatched up the dead man's spear, ran forward with one in each hand.

The hunter nearest to him backed, holding up his weapon. A man afraid; quarry should be helpless, cringing, easy to kill. A hunter's sacrifice dispatched at a safe distance with bullet or laser-burn. Now he faced a man, hurt, stained with blood, armed as well as himself, intent on taking his life. Too late he realized that he had to fight to save it. Fight and win. He decided to run and died as steel found his heart.

As the unarmed man died as Dumarest threw his other spear; receiving the same mercy as he would have given.

"Fast." Carl Indart threw back his hood. "Fast but a fool. You've disarmed yourself."

He stepped closer, feeling safe against an unarmed man, his face ugly with a gloating satisfaction. A man confident of victory. One who felt the need to talk.

"You're good," he said. "I knew it from the first. What you did to Albrecht proved it. But, as good as you are, I'm better. This proves it." He lifted his spear. "Steel against flesh—what odds would you give on your survival?"

Dumarest said, "You killed Claire Hashein. Why?"

"Does it matter?"

"To me, yes. Was it orders or—"

"No one gives me orders!" Rage flashed like a storm over Indart's face. "No one!"

"Who sent you after me? The Cyclan?" Dumarest read the answer in the shift of the other's eyes. "You fool. Didn't they tell you they wanted me alive?"

Talk to distract as he eased forward. Words which stung and diverted the hunter's attention. Made him forget the speed on which he had com-

mented. Even so, native caution made him wary.
Steel shimmered as he moved the spear in his
hands.

Shimmered and flashed as Dumarest lunged.

He felt the kiss of it as it brushed his cheek,
the burn as it sliced through fur to hit his shoulder then the shaft was in his hand, the fingers of
his other stiffened, stabbing at Indart's throat,
hitting the chin as the hunter lowered his head.
A wasted blow, followed by another to the eyes,
hitting the brows, the heel of the palm following
to smash against the temple.

As Indart fell Dumarest jerked the spear from
his hand, twisted it, thrust the tip of the blade
beneath his chin as together they hit the snow.

"Talk, you bastard! Talk!"

"Go to hell!"

Indart was stubborn to the last. Lifting his
hands, his arms to rest above his head, writhing
as the steel drove into his throat. Dying as the
woman had died—but slowly, slowly.

Chapter 5

Hagen stormed his fury. "You lied! You cheated! You made me look a fool! A finish like that and I missed it! How could you be so wrong?"

Karlene watched as he paced the floor, hands clenched, mouth cruel in his anger. A man who had hinted at his love for her now betraying his true motives.

She said, "You know I can never be certain. I've told you that again and again. I scent a node but time is a variable. The one to the west might happen next week or within the next few days." Or never; she had lied as to the scent. Deliberately she let anger tinge her voice. "You demand too much. I gave you the beast-killing. You had scanners set for Albrecht's death."

"Trivialities." With an effort he calmed himself. "Good but not enough—to those who follow the games the end is all-important. I was sure it

304

would happen to the west. I had Thorn set up the scanners. I even told—" He broke off, shaking his head. He had almost said too much. "Five dead," he moaned. "The quarry victorious. And I missed it."

"You had one scanner, surely?"

"One," he admitted. "But the coverage was poor." And would continue to be so without her help. A consideration which smothered his diminishing rage. A mistake, it had to be that, but there would be other opportunities. Smiling, lifting his hands toward her, he said, "Forgive me, my dear. I know you did your best. Blame the artist in me—an opportunity to record a finish like that comes but once in a lifetime."

The artist in him and the greed she could recognize. The tapes he wouldn't be able to sell and the money he had to return to the hunters who, trusting him, had loped to the west. Money in bets and money in blood—God, how had she been so blind?

"You look tense, my dear." His concern was as false as his smile. "You need to relax. A hot bath, perhaps? A massage? Some steam?"

"No," she said. "I'm going downstairs."

The cheers were over, the congratulations, but the party would last until dawn. Dumarest, neat in his normal clothing, his wounds dressed, lifted the glass in his hand as she entered the room in which he held court.

"My lady!" He sipped and added, "It is a pleasure to see you again. How may I know you?"

She smiled at the formal mode of address. "My name? Karlene."

305

"Just that?"

"Karlene vol Diajiro. Karlene will do." As he handed her a glass of wine she said, "Do I remind you of someone?"

"Why do you ask?"

"You smiled when you first saw me as if—well, it doesn't matter. But I was curious. May I add my congratulations to the rest? If anyone deserved to win the trophy it was you. I assume you are a skilled hunter? None other would have stood a chance. A fighter too, no doubt, it took skill to dispatch those men as you did."

Small talk, flattery, empty words to fill out silence. The ritual used by strangers when meeting other strangers. She felt irritated at herself for emulating the harpies clustered around; painted matrons eager to taste a new delight, others eager to boast of having conquered the conqueror. Why was she acting so awkwardly? A young girl meeting her first man could not have been worse.

Dumarest said, "I had help."

"What?" She blinked then realized he was answering her babble. A man discerning as well as polite. "Help? From whom?"

From those she had never known and would never meet; men who had taught him the basic elements of survival, women who had taught him how to read the unspoken messages carried in gestures and eyes. Others closer to the present; Vellani, the guard, herself.

She shook her head as he mentioned it. "Me? No, you must be mistaken."

306

"Of course." Dumarest didn't press the point. "Would you care to sit?"

She was tall, her head almost level with his own as he guided her from the room, her flesh cool beneath his hand. Outside a niche held a table and three chairs. Seating her, Dumarest removed the extra chair, setting it well to one side before taking the other. As he settled, a man came bustling toward him, a bottle in his hand.

"Earl! You'll share a drink with me?"

"Not now."

"But—" The man broke off as he saw Dumarest's expression. "I—well, at least accept the wine."

A woman was less discreet.

"Earl, you have my room number. Don't forget it. I'll be expecting you—don't keep me waiting."

As she left, Karlene said, dryly, "To the victor the spoils. I hope you're enjoying them."

"I'm enjoying this." His gesture took in the table, the seclusion, herself. "You were right when you thought you reminded me of someone. You do." He poured wine for them both. "Someone who died a long time ago. I drink to her memory."

"Her name?"

"Derai."

"To Derai!" She sipped and then, following a sudden impulse, drained the glass. "The dead should not be stinted."

"No."

"Nor ever forgotten." Her hand shook a little as she poured herself more wine. "What are we if none remember us when we are gone? Less than the wind. Less than the rain, the sea, the fume of spray. Less than the shift of sand. Nothingness lost on the fabric of time. All ghosts need an anchor."

Friends, a family, children, those who cared. Looking at her, Dumarest saw a lonely woman— haunted by the fear of death.

He said, "You have a way with words. Are you a poet?"

"No, just someone who likes old things. As you do." She smiled at his puzzlement. "The book," she said. "The one you were reading before the game. It looked very old. Did it give you comfort?"

"This?" He took it from his pocket and placed it in her hand. "I found it more a puzzle than anything else. Can you make sense of it?"

She riffled the pages, frowning, shaking her head as she tried to decipher the script.

"It's so faded. Chemicals could restore much of the writing and there are other techniques which could help. Computer analysis," she explained. "Light refraction from the pages—pressure of the stylo would have left traces even though the ink may have vanished. Machines could scan and reconstruct each page to its original content. Later wear could be eliminated." She turned more pages. "This seems to be a personal notebook. I had one when a child. I used to jot down all manner of things: names, places of interest, things I had done. Income and outlay, equations, poetry, all kinds of things. Even secrets." She laughed and reached for her wine. "How petty they seem now."

"The price we pay for growing up. What we thought were gems become flecks of ice. Castles in the sky turn into clouds. The magic in the hills becomes empty space. The secret we thought our own becomes shared by all."

"And childhood dies—as all things must die." She shivered as if with cold and drank some wine. "Why does it have to be like that?"

"Perhaps because we are in hell," said Dumarest. "What better name to give a universe in which everything lives by devouring everything else? Death is the way of life. Only the strong can hope to survive."

"For what? To die?" She sipped again at the wine, feeling suddenly depressed, overwhelmed by the futility of existence. The book moved in her hand and she opened it at random, studying a page with simulated interest. Light, slanting at an angle, enhanced faded script. " 'Earth,' " she said. " 'Up to Heaven's'—something—'door. You gaze'—" Irritably she shook her head. "I can't make it out."

"Try!" Dumarest controlled his impatience. "Please try," he said more gently. "Do what you can."

The wine quivered in the glass he held, small vibrations of nerve and muscle amplified to register in dancing patterns of light. He set it down as the woman frowned at the book.

"It's a poem of some kind. A quatrain, I think. That's a stanza of four lines. You know about poetry?"

"What does it say?"

"The first line is illegible but it must end in a word to rhyme with the last word in the second. My guess is that it goes one-two-four. The third line—"

"What does it say!"

"Give me a minute." She dabbed a scrap of fabric in the wine, wet the page, held it up so as to let the light shine through it. "That's better. Listen." Her voice deepened a little. " 'But if in vain down on the stubborn floor. Of Earth and up to Heaven's unopening door. You gaze today while you are you—how then. Tomorrow when you shall be no more.' No, wait!" She lifted a hand as she corrected herself. That last line reads, 'Tomorrow when you shall be you no more.' "

"Is that all?"

"Yes." She sensed his disappointment. "It would look better set out in lines. It's probably something the owner of the book copied from somewhere. Earth," she mused. "Earth."

He waited for her to say more; to tell him Earth was just a legendary world along with Bonanza and Jackpot, Lucky Strike and El Dorado and Eden and a dozen others. Planets waiting to be found and holding unimaginable treasure. Myths which held a bright but empty allure.

Instead she said, wistfully, "Earth—it has a nice sound. Is there really such a world?"

"Yes." He added, bluntly, "I was born on it. I left it when I was young."

He had been little more than a child, stowing away on a ship, being found, the captain merciful; allowing him to work instead of evicting him as was his right. Together they had delved deeper and deeper into the galaxy when, the captain dead, he had been left to fend for himself on strange worlds beneath alien suns. Regions where

310

the very name of his home world had become a legend, the coordinates nowhere to be found.

"You're lost," said Karlene, understanding. "You want to go home. That is why the book is so important to you. You think it might hold the answer you want."

"The coordinates. Yes."

"Did you really come from Earth?" She leaned toward him, her eyes searching his face. "Would you swear to it? Really swear to it?" As he nodded she added, "This is serious, Earl. It could mean your life."

"I've no need to lie." He caught her wrist, his fingers hard on the pallid flesh. "What do you know?"

"Tomorrow," she said. "I'll tell you tomorrow—after we've deciphered the book."

Cyber Clarge heard the blast of the sirens and lifted his head from the papers he was studying. A curfew? No, it was barely noon and, on Erkalt, sirens did not warn of impending night. A storm? A probability of high order but he was safe within the hotel. A fire, perhaps? Some other catastrophe?

His acolyte brought the answer.

"Master." He bowed as he entered the room. "A matter of local interest. The winds are rising and will establish a pattern yielding unusual phenomena. The sirens are to herald the entertainment."

The window was large, set high in the building, giving a good view of the city and the area beyond. To the south smoke seemed to be rising from the ground, writhing, twisting as it was caught by the winds which buffeted each other and created churning vortexes. Trapped in the blast the snow soared high in a shimmering panorama which filled the air with a dancing chiaroscuro.

Most found it beautiful. Clarge did not.

Against the window he resembled a flame; the scarlet of his robe warm against the snow outside, the great seal of the Cyclan gleaming on his breast. He was tall, thin, his body a functional machine devoid of fat and excess tissue. His face, framed by the thrown-back cowl, held the lineaments of a skull. One in which his eyes burned with a chilling determination.

A man devoid of artistic appreciation; looking at the external spectacle he could see only the waste of natural resources. The winds which blustered so fiercely should be tamed, their energy directed toward the generation of power with which to transform Erkalt into a useful world.

"Master. The information you requested is on the desk."

"Hagen?"

"Has been notified of your wish to see him."

And would report at the earliest opportunity if he was wise. The reputation of the Cyclan was such as to gain them respectful obedience; if he hoped to survive in business or expand his field of operations the entrepreneur would know he had to cooperate to the full. In the meantime other details could be attended to.

A gesture and Clarge was alone, the acolyte, bowing, leaving the room. One unnecessarily ornate with its ornaments and decorations, rugs and soft furnishings, but Clarge would not order their removal. Efficiency was not a matter of trivia but of the skillful application of resources.

Turning from the window the cyber returned to his desk. The papers he had been studying were laid out in neat array, those the acolyte had brought set in a pile to one side. Reports, data, schedules, statements—details of the past all set in concrete form. Studying them had given the cyber one of the only two feelings he could experience; not the glow of mental achievement but the cortical bitterness of failure.

The bait had been set, the trap sprung—yet again Dumarest had escaped.

How?

The details were in the reports but they begged the question. Luck, obviously, and luck of a peculiar kind. The combination of fortuitous circumstances which resulted in a favorable conclusion— a paraphysical talent which had saved Dumarest on too many occasions. Small things: the breaking of equipment, an illness, a sudden whim on the part of someone totally unconnected with the original scheme. Details which, apparently unaccountably, defeated the main purpose.

This time it had been jealousy.

An emotion Clarge would never experience as he would never know the impact of love or hate, fear or anger. Harsh training and an operation on the thalamus had robbed him of the capacity of emotion, turning him into a robot of flesh and blood, dedicated to the pursuit of logic and reason.

The plan should have worked. Instead it had failed.

The woman, Claire Hashein, selected because of her previous association with Dumarest. The man, Carl Indart, a trained hunter who had to do little but take and hold Dumarest should the need arise. A simple task; legs burned with a laser would have prevented movement. Drugs could have robbed Dumarest of consciousness. Guile could have distracted him until the ship bearing help could have arrived. His ship, his help, the cold decision made by a servant of the Cyclan.

Now he had nothing to report but failure.

Clarge moved a paper, studied another, eyes scanning, brain absorbing the information it contained, assessing it, combining it with other facts, earlier data. Details on which he could base an extrapolation of probable events. The talent of a cyber; the ability to predict the outcome of any situation once in possession of the facts.

"Master?" The acolyte's face showed on the screen of the intercom. "The man Hagen has reported."

"Have him wait."

More papers, further assessment—to operate on speculation and guesswork was unthinkable. Why had the prosecutor allowed Dumarest to volunteer for quarry? The case against him had been incontrovertible and murderers were not normally given such a chance. A need to enhance the games? The advocate's influence? Why hadn't Indart moved to prevent it?

A touch on a button and a screen flared to life on the projector at his side. It was blurred, unsteady, but the figures were plain. Dumarest and

Indart, the latter busy with words. Clarge watched as the scene ended, replayed it, darkened the screen as he sat assessing what the record had yielded.

A man obsessed, who had a monstrous ego—whoever had chosen Indart had been unwise and would pay the penalty for his negligence. As Hagen would pay for knowing more than he should. Had Dumarest guessed the scene was being recorded? Had his question as to the Cyclan been as superficial as it seemed? And the reminder that he was only valuable to the Cyclan if alive—to whom had that been directed?

Certainly Hagen hoped to gain from it.

"I came as fast as I could," he said after the acolyte had admitted him into the cyber's presence. "If there is anything I can do to help just let me know. I want to help—that's why I sent you the recording. Just the part of it I thought would be of interest." Pausing he added, "I know how generous the Cyclan can be."

Clarge said, "Tell me of the woman."

"The one who was murdered? I didn't really know her but—" He broke off, quick with an apology. "I'm sorry. You mean Karlene, don't you? Karlene vol Diajiro. Right?"

"Tell me about her."

"She was a help. Not much of one but she had the looks and the poise and it made it easier to get close to prospects and to make contacts. Window-dressing, mainly. I felt sorry for her. I even offered to take care of her but she didn't take to the idea. Now she's gone."

"Is that all?"

315

Clarge didn't alter his tone. It remained the same, level modulation devoid of all irritating factors but, as Hagen was about to nod, he felt the impact of the deep-set eyes. A stare which made him feel as if he was transparent and he shifted uneasily in his chair. To lie to the Cyclan was to ask for trouble. To strike a cyber was to commit suicide.

He said, "Not quite. I'll be honest with you. She has a talent. It's pretty wild but I found it useful. She can scent the approach of death." He elaborated the explanation, ending, "That's why she was really useful to me. The rest of it, too, but once we had located a death-node I could really go to town."

"Then why—"

"She cheated!" Hagen's anger spilled over. "The bitch cheated then ran out on me. Just when things were going well and were going to get better. She let me down. Took what she had and left. No warning. Nothing. No chance for me to arrange things. She just ran off with that quarry."

"Dumarest?"

"Who else?"

"You are certain?" Clarge pressed the point. "Absolutely certain?"

Hagen wasn't, he couldn't be, but he lacked the cyber's analytical mind. The pair had vanished and, as far as he knew, had shipped out. That was an assumption, but Clarge estimated it to be correct. He glanced at the reports the acolyte had left; details of ships and their complements, but none carried the names of either the woman or Dumarest. An elementary precaution.

316

"She sold her furs," said Hagen. "I checked. Took her jewels and all the money she had. Even borrowed on my credit and from my crew. They expect me to pay them. I'll have to see them square even if I have to sell that recording to do it." A hint, one he clumsily emphasized. "It's all I have, you understand. All I've got new."

Clarge said, "Tell me more about the woman. Where did you meet her? When? On which worlds have you operated? Has she any idiosyncrasies? Particular likes or dislikes? Allergies? Habits?" He listened then summoned the acolyte to show his visitor out.

Hagen lingered at the door. "You'll think about my problems? I mean—"

"You will be rewarded."

He, his crew, all who had knowledge of the recording, but it would be a reward they would not appreciate. An accident, an infection, sudden and unexpected death—the Cyclan settled its bills in more ways than one.

Alone Clarge dismissed the matter from his mind as he concentrated on things of greater importance. The woman had accumulated money, probably on Dumarest's advice, and he had cash of his own now augmented by that won with the trophy. Money enough and to spare, money to waste, to burn. Certainly enough to have left false trails.

Had they traveled together or apart?

On which ship?

Heading where?

Questions the cyber pondered as he sat at the desk oblivious to the snow which now hurtled against the window. The probability that they were traveling together was high, in the region of eighty-nine percent; she would not have left without him and would have seen no point in a later rendezvous. On which vessel? Three had left before his own ship had landed; two close together; the last only recently. Dumarest would not have waited. The *Tsuchida* or the *Gegishi*? Hagen had contacted the woman on Ryonsuke and the *Gegishi* was headed toward that sector of space.

Would Dumarest abandon the woman once they had landed?

A probability of high order—but his lead was small, his destination known and he could not be certain he was being followed. Even when dying, Indart had held his tongue.

The woman, Clarge decided. Find the woman and Dumarest would be close.

There was fire beneath the ice; a burning, hungry demand which left them both exhausted. He had first known such on Erkalt, then on the vessel in which they had traveled, now again here on Oetzer. Rising, Dumarest looked down at her where she sprawled on the bed. Even in sleep Karlene was beautiful, the planes of her face bearing an odd, detached serenity, enhanced by her pallor, the gleaming mass of her hair.

Silver repeated on her nails, her lashes, the intricate tattoo above her left breast. A design almost invisible against the flesh, revealed in gleams and shimmers when she moved and light reflected from the metallic ink buried beneath her skin. The pattern of a flower; slender petals set around a circular center, the whole adorned with curlicues—twelve petals and a circular area quartered by two crossed lines.

A symbol Dumarest had seen before.

"Darling!" She woke as he touched the tattoo. "I've had the most wonderful dream."

"Of home?"

"Of you." Her arms rose to embrace him, pulled him close. "Darling—hold me!"

She sighed contentedly as he obeyed, cradling her head on his shoulder, naked flesh glowing in the diffused sunlight beyond the window of their room. The chamber was large, set with a wide bed and adorned with objects of price. One soft with luxury, scented with delicate odors from cooled and perfumed air that wafted through fretted grills.

The Hotel Brisse was noted for its comfort.

He said, "It's time I was moving. Do you want to sleep longer or—?"

"I'll join you in the shower."

She stood before him beneath the aromatic spray, her fingers touching his torso, following the thin lines of old scars. Brands earned in a hard school where to be slow or weak was to be dead.

"Did it hurt, Earl? When these were made, I mean."

"Did that?" He touched her tattoo.

"I don't know. I can't remember." As before, she dismissed the subject. "But a needle isn't a knife and doesn't cut as deep." Her fingers lin-

319

gered on his body. "Darling, you must never fight again. Promise me."

"How can I do that?"

Honesty she had learned to admire. Hagen, a score of others she had known would have given the promise without hesitation; lying, treating her like a child. Now, she realized, she was acting like one. Did love always make a woman so stupid?

"I was thinking of the arena." Her hand fell from his chest as she changed the subject. "What are your plans? The book?"

Preoccupied, he didn't answer, prepared himself to go out—alone.

There had been no time to use facilities on Erkalt to decipher the text and further study had yielded little. The man in the laboratory where Dumarest had taken the book the previous day smiled a greeting as he entered.

"My friend! An early bird, I see."

"Did you do as I asked?"

"Of course." The promise of double pay had stimulated his energies. "You could probably get better resolution with more sophisticated equipment but I doubt if it would be worth it. Here." He rested the book on the counter and added a pile of individual sheets. "The pages of the book lacked numbers but I took the liberty of adding them so as to make it easier for you to compare the resolutions with the originals. The marks can be erased quite simply if you wish."

"It isn't important." Dumarest riffled the sheets. The script, enlarged, was far clearer than that in the book. In places certain words or passages were tinted red. "This?"

"The computer simulation of what was most probably present in the original form." The man swept up the money Dumarest set before him. "Thank you, sir. Glad to have been of service."

The Hotel Brisse lay to the north. Dumarest headed south, after leaving the laboratory, following a boulevard flanked with shops, taverns, casinos, restaurants. He halted at one, taking an ouside table, a brightly hued umbrella giving protection from the sun. A waiter served coffee and cakes, both of which he ignored as he studied those passing by.

One, a woman, young, her skirt slit to the hip, mirror dust on eyelids and lips, her blouse carelessly open so as to reveal the curves beneath, slowed, smiling as she saw the book on the table, the papers set to one side.

"Hi there!" She halted at Dumarest's side. "A fine day for reading."

"And walking." She didn't take the hint. "You're wasting your time."

"It's my time. Are you a student?"

"No."

"I didn't think so. You don't look the type. Lonely, perhaps?" She sighed as he shook his head. "A shame. Well, no harm in trying." Boldly she helped herself to a cake. Took another as he made no objection. "It's a hell of a life when you can't compete with a book."

He could see the book had a dangerous potential. Had it been set as bait? The tale of Loffredo a lure to draw him to Erkalt where Claire Hashein and Indart had been waiting? A trap the hunter's rage had aborted—if he had not yielded to jealous fury what would have happened? Dumarest could guess; delay piled on delay giving the Cyclan time to move in. Even had he been sentenced to slave labor no harm would have been done as far as his pursuers were concerned. They could have easily bought his indenture.

Karlene?

Dumarest reached for the papers and found the one he wanted; the one from which she had read. Now the quatrain was clear.

> But if in vain, down on the stubborn floor
> Of Earth, and up to Heaven's unopening Door
> You gaze Today, while You are You—how
> then Tomorrow, when You shall be You no
> more?

Earth—the one word sure to attract his attention. The tattoo she wore—the crossed circle was the astronomical sign of Earth. The hint that she knew of someone who could help him—if he was genuine.

Another trap?

The Cyclan would spare no trouble or expense to recover the secret he possessed, for it would enable them to dominate the known galaxy. It would be logical to pile trap on trap so that, if one failed, another would hold him fast. The Cyclan were masters of logic. They must know of his determination to find the world of his birth.

Was Karlene an agent of the Cyclan?

Dumarest rose and walked farther south to where the landing field sprawled well beyond the edge of town. Oetzer was a busy world and the field was heavy with ships. The air thrummed to the shouts of handlers, yells of porters, the hum of machines loading and unloading vessels eager to return to space. Even as he watched, a siren cut across the babble, and a ship, limned in the blue cocoon of its Erhaft Field, lifted to vanish into the sky.

He could have been on it. He could leave with any ship on the field, and, like them, he would vanish into the sky. Safe from Karlene and any who might be using her.

Safe to do what?

He looked at the field, the ships, seeing not the sleek or battered hulls, but the long, long years of endless travel and frustrated hope. How many more years must he search? How many more worlds must he visit? How many journeys, dangers, gambles must he face and take? And, if Karlene was what she claimed to be, he would have lost the chance now in his hand.

She could lead him to Earth—or she could lead him to death.

Which would it be?

"Earl!"

He turned, freezing the movement of his hand to the knife in his boot. The scarlet she wore was not a robe but a mantle to protect her skin from the growing savagery of the sun. Soon it would be too hot and all work would stop for the siesta.

"Earl!" She halted before him, panting, the mantle casting a warm glow over the pale face

323

shadowed in its hood. "A coincidence but a happy one. I had word and—"

"Word? From whom?"

"The man I told you about." Karlene smiled her pleasure. "It's all right, my darling. He agrees to help you, providing—but you know about that. So I came to find a ship and book passage."

"You?"

"I've engaged a Hausi. He will get us the best and fastest journey." She gestured at the field, the ships standing wide-spaced on the dirt. "It saves time and it's too hot to go shopping around. With luck we could leave tonight." She stared into his face. "What's the matter? Is something wrong?"

"No." He forced a smile. "Nothing."

"Maybe I should have waited," she said. "But I wanted to please you."

Or to sweep him along in the rush of events, giving him no time to think or plan? In turn, he searched her face, seeing the blank stare of mirrored eyes, his own features reflected in the silver lenses she wore.

He said, "Where are we bound?"

"Driest. That's all I can tell you."

A fact he would have learned as soon as he had boarded the vessel and any name she chose to give would be meaningless. Again he searched her face, seeing his own reflection waver a little, blurring as she blinked, vanishing as she turned her head. A time for decision, of knowing that here, now, was the moment of no return.

"Earl? About the booking—did I do right?"

He nodded. A gamble—but all life was that

324

and he was tired of running, of hiding, of living in dirt and shadows. If Earth was to be found he would find it or die in the attempt.

As the man on Driest would die if he had lied.

Chapter 6

Rauch Ishikari reminded Dumarest of a snake. A tall, slim man, aged, dressed in expensive fabrics which shimmered like scales. His thin, aquiline features bore the stamp of arrogance afforded by position and wealth. His voice, though melodious, bore a trace of cynical mockery. But it was his eyes which dominated the rest: almond slits of enigmatic gray. Set in the creped face they looked like polished shards of stone.

He said, "A final warning, Earl. I have no wish to destroy the innocent."

A chair stood bolted to the floor before the desk behind which he sat. Steel clasps were set in the arms; more on the legs to hold the ankles. The point against which the head would rest was of polished wood. Abruptly it smoked and burst into flame from the invisible beam which ate into the wood. A moment, then the flame was gone, the charred patch a blotch against the rest.

"Lie and the beam will pass through your brain. Are you ready?"

Silently, Dumarest sat in the chair.

He relaxed as the manacles closed to hold him tight. If this was a trap he was in it and there had been no chance to escape. Not from the moment of leaving the vessel when waiting guards had closed in to escort them both to a spired and turreted mansion set high above the town. The palace of a ruler, into which Karlene had vanished leaving him to the ministrations of men more like guards than servants. Then the meeting with Ishikari, the verbal sparring, the abrupt cessation of preliminaries.

Now the manacles, the chair, the laser which, at a touch, would burn out his life.

He said, "You play a hard game, my lord."

"Game? Game? You think this is a game?" Anger edged Ishikari's voice. "If it is you play with your life as the stake!"

"And you?"

Almost he had gone too far and he tensed, watching as the man behind the desk reared, stiffening as if he were a reptile about to strike. There was a long moment during which tiny gleams of light splintered in trembling reflections from the rings he wore, then, as if with an effort, he relaxed.

"I play no game," said Ishikari. "Unless the search for truth be a game. But the path you tread is a dangerous one. Did you tell the woman the truth?"

"About Earth, yes."

"You were born on that world?"

"I was."

"And?"

Ishikari listened as Dumarest went into detail, then fired other questions, probing, inhaling with an audible hiss as Dumarest spoke of the night sky, the moon which looked, when full, like a silver skull. A long time but then it was over, the manacles opening to allow Dumarest to rise. As Dumarest rubbed his wrists his host offered him wine.

"An unusual story," he said, lifting his own glass. "But a true one if the detectors are to be believed. I drink to you, Earl—man of Earth!"

The wine was like blood, thick, rich, slightly warm, traced with a tang of spice and the hint of salt. Dumarest sipped, feeling the liquid cloy on his lips and tongue.

"Earth," mused Ishikari. "A world of mystery. Ask after it and you will be told that it is a legend. A myth. A dream of something which never was. Details bolster that belief; why aren't its coordinates listed in the almanacs? If it is the repository of such enormous wealth why hasn't it yet been found by the expeditions which must have searched for it? Obvious questions but other claims negate them. You know of them?"

The question was like a bullet.

Another test? If so Dumarest passed it. His host nodded as he listened, added his own comments as Dumarest fell silent.

"The mother world from which all men originated—a ridiculous concept when it is remembered how many divergent races inhabit the galaxy. Yellow, white, brown, black—how could one world produce so many different types? We are all one basic race, true, the ability to inter-breed proves that, but—"

"We evolved on widely scattered worlds from the impact of space-borne sperm? Seeds driven by the pressure of light to settle on a multitude of planets? Spores which all produced the same basic type?" Dumarest shrugged and sipped at his wine. "I find the one-world concept easier to swallow."

"As a concept, perhaps, but is it the answer?" Ishikari shook his head in doubt. "What to believe? How to unravel the one thread which will guide us through the maze of legend and myth?"

"I thought you had the answer. Karlene said—"

"She told you that I would help you and I will. Follow me."

He led the way into another chamber, one with a high, vaulted roof set with lambent panes now filled with the dying light of day. Tinted squares which threw a dusty shadow over racks of spools, shelved of moldering volumes, oddly fashioned artifacts. Stray beams glinted on metal, crystal, plastic; things which could have been vases or toys or illustrations of tormented mathematical systems. At the far end rested the screen and controls of a computer.

"It is voice-activated," said Ishikari. "I want you to sit at it and tell it all you know about Earth. Everything, each tiny detail, every small item. That and more. All you have learned in your traveling among the worlds." He added, "It will join other information already in the data banks. The machine will correlate the information, find associations and meaningful relationships. Determine probabilities and yield valuable conclusions."

"The coordinates?"

"Perhaps. It's a possibility."

But not good enough. Dumarest looked around the room, guessing at the guards who must be watching, the weapons which had him as their target. A man of Ishikari's position would never risk his life as he appeared to be doing. Was this pretense to gain trust? To lull suspicions? Yet where was the point; if he was in a trap it could be sprung at any moment.

Casually he moved through the room to a table which stood against a wall. A convoluted abstract stood at one end. On the other rested Loffredo's volume and the enhancement he'd had made.

"You doubt my good faith." Ishikari came to join him. "I took the liberty of copying your papers, and the computer is assessing the detail they contained for anything of relative value. Not proof of my intentions, I admit, but one thing is. Look." He lifted the sheet bearing the quatrain. "Now this."

He lifted a book from where it rested in the shadow of the abstract. It was old, thick, stained with mold and wear. The pages were fretted beneath their protective covering of transparent plastic. Dimmed illuminations shone with the ghosts of silver and gold, ruby and emerald. The script, once thick and black, now sprawled like the gray and tangled web of spiders.

"Look," said Ishikari again, and touched something on the abstract sculpture. Light shone over the book from some source within the convolutions; electronic magic which thickened the script and brightened the hues as if defeating time. "The quatrain. See?" The tip of his finger traced the words. "And here. The word 'Earth' as before." Pages rustled. "Here again, you notice?"

Dumarest said, "What is it?"

"The book? A collection of verse containing pertinent philosophical concepts regarding life and reality." Ishikari riffled the pages. "Life, death and reality. The verse in the book you found shows that. Odd how an itinerant trader could have come by it."

"He could have seen that book." Dumarest gestured to it. "Or one like it."

"A remote possibility. It's more likely he saw it written somewhere. On a wall, perhaps? If so, why?"

Dumarest sensed that he was being led down a path the other had followed before. Spurred to reach a matching conclusion.

"A wall," he said. "But who would write such a verse on a wall unless it was a special place? As a warning? As a concept to bear in mind? A creed, perhaps, or the part of a creed?"

"In which case it surely would have been carved, not written." Ishikari put down the book. "Where would you find such a thing carved on a wall?" He paused, waiting. "A special place," he urged. "You've already mentioned that."

A special place, a carving, a creed. Verses dealing with life, death and reality. Words cut deep into adamantine stone so as to carry their message endlessly through time.

"A church?"

"A temple," corrected Ishikari. "The temple of Cerevox." He add quietly, "I believe it holds the answer we both are seeking."

At dusk Driest became alive with a brash and raucous vitality. Barely had the sun lowered beneath the horizon than lanterns were lit, casting lurid pools of lambent color on pavement and road, the sides of buildings, those thronging the streets and market. Men and women, drinking, laughing, selling produce, skills and, failing all else, themselves.

A crowd in which Dumarest wandered. He had had no trouble in leaving the palace though he was aware of the two men following him at a discreet distance. Guards like ghosts more sensed than seen and he wondered at Ishikari's caution. The bait the man had set was stronger than bars.

"My lords! Ladies! I beg your attention!"

A grating voice accompanied by the clash of metal and Dumarest halted to stare at a peculiar figure. One who wore red, blue, yellow, green—a plethora of vivid hues forming the bizarre depiction of a face. A ragged shape which capered and chanted to the rattle of a sistrum he held in one hand.

"I can dress wounds, treat minor ills, alter a garment. I am adept at massage. I can sing and relate stories to while away the tedium of monotonous hours. I have served as a valet, cook, guard, tutor. I can handle a raft. Hire me and have no regrets."

Next to him stood a vibrant thing which keened; an alien creature from some distant world. It's owner jerked at its leash and, as it reared, snarling, displaying fangs and claws, yelled of its value as a watchdog.

Beyond, a cripple lifted the stump of an arm.

"Lost in the Zhenganian conflict. Supply a prosthesis and I will serve you for a year."

A woman, veiled, silent, the card on her breast telling all she was a bountiful nurse.

Another, young and lissom, who smiled at Dumarest with frank admiration. "My lord? I am trained in the dressing of hair. A seamstress. Hire me for your lady and she will thank you."

He said, "I have no lady."

"Then, perhaps, the greater need of my services. Who else to tend your clothing and give you equanimity of mind?" She stepped a little closer. "Hire me for a month. Test my abilities. A week? A day?" She sighed as he shook his head. "Remember me should you have need."

Dumarest moved on to a plaza where stalls sold refreshments and beggars lay in wait.

"My lord! Give of your charity!"

A man with a face raw with oozing pustles, the orbs of his eyes white with a nacreous film. His bowl remained empty; there were a dozen ways of counterfeiting such sores and the membrane of an egg would emulate true blindness. Another, legless, had better luck. A monk better still.

He stood, his bowl of chipped plastic in his

hand, tall and gaunt in the brown homespun of his robe. His feet were bare but for sandals. His hair, cropped, surmounted a face too old for his years. One with cheeks sunken in deprivation, eyes which stared with compassion at the universe.

"Thank you, brother." He looked at the coins Dumarest had dropped into his begging bowl. "You are generous."

"Your name?"

"Fassar."

"Are you in charge of the Church here?"

"No. Brother Tessio leads us." He added, "Should you wish to ease your heart the church is close to the field."

The usual place but Dumarest had no intention of kneeling beneath the benediction light, of confessing his sins and receiving subjective penance and absolution. Never had he gone through the ritual of a suppliant, not even for the sake of the bread of forgiveness given at its termination. The wafer of concentrate which, to the hungry, was reason enough to feign true remorse.

The monks did not object—each who knelt beneath the benediction light was hypnotically conditioned never to kill. A fair exchange.

Dropping another coin into the bowl he said, "Perhaps you could help me. Cerevox." He repeated the word. "Does it mean anything to you?"

"Cerevox?" The monk thought for a moment, then shook his head. "No."

"Would the others know?"

"I can ask them."

"Please do. Just the monks. I'll ask later at the church."

Dumarest moved on. To one side a stall sold skewers of meat, pasties, spiced bread in flat wedges. It was busy and he passed it then halted at another selling mulled wine. Holding the mug he stood beneath a lantern which bathed him in violet brilliance.

Had Ishikari lied?

If he had he had done it with professional skill. An actor, judging time and emotion, triggering reactive patterns as if he played an organ. Building on Dumarest's natural relief of being freed from the chair and seeing a display of his old things, the talk concerning the computer and then, as if by happy chance, the book and papers and the old volume and the verses it contained.

The temple of Cerevox.

Cerevox?

An odd name but one with a haunting sense of familiarity. Dumarest ran it through his mind; cerevox . . . cerevox . . . cerevox . . . cerevox. Cere. Vox. Cere? Cere?

Erce?

A simple anagram—was that the answer? No, the change made no sense. Ercevox? Vox? Vox?

The monk stood where he had left him. Without preamble Dumarest said, "Vox. The word Vox. What does it mean?"

"I'm not sure. It is very old but, I think, yes, it means voice or voices. I will check if you wish."

"It doesn't matter. And forget the other. Cerevox. Forget it."

Two words, not one, and the simplest of anagrams. Had the meaning intended to be hidden? Or was it a secret known only to those who knew more than most? Earth had more than one name. Terra was another. Erce yet another but with a slightly different connotation. Not just Earth but Mother Earth. And Vox?

Earth voices? No. The voices of Earth? Not that either. What then?

Dumarest halted, mind alight with sudden understanding, careless of the crowd around him, the man who bumped into him and swore then moved quickly away as he saw his expression.

The Cerevox Temple.

The Voice of Mother Earth!

Karlene's room was on an upper floor, the servant who had guided him running, squealing away as the panel burst open beneath his boot.

"Earl!" Karlene turned from where she stood at the side of her bed. Her eyes widened as she saw his face. "Earl! For God's sake! Don't look at me like that!"

She backed as he closed the gap between them, her legs hitting the edge of the bed, her body toppling, hanging suspended as he caught her arms and held her against the pull of gravity. In her eyes he could see the snarling image of his face.

"I want the truth," he snapped. "All of it. What is Ishikari to you?"

"A friend. I—" She gasped as he set her jarringly on her feet, mouth opening with terror as steel shimmered in his hand. "No! Please, no!"

"Talk!" Light shone from the blade as it neared her throat. An empty threat but she couldn't know that. "Tell me about Ishikari!"

"He helped me," she said. "A long time ago now. I was in trouble and he helped me."

"And?"

"What do you mean?"

"Did he send you to Erkalt?" He read the answer. "Why?"

"I had—" She broke off, swallowing. "Please, Earl. You're hurting me."

With the threat of the knife, the fingers which left ugly welts on the delicate pallor of her skin. The threat vanished as the blade slid into his boot. The welts would take longer.

He said, less harshly, "He gave you instructions, right? And you can't tell me about them. But you can tell me if you left instructions with the Hausi on Oetzer to use hybeam to radio ahead so that we would be met. Did you?" Her nod was an admission. "Did you tell him to radio anyone else? The Cyclan?"

"No. No, Earl, I swear it!"

"What do you know of the temple?" He saw the sudden laxness of her face. "Damn it, girl! I won't hurt you. Just tell me about Cerevox."

From behind him Rauch Ishikari said, "You're wasting your time, Earl. She can't."

He stood within the room, guards flanking him at the rear, the snouts of their weapons ready to lower a barrier of destruction from either side.

Dumarest said, "If they fire they will kill the woman. You wouldn't want that."

"Would you?"

"No."

"Then we are agreed." Ishikari stepped to one side his hand gesturing toward the door. "I can find us a better place in which to talk. If you will precede me?"

A matter in which he had no choice; beneath the empty courtesy lay the cold determination of steel. The passage was empty, a door standing open a short way down. The room held a table, chairs, ornaments, a flagon of wine and glasses on a tray. Wine which could have been drugged. Dumarest shook his head as Ishikari gestured for him to help himself.

"I'd rather talk."

"About Karlene? What do you want to know." Before Dumarest could begin Ishikari lifted a hand. "First let me explain something. There are certain things she cannot talk about. I mean that literally. As a child she was conditioned never to reveal certain things about herself. You have seen her tattoo? Asked her about it? She couldn't answer you. Couldn't remember. Am I correct?"

"Perhaps. She dodged the question."

"As she did when you asked her about the temple?" Ishikari stepped to the flagon and helped himself to wine. Lowering his glass he said, "She *cannot* answer that question. Demand a reply and she will escape into fugue."

A loss of memory in which she left reality. A safeguard against her betraying secrets—but there were ways to break such conditioning. Had Ishikari found such a method?

Dumarest looked at the man. The wine he sipped was a demonstration of its harmlessness or an act to lull Dumarest's suspicions. As his own demonstration of violence had been designed to gain quick answers. If nothing else it had

338

brought his host running, eager to guard the woman or the knowledge she held.

He said, bluntly, "Can you?"

"Answer the question? No, but I can guess. When young, perhaps only a child, she was bound to the temple. Later she was forced to leave or she may have escaped. When my agent found her she was working with a fortune teller who claimed the ability to predict the moment of death. You are aware of her talent?" As Dumarest nodded, Ishikari continued, "It is wild but was good enough to impress the clients of the charlatan. My agent bought her and sent her to me. Once she was established I tried to question her but—" His shrug was expressive.

Dumarest said, "Then you have no real proof she was ever connected with the temple."

"There is the tattoo. Twelve petals surrounding a circle quartered by a cross. You know what that signifies. Look closer and you will see that the cross is set within a pentagram. Five sides, one for each of the senses, the common hallmark of humanity. The curlicues resemble schematics. The twelve petals symbolize—"

"The Sign of the Zodiac," snapped Dumarest. "That still isn't proof. Anyone can copy a tattoo."

"I have other evidence. The association is undeniable. She was attached to the temple and must know what it contains."

The answer to where Earth was to be found but, Dumarest sensed, Ishikari hoped for more. He stood by the table, apparently calm, but the wine in the glass he held quivered a different message. Then, as if aware of the betrayal, he set down the container.

Dumarest said, "Was Karlene indentured? You said your agent bought her."

"The charlatan claimed debts due to maintenance. It was easier to pay than argue. She was found on Threndor—a world of the Sharret Cluster."

"I want to see her."

"No. She must not be bullied."

"I want to apologize, not threaten. I was a little rough with her." A mistake, the shock hadn't achieved its objective. Dumarest added, "I might even be able to find out what you want to know."

"I told you—"

"Fugue, yes, but there are more ways than one of reaching the truth. I could be lucky—and what have you to lose?"

She sat in her room like a broken doll, a toy used and discarded, slumped on the edge of her bed, head lowered, face hidden by the cascade of her hair. Dumarest touched it, caressed the fine strands, the soft flesh of her naked arms. Beneath his fingers he felt the jerk and twitch of muscles. A woman locked in the grip of conflicting emotions. A child, lost, bewildered, needing help.

To the maid standing by he said, "Leave us."

"But—"

"Do it!"

As she obeyed Dumarest sat at Karlene's side, his thigh touching her own, one arm around her shoulders, the other parting the hair before her face. Tears marred her cheeks and her lips held the moist looseness of a frightened child.

"Karlene." His tone was gentle, soothing. "Come back to me, darling. Come back now. Wake up and join me. I need you. Come back to me. Karlene, come back to me."

"Earl?" Her voice was small, empty. "Earl?"

"You're safe, darling. Nothing can hurt you. There's no need to hide." He continued speaking, words which formed a comforting drone as his hands stroked her hair, her body. The treatment he would give to a frightened animal. "Come back to me, Karlene. Come back to me."

"Earl?" Her voice was stronger as she turned toward him. Emptiness vanishing as if she woke from sleep. "Is that you, darling?" Her hands groped, found his, closed with crushing intensity. "You attacked me. I thought you were going to kill me. A dream. Was it a dream?"

"I asked you a question. Don't you remember?"

"No."

"It seemed to upset you."

"Why should it do that?"

"I don't know. Tell me about your life on Threndor. The man you worked for before you joined Ishikari. How did you meet?"

"He found me. He must have found me. I was lost and cold and frightened and ... and...." She shook her head, frowning. "I can't remember."

"Never mind. Did he ever talk about your past? Ask what you'd done before you met?"

"I don't think so. No."

"Wasn't he curious?" Dumarest waited then said, gently, "Surely he must have wanted to know something about you. A beautiful young girl. Others could have been looking for you. There could have been the possibility of a reward." Casually he added, "How old were you when you met?"

"I don't know. I don't think he liked me much. Not before he found out about—" She fell silent then, in a different tone, said, "I don't want to talk about it."

"Then we won't."

"Not now. Not ever."

"I understand." Dumarest freed his hand from the woman's grasp. "I wish you could trust me as much as you trust Ishikari."

"What do you mean?"

"Surely he must have asked you about your past? He took you in, looked after you. Maybe you're related in some way. Why did he send you to Erkalt?"

"I was working. With Hagen. You know that."

"But you told Ishikari about me. Why?"

"You needed help. He said he could help you. You agreed to meet him. You know all this."

Dumarest said, "What I don't know is what he wants. What he hopes to find. Why is he so interested in the temple?" He saw the sudden blankness of her eyes. "Karlene! Stay with me!"

"I'm sorry." She drew a shuddering breath. "I feel confused. All these questions. "Earl—what do you want of me?"

"Answers. About Ishikari. Don't you remember the questions he asked? The details he wanted?"

Her face gave the answer. She remembered

Ishikari's probing no more than she remembered his own recent violence. The fugue into which she escaped blurred the cause of its creation and turned real events into the figment of a dream.

Chapter 7

By day the church was bright with pennons of blue and white; colors of purity and hope. At night lanterns of the same hues signaled to all that here was to be found help and comfort both of body and mind. And, always, throngs came to partake of both.

Brother Tessio walked among them, tall, austere in his brown robe and sandals. A costume designed for utility, devoid of ostentation. Not even the heads of the great establishments wore a different garb. Not even those who ruled the great seminaries on Peace and Hope. The Church of Universal Brotherhood had no use for hypocrisy; a jewel would buy food for the starving, gold braid provide medicine for the sick, expensive fabrics make a mockery of the humility which alone could alleviate the suffering of humanity.

"Brother!" A woman caught at his hand. "Please

help me. My child—" The small bundle beside her stirred with a fitful wailing. "Please!"

"You will be seen," promised Tessio. "And the child will be helped."

With medicines, antibiotics, drugs. With the skill of monks trained in manipulation, hypnosis, natural healing. As the others waiting in the annex would be helped and sent on their way. Some would leave a donation; others, too poor to give even that, would mouth thanks; and some would offer their labor at menial tasks.

But none would ever be refused.

Tessio sighed as he reached the far end of the room and passed through a door into a passage. From behind drawn curtains he heard the murmur of voices and lingered at the cubicle containing Brother Vendell. A good man, if inclined to be impatient. One who chafed at the irksome necessity of making haste slowly.

"Look into the light," he heard the monk say to the suppliant kneeling before him. "Relax. Concentrate on the colors. See how they shift and change. The patterns they make. Try to follow them. So soft. So restful. Watching them makes you feel so relaxed, so tired ... so tired ... tired...."

There was the hint of the mechanical in the voice and Tessio made a mental note to speak to Vendell about it. To deal with the endless line of suppliants could not help but be boring but never, ever, should it be shown as that. Each was an individual and needed to be reassured of his or her particular importance.

Pride, concern, consideration—words Tessio

345

turned in his mind as he went on his way. Pride in personal ethics, concern for the general environment, consideration for all other individuals. If men would keep their word, cease from wanton destruction, have the imagination to realize how their actions affected others. If each could look at others less fortunate and say "There, but for the grace of God, go I," the millennium would have arrived.

Something he would never see. No monk now living would ever see—men spread too fast and wide for that. Yet it was the objective for which he strived and to which the Church was dedicated.

"Brother!" The monk was young, still idealistic, yet to experience the full measure of pain and degradation which was the inevitable price paid by all who aspired to wear the brown robe. "You have visitors."

They waited in a small room containing a table, chairs, a patchwork rug on the floor. The walls were bare aside from a crude painting, a mask carved from wood, a bundle of thin reeds, a knife made from flints set into a scrap of wood. Mementoes, each with its history and each punctuating a period of his life. Tessio would use them if the need arose; making conversation, illustrating various points as he strove to reach the heart of a problem. No monk of his standing was less than a master in applied psychology.

Dumarest saved him the trouble. Rising to his feet as the monk entered, he said, "Brother, we need your help."

"We?" Tessio glanced at Karlene where she sat. "You speak for both?"

"Yes." She met his eyes, her own direct. "I am under no duress but—" She broke off, hands together, knuckles taut beneath the pallor of her skin. "Earl, do you think this wise? I mean—"

He said, abruptly, "Tell me about Cerevox."

Tessio inhaled as she slumped, face lax, eyes rolling upward beneath her lowering lids. Dumarest caught her, steadied her in the chair. His touch, Tessio noted, was gentle, almost a caress.

"An illustration," said Dumarest. He straightened, one hand holding the woman upright in her chair. "Do you know what you're looking at?"

"Fugue." Tessio touched the pale skin of her throat and forehead, lifted an eyelid, pressed a finger beneath the cascade of her hair. "A natural infirmity?"

"Artificial."

"Conditioning?"

"Yes. She has been deliberately sensitized against certain words or concepts and acts, as you have seen, when stimulus is applied. I want you to remove that sensitivity." Dumarest saw the doubt in the monk's eyes. "Listen," he said urgently, "She is under no duress—she told you that. She is here of her own volition. She is sick and asks for your help. If what you believe has any validity at all—how can you deny her?"

A good question but the answer was not so simple. The man was what he appeared to be but the woman wore fabrics of price and could be under emotional constraint. Too old to need the consent of a guardian but should he arouse the anger of her family the Church would suffer. If it was abolished from this world who would help those now waiting for succor?

One against many and yet ... and yet. ...

There, but for the grace of God, go I!

Dumarest said, quietly, "If I brought you a bird with a broken wing what would you do? Kill it? Heal it? Ignore it and leave it to suffer? Tell me."

"This woman is not a bird."

"She is still a cripple. An emotional one, true, but a cripple just the same. I'm not asking you to find out who applied the conditioning, or when, or why. I'm asking you to remove it. To heal her as you would heal an injured bird. To make her whole again. To give her free choice. To restore her pride."

Pride which, if it became overweening, would be a sin. As concern for another would become if allowed to grow into interference. As consideration could never be.

Could he show less consideration to a woman than he would to a bird?

Tessio said, "I can promise nothing. I will do my best but my skill is limited. You must understand that."

"You will help?"

"I will do what I can."

Dumarest waited in the annex, striding down the rows of those wanting aid, disturbing them and the attendant monks both. A thing he recognized and he left the church to stand looking at the field. The perimeter lights made a harsh circle of brilliance around the area, small glitters reflected from the barbed points of the mesh. A hard fence to climb; too high to jump and the barbs would rip flesh and clothing. Guards stood at the gate and others, not so obvious, stood close in the shadows. Men without uniforms but with watchful eyes and Dumarest had no doubt as to their orders. They, the lights, the savage barbs were all a part of his cage.

As was Karlene herself.

He moved on, edging around the church as he thought of her. Imagining her face beneath the glowing, ever-changing colors of the benediction light. Tessio would be using his skill and trained ability, questioning, suggesting, directing. Easing the burden others had clamped on her mind. The guardians of the temple? The charlatan she had worked for? Others?

A wall rose before him and he turned to retrace his steps. It would have been easier for the guardians to have killed. Safer, too, if their secrets were so important, her knowledge so dangerous. The charlatan would have had no reason. A pretense? The fugue had been genuine enough. The conditioning was real. But who had established it? And why?

"Brother?" A young monk headed toward him. "If you would return to the church?"

Karlene waited in the room in which he had left her. She turned as he entered, radiant, smiling, arms lifting to merge into his embrace.

"Darling! I feel so well! So alive!"

"I'm glad." Dumarest touched the softness of her cheek, her hair, his fingers imparting kisses. They were alone. Tessio, as well as being a psychologist, was also a diplomat. "Tell me about Cerevox. The Temple of Cerevox."

"What?" She stared at him, frowning, and for a moment he wondered if the monk had failed. But there was no sign of withdrawal. No hint of fugue. Then she smiled. "Cerevox? Of course, darling. What do you want to know?"

It was the fabrication of a dream; a mass of chambers and passages, of halls and promenades, open spaces and soaring pinnacles. An edifice of stone which had grown during the course of time to rest like a delicate flower in the cup of misted hills.

Dumarest pictured it as he sat in the tavern to which he had taken Karlene. A mental image enhanced by the dancer who spun with a lithe and supple grace to the music of pipe and drum. The fabrics she wore echoed the vibrant hues of gems set to adorn arch and pillar, the tinkle of her bells the clear chimes of instruments stirred by the wind. The pipe and drum matched the tramp of marching feet, the chant of devoted worshipers. Even the serving maids emulated young and nubile priestesses.

"It is beautiful," said Karlene. "I can't begin to tell you how beautiful it is. The wind is always gentle. The air is always warm. At night the sky is a blaze of stars. There are two moons and, when they are close, there are ceremonies."

"Special ones?"

"Yes. To the Mother."

"How about those who live there?"

"All are bound to the Temple. Some gather

fruits and tend the land. Some build. Others weave fabrics for robes and garments. The elders teach. Those who come to make their devotions bring offerings. Usually it is money or goods of value. Sometimes they offer the fruit of their bodies."

"Children?"

"Those barely able to walk. They are examined by the priests and, if found to be without flaw, are bound to the Temple." Her hand rose to touch the place above her left breast. "If accepted they bring honor."

Dumarest said, "Who are these devotees? The Original People?"

"Who are they?"

"A religious sect with a mania for secrecy. They neither seek nor welcome converts; new adherents are gained from natural increase." Watching her, he quoted, in a tone which held the roll of drums, "From terror they fled to find new places on which to expiate their sins. Only when cleansed will the race of Man be again united."

Karlene said, frowning, "What does it mean?"

"It's part of the creed of the Original People. Do you recognize it? No? A pity. Once things happen as they say there should be a paradise like the one you've described. The Temple," he explained. "I can't understand why anyone should want to leave it."

"Are you saying I lie?"

"I'm saying I'm curious. You agreed to talk. What happened? Why did you leave?"

"I didn't fit. I wasn't wanted." Her tone was tense, hurt. "And I grew worried. I kept feeling

351

that thing in my mind. At first I asked about it then I just kept it to myself."

"Why?"

"They told me I was imagining things. That I was contaminated. I knew what happened to contaminated things and I was frightened it would happen to me. I thought it was going to happen, that I was going to die in the fire like the other things. The dead animals and spoiled fruits so ... so. ..." She broke off and took a deep breath. Then, in a calmer, more adult tone said, "So I left. I disguised myself and mingled with a bunch of worshipers. I was lucky—when a man discovered I didn't belong I made him believe I was on a secret mission for the Temple. He aided me."

As had others in ways and for reasons Dumarest didn't go into. The charlatan had provided a temporary refuge. Rauch Ishikari a more permanent one. But what was his real interest in the Temple?

"He wanted me to describe it," said Karlene when he asked. "In detail. He wanted to know all about me, everything I'd done. He made me tell him about the rituals and—"

"Made you?"

"He kept on and on. It was easier to talk than remain silent. Anyway, I owed him. He was good to me. I wanted to help as much as I could. Then, I guess, he must have lost interest or grown tired of asking questions because he let me live much as I wished."

The dancer finished her performance to a burst of applause and left the floor, bowing, an assistant gathering up the coins thrown in appreciation of her skill. A tumbler replaced her, a man who spun and twisted in a glitter of sequins. One who kept shining balls balanced in the air above head and feet.

As Ishikari had kept the truth spinning just beyond his reach.

It had to be Ishikari.

Dumarest looked at his hands, at the goblet he held between them. Wine he didn't want but its price had paid for the shelter of the tavern, the privacy he had needed. Time to learn what he could away from prying ears and eyes but it had been little enough, as his host must have known. Was he even now smiling at his jest?

If so it was time to wipe the grin off his face.

He sat in the chamber with the vaulted roof, the panes now dark with the nighted sky. Lanterns glowed from brackets set high on the walls, their light adding to the nacreous glow from the computer. Limned against the screen Ishikari looked thin and insubstantial, then he moved, light splintering in dying reflections from gems and precious metal, the braid edging the fabric he wore so that, for a moment, he was adorned with glinting scales.

"My friend." His gesture dismissed the guard attending Dumarest. "You are impetuous."

"Impatient." Dumarest strode closer to the screen, his host. "Why did you lie?"

"Did I?"

"The conditioning—"

"Was applied by me, true, but did I ever tell you otherwise?"

353

"You told me she had been conditioned when a child."

"As she was. Surely you must have realized that. How did she describe the Temple? As a paradise, right? Warm air and gentle winds and all the rest of it. What else was that but a picture impressed on her mind when young? Tell a child often enough that dirt is bread and he will believe it. Heat will become cold, stench become perfume, pain turn into pleasure. As for the rest?" Ishikari shrugged. "A man is a fool who doesn't guard his treasure."

"You sucked her dry," said Dumarest. "Learned all you could then made sure she wouldn't be able to talk to others. Why didn't you stop me? You must have known I'd taken her to the monks."

"Of course. I would have been disappointed if you had not."

"You wanted me to question her?"

"I want you to believe," said Ishikari. "In her. In me. In what I have to tell you. Cerevox is real but, like Earth, not easy to find. Did you ask her where it was?"

"She didn't know. She thought the world and the Temple had the same name."

"They haven't. Cerevox is located on Raniang. It is a world of the Sharret Cluster."

"As Threndor is," said Dumarest. "She didn't travel far."

"Farther than you think." Ishikari touched a button on the computer. As the screen flared he said, "The Sharret Cluster."

The answer came in a mellifluous female voice

354

which matched the graphic symbols illuminating the screen.

"The Sharret Cluster: central coordinates 42637/69436/83657. A collection of thirty-eight suns in close proximity together with strands of cosmic dust. There are a multitude of worlds most of which have neither been explored nor noted. A total of twenty-seven are habited some with only minor installations. In alphabetical order they are—"

"Cease! Name only major worlds."

"In order of population-destiny based on the latest almanac-entries: Dorgonne, Brauss, Stimac, Berger, Threndor—"

"Cease! Where does Raniang lie? In population order?"

"Nineteenth."

"Position in relation to Threndor? In spatial terms."

"Almost diametrically opposite in cluster."

"A long way," commented Ishikari as the computer-screen resumed its blank glow. "And none of it easy. Can you imagine what it was like to a young girl, frightened, totally unsuited to what she went into? It must have been a living nightmare."

One Dumarest had known. He said, "What is your interest in the Temple?"

"The same as yours."

"I doubt it. I want to find Earth. I think you want to find something else. Why else all your questions as to robes and rituals? Just what does Cerevox mean to you?"

For a long moment Ishikari made no answer,

then, abruptly, he said, "You know of the Original People?"

"Yes."

"Their creed?" As Dumarest nodded, he continued, "From terror they fled. Terror. Or maybe it should be Terra. Another name for Earth as you must know. A slight change, natural enough, but one word becomes another. Now, if we say, From Terra they fled—you grasp the significance?"

"They left Earth, yes."

"But why?" Ishikari leaned forward as if he were a snake about to strike. "They fled—from what? They ran and settled on other places. Those other places could only have been worlds. And the cleansing they mention. The need to expiate their sins. What sins? Against whom?" Pausing he added, "And why should Earth have been proscribed?"

"You know?"

"Don't you?" Ishikari rested his hand on the computer. To it he said, "On the basis of all information you have, give the most probable location of the mythical planet Earth."

The screen flared, became a mesh of drifting lines, of slowly rotating graphics and transient figures. A background to the mellifluous voice.

"The firmest guide to the location is the zodiac. The zodiac consists of twelve symbols, each representing a portion of a band of the sky in a complete circle. A configuration of stars represents each of the symbols. Earth is supposed to lie within the center of the circle. The signs are: Ram, Bull, Twins, Crab, Lion, Virgin, Scales, Scorpion, Archer, Goat, Pot, Fish. The point in space from which these signs are recognized in a surrounding circle is the most probable location of Earth."

"The actual design of the configurations?"

"Unknown."

"Give details of all other worlds which have been proscribed."

"None."

Dumarest said, "How do you know Earth was proscribed?"

"The fact worries you?" Ishikari touched the computer and, as his hand fell from the control, added, "I found a reference in an old book. There is also a mention in the Cerevox rituals, but you wouldn't know about that. Now, given the findings of the computer, could you find Earth?" He smiled as Dumarest shook his head. "Of course not. The clue of the zodiac is useless. The patterns to look for are unknown and even if we had the information where would we start? The books tell us nothing. Those to which we have access, at least. To me it is obvious that all references to Earth were deliberately suppressed and all almanacs giving its location destroyed. How else to proscribe a world other than by isolating it? And again we come to the question—why? Why was a world abandoned? Condemned?"

The answer he hoped to find. His real interest in the Temple. Dumarest wondered why he had made no reference to his failure to add his own information to the computer, then decided Ishikari had either forgotten his command or thought it had been obeyed. The latter, he decided, the man was not accustomed to disobedience.

"The Original People," said Ishikari. "They have the answer, I'm sure of it. They have kept the past alive. Distorted, altered, wrapped around with symbolism and myth, but the truth is in their keeping. All we have to do is find it."

"How? They value their secrecy."

"But you know of them and so do I?"

"Fanatics existing on backward worlds," said Dumarest. "Small groups living in primitive conditions. Everyone knows that."

"How?" demanded Ishikari. "If they are so secret how do we know even that? No, my friend, nothing is so secret that it cannot be learned by others. The Original People know that. Know too that a secret that is not a secret is safe. I confuse you? Tell me, how better to keep a secret than by persuading everyone that it isn't really a secret at all? Look for your primitives and you fail to see the civilized men beneath your nose. The primitives are hard to find, true, but who wants to find them anyway? Who really has interest in a bunch of fanatics conducting bizarre and esoteric rituals? And yet, in order to maintain cohesion, certain ceremonies must be maintained."

"The Temple?" said Dumarest. "Cerevox?"

"The heart of the Original People. The center of their worship. I am certain of it." Ishikari left the computer and moved with long, loping strides. A man burning with conviction. He halted and caught at the edge of a table while sucking air deep into his lungs. More quietly he said, "I have been advised against exciting myself but at times I forget."

"You are ill? Shall I call for help?"

"No."

"Is there anything I can do?"

"Listen. For now just listen." Ishikari drew more air into his lungs. "Mysteries have always fascinated me. Even as a boy I yearned for answers. My position makes it impossible for me to follow a scientific pursuit but, even so, it has compensations. I can question and those I question know better than to lie. I can order and be obeyed. I can punish and I can reward. Do I make myself clear?"

Power displayed as the threat of a naked blade and his own position made obvious. Dumarest waited, saying nothing.

"Cerevox is a mystery and one I intend to solve. I want to know what lies at the heart of the Temple." Ishikari paused to breathe, his hand tight on the edge of the table. "Think of it! The secret they have guarded for so long. Not just the location of Earth but all the rest. Why was it abandoned? Why proscribed? What terrible sin needs to be expiated? The answers can be found. You will find them."

He stared at Dumarest, his eyes wide, bright, glowing with fanatical determination. Foam showed at the corners of his mouth.

"You will find what lies at the heart of the Temple," he said. "And, finding it, you will discover how to find Earth."

Chapter 8

Ellen Contera was as dark as Karlene was fair. A small, hard, self-assured woman with close-cropped hair, a face which showed her age and a restless, impatient manner.

To Dumarest she said, "So you're the appointed. How good are you with that knife?"

He smiled, not answering, looking at the enclosed garden they were in: a walled extension of the palace, the walls high and topped with vicious spikes. A stone promenade followed the inside of the wall, shrubs and bushes edging it to surround an inner lawn set with a band of flowering plants. The air was soft, scented, the heat trapped from the noon sun reflected from the walls and created shimmers in the air.

"I asked you a question." Ellen moved three paces, halted, moved back to the bench against which she had been standing. The fabric of her

360

clothing made a dry rustling. She wore pants, shoes, a mannish blouse. Her hands, broad, the fingers spatulate, were marred with livid blotches. She wore no rings. "Need I repeat it?"

"You made a statement and asked a question," corrected Dumarest. "One I don't have to answer. Why did you say I'm the appointed?"

"Rauch gave us the word. You're going to lead the team to rob the Temple. Didn't he tell you?" She frowned as he shook his head. "Did you think you'd be operating alone?"

A possibility he had considered during the night—but had rejected. To a madman all things were simple and Ishikari, he guessed, was far from sane. He remembered the eyes, the glare, the foam on the lips. A man obsessed. A dreamer driven insane by his dream. Such a man was dangerous in more ways than one. Rather than follow him Dumarest had decided to go his own way.

"He's consumed with an ideal," said the woman. "But I guess you noticed that. For years he's been trying to solve the mystery of Cerevox. I've helped him. The girl," she explained. "Karlene vol Diajiro. A mess if ever I saw one. God knows what they did to her in the Temple but I managed to bury most of the traumas."

"You?"

"I'm Ellen Contera. Profesor of applied psychology. Doctor of medicine. Doctor of hypnotic therapy. Professor of psyche manipulation. I'm among the top of my field. Something else you didn't know, eh?"

"No." There had been pride in her voice when

she had mentioned her name and titles. "Why does Ishikari need me?"

"If I'm so good?"

"I didn't say that."

"No, you didn't." Her eyes searched his face. "The answer's simple: I work in one way and you in another. That's why I asked if you could handle that knife." She paused as if expecting him to demonstrate, then, as he made no attempt either to speak or reach for the blade, continued, "He's been looking for the right kind of man. One with guts, courage and intelligence. He figures you fit the bill."

Dumarest said, dryly, "I gained the impression he wanted a thief."

"He has a thief. Someone caught trying to rob the palace. He's alive now only because he was so good. You'll meet him later. For now I'd like to know how you feel about it."

"Robbing the Temple?"

"Call it that if you like. I was thinking about the religious aspect. Some men can't kill. Some can't stand the sight of another in pain. Some won't commit sacrilege. We all have our weaknesses. Are you superstitious?"

"No."

"Does the thought of violating a sacred shrine bother you?" As Dumarest shook his head she said, "I'd like to check your psyche. Would you object to hypnotic interrogation? It would do no harm."

"To you, no."

"Then you object?"

362

"Strongly. I don't like anyone probing my mind. Call it a weakness if you like."

"I'd call it a strength." Again she strode from the bench, but this time did not return. "Well? Aren't you interested in what's facing you?"

She led the way from the garden into a room bright with diffused sunlight. Cold air gusting from vents gave the place a stimulating coolness. In the center of the chamber stood a large table. On it was the model of a patch of countryside together with a building.

"That's it," said Ellen. "The Temple of Cerevox."

It wasn't what Dumarest had expected.

Karlene had described a place of delicate construction, of walks and promenades, soaring arches and open spaces filled with the perfume of massed flowers. The spaces were present together with the walls but the spaces were bare and the walls had been constructed of rough stone which sprawled in a mazelike pattern around the central mass of the building, which was low, domed, set with stunted towers and flanked by the sloping roofs of attendant buildings.

"No gems," said Ellen. "No polished stone. No soaring arches, flowers, scented air. And you can forget about the warm air and gentle winds. Raniang isn't known for clement weather."

"She lied."

"Karlene? No. She told you what she thought to be the truth."

"Conditioning?"

"From the moment she was bound to the Temple. The rituals are strongly hypnotic. They usually are, of course, but these are something special.

363

Chants, drums, incense, suggestion, fasting, pain, soporifics—they use the whole spectrum and they're damned good at what they do. First they blurred her early memories then imposed a false reality. She told you they only accept the very young?"

"Those barely able to walk."

"That, in itself, is suspicious." Ellen gestured at the table, the model it carried. "What would they want with people so young? Children are a burden until they can at least fetch and carry. The Temple needs servants, workers, guards and a supply of new priests and priestesses. Those in charge would have neither the time nor resources needed to bring up the very young and helpless."

"So you dug into her mind," said Dumarest. "You and Ishikari. And found, what?"

"I did the digging, she only thinks Rauch did. And what I found isn't nice. She must have been about eight or nine when they took her. Suggestion made her think the air was warm and all the rest of it. An invented paradise to keep her and the rest happy. Fair enough—on a world like Raniang that's good therapy. But later, when her talent began to worry her, things changed for the worse. Can you tell me how and why?"

She was serious. Looking at her Dumarest recognized the expression in her eyes, the blank attentiveness of her face. Another test? One to determine his level of intelligence?

He said, "She was in a closed society. A religious one. For such a society to work all must share the same beliefs and have an unquestioning obedience to authority. Her talent would have set her apart."

"And?"

"Differences, in such a society, cannot be tolerated. All must conform."

"You've got it!" Ellen turned, relaxing, and he guessed he had passed her test. "To them she became a heretic. Her talent was a nagging ache; a question to which she could find no answer. Instead of trying to understand it they tried to eradicate it. To beat it out of her." Her voice thickened a little. "I mean that literally. I'll spare you the details but there are none so cruel as the righteous. If Karlene hadn't run they would have killed her."

"So the story she told me—"

"Was the edited version of what I put in her mind." Ellen gestured at the table. "What do you think? Can you get in there and find what it contains?"

Dumarest said, "I'll need a lot more information before I can answer that."

"You'll get it. Now come and meet those who are going with you."

The thief was Ahmed Altini, a slim, lithe man with a solemn face and grave eyes. His hands were designed to handle locks as a surgeon handled a scalpel. Neat hands, deft, the kind Dumarest had seen often before. Gambler's hands trained to manipulate cards.

One touched his own in greeting. "An old custom," Ahmed explained. "But one we must become accustomed to using."

"The pilgrims use it." Kroy Lauter was big, bluff, one cheek pocked with scars. "But I'll greet

365

you in a more familiar fashion." He extended both hands, palms upwards in a mercenary's welcoming salute.

Ramon Sanchez smiled as he stepped forward. A fighter, light on the balls of his feet, shoulders hunched as if ready to drop into a familiar crouch. His touch was cool, assured.

"We are of a kind, it seems. Unlike Dietz."

Pinal Dietz was an assassin, a stealer of lives as Altini was a stealer of wealth. A small, neat, precise man devoid of any outstanding feature. One who would be easily lost in a crowd and as quickly forgotten by any who saw him. Only at times, when his eyes betrayed him, did he look what he was.

"A gambler," he said. "Although he's tired of the risks a gambler must take. Once we have won the wealth of the Temple I shall retire to some secluded world. I may even write a book."

"On the art of killing?" Ellen gave him no time to answer. "Rauch had him hired," she explained to Dumarest after she had drawn him to one side. "Paid to kill a man from whom he wanted a favor. He warned the man what to expect and, when Pinal made his attempt, he was taken. The victim, of course, was grateful. Pinal decided to work for Rauch rather than face the penalty of failure."

"Ishikari trusts him?"

"Now, yes." Her smile was enigmatic. "An elementary precaution. Pinal is a snake without fangs until given the word. I shall teach you that word."

"The others?"

"Ahmed you know about. Kroy is what he seems—a mercenary willing to do anything for the hope of reward. Ramon comes from the arena which is why I asked if you were good with a knife. Such a man may decide to question your authority." She glanced to where he stood with the others. "Come, now, let's eat."

The room was next to the one holding the model; a spacious chamber containing tables, chairs, a bookshelf and computer terminal. A door opened to baths and showers. One table bore scattered cards; another, chessmen in neat array. The center table, flanked by chairs, bore wine and plates of succulent dainties. Salvers bore cold meats and an assortment of bread and pastry.

As he helped himself Kroy said, "What do you think we'll find in the Temple, Earl?"

"Probably nothing."

"What?"

"He could be right." Altini helped himself to wine. "I once robbed a shrine on Matsuki. It was reputed to hold a fabulous treasure. A thing so holy that it was virtually beyond price. I found an egg."

Kroy stared his disbelief. "An egg?"

"Just that. It was made of stone."

"A jewel? Well—"

"Stone," repeated the thief. "Some hard, black stone. Smoothed and polished, of course, but about as valuable as any other you can pick up on the shore. A symbol valuable only to those who worshipped it." He sipped his wine with the fastidiousness of a cat. "I could tell you other stories."

"We can all tell stories." Dietz reached out and

lifted a pastry from the salver. "I'm only interested in rewards. Gems, precious metals, things of price. The Temple must be full of them. Think of all the pilgrims who make offerings. Over the years they would fill a hundred rooms the size of this."

"One would be enough for me." Sanchez leaned back in his chair, smiling, a grimace without humor. "A private arena, a stable of fighters, a selected audience. Easy money, Earl, don't you agree?"

"Is that what you want?"

"As a hobby, of course. Even a rich man must have something to occupy his mind. With what I get from the Temple I'll build the finest establishment ever seen. Inlaid chairs, a ring of precious metal, attendants all dressed in silk. The epitome of luxury. The peak of fighting skill. Surely you've dreamed of owning such a place, Earl? Of being on the winning side for a change."

Ellen Contera said, "What makes you think Earl is a loser?"

"Could Rauch buy anything else?" Sanchez met her eyes. "We are all after the same thing. The Temple has it and we are going to rob the Temple. Money with which to establish ourselves."

"Just walk in and take it, huh?" Ellen shrugged. "You think it will be as easy as that? Even a fool would know better."

"Are you calling me a fool?" Sanchez glared his anger. "Are you?"

"Anyone's a fool who walks blind into a trap," snapped Dumarest. "And before loot can be spent it has to be won."

"Meaning?"

"You've been in the arena. What happens when a fighter is convinced he's already won? That he's got it made. When all he can think about is the money he'll get and the woman he'll pick and the feast that's waiting. What would you call such a man?"

"A suicide." Sanchez puffed out his cheeks. "I get the point."

"Keep it in mind. That goes for all of you." Dumarest looked from one to the other. "We don't know what's in the Temple. It doesn't matter. First we have to get to it. Any ideas?"

Kroy Lauter led the explanations, jabbing a thick finger at the map he unrolled, moving it to illustrate points.

"Raniang's a hard world. One little better than a cinder. The Hsing-Tiede Consortium has an installation there but it's on the other side of the planet from the Temple. Pilgrims usually arrive in groups on chartered ships which land here." His finger jabbed. "Well away from the Temple and down in this depression. Pilgrims march toward the Temple and enter the complex here." Again his finger rapped the paper. "They are met and escorted by priests. After certain ceremonies they are led into the Temple proper."

"Which is where the hard part begins." Altini leaned over the map. "We can only guess as to what really lies inside."

"Why guess?" Dumarest glanced at Ellen. "Don't we have maps? Diagrams?"

"The best I could get," she admitted. "But—"

"Things change," said Altini quickly. "Walls

369

built or removed. New paths opened in different chambers. Traps set in the floor. Even the rituals can vary. Those guarding the treasure aren't fools and we can't be the first to want to rob them."

Dietz said, "No matter how things vary the basics remain the same. A thing I learned when young at my trade. To hunt down a man, to place him in the right position for the kill, to strike home and escape capture—all depends on established habit-patterns. Discover them and the victim is helpless."

"An assassin's philosophy," sneered Sanchez. "You are saying a man cooperates in his own murder."

"Unconsciously, yes. As you may easily cooperate in your own defeat when—"

"Nonsense!"

"No," said Dumarest. "A fighter, any fighter, can't help but follow a certain pattern. He will repeat winning maneuvers, hold his blade in a familiar way, stand in a workable position. Watch him long enough and you can plan his defeat." He changed the subject; if he had to fight Sanchez then the less he knew the better. To the assassin he said, "You were talking about the basics, Pinal. Would you please continue?"

He listened, checking points, evaluating available data. Too little was based on known fact, too must rested on assumption. Yet it was logical to expect that the treasure, whatever it was, would remain in its shrine. That ceremonies would remain basically unaltered. That Karlene, despite her conditioning, would have yielded essential data as to the interior of the Temple.

He remembered how Altini had cut Ellen short and wondered at his reason. Later, when the discussion was over and the others had drifted apart, he spoke of it to her as they walked beside the garden wall.

"Ahmed is a thief and as such he tends to be cautious. Also he is proud and wants to enhance his prowess."

"Is that all?"

"Of course." She turned to look at him, smiling. "What other reason could there be? You can trust him, Earl."

A conviction Dumarest didn't share. He said, "Are you coming with us?"

"Yes."

"I meant into the Temple."

"I can't do that." She walked seven paces in silence then added, "Remember we talked of weaknesses? Mine is pain. I can't stand it. I found that out on Kampher when some people I knew staged a rebellion. I didn't take part but I was taken in for questioning. They weren't gentle." She lifted her hands so as to display the livid blotches. "I told them everything they wanted to know."

"You can't be blamed for that."

"You are kind to say so. Not everyone would be so understanding. But I dare not go into the Temple and risk discovery by the priests. I learned from Karlene what will happen."

"Bad?" As she nodded, Dumarest added, "Is that the real reason Ahmed stopped you? Was he afraid you'd tell us what we'd face if we were caught?"

"Possibly. But, as I said, he can be trusted."

As the assassin, the fighter, the mercenary—all trusted to be hungry to make their fortunes. All united by greed. Not the best of motivations.

Ellen said, as if reading his thoughts, "Rauch had to take what he could get, Earl. That's why he wants you to take command."

Dumarest said, dryly, "Because I've guts, courage and intelligence?"

"You've got all that," she admitted. "But so have the others. What makes you special is that you have something else. A greater motivation." Halting, she turned to face him, to look up into his eyes. "They just want loot—but you want to find a world."

The air of Driest was far more salubrious than that of Erkalt and, instead of snow and ice, the window gave a view of rolling plains and distant hills all covered in a rich brown and green. A difference Clarge noted and dismissed as unimportant as he had the comfort of the room, the furnishings, the cool air vented through decorated grills. The room, the planet meant nothing.

Dumarest was gone.

The data lay before him: a mass of facts, reports, observations—the results of time-consuming but essential verification of statements made by those willing to help the Cyclan.

Again he checked them, feeling the mental glow of achievement which was the only real pleasure he could ever experience. His prediction had been correct—finding the woman had guided

372

him to the man. Had he arrived a week earlier the hunt would now be over.

He rose from the desk, banishing thought of what might have been. To speculate in such a manner was a waste of mental direction and as useless as regretting the past. And all was not lost; when Dumarest had moved on he had not gone alone.

Mentally he reviewed the data he had obtained. An agent of Rauch Ishikari had chartered a vessel, the *Argonne,* and none knew where it was bound. Dumarest and the woman had resided with Ishikari. Investigation had shown they no longer occupied their quarters. A party had left in the chartered ship; a score of persons all muffled in masking robes but one of them, caught in a sudden gust of wind, had revealed a mass of shimmering white hair.

A genuine mistake or a deliberate diversion? A moment of accident or a false clue planted to lead any followers astray?

The former, he decided, the woman had left on the ship.

But where would it land?

Dumarest was on it; Clarge set the probability as high as 99.9 percent. As near as any cyber would go to predicting certainty. The woman also—but why was he still with her? What had she to offer?

The acolyte came at his signal, bowed as Clarge said, "Total seal."

Within his own quarters Clarge lay supine on the bed. A touch activated the wide band circling his left wrist, the device ensuring that no electronic scanner could focus on his vicinity. Relaxing, he closed his eyes and concentrated on the Samatchazi formulae. Gradually he lost the use of his senses; had he opened his eyes he would have been blind. Locked within his skull his brain ceased to be irritated by external stimuli. It became a thing of pure intellect, its reasoning awareness its only connection with normal life. Only then did the grafted Homochon elements become active. Rapport followed.

Clarge blossomed into a new dimension of existence.

Each cyber had a different experience. For him it was as if he were a point of expanding parameters; rings which widened to the end of the universe, renewed and replenished by further rings. A point which pulsed and moved through realms of scintillating brilliance, connecting, interchanging, embracing everything in a composite whole. The living part of an organism which had transcended the limitations of flesh and moved with the freedom of unrestricted thought.

And all was rooted in the heart of the Cyclan.

Buried deep beneath layers of adamantine stone Central Intelligence absorbed his knowledge as a sponge soaked up water. Mental communication, almost instantaneous, made him one with the massed brains.

Information given and orders received—but this time Clarge wanted more.

"Check on the origins of a tattoo." He described it in detail; information gained from Hagen. "Worn on the region above the left breast."

A question.

"The woman, Karlene vol Diajiro."

A query.

"Dumarest is with her. She must be leading him. The tattoo could provide the answer to where."

A command.

Clarge waited as Central Intelligence searched the massed intelligence which made it what it was. Brains removed from the skulls of cybers who had earned the reward of near-immortality, lying still alive and aware in sealed vats of nutrient fluid, all hooked in series with each other to form a composite whole. An ideal state in which to ponder the problems of the universe. A combination which formed a tremendous organic computer of incredible complexity working to establish the rule and dominance of the Cyclan.

Once, perhaps centuries ago, a cyber had seen or learned of the tattoo. Or had been told about it when an acolyte. A memory which, like all memories, would never die. Now, stimulated by need, it woke to provide the answer.

Clarge spun in an intoxication unsurpassed by any drug. A mental euphoria in which he sensed strange memories and alien situations—the scraps and overflow of other minds. The residue of other intelligences. A stimulation which always followed rapport but was now enhanced by an added dimension. One which would ensure his reward.

Clarge opened his eyes, waiting until the ceiling grew clear and small sounds adopted meaning. Always it took time for the workings of the body to become realigned with the dictates of the mind. He swayed a little as he rose from the bed and sat again knowing he had been too impatient. A fall now would demonstrate his inefficiency; minutes were not important now that he knew where Dumarest was heading.

Chapter 9

Raniang was worse than Lauter had described: a cinder scoured by abrasive winds, the air acrid with chemical taints, the whole lit by a sullen red giant which tinged everything with the color of blood. Lying prone on a crest, head and body masked by massive boulders, Dumarest stared through binoculars at the Temple below.

It was uncannily familiar; Ellen had done a good job of interpreting Karlene's memories in order to build her model. Rugged walls enclosed open spaces with openings in a complex pattern which would trap the unknowing in a maze. The central dome, the squat towers, the flanking buildings all looked the same but the basic mystery remained. The inner part of the Temple was still an unknown quantity.

"Earl?" The voice came from the speaker in his ear. Altini's voice. "Anything new?"

"No." Dumarest sub-vocalized, the vibrations of his larynx transmitted by the throat-mike. "They're still in there."

A party of twelve all muffled in black robes who had wended their way from the landing field. Robed priests had met them at the entrance to the external complex and had guided them through the labyrinth. A path Dumarest had memorized but, even as he watched, laboring figures were busy blocking some openings and creating others. Windblown dust would form a patina over the alterations and make a mock of any memorized path.

"Neat," said the thief when Dumarest transmitted the information. "Enter one way and leave by another and both will be changed before the next party of worshipers arrives. I'll bet they operate the same way inside. Earl, see—"

"Wait!" Dumarest adjusted the binoculars. "They're coming out."

Wind gusted, blurring the view, but he could see the small column as it wended its way from the heart of the complex. The devotees wore black robes devoid of any insignia or decoration. Those worn by the priests, also black, bore a stylized sunburst on breast and back. Dumarest counted, frowned, counted again as the column crossed an open space.

Altini said, as he reported, "Two short? Are you certain?"

"Fifteen went in: the party and three priests. Thirteen are coming out. Three of them are priests." He waited as the column reached the

378

outer wall and separated into two groups. "Ten heading back to the landing field."

"But—"

"Cut it!"

The radio operated on a scrambled frequency, but an electronic ear could pick up the noise and a monitoring guard could become suspicious. If the Temple had electronic ears and guards on watch—but Dumarest, willing to take a small risk, was reluctant to take unnecessary chances. Now he slipped the binoculars back into their case and began to ease himself back from the crest. Dirt scraped harshly beneath his stomach and chest, a gritty, rasping sound, that was repeated as he drew free of the sheltering boulders.

Nightmare reared from the dirt inches before his face.

It was black, spined, edged with hooked and spindled legs. An insect, two feet from barbed tail to gaping mandibles. Curved and serrated arcs of shearing destruction. They swung toward his throat as acid sprayed at his eyes.

The acid caught his cheek, the jaws closing on his left arm as Dumarest threw himself sideways to roll on the dirt. As the barbed tail slammed against his chest he tore the knife from his boot and sent the razor-sharp edge to slash at the segmented body. As the swollen abdomen fell he thrust the point between his sleeve and a mandible, twisted, heaved, the broken jaws joining the rest of the body.

The body eaten even as he climbed to his feet by other nightmare shapes; predators who lurked in the dirt, attracted to their prey by the vibrations of movement, the scent of flesh and water.

Ellen Contera pursed her lips as she examined Dumarest's cheek.

"Nasty. If it had hit your eyes you'd be blind now. Here." A spray took away the pain. Another sealed the raw patch beneath a transparent dressings. "Anything else?"

"No." The mesh beneath the plastic of his clothing had saved him from all but bruises. "Why didn't Karlene mention the local wild life?"

"She probably never saw any or, if she did, she was told they were other than dangerous. Pets, maybe." Ellen shrugged. "Is it important?"

"It stops us hanging around."

Dumarest stepped from the woman's cabin into the passage. The *Argonne* was small; a ship little larger than a rich man's pleasure craft, but the engines were good enough to have carried them into the Sharret Cluster and strong enough to have beaten the hazards always present in such a conglomeration of suns. An expensive vessel to operate and far from cheap to charter. Dumarest wondered just how far Ishikari was willing to go to chase his dream.

He sat with the others in the salon, old, withered, only his eyes truly alive.

As Dumarest entered the compartment he said, "Are you certain about the diminished party?"

"Yes."

"How do you account for it?"

Dumarest looked at the man, saying nothing.

He had traveled fifty miles by raft back to where the ship rested in a shallow valley. But for his natural quickness he would be blind now, dead.

Altini said, quickly, "Some wine, Earl? You look as if you could use it. How bad was the thing which attacked you?"

"Bad enough." Dumarest took the goblet the thief handed him. "The predators limit our course of action. We can't make camp and wait and watch until we pick the right time. I wasn't too keen on doing that anyway—the longer we hang around the greater the chance they'll discover us."

"If they do we'll be staked out on the dirt." Lauter rubbed at his chin. "I still think a frontal attack is the best policy."

"A hundred men," said Sanchez dryly. "Lasers, gas, heavy weapons. Explosives to smash down walls. Attack the Temple as you would a fortress. Well, I guess it would work, given enough men and had the money to pay for them." He glanced at Ishikari. "Or could swear there was enough loot to compensate for their time, trouble, dead companions and wounds. Of course, if there wasn't, they wouldn't be gentle."

Dietz said, "Those in the Temple must have friends. My guess is that any frontal attack would be crushed before it got very far. The Hsing-Tiede Consortium," he explained. "It has to be more than it seems."

"Which leaves us where?" Altini poured himself more wine. "Earl?"

"We head for space," said Dumarest. "Wait for a ship to arrive with worshipers. We follow them

381

down and join their party." He lifted a hand to still any protest. "If we come in alone we'll be too small a group to get by. If we hang around waiting for a party and then try to join it we could be noticed and, anyway, the predators don't make that a good idea."

"We could drive a shaft into the dirt," said Ellen. "Rig a motor to give vibration. It would draw the pests to it."

"Some yes," admitted Dumarest. "But we can't move around without causing vibration; our footsteps, the beat of our hearts, the pulse of our blood. And why do things the hard way?"

"Land," mused the assassin. "Step out of the ship and catch up with the other party. Mingle with them until we're in the Temple. Learn what we can and then—" His hand made a chopping motion. "We may need to make a speedy retreat."

"The raft can provide it." Dumarest rose to his feet. "I'll work out the details later."

He was tired, the wound beginning to burn again and he guessed the acid must have contained a soporific of some kind. The edge of the salon door hit his shoulder as he left the compartment and twice he staggered and almost fell. A door opened beneath his touch and he caught the scent of perfume, saw the muted sheen of silver in softly diffused lighting.

"Earl!" Karlene came toward him, embraced him, held him close. "Darling! I'm so afraid!"

"It was nothing." He reassured her as he stroked her hair. Against his body he felt the faint quivering of her flesh. "Barely a scratch, see?" He

382

tilted his head to display the wound on his cheek then noticed the blank stare of her eyes. "Karlene?"

She made no response and he guessed she hadn't heard him. Guessed, too, that her fear wasn't for him but stemmed from something far deeper. The working of her talent which had made this world a living hell. The world and the Temple which had been her home.

"Karlene!"

She moaned like an animal in pain, one lost and helpless and unable even to run. Cringing in his arms, her eyes glazed, little bubbles frothing the corners of her mouth. The sting of his hand barred her cheek with livid welts.

"Karlene! Karlene, damn you! Snap out of it!"

Crude therapy but it worked. The glaze left her eyes and she straightened a little, the tip of her tongue destroying the foam on her lips.

"Earl!" Her hands clutched at his neck, his shoulders, "The scent, Earl. So strong. God, so strong!"

Death and terror lying in the future, waiting to pounce, to become real.

"Be calm, darling." His hand soothed her hair, her body. "You're safe now. Just relax. Take deep breaths and relax. Relax."

Loosen the muscles and slow the pounding of the heart. Let the nerves unwind and the screaming tension dissolve. Ignore the threat of the future in the comfort of the present. Relax and sleep. Sleep.

But, later, when the captain had lifted the

Argonne into space, she jerked and writhed in his arms as she threshed in the nightmare of her dreams.

The robes were thin, cheap, black, cowling faces, concealing bodies, their hems trailing the ground. Copies of those worn by the worshipers Dumarest had watched and the uniform of those moving ahead. A score of pilgrims vented from the bowels of a battered vessel bearing indecipherable markings. Barely had they embarked when the *Argonne* landed to discharge its own load. Now the gap between the parties was closing.

Dumarest glanced back at the valley and the ships it contained. They stood wide apart, each a locked and isolated fortress, and he admired the captain's skill in handling his vessel. Before him rose the slope broken at the crest with undulating mounds like worn and fretted teeth. Those in the van ahead had reached it and were moving sideways as they followed an as yet invisible path.

Lunging forward Dumarest lessened the gap, the others following. There was no need of conversation; the plan and details had been worked out while waiting in space. Now, as he joined up with the major party, Dumarest stumbled, almost fell, caught at the arm of a man to regain his balance.

"Steady!" The man was middle-aged, soft beneath his robe, his face round and bland in the frame of his cowl. "This is no time to get hurt."

"Sorry." Dumarest straightened. "I guess I must have twisted my foot. I hope that's all it is."

"Lean on me if you want." The offer came without hesitation. "Each should share another's burden."

"As each should lighten another's path." Scraps of ritual learned from Karlene. Dumarest tested his weight, grunted, kept pace with the other as he moved on. "Have you been here before?"

"Twice." Pride edged the man's voice. "Your first time? I thought so. In a way I envy you—there can only ever be one first time. But this will be my last." He paused as if waiting for an expected response. One Dumarest didn't know. Instead he coughed, doubled, kept coughing, finally straightening to wipe his mouth. "Bad," said the man at his side. "With me it's cancer. In the stomach, early as yet but there's no point in waiting. In a way it's a relief. Now I don't have to make a decision—just serve the Temple for as long as I'm able."

The man stayed behind when the others left—had the two who had stayed earlier also been diseased? Was this the way the worshipers chose to end their days? But what care could they hope to get in the Temple?

Dumarest looked around. The path wended between soaring mounds, dipping, rising but never leaving the flanking shelter of dirt and stone. The others had forged ahead to mingle with the main party and he saw Altini walking close to a slender shape which could have been a woman. A suspicion verified as she turned to display her face—old, drawn, ravaged by time.

"Pollonia," said his companion. He had noticed Dumarest's interest. "She's staying too."

385

"Have you known her long?"

"We met on the ship. She joined it late."

He didn't say where and Dumarest didn't ask. It was enough to learn that the main party were mostly strangers to each other. A hurdle passed—but there would be others.

Dumarest left his companion as the line began to straggle, moving ahead, spotting the others. As the path finally left the shelter of stone and dirt and began to descend the slope toward the Temple the thief fell into step beside him.

"There's a grip," said Altini, his voice low. "A recognition sign. Give me your hand." His fingers gripped, pressed. "That's the question. Now for the response." Again his fingers pressed but this time in a different pattern. "Got it?"

"Have the others?"

"They will. Once more, now, just to make sure."

His fingers gripped and then he was gone to give the others the secret he had stolen. Before them waited priests, seven of them, tall, enigmatic in their robes, the sunburst insignia bright in the light of the scarlet sun.

"You are welcome."

Dumarest looked at the priest who had come to stand before him. Watched as a man went forward, knelt, hands lifted as if in supplication. As he rose to move toward an opening, Dumarest took his place.

"You are welcome."

Hands took his own; he felt the wide-spaced fingers press, linger until Dumarest returned the signal. Rising he followed the others to the opening, stood waiting as all were greeted, all tested.

"So far so good." Sanchez breathed the words,

not looking at Dumarest, his cowled face pointed toward the Temple. "What now?"

"We are friends. We traveled together. It would be suspicious if we acted as if we didn't know each other." Dumarest kept irritation from his voice—some men found it hard to remember simple instructions. "Just act as if you were genuinely what you claim to be."

A pilgrim, one a little overawed, more than a little overwhelmed by the majestic expanse of the Temple. A man enamored yet constrained by respect. One who couldn't help but show his interest but one who wouldn't stare for too long.

A role Dumarest acted as the priests guided them through the maze. A long, convoluted journey which ended at the massive walls of the central complex. Great doors decorated with abstract designs stood open beneath overhanging eaves, then closed behind them with the sonorous throb of a beaten drum.

"Welcome to the Temple of Cerevox."

The priest was tall, old, thin within his robe, adorned not with the sunburst insignia but a design composed of interconnected circles. Staring at it Dumarest was reminded of the Seal of the Cyclan and looked to where the pattern was repeated on the altar at which the priest stood. A block of stone as black as night set on a raised platform so as to dominate the entrance hall. Flames from flambeaux set to either side threw a dancing, ruby sheen over those assembled.

"For time beyond the count of mortals has the truth here being guarded. From the very first, when those bearing the fruit of true knowledge settled and dedicated their lives to the preservation of the heritage of Man, has the Original Secret resided within these walls. Only those who share our heritage may enter this place. Only those who are true in heart, in mind and spirit, may unite with us here in harmony."

Like the priest, the voice was old but, again like the speaker, it held the strength of burning conviction. The voice of a fanatic.

Those answering it were like the dry rustle of leaves.

"All praise to the Guardians."

"Here, now, the past and the present are one!"

"As it was so let it be."

"Let your hearts be humble!"

"We grovel in the dirt at the feet of truth." A concerted movement and the floor was covered with the black-robed bodies of the worshipers. "We are blinded by the light of revelation."

The introductory ceremony, at least, presented no problems. Dumarest mouthed as if making the correct responses, bowing, lying prone as he darted glances to either side. The walls appeared solid. The roof was heavily groined with carved supports of inset pillars. Dimly, in the flaring light of the flambeaux, he could see the shapes of attendant priests. They bore touches of scarlet on their robes. A higher rank, he guessed, or those who were entrusted to do the bloody work of executioners. Speculation ended as the old priest fell silent, stepping back as, in a line, the worshipers moved past the altar to make their donations.

"For the Temple." A woman, not Pollonia,

tipped a bag and let gems fall like glinting rain on the black stone. "May it stand always as Guardian of the Truth."

"For the Temple." A man set down a small bar of precious metal.

Another had coins, thick, gemmed, easily negotiable wealth. He followed the others who had gone before to stand at a door flanked by priests. Beyond it, Dumarest guessed, would lie the inner precincts of the Temple, more ceremonies, a service of some kind, a view of sacred objects, incense, chanting, hypnotic repetitions. The basis of any ritual designed to reenforce obedience to authority.

The worshipers would be led like sheep, treated like sheep, herded the same way. To follow them would be to learn little.

"For the Temple."

More gems. More portable wealth. Dumarest glanced back at the line. Sanchez was closest; the assassin beyond him, Lauter, looming over a woman close to the end of the line. Altini, the thief, was last. For a moment their eyes met, then Dumarest turned away. Three others stood before him, one the man he had spoken to on the trail.

"For the Temple." He made his donation. Then, instead of moving on, he rested both arms on the altar. "I also dedicate my heart, my spirit, my body, my life. To be used as a bastion for the truth."

The priest said, "You choose a hard path."

"Willingly."

"The step is irrevocable."

"That I accept as I accept all things. Grant me the supreme joy of serving to the end of my days the truth which has dominated my existence."

After a moment the priest lifted a hand. "It is so granted."

Attendants led the man to one side, to where a door gaped in the wall, one set far from that before which the others waited.

"For the Temple."

A man made his donation.

"For the Temple."

Another did the same and Dumarest stepped forward to take his place. He coughed as he reached it, doubling as he had on the journey, straightening, the cowl falling back from his face.

"For the Temple." He set down the small bag containing items of jewelery. He followed it with both arms set on the stone. "I also dedicate my heart, my spirit, my body, my life. To be used as a bastion for the truth."

Ellen Contera said, "Earl dedicated himself? What the hell made him do that?"

Altini shrugged. He sat in the salon of the *Argonne,* his face marked with lines of fatigue. The wine he held did little to refresh him. Later there would be drugs but, for now, it was good just to sit and rest and savor the sweet comfort of the wine.

"And the others?" Ishikari was impatient. "What of them? Speak, man!"

"They followed Earl. A contingency plan."

Altini sipped at his wine. The *Argonne* was in space, drifting high above Raniang, the captain following his instructions. Karlene, drugged, was somnolent in her cabin. Far below, night had closed over the Temple. When it thickened he would return.

"Earl saw his chance and took it," explained the thief. "A way to get close to the heart of the Temple. Ordinary worshipers don't come close. Earl must have guessed that. He gave me the signal to stay out of it and went ahead. The others joined him. I followed the rest."

"Into the Temple?" Ellen leaned closer. "What did you see?"

"I'm not too sure."

"Try to remember. I could help you if you want."

"No." He smiled and lifted his glass. "I've had enough hypnotism. You were right about that: chanting, drums, flashes of light, repetition, ritual responses, movements, all of it. I dug my nails into my palms and managed to keep a clear head. It wasn't easy."

"But you managed." Ishikari gnawed at his lip. "But what did you see?"

A chamber reached by a sinuous passage decorated with a host of beasts and birds, reptiles and all manner of living things. A roof glistening with artificial stars. Priests chanting to either side, some with the scarlet insignia, others with the sunburst, few with the convoluted rings.

"No women?" Ellen fired the question. "No priestesses?"

Not in the passage but in the great hall to which it led nubile girls had offered small cups of pungent liquid which had to be swallowed at a gulp. Symbolic blood of a symbolic world, or so

Altini had guessed. He had managed to retain most of the fluid, spitting it out later when unobserved, but the little he had swallowed had made his ears buzz. As had the pound of music; the wail of pipes and the throb of drums. A beat designed to match that of his heart, to slow it, to weave about him a strange, almost mystic detachment, enhanced by the dancing of the girls, the directed movements of the worshipers. Before him a world had opened, strange, alien, brightly exciting. One which held a touch of fear.

"It was creepy," he said. "I can't describe it better than that. A feeling of danger."

Of danger and excitement as would be felt by a child exploring a reputedly haunted house. An adult teasing a serpent. One who yielded to the desire to test personal courage by risking an action which could destroy if followed too far.

And then came the climax of the ceremony.

"You saw it?" Ishikari was intent. "You saw what the Temple contains?"

"I don't know. A part of it, perhaps, but that's about all. It was—" Altini broke off, shaking his head. "It was—strange."

Objects set in cases encrusted with gems and precious metals. Things which the priests displayed as if they were sacred relics. Most had knelt and kissed the containers. Others had stood as if entranced. All had given their total attention to what they were shown. And then had come the climax.

"A light," said Altini. "A blue glow which seemed to pulse. One without heat."

"You saw it?"

"I saw something." The thief swallowed more wine, not looking at the old man. "A reflection, maybe. A glow seen through complex mirrors. I had that impression. I also felt that, if I had seen it direct, I would have lost my eyes."

"The living God shining in resplendent glory at the heart of the Temple," mused Ellen. "In the Holy of Holies. Is that what they said it was?"

"Not exactly. The hint was there, maybe, and some could have taken it for that. But they didn't talk of God. It was Earth, they said. Mother Earth."

"Which they worship. Anything else?"

"Not much. There was bowing and chanting, then the light vanished and it was over. The priests made gestures, a blessing of sorts, maybe, then we were led out." He added, "It seemed a hell of a long way back to the valley."

"Is that all?" Ishikari made no effort to mask his disappointment. "Damn it, man, you went—"

"I was doing a job." Altini finished his wine and slammed the goblet hard on the table. "I wasn't there to enjoy the sights. You want to know just what happened? Every word spoken? Every gesture made? Then join the next batch of pilgrims. You might be lucky and get away with it. Then, when you come out, you'll have your answers."

But not all of them. Ellen said, quickly, "You're tired, Ahmed. Short-tempered and I can't blame you. Did you find out what you wanted to know?"

He was a thief and had noticed things others would have missed; the layout of the passage and chambers, nooks in which a man could hide, vents through which he could crawl. While the others had bowed, chanting, he had watched and studied; the twist of smoke in the air as it rose pluming from smoldering incense, the touch of subtle drafts, the echoes of shuffling feet, the set of shadows and the texture of walls and floor. A master of his trade who scented weakness like a dog scented blood.

Later, when he rested in his cabin, pipes feeding energy into his veins, metabolism speeded by the use of slowtime which stretched minutes into hours, Ellen returned to join Ishikari.

He sat, thoughtful, spinning an empty goblet in his fingers, small droplets of wine clinging to the interior, moving so as to trace elaborate patterns on the glass.

Without looking up he said, "Will he be ready in time?"

"I've given him forty hours subjective. He'll wake hungry but fit." She added, "By the time he's eaten and aligned himself it'll be two hours from now."

"The moon sets in three." It was barely a crescent but a little light was more dangerous than none. "He'll have plenty of time."

"Plenty," she agreed. On Raniang the nights were long. "It'll work out."

"Maybe." Ishikari turned the goblet again then blinked as, without warning, the stem shattered in his hands. "Earl," he said. "Why—"

"Did he split his forces?" She shrugged, impatient with his lack of understanding. "A wise move. He and the others on the inside and Altini free to operate on the outside. Who better than a

394

thief to break into the Temple? If Earl makes a distraction he could make his way to the inner chambers. Or it could be the other way about. I'm not worried about that."

"Then what?"

"The glow," she said. "The mystic chanting. The worship of a God-like something. The way some pilgrims offer themselves to the Temple. And the way Karlene's acted ever since we arrived here. Her terror. That's why I've kept her drugged. The thing which made her run in the first place is tearing at her mind. The foreknowledge of death and fear—and it's so strong, so close."

He looked up, ignoring the broken glass, the blood which welled from a tiny wound on a finger to form a ruby smear.

"What has that to do with us?"

"Religions change," she said. "Like all institutions. What begins as one thing ends as another. Sometimes circumstances dictate the change, sometimes expediency. In times of stress it can be the worshipers themselves. They need to take a greater part, to bind themselves closer to the object of their veneration and, always, the priests will accommodate them. Those who serve a god serve the greatest power they can imagine. They share in that power. And the more demanding their god the greater it becomes. Maybe the Temple has passed the line."

She saw he didn't understand.

"Donations," she explained. "Personal attachment. The binding of the young to serve. But it needn't stop there. The line between symbolism and reality can be passed. When that happens token surrender isn't enough." Pausing she added, "I think Earl could have offered himself for sacrifice."

Chapter 10

The man with cancer was Nakam Stura, a merchant, he explained and, from his clothing, Dumarest guessed he had been successful. The robe covered soft fabrics of expensive weaves and he wondered why the man hadn't used his wealth to buy medical treatment.

"We all follow the Wheel." Stura answered his unspoken question. "The Mother knows what is best. To fight against what is to be is to act the child. Better to accept with dignity and to serve as one is able. As you chose to do, my friend. As Pollonia and Reigan. In submission lies contentment."

They waited in a room to which a priest had guided them. One with bare stone walls and a floor of tessellated segments of black and amber. Light shone from sources beyond tinted panes: a luminous glow enhanced by the minute flames of vigil lights set before various places on the walls. Reigen knelt before one, hands clasped, head lowered, words a soft mumble as he prayed before the stylized depiction of a quartered circle. A man like the woman, old, drawn, his face ravaged by time. One with eyes lost in a vision of things Dumarest couldn't discern.

"He lives only for the Mother," said Stura. "Always he has longed for her embrace."

As had they all—if they were what they purported to be.

Dumarest edged away, sensing danger, not knowing when a word or remark would reveal him for what he was. Lauter, big, solemn, sat to one side, his face blank, eyes glazed as if lost in a world of his own. Dietz, small, restless, paced to one side. He slowed as he caught Dumarest's eye and turned to concentrate on a vigil light, the round, blotched circle it illuminated.

Sanchez said, softly, "How long are we supposed to wait here?"

He had drifted close and spoke without looking at Dumarest but, even so, he was being unwise. As he had been willful when dedicating himself to the Temple. He should have followed Altini; instead, greed for loot had made him ignore the plan.

Now he said, "We could break out. Grab a few of the priests and find out what they know. Gather what we can and get on with what we came to do."

Dumarest said, "The Mother is merciful."

"What?"

"If you have sinned then there will be forgiveness."

398

"Earl—"

"Be patient." Dumarest glanced at the ceiling, the tinted panes, the frieze cut into the wall of the chamber. Who knew who could be watching? Listening to every word? In a whisper he added, "Act the part you chose to play. Settle down. Pray. Look blank and wait. Damn you, wait!"

Beyond the chamber there would be ceremonies under way. Priests busy with the function of the Temple. The worshipers who would leave needed to be attended to—those who had dedicated themselves could be left for a time. He sat, hearing the soft mumble of Reigan's voice. Pollonia sighing as she sat in an apparent trance. Even the merchant was silent, head lowered, chin resting on his chest.

What would happen if he should change his mind and buy the treatment which would save his life?

A question Dumarest knew he dare not ask. He leaned back, shoulders against the wall, forcing himself to relax as he had done so often before when waiting to enter the arena. He drifted into a calming detachment during which his powers were conserved and vital energies husbanded.

In his mind he saw the model of the Temple, the plans of its interior. Guesses, but better than nothing and, so far, they had confirmed Karlene's memory. The great entrance doors, the altar, the passage which must have lain beyond, the one they had followed to this room—a chamber set on a lower level; others would adjoin it. Halls, more chambers, more passages. Places where she had worked and others where those serving the Temple had eaten, cooked, slept. A lot of people, a lot of rooms—but still the inner chambers posed a mystery.

How long had it been?

Dumarest glanced at the chronometer strapped to his wrist; an instrument which was more than it seemed. Time had moved faster than he had guessed and he inhaled, filling his lungs with air drawn through his nose, catching a pungent sweetness, a hint of acridity. Incense and something else, a truth-inducing vapor of some kind, perhaps, if they were under test it would be natural.

Lauter must have scented it too. He rumbled and sat upright and snorted as if to clear his nose. Rising, he crossed the room and checked the door. It resisted his pressure.

To Dumarest he whispered, "I don't like this. We're in a cage. The air stinks and I've the feeling trouble's on its way."

"So?"

"Why wait for it? We've got to do something."

Dumarest said, softly, "Use your head, man. We're outnumbered by the priests. We don't know where the treasure lies. We don't even know the way out and, even if we did, where would we go?"

"But—"

"They have to make the first move. Until then we wait." He added, "And watch Sanchez. He's as jumpy as you are."

As Dietz could be but, if so, he didn't show it. A gambler who had learned to mask his features. An assassin who knew that he could be his own worst enemy. He glanced at Dumarest as if about to speak, then changed his mind as the door swung open.

Girls like angels stepped into the room.

They were young, lithe, nubile, neatly dressed in gowns which fell to just below the knee. Each had the left shoulder bared and on the soft flesh the imprint of a tattoo shone in reflected splendor. Each bore a tray on which rested a bowl, a plate, a steaming cup.

"Food." Sanchez smiled at the girl who proffered him her tray. "At least they aren't going to starve us. And what of you, my dear? Are you also a gift of the Mother?"

A fool, careless with his tongue, Dumarest saw the stiffening of Stura's face, the expression in Pollonia's eyes. Only Reigan, lost in his private world, seemed not to have noticed.

"All things are gifts of the Mother." The girl lifted her tray. "Eat so as to gain strength to serve her."

"And after?"

"Eat!" Dumarest took the tray from the girl and thrust it into the fighter's hands. To the girl he said, "How long must we wait before we can serve?"

"The ceremonies are almost over. When the worshipers have left, the priests will come for you." Her hand reached out and rested on his own. "You are strong and that is good. You must stay strong for the Mother needs you. Now eat and be patient."

The bowl held a thin stew composed of stringy fibers which could have been meat together with an assortment of vegetables. The plate bore a portion of hard, dark, gritty bread. The cup held hot water into which herbs had been infused.

"Today is a special day," said the girl who had given Dumarest his tray. "And so we eat the feast of celebration."

"Will you share it with me?" He read the answer in her eyes. "Here."

He watched as she spooned up the stew and dug sharp teeth into the bread. Not drugged, then, or if it was she didn't know it. And there was no mistaking her pleasure. He remembered what Ellen Contera had told him and wondered if the girl thought she was eating rare and expensive viands, drinking fine and special wine.

"Where will the priests take us?" Dumarest smiled as she stared at him. "After the meal," he urged. "Where will we go?"

"Down toward the inner chambers."

"And?" As she didn't answer, he said, "Do all those who dedicate themselves to the Temple go down to the inner chambers?"

"Of course. The old and flawed and those who are ill." She glanced at Pollonia. "Those who seek comfort and to rest. And the strong." Her eyes met his own. "Those who are not young."

"What is down there?" He saw the sudden blankness of her eyes. "Do you know? Can you tell me?" Then, quickly, knowing he had pressed too hard, he said, "Forget it, my dear. Just finish the wine."

It was night before the priests came. Five of them, tall, their robes adorned with the sigils of convoluted circles. The eldest, a man with a face ravaged with pits and lines, stared at them with deep-set, burning eyes. A fanatic who strode from one to the other as if reading their secret thoughts. The woman he ignored as he did Reigan who was still on his knees.

To Nakam Stura he snapped, "What ails you?" He nodded at the answer, turned to Dumarest. "You?"

"My lungs." Dumarest coughed and fought for breath. "A parasitical spore. I guess I haven't long to go."

"You?"

"I am fit," said Ramon Sanchez. "Strong and eager to serve."

Dietz whispered that he had an affliction of the heart. Lauter complained of his wounds.

"A laser burn in the gut," he explained. "Plates in both legs. A bullet still riding near my spine. I could get fixed, I suppose, but what's the point? I'd rather serve while I still have something to offer."

"You come from where?"

"Chalcot. I was a mercenary."

A mistake—the Original People did not follow paths of violence. Lauter had betrayed himself by volunteering his profession. Yet the priest made no comment and Dumarest wondered at his indifference as he led the way from the room down winding passages which fell in a spiraling decline beneath his feet.

A long journey ending in a gallery flanked with doors. Light blazed from the ceiling, a cold, blue luminescence which drained the natural color from flesh and left it the grim hue of lead.

"Later you will be given instruction," said the priest. "Now you will rest. You," his finger stabbed at the woman. "In there." The finger stabbed again as Pollonia moved toward a door. "You and you in there." He moved on as Reigan and Stura hastened to obey. At the end of the gallery stood wider doors, the air tainted with an acrid stench. "You in there and you," the finger pointed at Lauter, "in there."

A division Dumarest didn't like, for it had separated the false from the genuine and had split the mercenary from his companions. At his side Dietz murmured, "He spotted Kroy for a fake."

"Us too, maybe."

"Does it matter?" Sanchez looked up at the glowing ceiling, down at the room, the long row of cots it contained. "The priests are fools. They didn't even trouble to search us."

"What would you have done had they tried?"

"Fought, what else?"

"They could have guessed that. Why risk their skins when there is no need?" Dumarest looked at the nearest of the cots. "We don't seem to be alone."

A man lay on the fabric stretched on a frame. His face was mottled with sores as were his hands, his arms and naked torso. Ugly, oozing pustules which had stained the cot with crusted smears. He was asleep or drugged, moaning a little, a thin skein of white hair fringing the dome of his skull.

Another, not so badly afflicted, lay beyond him. A third lower down. As Dumarest walked along the cots a man reared toward the end of the room, turning his head, blinking eyes glazed with a nacreous film.

"Master? Is that you, Master? Am I again to serve the Mother?"

"Not yet," soothed Dumarest. He touched the man's naked shoulder. "Rest while you may and peace attend you in your dreams."

As they moved on, Sanchez said, softly, "They stink. They all stink of sickness and disease. Why the hell did the priests put us among them?"

"To serve."

"Not me. I'm no nurse."

Dietz said, patiently, "You do not understand, Ramon. We, they, are all of a kind. You heard the blind man. He yearns to serve. He must have offered himself for that." Pausing he added, "Just as we did."

To be used as the needs of the Temple demanded offering their hearts, spirits, lives, bodies. Dumarest remembered the meal, the thin stew with the stringy shreds of meat. The Temple was on a harsh world and those running it could not afford to indulge in the luxury of waste. Those dedicating themselves would be used to the full and, even when dead, they would still be of value.

He strode down the length of the room, counting the sick, the empty cots. About half and half which, if some were now working, explained the apparent carelessness of the priests. Labor was in short supply, especially the kind which was provided by those on the cots, and soon he and the others would be swallowed among them.

."It's crazy," said Sanchez. "If they suspect us why leave us free?"

"They suspect Kroy," said Dumarest. "We were separated from the others because we are more fit. But they don't know we arrived as a group."

"Are they stupid?"

"No," said Dietz. The assassin knew the strength of the established habit-patterns better than most. Knew too the encysting effect of established authority. He said, "We're operating on momentum. They take us for what we claim to be. We'll get by if we don't draw attention to ourselves as Kroy did."

"Or unless he betrays us." Sanchez looked at the door, scowling. "They could be working on him now. Coming for us at this very moment. I say we move."

"When they come for us," said Dumarest.

"Now."

"No. We wait."

"Like hell!" Sanchez strode toward the door, halted as Dumarest stepped before him. His teeth shone white between his snarling lips. "Get out of my way, damn you. Shift or—"

Dumarest moved, his left hand darting forward, catching the fighter's right forearm, jerking it from his body, the weapon he guessed the man was reaching for. His right hand stabbed forward and upward, fingers closing on the other's throat, fingers gouging deep to rest on the carotids.

"Relax," he said, coldly. "Kick or struggle and I'll close my hand." His fingers tightened in warn-

406

ing. Tightened more as Sanchez lifted his free
hand. "Don't try it!"

"Don't!" Dietz was beside them. "Earl! Ramon!
This is madness!"

Dumarest said, not looking at the assassin, "I
agree, but so is running blind in the Temple. The
place must be thick with priests. We could get
some but the others would have us trapped. We
must wait until they come for us. If necessary
we'll defend ourselves but, if they've come to
guide us, we play along." He eased the pressure
on the fighter's throat. "I'm running this operation, Ramon. If you don't like it too bad. Do you
play along or not?"

"I—" Sanchez swallowed as Dumarest lowered
his hand. "You—"

"Forget the threats. I want an answer." He
would get the answer he wanted or the fighter
would lie dead on one of the cots. Sanchez recognized this. "Good." Dumarest glanced at his wrist
as the man yielded. If the priests left them alone
they would have to move but there was time yet.
"Get some rest."

As Sanchez, smoldering with rage, moved to
an empty cot Dumarest added, "That goes for you
too, Pinal."

"You're a fool, Earl." Dietz spoke in a whisper.
"Ramon will never forgive how you shamed him.
You should have killed him. Give me the word
and I'll do it for you."

"We can use him."

"Then, at least, give me the word." A different
word, one which would free his mental restraints,
and Dumarest wondered how the assassin knew

he had been chained. "I tried," he explained, anticipating the question. "It wasn't hard to figure out how Ishikari had tricked me. Twice I tried to even the score. Twice I failed. The second time he told me why."

"Did you expect him to trust you?"

"He made me eat dirt," said Dietz bitterly. "Had me sweating with fear. But, worst of all, he trod on my pride." He looked at his hands, the minute quivering of his fingers. "He left me less than a man. I want to be whole again."

To use his skills, his drugs, his poisons, his trade. Hampered, he was safe but a tool which had lost its temper. A knife which had lost its edge. And no man should be a cripple.

Dumarest said the word.

And watched as a veil seemed to fall from the assassin's eyes. He straightened a little, breathing deep, the quiver now absent from his hands. A man as deadly as a serpent.

"Get some rest now," said Dumarest.

He felt the sting of the chronometer against his wrist as the man obeyed. Altini was on his way.

It was hard to move in the night. There was no moon but starlight cast a silver sheen and created deceptive shadows which masked stones and potholes and uneven footing. Terrain over which the thief raced with trained grace, sensing obstacles, avoiding them, moving on until he reached the outer complex of the Temple. His path was already plotted: not through the maze but over it. Dust gritted beneath the soft soles of his shoes as he ran along the tops of the walls, crouching, dropping to run over bare spaces, jumping gaps, moving like a flitting shadow toward the flanking buildings, the dome, the squat towers.

They would hold defenses, watchers, weapons to burn down unwanted rafts, to sear the bodies of any trying to gain unauthorized entry to the sacred precincts. Flattened against stone he studied them, the black grease on his face and neck merging with the color of the clothing he wore, the gloves hiding his hands. Carefully he lifted an arm, his fingers moving with the delicacy of spiders traversing shattered glass, pausing as they felt an invisible strand. An alarm, one he avoided as he climbed, a second he left behind him, a third which he neutralized with small instruments he took from a pouch at his waist.

Cracked stone provided easy holds and he rushed upward to move into the inward facing side of a tower, to freeze as he strained both eyes and ears.

He saw nothing but the loom of other towers, the silent barrenness of sloping roofs and the sweeping curve of the central dome. Were the towers deserted? He climbed higher and froze again at the sound of a shuffle, the drone of a voice.

It stilled, yielded to silence, commenced again as if it were a repetitive recording played on a machine. A routine prayer mumbled so often it had become as normal as breathing to the man on watch.

Altini climbed higher to where openings gaped in the stone toward the summit of the tower. Hanging by one hand he dipped the other into his pouch, found a small cylinder, thrust his thumb hard against an end and threw it into an opening.

He heard it hit, a startled exclamation, then the sound of something heavy slumping to the floor. One impact which meant a solitary guard and he guessed the other towers would be as sparsely manned. It was tempting to climb up and into the tower. There would be a door of sorts giving to the lower levels and access to the main body of the Temple but to try that route was to take too big a gamble. To maintain efficiency single guards would need frequent reliefs and a change could be due at any time. It would be safer to descend and cross the roofs in the "blind" spot he had created. Shadows clustered thick beneath the eaves and gave good cover.

Altini reached it, avoiding alarm wires and pressure points which would have bathed the roof in revealing light. Stone pierced with grills ran beneath the eaves and he crouched beneath one, sniffing, catching the heavy odor of incense. Air vented from the hall below as he had suspected; now he needed to find a way into the heart of the Temple, the inner chambers where the loot would be found.

Thieves' work and he was good at it. Like an insect he moved from place to place, sniffing, questing, careful of wires and traps. The openings in the towers were like blind eyes, the stars distant, hostile, indifferent to sacrilege and the impending rape of cossetted treasures. Soon now he would have forced a way in, the Temple violated, the priests impotent in their power to protect their charge.

"Ahmed!" The voice whispered in his ear. Ellen's voice from where she waited with the raft. "Answer, damn you!"

"Trouble?" silently he moved his lips.

"Maybe. How are things going?"

"Well." He looked at the chronometer on his wrist. A twin to the one carried by Dumarest. "Is that what you called to ask about?"

"No. There's a raft heading your way. From the Hsing-Tiede Consortium, we think."

"Close?"

"Too close for comfort. It might be expected. Best to take cover."

"Out!"

Talking was dangerous in that it took concentration as well as time. Altini moved, eyes wary, feet and hands moving in neat precision. Grit made small, scratching sounds and something shifted to roll down the slope with a fading rattle. Broken stone or a shard of aged mortar but enough to betray him, and Altini tensed, his stomach tight to the anticipated challenge, the blaze of revealing light, the searing burn of a laser.

Then, abruptly, the raft was above him.

It rode high and straight, circling, bearing lights which flickered in a recognition pattern. It lowered, hovering, as searchlights bathed it. Lower until it passed the summits of the towers, the flanking buildings, to land in the outer complex close to the great doors. Watching, Altini could see the men it carried, the scarlet of the robe one of them wore.

Chapter 11

Dumarest rose from the cot as he felt the sting of the instrument on his wrist: Altini's signal warning that the thief was in position. Sanchez joined him as he headed toward the door, Dietz at his heels.

"We move?"

"Yes."

"Not before time." The fighter lacked patience. "What about Kroy?"

"We'll pick him up on the way." Dumarest looked at the cots, the men they contained. Already he'd made his choice. "Get the door while I collect a guide."

He was thin, ravaged, jerking awake at a touch, eyes wide as he saw the loom of Dumarest's body, the nighted color of his robe. A man confused, thinking he had been wakened by a priest.

"Get up," said Dumarest. "Come with me. I want you to show me where you work."

"I—"

"What is your name?"

"Ritter. Chang Ritter."

"Hurry, Chang. Come with me. The Mother commands it."

Sanchez was busy at the door. It was thick, heavy, fastened with a metal catch. It swung open beneath the fighter's hands and Dietz stepped into a passage, that was deserted and he led the way to the room where the mercenary had been taken. Dumarest heard him cry out as he entered.

"God! The swine!"

The room was small, holding only five cots, four of them empty, Lauter sprawled on the fifth. He was naked to the waist, his torso blotched with ugly wounds. Blackened rips as if hot pincers had torn at the flesh, charring tissue and releasing blood which had clotted to form carmine mounds.

"Kroy?" Dietz was at his side. "Kroy?"

Dumarest looked around. Water stood in a bucket on the floor and he lifted it, flung it over the mercenary where he lay. Before Lauter could move he was at his side, hand clamped over his mouth, nose closed by the pressure of thumb and finger. A hold which could kill but one which stimulated the mercenary's survival instinct. Lauter shuddered, heaved, lifted a hand to tear the constriction from his mouth.

"No noise," warned Dumarest. "Just take it easy."

Air made a rasping sound as Lauter filled his

lungs. He tried to sit upright, almost fell, made it as Deitz thrust an arm beneath his shoulders. For moments he could do nothing but sit and fight for breath then, as his tenacious grip on life asserted itself, he snorted, coughed, winced, as he swung his legs over the edge of the cot.

"What kept you?"

"Ask Earl." Sanchez glanced at Dumarest. "He made us wait."

"Just as well he did." Lauter looked at his chest. "Those bastards weren't gentle. They took me down the passage to a place they've got. Tied me up and had themselves some fun. Amateurs!" His contempt was real. "I could have had them spilling their guts in half the time."

"They questioned you?" Dumarest checked to see if Ritter was safe. "What did they want to know?"

"Who I was. Where I'd come from. Was I alone—stuff like that. I pretended I didn't know what they were talking about. When they put the irons to me I just yelled and slumped. I wonder you didn't hear me."

And lucky they hadn't. To have attempted a rescue would have been to join him in danger, as it was, the mercenary served to warn of what would happen if they were careless. As he straightened to his feet Dumarest studied the instrument on his wrist. Time was running out. Altini was on the roof. They had to find the secret the Temple contained, make their way upwards to the opening he would have made, join with him in the final run to safety.

A simple plan but one depending on speed. To

hit, to take, to run and, with luck, to do it before the alarm could be sounded.

"Let's get moving." Dumarest stepped toward the door, listened, thrust himself through the portal into the passage. It was still deserted and he stared at the guide. "Which way, Chang?"

Sanchez snarled as the man made a vague gesture. "The creep. Hasn't he any brains? I'll make him talk."

"You watch the rear." Dumarest was harsh. "You're too big with your mouth. I won't tell you again. Now, Chang, which way?"

Down the passage to a junction, to turn left, to follow a slope, to move through a door into another chamber. The cold, blue light ended, replaced by a warmer glow cast from scattered lanterns. Another passage swallowed them, the floor cracked and seemingly neglected, and Dumarest guessed it was used only for the passage of workers. Deeper into the maze of the Temple and he tensed to the sound of chanting.

"Kroy, drop back to stand beside Chang."

Dumarest moved to take his place as the mercenary obeyed. Himself and Dietz in the front, Sanchez at the rear, the two apparent workers in the middle. In the dimmer lighting they might just get by. Another gamble to add to the rest.

"Robes," whispered the assassin. "We need camouflage."

A need which grew as they progressed. The empty places were far behind now and more voices could be heard together with the rasp of sandals, the moving shadows which created soft rustlings. Even at night the Temple was busy.

"There." Dumarest halted as he heard Chang's voice. "No! Not on! There! There!"

He stood pointing at the wall, at a carving depicting a fanged and monstrous beast. His face was twisted as he stubbornly fought Lauter's dragging hand. A man like a machine which had been set in motion. One clinging to a familiar path.

Again his hand stabbed at the beast. "There!"

Dumarest said, "Is that the way the priests took you? Through the wall?"

"He's lying. It's solid." Lauter snorted his impatience. "You can see it is."

"Perhaps not." Dietz moved toward it, ran his hands over the carved stone, grunted as he felt a movement. "It's on a pivot. A secret door of some kind."

A convenience which enabled workers to attend their duties without encroaching on the devotions of those in adjoining chambers. Opened, it gave on to a narrow passage which led to a room stacked with brooms, cloths, jars of wax, other assorted materials. The passage continued to open in the well of an area brilliant with light.

"Hell!" Sanchez narrowed his eyes. "What's this?"

A door faced the one through which they emerged. It was set far back beneath an overhang and stood deep in massive blocks of stone. The symbol of the quartered circle was prominent over an ornate lock. To either side stairs led up to a gallery which swept in an arc to either side. Climbing them, Dumarest saw walls of polished stone heavily carved, the quartered circle

416

predominent. Light shone from panels set into the roof. A clear, blue illumination which threw the troughlike bench running around the inner wall of the gallery into prominence.

From within it came the wink and flash of jewels.

"Loot!" Sanchez thrust himself forward. "This is it! This is what we came for!"

The donations of worshipers stored and accumulated over countless years. Rare books their covers crusted with gems, ornaments, necklaces, rings, torcs, bracelets, objects of intricate loveliness, the work of long-dead craftsmen, the valued treasures of generations set as votive offerings to what the Temple contained.

"Leave them!" Dumarest was sharp. "This isn't what we came for!"

The fighter ignored him. "Look at this?" Sanchez held a flower of metal, the petals composed of matching stones which glowed with ruby and emerald, sapphire and diamond. Precious metal beneath his fingers as he tore them from their settings. "And this!" A chalice of shimmering perfection. "And this!"

He ran down the gallery, caution forgotten, entranced by the treasure spread before him. A rapacious child snatching at scintillating toys, destroying them, thrusting handfuls of gems into his pockets.

"No!" Chang cried out in protest at the sacrilege. "Don't! Please don't!"

He ran forward, frail arms lifted in a hopeless attempt to stop the fighter. Sanchez turned, snarling, striking out with brutal force. Chang flew backward to hit against the edge of the trough, to slump like a broken doll, to lie on the polished stone of the floor, his head at a grotesque angle.

"No, Earl!" Lauter caught at Dumarest's arm. "He's mad. Crazed. Try to stop him and he'll kill you. I've seen it before. An entire squad. All they could see was loot."

And all Dumarest could see was the blood staining the dead man's mouth. A carmine smear which grew and grew until it filled the gallery, the entire universe.

There had been formalities which had added more time to that already lost but Clarge had had no choice but to yield to ancient tradition. Even while waiting for the ceremonies and rituals to end, his mind had been at work. The Temple was, to him, almost an open book. He could visualize what it must have been in the beginning; a shrine attended by dedicated attendants. One which had enlarged over the years, gaining status with bulk, stature from the donations of worshipers. Enhanced power and prestige would have accelerated the growth until the peak of optimum efficiency would have been reached and passed. Now revenue would have fallen, attendants fewer and of a lesser quality, those adhering to the creed it preached content to do so from afar, less inclined to make the arduous pilgrimage.

The way of all such institutions. Only the Cyclan would continue to grow and expand its influence over an endless succession of worlds. The secret domination which already controlled the destiny of a myriad planets and would lock more into its expanding web. One day the entire galaxy would be under that domination and then there would be a final end to waste and stupidity.

Clarge could visualize it as he could the origins of the Temple in which he stood. It, like so much else, would be swept away, the stones used in its construction devoted to rearing buildings dedicated to the pursuit of knowledge. Poverty would end—able beings would be put to work, fed, housed, maintained in a state of efficient health, set to work to create the new way of life. The whims of petty rulers would be abolished. Emotional poisons eradicated. Birth, growth, death and development controlled. Selected types bred and genetic advantages incorporated into the human race. There would be no disease, no irrational loyalties, no catering to superstition. The mind would be all. Logic, reason, intelligence, efficiency—the cornerstones of the new, bright and glittering order to come.

The whisper of a gong brought him to full concentration on the matter at hand. He stood within the small room to which he had been escorted, the hue of his robe warmly scarlet against the dull brown of the walls, in sharp contrast to that worn by the old man who came toward him. But if his robe was black the insignia covering the breast was not. It glowed with gems and precious metals, an elaborate sigil surrounding a quartered circle.

"My lord!" The cyber inclined his head. "I am most honored that you have condescended to grant me this audience. It is something you will never have cause to regret. I would not have imposed my presence in this sacred place but for the urgency of my mission."

Deference and polite words to a man who was little better than a superstition-ridden fool, but here, in the Temple, the High Priest held supreme power. A fact never to be forgotten if he hoped to enlist Varne's aid.

"Sit." A withered hand gestured toward a chair. As Clarge took it the High Priest dropped into another. "You are importunate, cyber."

"With reason. The need is great."

"Nothing is greater than the Mother." Varne waited as if expecting a comment. When none came he added, "Those who sent you assured me that you intend no harm. Did they lie?"

"They told the truth. I have come to make you an offer. I have cause to know that a man is interested in the Temple. He is not of your following. He would not hesitate to violate your sacred places. He—"

"That is impossible! The Mother would never permit it!"

"Yet—"

"No! The thought is sacrilege!"

To press the point would be to alienate the priest and Clarge recognized the danger. Recognized, too, the brittle situation he was in. Too much time had been wasted at the Hsing-Teide establishment before those in charge had even admitted the existence of the Temple. Then had come the tedious delay before permission had been granted for him to be received at the Temple. Time in which Dumarest could have come and gone—once again escaping the grasp of the Cyclan.

Clarge knew the penalty should he fail.

He said, "Have none appeared who are not what they claim to be?" He elaborated the question. "I am thinking of someone who seems unsure of the rituals. Who hesitates or avoids a direct response. He could pretend to be dumb or even blind. Or he could ask too many questions. Have you no check on those visiting the Temple?"

"The secrets of the Temple must remain inviolate."

"That is understood. But surely a stranger, pretending to be a pilgrim, would have been noticed? Or could be noticed?" Pausing, Clarge added, "If such a one should be discovered the Cyclan would pay well if he were to be handed into their charge. If you already have such a one I can assure you he will never be able to tell what he may have seen."

A bribe, a promise, trusted currency in all such negotiations and, despite his position, Varne was little different from any ruler intent on safeguarding his power. A hard, ruthless, ambitious man—none other could ever have achieved his eminence. Clarge was accustomed to the type: all that was needed was to guide him the way he wanted to go.

Varne said, "What is your interest in this man?"

"The Cyclan needs him."

"Which tells me nothing."

"Need more be told?" Clarge let the question hang, unwilling to say more yet knowing that the High Priest would demand it. "The man I am

421

looking for is in possession of a secret stolen from the laboratories of the Cyclan. It is important that it be regained. Now, my lord, if we can come to some agreement?" He added, before the other could answer, "It is, of course, imperative that the man be handed over alive and unharmed."

"You add conditions to your demands?"

"Dead, the man will be useless," said Clarge. "Injured, his memory could be impaired. I demand nothing you are not prepared to give, my lord, but think of the advantages gained if you cooperate. The skill of the Cyclan at your disposal, advice and guidance as to investments, predictions as to the most probable outcome of events. Warnings as to hazards which might lie ahead."

"As you now warn of interlopers?" Varne's tone held irony. "It seems—" He broke off as a priest entered the chamber, stooping to whisper in his ear. Watching, Clarge saw the thin hand clench as it rested on the ebon robe.

As the man left, Clarge said, "News, my lord?"

Varne was terse. "You predict well, cyber. Men have violated the treasury. They were gassed and taken."

"Dumarest? Is one named Dumarest?"

"Perhaps." The High Priest rose from his chair. "Names are unimportant—all must die!"

Karlene woke, crying out, sitting upright in the bed, seeing on the bulkheads the fading traces of vanished dreams. Nightmares which had turned her drugged rest into a time of horror so that she clutched her knees and felt the thing in her mind

422

coil and move like a writhing serpent, that left a trail of fear and terror.

Strong!

So close and strong!

"Karlene?" Ellen was at the opened door of the cabin. "Are you all right?"

She entered as the question remained unanswered, one hand reaching to brush aside the cascade of silver hair and rest on the pallid forehead, the other resting fingers on the slender wrist as she checked the pulse. Fast—Karlene's heart was racing and Ellen could feel the perspiration dewing the forehead.

"You were crying out," she said. "In your sleep. Did you have a nightmare?"

Karlene nodded.

"A bad one?" She was gently insistent on gaining an answer; talk, in this case, was good therapy. "Was it a bad one?"

"Yes."

"I thought so. Your heart is racing but that is to be expected. Temperature is high, too, but it will quickly fall. Why don't you take a shower? It will relax you."

"Later, perhaps." Karlene moved away from Ellen's hand. "Has there been any word?"

"From Earl? No. Not as yet but we didn't expect any, did we? Ahmed has the radio."

"From him then?"

"A routine report. He made it to the roof and was checking the structure for a suitable place to make an opening." Ellen was determinedly cheerful. "There's nothing to worry about. Everything is going to plan."

A lie, there had been no real plan, just opportunities seized as the chance occurred, but Karlene didn't question the statement. Instead she sat, staring at the bulkhead, eyes misted with introspection.

"I saw it," she said. "In my dream. Something terrible and bright. So very bright. It grew and grew and I tried to run from it but it grew too fast and I didn't seem able to move."

"A common dream." Perfume stood on a table beside the bed. Ellen reached for it, dabbed it on Karlene's temples, the hollow of her throat. "There's a psychological explanation for it but I won't bore you with it now. Just take my word for it that everyone has dreams like that. Just as they do about falling. You've had a dream about falling, haven't you? Of course you have. You wake up with a jerk, your heart pounding and all in a sweat as you did just now. But the dream doesn't mean anything. Dreams never do."

Her voice deepened a little as she applied more perfume.

"Why not relax now? You must still be tired. Just lie back and look at the ceiling. You don't have to close your eyes but there's no reason why you should keep them open. Yet the lids are so heavy. So very heavy. It would be much more comfortable to close them and sink into the soft, warm darkness. So very nice just to drift and think of pleasant things. To drift ... to sleep ... to sleep ... to sleep ..."

Hypnotic suggestion, a useful tool and one easy to use on a preconditioned subject. Ellen looked back at Karlene as she reached the cabin door hoping that the next time she woke she wouldn't fill the ship with the echo of her screams. It had been a mistake to bring her. She hadn't wanted to come. The Temple held too many unpleasant memories, but Ishikari had insisted and what he wanted he got.

Ishikari looked up from the table as she entered the salon, watching as she poured herself a drink, saying nothing until she had gulped it down.

"Is she settled?"

"Yes."

"Another dream?" He frowned at her nod. "I shouldn't have brought her with us but I didn't know she would react as she has. And we needed all the help we could get."

"We had all she could give."

"True, but I didn't know that. I thought she could act the part of a pilgrim, go into the Temple with the others, give them help and guidance."

"I would never have permitted that."

"No?" For a moment anger flared in his eyes then he shrugged. "Well, it can't be helped. Still nothing from Altini?"

"No."

"Why doesn't he keep in touch?" Ishikari pulled irritably at his chin. "He should make regular reports. He must know I want to keep abreast of what is going on."

"The radio was for emergency communications only." Ellen was patient, recognizing his anxiety, the strain he was under. "The mere fact we have heard nothing is a good sign. He may have decided against responding to our signals. He could be in a precarious situation. There could be monitors, anything. He wouldn't want to trigger an alarm." Suddenly she was tired of pandering to his conceit. "He's not fool enough to risk his neck just to satisfy your curiosity. You must trust his judgment."

A matter on which he had no choice. He rose from the table, pulling at his chin, a gesture she had never seen him make before. Once, perhaps, in years gone by, he had worn a beard and pressure had revived an old habit. Now he paced the salon, quivering, restless, a man yearning to grasp the concrete substance of a dream. One terrified lest the dream itself should vanish like a soap bubble in the sun.

"Relax," she said. "There's no point in wearing yourself out."

"It's getting late."

"It isn't that bad. Your time sense is distorted. It happens in times of stress. Here." She shook blue pills from a vial, handed them to him together with a glass of wine. "Get these down and you'll feel better." Her voice hardened as he hesitated. "Do it! I don't want another neurotic on my hands!"

And she didn't want to become one herself. She strode from the salon, feeling a sudden claustrophobia, a need for unrecycled air, the ability to stretch her vision. The *Argonne* had landed in a wide cleft to one side of a line running from the Temple to the Hsing-Tiede complex. Hills loomed to all sides making a framework for the night sky. One blazing with the stars of the Sharret Cluster. Suns which threw a diffused illumination over the area and created pools of mysterious shadow.

The crewman at the port killed the interior lights before opening the panel, catching at her arm as Ellen stepped to the edge.

"Careful. Don't get too close. There could be things out there."

Good advice and she took it, staying well back from the rim, looking up and breathing deep of the natural air. It caught at her throat and lungs with a metallic acridity and she was shocked then surprised that she had been shocked and then annoyed at herself for the conflicting emotions. The air was bad as was the planet, but the sky compensated for everything. A span of beauty graced with scintillant gems constructed of fire and lambent gases and swirling clouds of living plasma. The glory of the universe against which nothing could compete.

"My lady?" The crewman was anxious, eager to regain the safety of his sealed cocoon.

"All right." Ellen took a last breath of the acrid air. "You can close the port now."

She heard the clang as she headed toward the salon, back to the harsh metal of decks and bulkheads, the prison men had created to travel between the stars. Even as she walked her hand was fumbling at the vial for the blue pills. There was nothing to do now but wait—and, for her, waiting had never been easy.

Chapter 12

The priests had not been gentle. From where he stood Clarge could see the crusted blood marring Dumarest's left cheek, the ugly bruise on his right temple. Red welts showed at his throat and his lips were swollen. Injuries which could have been caused when he fell but which had more likely been given by those answering the alarm in the treasury. And there could be no doubt as to his bonds; thin ropes tied with brutal force clamped him to a thronelike chair. His boots gave his legs some protection but the flesh of his hands was puffed, purpled from the constriction at his wrists.

To the priest who had accompanied him Clarge said, "Bring water."

A table stood in one corner of the room. Clarge moved it, set it down before Dumarest. A chair followed and he sat, waiting, looking at the man for whom the Cyclan had searched for so long. One now trapped, helpless, hurt and suffering. The fantastic luck which had saved him so often before now finally spent.

"The High Priest has given me permission to question you. I trust that you will not be obdurate."

Dumarest made no answer. His head still swam a little from the effects of the gas and, like an animal, he had withdrawn into himself to escape the pain of his body, his bonds. Retreating into a private world in which he saw again the deep-set door which Chang had indicated. The door through which they should have passed to the inner chambers, the secrets they had come to find. To learn them, take what they could, to escape by the route the thief had prepared. A daring plan which could have worked. One ruined by the fighter's greed. Well, Sanchez would pay for it as would they all. Now it was each for himself with survival the golden prize.

He moved his head a little as the priest returned with the water, accentuating his weakness. But there was no pretense as to his thirst and he gulped the water Clarge held to his mouth.

"Is that better? Would you like more?" There was no charity in the cyber's offer—it would be inefficient to attempt to hold a conversation with a man unable to speak. "Here."

"Thank you." Dumarest breathed deep, inflating his lungs, striving to clear his senses. Here, now, would be his only chance of life. A wrong word, a wrong move and it would be lost. "I must congratulate you for having found me."

"It was a simple matter of logical deduction."

429

"Simple?" Dumarest shook his head. No cyber could feel physical pleasure but all shared the desire for mental achievement. It would do no harm to let the man bask in his success. "You have succeeded where others have failed."

As yet, but the real success still had to come. Clarge glanced at the priest. "That will be all. Withdraw now. Wait in the passage."

"The High Priest—"

"Ordered you to attend me. Must I report your disobedience?"

Dumarest waited, then as the door closed behind the priest he said, "I am in pain from my hands. Would you please loosen the bonds."

"There is no need."

"The pain makes it hard to think. Harder to remember."

"You know what I want?"

"Of course. Loosen the bonds and we'll talk about it." Dumarest looked down at his hands. "It would be better to cut the rope. Use my knife."

It was still in his boot—an apparent act of criminal stupidity on the part of the priests but Clarge knew better. The knife, Dumarest's clothing, the chronometer he wore, even the thin, black robe were, like himself, a violation of the Temple. Symbolic dirt to be kept together for united disposal.

Clarge pulled free the blade, ran the edge against the ropes, backed as they fell from Dumarest's arms. Placing the knife on the table he produced a laser from within his wide sleeve.

"Do anything foolish and I will use this. I will not kill you but—"

"I know." Dumarest stretched his arms and flexed his fingers, baring his teeth at the pain of returning circulation. He was still fastened by legs and body to the chair but something had been gained. "You'll burn my knees, char my elbows, sear the eyes from my head. I've heard it all before. Crippled I would still be of use to the Cyclan—but not this time. Or have you forgotten what they intend doing with me?"

Clarge had no doubt. Dumarest was to die—but when he died the precious secret would die with him. Escape was impossible and logic dictated the inevitable should be accepted.

"The affinity twin," said Dumarest. "The secret of how the fifteen biomolecular units should be assembled. You want me to tell you the correct sequence."

Fifteen units—the possible combinations ran into the millions. Since it had been stolen the laboratories of the Cyclan had been striving to rediscover it but time was against them. It took too long to assemble and test each combination. Eventually the secret would be found but it could take millennia before it would happen.

Clarge said, "Give me the secret and I will speak to the High Priest on your behalf. It may be possible to avoid your execution."

"I will be allowed to live?" Dumarest stared at the cyber. "What is your prediction as regards that probability? High or low? What are my chances?"

"I will do my best."

As he would butcher Dumarest cell by cell to get what he wanted. As he would tear and rend

431

his brain with electronic probes, to leave him a thing of blind and mewling horror devoid of any claim to humanity. Garbage to be seared to ash, to be flushed away and forgotten once he had yielded what he knew.

Dumarest lowered his face to conceal his eyes, the raw hate he knew they must contain. The Cyclan had cost him too much. Turning him into a hunted creature forced to run, to hide, to forgo happiness. To see those he loved destroyed before his eyes. He had no cause to love the scarlet robe.

Yet the cyber was his only chance of life.

"The secret." Dumarest looked at his hands. "I'll give it to you—but you must promise you'll do your best to save me. You must swear to that."

"You have my word."

One he would keep; the Cyclan did not deal in lies. Clarge would speak to the High Priest but what the outcome would be was immaterial. Once he had the secret Dumarest would cease to be of value. The cyber looked at him where he sat, a man tense, afraid, advertising his fear. One willing to do anything in order to stay alive.

An impression Dumarest did his best to maintain. The cyber didn't know him; recognizing him from a remembered description, accepting his own admission of identity. Those who could have warned him were dead, victims of their own false assessment. Logic could, at times, turn into a two-edged weapon.

Dumarest said, "A secret's no good to a dead man. You can have it. Give me paper and a stylo and I'll write it down."

He flexed his fingers and rubbed his hands together. It was inevitable they should have been freed—a man cannot write with his hands lashed fast.

"Here." He flipped the paper across the table with the tip of the stylo. "This is what you want."

Fifteen symbols scrawled in the order of correct assembly. Clarge studied them then looked at Dumarest.

"Write them again."

The second set matched the first and was just as worthless; a random pattern Dumarest had long since committed to memory. A possibility the cyber couldn't fail to consider. Had Dumarest, desperate to survive, set down the truth? Or was he being stubbornly uncooperative for the sake of some emotional whim?

"You don't trust me," said Dumarest. He was deceptively casual. "But I'll give you more. Help me and I'll give you all you could hope for. I'll give you the affinity twin!"

It rested in the hollow of the cyber's hand; two small ampoules each tipped with a hollow needle, one the color of a ruby, the other that of an emerald. Twin jewels but far more precious than any to be found in the entire universe. The secret for which the Cyclan had searched for so long.

The knife in which they had been housed lay to one side on the table, the pommel unscrewed and resting beside the blade, the hollow hilt now filled with nothing but shadows. A neat hiding place; the pommel had been held by an unbroken weld and Clarge had bruised his hands in the

433

effort needed to break it. Now both knife and bruises were ignored as he looked at what lay in his palm.

The artificial symbiote which was the affinity twin.

Injected into the bloodstream it nestled at the base of the cortex and became intermeshed with the entire sensory and nervous system. The brain hosting the submissive half would become an extension of the dominant partner. Each move, all sensation, all tactile impressions and muscular determination would be instantly transmitted. The effect was to give the host containing the dominant half a new body. A bribe impossible to resist.

An old man could become young again, enjoying the senses of a virile healthy body. An aged crone could see her new beauty reflected in her mirror and in the eyes of her admirers. The hopelessly crippled and hideously diseased would be freed of the torment of their bodies, their minds given the freedom of uncontaminated flesh.

It would give the Cyclan the domination of the galaxy.

The mind and intelligence of a cyber would reside in the body of every ruler and person of power and influence. Those dominated would become marionettes moving to the dictates of their masters. Slaves such as had never before been known, acceptable façades for those who wore the scarlet robe.

"That's it," said Dumarest. "Now it's yours. I guess it will win you a rich reward."

The highest. Clarge would be elevated to stand

among those close to the Cyber Prime himself. To direct and plan and manipulate the destiny of worlds. To set his mark on the organization to which he had dedicated his life and then, when his body grew too old to function with optimum efficiency, to have his living brain set among those forming the heart of the Cyclan. To gain near immortality.

And now he had regained the secret of the affinity twin to spend the endless years in body after body.

If he had regained it.

Clarge looked up from what he held in his hand, seeing Dumarest seated before him, the casual attitude he wore, the hint of a smile curving his lips. A man who had given in too quickly; demanding nothing more than a bare promise to help save his life. Odd conduct from someone who had run so far, hidden so well, fought so stubbornly to retain what he had now so willingly given.

Was he so fearful of death? If so why hadn't he demanded stronger guarantees? Why had he so meekly surrendered?

"Your prize," said Dumarest as again the cyber looked at what he held in his hand. "I wish you joy of it."

A jibe? Had there been mockery in his tone? Those poisoned by emotional aberrations took a distorted pleasure from illogical behavior. Was Dumarest enjoying an anticipated revenge?

Clarge moved his eyes from the ampoules to the papers, the symbols they bore. It was as easy to write falsehood as truth—the information so freely given could be worthless. The vials could contain nothing more than colored water. Was he the victim of a preconceived plan? Would Dumarest, even while dying, gloat over his victory?

"I say I wish you joy of it." Dumarest leaned back in his chair, now openly smiling. "I'm not being generous, cyber but, as I said, what good is a secret to a dead man? You don't really believe they will ever let you leave the Temple, do you?"

"They have no reason to prevent me."

"Since when has superstition had anything to do with reason? You know too much. You know where the Temple is and you have been within it. You know what lies inside. You have details of the treasury—they think I will have told you. Now, cyber, be logical—why should they let you stay alive?"

Logic and the acid test of reason. Clarge remembered the High Priest, the fanaticism dwelling in his eyes. A man, by his standards, hopelessly insane. One dedicated to the Temple and what it stood for. He had been adamant as to Dumarest's release, blind and deaf to the fortune offered for his unharmed body. Dumarest was to die as the others were to die and, in the end, Varne had lost his patience.

"You may talk to the man but that is all. You will be attended. The interview will be short. Do not ask again for his release. To do so would be to spit in the face of the Mother."

Would such a man fear the might of the Cyclan?

Clarge knew the answer—Varne wouldn't recognize any power but his own. Already he could be regretting having yielded to those who had

436

arranged the interview. Torn with religious unease at the thought of having committed sacrilege.

Dumarest said, guessing his thoughts, "You'll be eliminated. Wiped out before you leave the Temple. You'll never even reach your raft. You have a raft?"

"I came in one. It was to have waited. The men escorting me are servants of the Temple."

"So you're alone. An easy victim. Who will miss you? Who can help?" Dumarest added, dryly, "You have the facts, cyber. Now extrapolate the probability of your leaving here alive."

Too low an order for comfort. Clarge looked at the papers, the ampoules in his hand. Dumarest's revenge: to give him what he could never use.

"I want to live," said Dumarest. "I assume you want to live also. Together we can manage it. There's a way it can be done. You have it in your hand."

"What?"

"The affinity twin." Dumarest was no longer casual, no longer smiling. He spoke hard, quickly, conscious of the passage of time. "Use it on the priest attending you. He will take over my body. Release it, change robes and put his own in the chair. He will be able to guide you from the Temple and take you to your raft."

"As you?"

"Yes. He will be confused but tell him he has been blessed by the Mother. Anything. Just get him to obey."

"And then?"

"I will be myself again when he dies. That must be arranged before you leave. He will be

437

unconscious, in an apparent coma. Open a vein so that he will slowly bleed to death. That will release me. I'll be alive, you'll have the secret and we'll both be free." Dumarest glanced at his chronometer. "But hurry. You'll only get the one chance. Inject me now then get the priest after you've called him in."

"Which is the dominant half?"

"What?" Dumarest's hesitation was barely noticeable. "The green one."

The truth, but Clarge didn't believe it. Already he had assessed the potential danger of the plan; should Dumarest take control he could kill, free his body, carry it from the room and make his own escape. It would be natural for him to lie and the slight hesitation had betrayed him. The liar's pause in which one answer was changed for another. And another factor influenced his decision; red was the hue of power, of domination, of the robe he wore. Red—the color of victory.

Transition was instantaneous. One second he was sitting, bound and slumped in the chair, the next he was standing, swaying a little, hands lifting as he turned toward the cyber. Hands which were not as he remembered, muscles not as familiar. Instead of clamping on the cyber's throat the fingers missed, tore at the robe, closed on bone and sinew. Before Dumarest could shift his grip Clarge was on the attack.

He twisted free, eyes betraying his belated recognition of the trick Dumarest had played. One hand dived into his sleeve as Dumarest reached for his throat, reappeared holding the laser as

438

the fingers tightened, fired before they could take his life.

A shot which would have killed had not Dumarest jerked aside his head, the beam ruining an eye and charring half his face. Dropping his hand he snatched at the weapon, twisted it as again it vented its shaft of destruction. Again it hit, lower this time, the muzzle aimed at the stomach, driving a charring beam into the intestines, searing the liver and creating a lethal wound.

Dying, Dumarest fought back, grinding the wrist he held, the weapon, turning it, thrusting the muzzle against the body of the cyber as he pressed on the finger riding the release. A moment and then suddenly it was over, the cyber's dead weight sagging against his body, the scarlet robe charred in the region over the heart.

As he fell Dumarest leaned on the table, gasping, fighting the waves of darkness which threatened to engulf him. The knife caught the sight of his remaining eye and he snatched up the blade, dropping to his knees beside the chair holding his limp body. Ropes parted beneath the edge and he slumped, hovering on the edge of darkness. An oblivion which could last too long— already the priests could be coming for him.

Turning the knife in his hand he drove the blade into his heart.

Dumarest rose from the chair, feeling the sweat dewing his face and body, the tension which knotted his stomach. To kill himself, even in a surrogate body, had not been easy. Stooping he pulled the knife from the dead priest's body, frowning at its feel, the loss of balance. Stability regained as he screwed back the pommel. Wiping the steel on the cyber's robe he thrust the knife into his boot then heaved the man into the chair at the end of the table. Quickly he stripped off his thin, plain robe, exchanged it for the blazoned one of the priest, lifted the man and set him into the throne-like chair. Ropes held him, the cowl masked the ruin of his face, the robe covered the blood from heart and stomach.

If anyone should look into the room they would see the cyber interrogating the prisoner, the priest in attendance standing by.

One armed with knife and laser—small weaponry to defeat the might of the Temple. And the pretense couldn't last for long. Dumarest cursed the cyber's too-quick recognition of the trap. He should be standing as the priest now with his own body wearing the scarlet robe cradled in his arms. He could have walked from the Temple to the raft and safety. A plan ruined by the cyber's belated realization that, to the vast majority of emotionally normal people, red is the color of danger.

Now he no longer wore the body of the priest. The robe with its red touches was stained with even more. To follow the original plan would be to invite death—there had to be another way.

He looked at the instrument on his wrist, pressed a stud, watched as the hands spun then came to rest. Up and toward the center of the Temple. The place where Altini would have made his opening and set the guiding beacon.

Dumarest remembered the treasury, the enigmatic door, the inner chambers which could contain the information for which he had searched so long. It could be lying waiting for him. Close. So very close. Too close for him to walk away now.

He had just one gamble, probably the greatest risk he had ever been forced to take. Now he had no choice but to follow his winning streak.

The passage outside was wide, flanked with doors, the roof bright with illumination. Servitors moved slowly along busy with polishing cloths, dusters, brooms. Two priests wearing the sunburst insignia passed him without comment. Another, wearing circles, glanced at Dumarest and lifted a hand in an esoteric gesture. One Dumarest returned far too late for it to have been clearly noticed. The priest walked on unaware of how close he had been to death.

More servitors, a small group of women dressed in ceremonial regalia, a priest wearing a robe blazoned with a quartered circle who strode, head bared, arrogance stamped on his thin features.

Dumarest hurried on, intent on a task of momentous importance. He reached a junction, chose a path without hesitation, found what he was looking for in a passage less brightly lit than the other.

"You!" His finger stabbed at a priest wearing a robe similar to his own. One with a face younger than most and with an air of recently acquired importance. "Accompany me to the treasury. Go before."

In the Temple age carried seniority and the snap of command induced the reaction of obedience. The priest looked at Dumarest, failed to see the face masked by the cowl, took him for what he purported to be. Even so he had questions.

"The treasury? Is there trouble, master?"

"The violators. More has been learned. One has confessed to leaving an explosive device." Dumarest had no need to counterfeit urgency. "There is no time to waste. Hurry!"

He fell into step behind the other as the man led the way. A willing guide through a tortuous labyrinth in which Dumarest would have quickly been lost. As they reached a familiar area he slowed.

"This will do."

"You wanted my help."

"You have given it." Dumarest lifted his hand as if in blessing. "Remain here. Others will be following."

He moved on down the passage, to the wall where the carved beast crouched snarling, locked in stone. As before the passage beyond was empty. As he reached the room containing the cleaning materials he heard the pad of running feet. Turning he saw the priest running toward him. Recognized danger in his face.

"You are not of the Guardians!" The priest's voice held triumph. "I had my suspicions and now I am certain. Twice I led you wrong and neither time did you notice. And your robe is soiled."

"You fool," said Dumarest. "I gave you your chance."

"To wait while you violated the treasury? How many of you are there? Never mind, you will tell us—and then you will make reparation to the Mother."

He came in a rush, hands lifted, opened into blunted axes. A man trained in the skills of unarmed combat, using feet, knees, hands, elbows, the battering ram of his skull in order to gain victory. One with his mouth opened to scream a warning and summon aid.

Dumarest met the rush, blocking the slash of a hand with his forearm, sending the heel of his palm to slam against the other's jaw. A blow which did no real harm but delayed the warning shout. As the priest again opened his mouth Dumarest snatched at his knife and sent the pommel hard against the man's temple. A second blow and the fight was over, the priest slumped on the floor, unconscious, blood on the broken skin.

Laser in hand Dumarest ran to the far end of the passage, the lighted well, the sunken door. Like a shadow he passed through it into the area beyond.

Chapter 13

He had expected mystery, he found enchantment: a curving hall truncated at each end to form a segment, the outer wall rising up and sweeping over to meet a circular central area. The door through which he had passed gave on a narrow gallery which ran up and down the curving wall. Dumarest followed it down, seeing blazing words set into the stone; gold and silver polished to a mirror smoothness and forming abstract symbols, quartered circles, regimented quatrains.

The floor was of tessellated stone shaped in diamonds of red and grey. Scattered lanterns threw a diffused illumination, creating shadows in high places; pools of dimness touched by gleams of gems and precious metals. The place was almost deserted and he guessed it was a hall reserved for special ceremonies held at predetermined times when priests and priestesses would conduct ancient rituals.

He trod softly to the nearest wall, to a door set in an arch of stone. It gave on another chamber similar to the one he had just left but larger in that it encompassed more of the central area. The lighting here was brighter, the place crowded with robed figures, and Dumarest turned, hugging the wall, checking the instrument on his wrist.

It was getting close to dawn when the Temple would wake to thronging activity. The swinging hands pointed up and in as they had before, the angle steeper now. The beacon must be at the edge of the central dome which, he judged, topped the central area. To get into it, to climb, to find the opening and escape before the new day bathed the external area with light. To do all this and discover what he had come to find.

Dumarest scanned the walls, seeing the flare of gold and gems, the symbols now grown familiar, the marching quatrains. Philosophy repeated in every chamber, inscribed on every wall. Words which like the engraved flowers, the soaring birds, the fish and wide-eyed beasts touched with jewels and delineated with skins and feathers of laminated foil glowed like the denizens of paradise.

One which held a bloody fruit.

They hung at the far side of the chamber, arms lifted, wrists fastened to a ring which encompassed an upright pole. Men, stripped, bodies ugly with wounds, faces tormented with the agony inflicted on them. Nighted robes surrounded them as if they had been animals set out to feed preda-

445

tors and the faces turned toward them held expressions Dumarest had seen before. The gloating sadism, the blood-lust, the avid hunger of the degenerate to be found in every ring. But these were not watching men fight with naked steel but spectators reveling in the spectacle of pain. Of the agony of men impaled on cones of polished glass.

Dietz, Lauter, Sanchez.

But for the cyber he would have been among them. Would still be among them if he was caught.

Dumarest moved, edging to one side, careful not to attract attention. A man among others trying to get a better view. His lips moved in emulation of those around him as they droned invective. Shielded by his sleeve his hand clasped the laser as his eyes gauged angle and distance. One chance and if he failed he would be impaled with the others. But it was a chance he had to take.

He moved again, edging closer, working his way to the front of the crowd. Dietz hung, sagging in his chains, head slumped forward on his chest. The blood between his thighs was crusted and dark but there had been no time for his weight to have driven the pointed cone deep and he could well be still alive. As could Lauter despite his earlier wounds. There was no doubt about Sanchez. The fighter had a virile strength and an anger to match. Even as Dumarest edged into position, Sanchez lifted his head, eyes opening, mouth working to create a gobbet of spittle.

"To the Mother!" Deliberately he spat. "To the Great Whore of Creation!"

Dumarest surged forward with the rest, screaming his rage, taking his chance. The laser was a short-range weapon, silent, devoid of a guide beam, efficient only at close quarters. Sanchez slumped as it charred a hole in his heart. Lauter was next, an ooze of blood at his temple showing where the beam had hit. Dietz didn't move as Dumarest shot him in the throat, searing the carotids, releasing a turgid stream.

Death delivered with mercy—but there would be none to give him the same should he be caught.

Dumarest backed, the laser hidden, leaving the crowd as inconspicuously as he had joined it. Within seconds he was clear of the throng. A minute and he was again edging along the wall leading to the central area. An opening gaped in it, high, pointed, surmounted by a quartered circle shining with the gleam of polished gold. Two priests stood before it armed with heavy staves, weapons which clashed together to form a barrier as Dumarest approached.

"Halt! None may enter the Holy Place."

"My forgiveness but the insult done to the Mother—"

"They have paid and will continue to pay."

The robes concealed armor; Dumarest had caught the glint of metal beneath the fabric. Scales which would resist the beam of a laser, the thrust of a knife, and he guessed their faces would be also protected. He stepped closer, his hands lifted, open, obviously empty. A man apparently beside himself with rage.

"I must pay homage to the Mother. I—"

He stumbled and almost fell, lunging forward

447

to regain his balance, rising with the stave of the left-hand guard clutched in his hand. Holding it while the other became a fist which battered the robe, the flexible armor beneath, driving both fabric and metal against the man's throat. As he fell, gasping, spitting blood, Dumarest tore free his stave and sent the end like a spear into the other's cowl. Bone snapped and blood gushed from the shattered nose. A second thrust and the man had joined his companion on the floor.

Dumarest jumped over them, reached the opening, ran through it and up the stairs which wound in a tight spiral beyond.

They led to the Holy Place.

There was magic in it; the emanations of generations of worshipers who had taken stone and metal and created a thing greater than the components which had gone into its making. A sacred place, one set apart, a small area which held the condensation of belief. Here, for those who worshipped, was reality. Here the naked, undeniable truth. Here, if anywhere, would be what he had come to find.

Dumarest stepped from the opening at the top of the stairs, head tilted, eyes wide as he surveyed what lay before him.

A circular chamber topped by a dome the whole filled with a misty blue luminescence which softened detail and gave the illusion of vastness. One dominated by the figure which occupied the center. The statue of a woman, seated, her head bent as she stared at her cupped hands, the ball which hovered above them.

The Mother. The sacred image of the Temple—it could only be that. A woman with a soft, grave face, hair which rested in thick coils about her head and shoulders. The gown was plain, full-skirted, the type often favored by those wedded to thé land. Her hips and breasts were swelling curves of fecundity. Her eyes held sorrow.

Dumarest stepped closer to where it stood. The statue was, he judged, about twelve times life-sized, the cupped hands some seven feet across. They, the entire statue, the stool on which it sat, was carved from some fine-grained stone the dull brown material unrelieved by any adornment or decoration. The ball hanging above the cupped palms was about ten feet across and he studied it, frowning, wondering as to its purpose, the markings blotching the shining, metallic surface. A ball poised before her, one she had just tossed upward or was about to catch. Or was it something more than that? The symbolism had to be important. A ball—or was it representative of something special? A world, perhaps?

A world!

Earth!

It had to be Earth!

Dumarest felt a rising tide of excitement as he studied it, the deep-cut markings marring its surface, the irregular shapes, the huge triangular continental masses. The Earth, he was certain of it. The Earth and the Earth Mother—there had to be more.

He turned, eyes searching the interior of the chamber. It was set with fluted columns which rose to converge like the interlocking fingers of mighty hands across the sweep of the dome. They matched the wall itself in its gray, metallic dullness. One broken at points with figures incised in gold.

Dumarest stared at them, at the dark mouths of openings giving on to the chamber. Some must lead to stairs such as he had climbed, others held the glint of crystal. All could soon vent a stream of guards. He could guess what would happen to him should he be caught.

He looked at his wrist and touched the stud of the instrument strapped there. The hands now signaled a point almost directly overhead. He threw back his head, eyes narrowed as he searched for the opening which was his only hope of survival. A flicker of movement caught his eye, another. Altini, crouched on a ledge which ran around the lower edge of the dome, gesturing with searing urgency.

"Earl!" His voice ran in echoes around the chamber before dying in fading murmurs. "Earl! Up here, man! Hurry!

Dumarest ran for the wall as sounds came from beyond the openings. Men, marshaled by priests, preparing to rush. A threat which gave strength to his hands, cunning to his feet. The fluted column held roughness and he found it, used it to climb like a spider over metal which crumbled in places beneath his fingers.

"You made it!" Altini sucked in his breath as Dumarest joined him. He was sweating, his skin unnaturally pale. "Get anything?"

"No."

"Me neither. There's damn all down there worth

450

the carrying." The thief gestured toward the statue, the misted chamber. "So much for Ishikari and his promises. The thing's a bust. What about the others?"

"We got caught. Gassed and taken. I was lucky. They weren't."

"How lucky?"

"A cyber arrived. He wanted to know things and chose me to provide the answers. He's dead now. Like the others."

"Dead? But how? I saw them. I'd set the beacon and was widening the hole when I heard voices. Chanting and such so I froze. Some priests came in and had the others with them. There was talk about homage being paid to the Mother and some other stuff then the priests left. There was a blue glow. I saw something like it earlier when I acted the pilgrim but this was different. It made the air taste peculiar. Afterwards I did some thinking. Then I took some action. Those bastards won't play any more games in the name of holiness."

"Tell me."

"Never mind." Altini shifted on his ledge and Dumarest saw the direction of his eyes. "You'll know all about it when it happens. How did the others die?" He blinked as Dumarest told him, looked at the laser in his hand. "Neat, clean, but it took guts. I'm glad you did it. I liked Kroy a lot and being stuck on a cone is no way to die. The bastards! But they'll pay!"

"How?" Dumarest was sharp. "What have you done? Tell me, damn you! Tell me!"

"That ball." Altini pointed. "They lower it and

it glows. It's hung from the dome, see?" Again he pointed. "Well, I've fixed thermite charges to the rod. Acid detonators. When they go the rod'll fuse and part. The ball will fall. The glow will start and they'll be too worried about it to think of us. Neat, huh?"

A man clever in his trade but with limitations. Altini could pick a lock, a pocket, rob a safe, break into a guarded place, steal without leaving a trace. But he had never acted as crew on a vessel, knew nothing of physics, was ignorant as to the workings of power plants and atomic piles. Dumarest looked at the suspended ball, the hands cupped beneath which now, he could see, held the same metallic shine as the globe. Metal set within the stone, blocks fashioned to follow the curve of the ball.

He remembered the workers, their sores, their emaciation.

Karlene's dreadful fear which caused her to wake screaming in the night.

"Out!" Dumarest rose to his knees on the ledge. "We've got to get out! Now!"

"Earl—"

"Out, damn you! Out!"

He thrust the thief before him to where a narrow opening gaped just beneath the lower edge of the dome. One cut on the slant to block the passage of light. Altini reached it, twisted so as to enter it feet first, looked to where he had been before.

"It won't be long now, Earl. If—"

"Move! Damn you, move!"

Dumarest turned as the thief obeyed, looking

again at the statue, the ball, the golden figures incised on the walls. Finally at the slender rod almost invisible against its background of matching color. The charges Altini had set made a swollen protrusion. Even as he watched, smoke seemed to rise like the plume of smoldering incense.

"Earl? I'm clear."

Dumarest dived into the opening, head first, wriggling, clawing his way past the riven stone. Cooler air touched his face and, with another twist, he was free, rolling down a slope, checked by Altini's hand.

"Steady." The thief's voice was a whisper. "Take it slow and careful. There are alarms, watchers—"

"We've no time." Dumarest rose to his feet, laser in hand. "Run for it."

"But—"

"Run!"

He set the lead, racing over the roof, the slope adding to his speed. A wire caught his ankle and he stumbled, falling as a man called out and the shaft of a guide beam seared the air where his head had been. Light accompanied by energy which cracked stone and left a glowing, vivid patch. As Altini rolled past him, Dumarest turned, firing, his own weapon making no betraying signal. Doing no damage either and he wasted no more time. Escape lay only in speed, the deceiving glow of starlight, the slowness of the guard's reactions. By the time they had spotted the flitting shadows, aimed their weapons, their target had vanished.

Dumarest fell again as he neared the edge,

something moving beneath his boot, and he rolled, catching vainly at the eave, missing to plummet down to the ground below. Luck was with him; the wall which could have broken his spine brushed his shoulder, the stone which could have smashed a knee or his skull rested an inch from his face when he hit the dirt.

"The raft!" Dumarest sprang to his feet as Altini landed beside him. "Where did you leave the raft?"

"To the west." The thief made a vague gesture. "Slow down, Earl. They'll forget us soon. They'll have something else to worry about."

"Keep moving!" Dumarest saw a shadow thicken on the summit of a wall, fired, saw stars gleam where the darkness had been. Stars which were beginning to pale. "There's another raft. The one the cyber came in."

"I saw it. Over at the main entrance."

"Let's get it!"

Altini led the way, slipping along in shadow, reaching walls, climbing them to drop on the far side. Cautious progress and far too slow. Dumarest forged ahead, ran along narrow ledges of stone, jumping, racing, taking chances as savage fingers of destruction reached toward him. Seared plastic stung his nostrils with acrid stench and hair flared over the wound on his scalp. Fire quenched by his own blood. The thief wasn't as lucky.

Dumarest heard his scream, saw the guard standing to one side, weapon lifted to send another blast of fire into the twitching body. A man

454

who shrieked as invisible death burned the sight from his eyes, the life from his brain.

"Ahmed?" Dumarest knelt beside the thief. "Bad?"

"In the guts." Altini writhed on the dirt, face silvered by the starlight. "Don't waste time." He beat at the hand Dumarest extended toward him. "This is no time to go soft. Take your chance—but leave me the laser."

He screamed as Dumarest raced on; the sound of an animal at bay, trapped, hurt, defying those who hunted him down. Deliberate noise which attracted attention, targets for his laser, as he provided a target in turn. Dumarest reached the last wall, sprang over it, crouched in the shadow at the far side. Luck was with him, the raft stood to one side of the great doors, the two men in attendance looking to where the thief had died.

The first fell beneath the hammer-blow of the pommel of Dumarest's knife. The second fell back, one hand lifted to the gaping slash in his throat, the other raised in futile defense. The body of the raft was empty. Dumarest threw himself at the controls, forcing himself to take his time, not to overload the initial power-surge. As men came running toward him the vehicle lifted, darted higher as he fed power to the generator and the antigrave units, which gave it lift.

From below a laser reached toward him and solid missiles from a tower chewed at the rail. He ignored both weapons, concentrating on height and speed, sending the raft hurtling toward the west.

Higher. Higher. Reaching toward the stars ur ·

til sanity checked him and he dived, riding low, dropping beneath the peaks of hills, following valleys, keeping rock and stone between himself and the Temple.

Flinging himself down into the body of the vehicle as, with shocking abruptness, the night vanished to reveal the terrain with ghastly clarity. Stroboscopic brilliance streaming from behind where a sunburst flowered to create a searing mushroom against the sky.

"A bomb," said Rauch Ishikari. "An atomic bomb. I find it hard to believe."

He sat in the salon of the *Argonne*, his clothing disheveled, his face bearing the marks of tension and strain. He looked older than he had, robbed of sleep, the culmination of a dream. As he reached for the decanter to pour wine, his hand shook a little so that thin, delicate chimings rose from the contact of container and glass.

"It's true enough." Dumarest leaned back in his chair. His throat was sore from explanations and his body ached from Ellen Contera's administrations. Drugs and other things to treat his wounds and wash the absorbed radiation from flesh, blood and bone. "It's what you wanted to find out. The secret of the Temple. The object of their veneration. I wish I could give you more but Sanchez—"

"Sanchez was a fool! One blinded by greed. I should have recognized his weakness—such men are never to be trusted." Ishikari gulped at his wine. "But a bomb? They worshiped a bomb?"

"They worshiped the Mother," corrected Dumarest. "The Earth Mother. The statue and the bomb were symbols and they may not have known it was a bomb at all. Once, maybe, but they could have forgotten. It had become a part of their ceremonies; the depiction of Earth cradled in the hands of the Mother. Both were radioactive substances which neared critical mass when brought close. When that happened there would be an intense blue glow."

"Radiation," said Ishikari. "Altini saw it."

And had seen it again without the protection of reflective surfaces. Dumarest wondered if the thief had guessed he was dying—that his body was doomed to rot just as those of the workers were rotting. Contaminated as the priests who had attended the Holy Place had been contaminated. Experiencing the affliction which had cursed a world.

Dumarest looked at the wine and saw in the ruby liquid images of an ancient horror. A planet riven with suicidal madness. One shunned, proscribed, set apart by those fearful of the contagion of insanity. One forgotten. A world deliberately lost.

Earth.

It had to be Earth.

"It's gone." Ishikari shook his head radiating his disappointment. "Everything I'd hoped to find. Now there's nothing left but a crater filled with radioactive slag."

"You blame me?"

"No, of course not."

But he would be blamed, Dumarest knew, if not now then in a week, a month, a year. When

Ishikari had brooded long enough over the votive offerings now lost, the books, the gems, the cunning artifacts. The history which the Temple must have contained. The secret knowledge which he would be certain had been there to find. The power he yearned to obtain.

By that time they would have parted—already the *Argonne* was heading to a nearby world. One where he could take a choice of vessels.

Leaving the salon Dumarest made his way down the passage. Ellen was within her cabin, wine at her side, a plate of small cakes resting beside her on the bed. She smiled as he knocked and entered; then reached for the bottle, halting the movement of her hand as he shook his head.

"No? Well, you know best. I thought you could use it. I guess Rauch has pretty well sucked you dry."

"There wasn't that much to tell."

"I agree—if you told me all there was."

"You doubt it?"

"Does it matter?" Shrugging, she held onto the bottle and filled her glass to the brim. "Some secrets should remain just that—secrets. You know what I'm doing?"

"I think so. You're holding a wake." He saw she didn't understand. "A party to say farewell to the dead."

"You'd know about such things. Just like Kroy. He told me how mercenaries operate. How to stop your enemies haunting you and how to settle with your friends. The few I had are still around. I was too close to them for too long. Help me, Earl. What should I do?"

He reached for the bottle and filled an empty glass and lifted a cake from the plate at her side.

"You do as I do. You sip and take a small bite and eat and swallow and take another sip. Each time you do it you say farewell." To Kroy and Ahmed and Pinal the assassin. To Ramon Sanchez and the man he had killed. Watching the woman, counting, Dumarest wondered why she had included him also. A man she had never seen and could know nothing about. Who else had died? "Where is Karlene?"

"Earl—"

"Take me to her!"

She lay on her bed like a woman carved from alabaster, white, pristine, pure, with the face of a child. She lay on her side, knees drawn up to her chest in the fetal position, one hand at her mouth, the lips closed around her thumb. Her eyes were open, wide, as vacuous as the windows of a deserted house.

"Karlene?" Dumarest stepped toward her. "Karlene?"

"It's no good, Earl." Ellen drew him back as the woman made no response. "She can't hear you. She's locked in a world of her own. Her talent drove her to it."

"The Temple?"

"It dominated her when young and stayed with her all her life. She knew what was going to happen. She *knew* it! It kept coming closer and in the end she had to run from it. But it was always there and Rauch, the fool, had to bring her back. She couldn't rest. All the time you were away I kept her under sedation but it wasn't enough.

When the Temple blew—Earl, can you guess how she must have felt?"

An entire community of men and women—how many he could only guess. All dying in a furious blast of ravening energy, seared, blinded, torn, broken—death had been fast but thought would have been faster. Each victim would have had a fraction of time to know the shock and fear of extinction.

The scent which had blasted Karlene's mind.

"She could only escape into the past," explained Ellen. "But, for her, the past was never a happy time. So she kept regressing until she went back into the womb. Catatonia. I may be able to do something with her eventually but she'll never be the woman you remember."

Another ghost to add to the rest. One who had smiled and held out her arms and embraced him with a fierce and demanding passion. A woman who had led him to the place where he had found the secret for which he had searched for so long.

The golden figures incised on the grey, metallic walls of the Holy Place.

Figures which he knew beyond question were the coordinates of Earth.

Soon, now, he would be home.

A Selection of Legend Titles

☐	Eon	Greg Bear	£4.95
☐	The Infinity Concerto	Greg Bear	£3.50
☐	Wolf in Shadow	David Gemmell	£3.50
☐	Wyrms	Orson Scott Card	£2.95
☐	Speaker for the Dead	Orson Scott Card	£2.95
☐	The Misplaced Legion	Harry Turtledove	£2.95
☐	An Emperor For the Legion	Harry Turtledove	£2.99
☐	Falcon's of Narabedla	Marion Zimmer Bradley	£2.50
☐	Dark Lady	Mike Resnick	£2.99
☐	Golden Sunlands	Christopher Rowley	£2.99
☐	This is the Way the World Ends	James Morrow	£5.50
☐	Emprise	Michael Kube-McDowell	£3.50

Prices and other details are liable to change

ARROW BOOKS, BOOKSERVICE BY POST, PO BOX 29, DOUGLAS, ISLE OF MAN, BRITISH ISLES

NAME...

ADDRESS...

....

....

Please enclose a cheque or postal order made out to Arrow Books Ltd. for the amount due and allow the following for postage and packing.

U.K. CUSTOMERS: Please allow 22p per book to a maximum of £3.00.

B.F.P.O. & EIRE: Please allow 22p per book to a maximum of £3.00

OVERSEAS CUSTOMERS: Please allow 22p per book.

Whilst every effort is made to keep prices low it is sometimes necessary to increase cover prices at short notice. Arrow Books reserve the right to show new retail prices on covers which may differ from those previously advertised in the text or elsewhere.

Bestselling SF/Horror

☐ The Labyrinth	Robert Faulcon	£2.50
☐ Night Train	Thomas F. Monteleone	£2.50
☐ Malleus Maleficarum	Montague Summers	£4.50
☐ The Devil Rides Out	Dennis Wheatley	£2.50
☐ The Shadow of the Torturer	Gene Wolfe	£2.95
☐ Contact	Carl Sagan	£3.50
☐ Cobra Strike (Venture SF 17)	Timothy Zahn	£2.95
☐ Night Visions	Campbell, Barker, Tuttle	£2.95
☐ Bones of the Moon	Jonathan Carroll	£2.50
☐ The Island	Guy N. Smith	£2.50
☐ The Hungry Moon	Ramsey Campbell	£2.95
☐ Pin	Andrew Neiderman	£1.50

Prices and other details are liable to change

ARROW BOOKS, BOOKSERVICE BY POST, PO BOX 29, DOUGLAS, ISLE OF MAN, BRITISH ISLES

NAME...

ADDRESS...

....

....

Please enclose a cheque or postal order made out to Arrow Books Ltd. for the amount due and allow the following for postage and packing.

U.K. CUSTOMERS: Please allow 22p per book to a maximum of £3.00.

B.F.P.O. & EIRE: Please allow 22p per book to a maximum of £3.00

OVERSEAS CUSTOMERS: Please allow 22p per book.

Whilst every effort is made to keep prices low it is sometimes necessary to increase cover prices at short notice. Arrow Books reserve the right to show new retail prices on covers which may differ from those previously advertised in the text or elsewhere.

Bestselling Fiction

☐ Hiroshmia Joe	Martin Booth	£2.95
☐ The Pianoplayers	Anthony Burgess	£2.50
☐ Queen's Play	Dorothy Dunnett	£3.95
☐ Colours Aloft	Alexander Kent	£2.95
☐ Contact	Carl Sagan	£3.50
☐ Talking to Strange Men	Ruth Rendell	£5.95
☐ Heartstones	Ruth Rendell	£2.50
☐ The Ladies of Missalonghi	Colleen McCullough	£2.50
☐ No Enemy But Time	Evelyn Anthony	£2.95
☐ The Heart of the Country	Fay Weldon	£2.50
☐ The Stationmaster's Daughter	Pamela Oldfield	£2.95
☐ Erin's Child	Sheelagh Kelly	£3.99
☐ The Lilac Bus	Maeve Binchy	£2.50

Prices and other details are liable to change

ARROW BOOKS, BOOKSERVICE BY POST, PO BOX 29, DOUGLAS, ISLE
F MAN, BRITISH ISLES

NAME...

ADDRESS..

....

....

Please enclose a cheque or postal order made out to Arrow Books Ltd. for the amount
due and allow the following for postage and packing.

U.K. CUSTOMERS: Please allow 22p per book to a maximum of £3.00.

B.F.P.O. & EIRE: Please allow 22p per book to a maximum of £3.00

OVERSEAS CUSTOMERS: Please allow 22p per book.

Whilst every effort is made to keep prices low it is sometimes necessary to increase cover
prices at short notice. Arrow Books reserve the right to show new retail prices on covers
which may differ from those previously advertised in the text or elsewhere.